Praise for *An African Rebound*

"With his familiar world of college and professional basketball as a backdrop, Dan Doyle's *An African Rebound* weaves a tapestry of success, failure, joy, pain, grief, and redemption as a seasoned basketball coach searches for his meaning in life and finds it in Africa. There's something for every reader: philosophy, psychology, religion, literature, and history. Not surprisingly, the themes of non-violence and anti-prejudice are prominent, given Dan's personal energy in promoting those two causes through his Institute for International Sport."

— Darrell J, Burnett, PhD, Clinical Psychologist,
Youth Sports Psychologist, author of *It's Just a Game!*

"The love of sport can overcome the sadness and selfishness of human problems. In this remarkable novel, Dan Doyle shows just how true this can be!"

— Judy Cameron, Naismith Basketball Hall of Famer,
President, All American Red Heads Alumni Association

"I've long regarded Dan Doyle's *Are You Watching, Adolph Rupp?* as the best basketball novel I've ever read. With his new book, Doyle, a gifted storyteller, has crafted a coach's tale of redemption within the milieu of the game's recent globalization. Any serious basketball fan is bound to find this novel an interesting and compelling read."

— Tom Konchalski, HSBI Report

"This novel takes us into a reality that most in the world of sports turn away from: failure. This culture likes winners. . . . In *An African Rebound*, Doyle makes his deepest concerns incarnate by taking us into the world of Jim Keating and forcing us to cheer for this 'loser.' As we follow Keating's struggle toward a redeemed life, we are led to reassess what really matters."

— Jack Ridl, author of *Losing Season*
and *Broken Symmetry*

"Do you hurt hard and long when the world confronts you with unfairness? Coach Keating weaves you into his struggle with fate as he enlightens you with his encyclopedic knowledge of the competitive basketball arena. Can we transcend the frustration that crushes our self-worth, supports guilt and depression, and fuels the harmful violence we abhor? Get wiser and happier as you grow your mental-spiritual strength with Coach Keating."

— Donald Pet, M.D., world peace activist

An African Rebound

An African Rebound

A Novel

By
Dan Doyle

Skyhorse Publishing

Skyhorse Publishing books may be purchased in bulk at special discounts for sales promotion, corporate gifts, fund-raising, or educational purposes. Special editions can also be created to specifications. For details, contact the Special Sales Department, Skyhorse Publishing, 307 West 36th Street, 11th Floor, New York, NY 10018 or info@skyhorsepublishing.com.

Skyhorse and Skyhorse Publishing are registered trademarks of Skyhorse Publishing, Inc., a Delaware corporation.

www.skyhorsepublishing.com

10 9 8 7 6 5 4 3 2 1

Library of Congress Cataloging-in-Publication Data
Doyle, Daniel E., 1949-
An African rebound : a novel / Dan Doyle.
pages cm
ISBN 978-1-62087-794-4
1. Basketball coaches--Fiction. 2. Americans--Burundi--Fiction. 3. Hutu (African people)--Fiction. 4. Tutsi (African people)--Fiction. 5. Burundi-- Ethnic relations--Fiction. I. Title.
PS3604.O95474A47 2013
813'.6--dc23
2012049794

Printed in the United States of America

Dedication

My Dream Team

This book is dedicated to a group of individuals who enhanced my love of the game. Most are from my early youth, the others I have come to know in adulthood. All have helped me develop an appreciation for the many wonderful benefits of basketball.

- Chi Rho League Coaches and Administrators: Father Donald Gonyor, "D" O'Donohue, Dan Sullivan, and Don Jubinville
- Jerry Alaimo
- Charlie Bibaud
- George Blaney
- Tommy Burns
- Bob Cousy
- Bob Devlin
- Jack "The Shot" Foley
- Paul "Frosty" Francis
- Chuck Hamblet
- Ray Handlan
- Noel Keating
- Joe Lane
- Richard Lapchick
- Larry O'Brien
- Dee Rowe
- Buster Sheary
- George Wigton
- My six favorite players: Matt, Andy, Meg, Carrie, Julie, and Charlie
- My parents and my Uncle Matt
- My brother Mike and my sister Jo
- The teams I played for and coached

I
Heading Home

1

Cherry Hill, New Jersey

(Fall 1989)

Jim Keating decided to pass on a final walk-through, one sellers often take to evoke nostalgia. For Jim, painful memories had smothered any pleasant remembrances, and he could not leave the house soon enough. He continued loading the last of his modest belongings into a car that looked to be on the critical list, moving as quickly as his weary body would allow. The last suitcase was the heaviest, and he had to heft it on his thigh to get it in the trunk. He went back, slammed the door, locked it, then saw his lawyer pull up.

"Thanks for coming, Joe," Jim said. "Here's the key. Hope the new owners have better . . ." Halting in mid-sentence, he checked his self-pity.

"Good luck in your new home, and be careful on the trip," said the lawyer. "And listen, Coach, things will get better."

Couldn't get much worse, thought Jim.

———

Several weeks before his New Jersey departure, Jim had asked the Chevrolet dealer who provided automobiles for the athletic department to sell him a cheap but reliable car. He got a '78 Malibu, eleven years old with more than a few dents and scratches. But at least it was comfortable.

The ride up I-95 to I-84 was smooth enough. Anxious to put Jersey behind him, he made only a couple of pit stops, but every exit sign triggered recollections of fast-food restaurants, entitled recruits, and blighted hope. Finally, he neared Hartford and managed to keep his concentration on a Ludlum audiotape. One more tape, just enough to get him to his old hometown.

An hour later, as several people crossed at a traffic light, none took notice of the rickety '78 Malibu, idling in an agitated state, or of the man behind the wheel. That no one paid any attention to the car or its aging driver was a big change from forty-odd years earlier, when a sighting of Jim Keating would have turned every head in the Main South section of Worcester, boy or girl, man or woman.

I've made it home, thought Jim.

Before the devastating events of the past couple of years, a four-and-a-half-hour drive would have been a lay-up for the old jock. Yet so severe was his despondency that he had seriously questioned whether he could handle the trip without breaking down. And if he didn't, then surely the damn car would. But now he had arrived safely in the city he had lorded over as a youth, where his athletic exploits, even decades later, had never been equaled.

At the Auburn exit of the Massachusetts Turnpike, just before the turn onto I-290 into Worcester, he decided to take a slightly longer route to his new residence. He wanted to see his old Main South neighborhood. Now that he was in it, he said to himself, *It's worse than I thought. Looks like I feel.*

Homes he remembered as attractive and meticulously kept were sadly decrepit: sagging porches, boarded windows, yards full of weeds and trash. Cops patrolled Main Street with taut looks and billy clubs swinging. The high hope that had resonated from most every household of Jim's youth was now displaced by a palpable sense of futility.

Stopped at a red light, Jim eyed a skinny black kid with unusually long arms loping across the street in front of his car.

Since he'd started coaching in '50, Jim Keating had always taken note of physical attributes that might give an athlete an edge in any sport. This kid's arms drooped below his knees, and the image caused Jim's face to break into a half smile, his first in some time.

The light turned green, and the Malibu proceeded up Main Street to his new home two miles away, just beyond the border of the urban squalor that now surrounded him.

Jim Keating drove slowly. There was nothing on his calendar.

———

Turning left onto Stoneland Road, Jim rested his Malibu next to the curb and studied the scribbled notes he'd received from his landlord, Bill Perkins. "Number 14, seventh home on right, three-decker with brown shingles."

Rolling to a stop at Number 14, the old Coach's eyes focused on the rotund figure seated on the front steps—a familiar face in a stranger's body.

"Well, if it ain't Mistah Jimmy Keatin'. Great ta see ya, Jim . . . been twenty years at least. Thought I'd wait for ya, give ya the key personally," said Perkins in his classic Worcester accent.

Both men noticed, though neither mentioned, how time had turned each of them into caricatures of their former selves. For his part, Perkins knew well of his old friend's recent torment, and he was ready with an ice-breaker: "Pulled this out of an ol' chest coupla weeks back—just after you first called me about rentin' the apartment. Thought you'd get a kick out of it."

Jim scanned a press clipping that chronicled his fourth-quarter heroics in some long-forgotten basketball game. The same article was no doubt glued to a page in one of the many scrapbooks his mother had kept.

"Let me take you upstairs, show you the place," said Perkins. The ascent was a Kilimanjaro climb for the landlord, and as the two reached the third floor, his slack-jawed mouth gulped fitfully for oxygen.

"Like I told ya on the phone, it ain't much, but it's clean and quiet," Perkins gasped as he handed Jim the key to the one-bedroom flat.

Perkins's description was on the mark, but Jim had no complaints. He was glad to be home and gladder still for the space that now separated him from some painful memories.

"Main South ain't what it used to be, Jim. It's fine down this end—still good people. But up past St. Peter's, the ass-end of the neighborhood, it's n—s and spics. N—s came first, then the spics, and they're even worse. If you go for a walk at night, stay in this area and you'll be fine. But listen to me advisin' Jim Keating on personal safety."

Recent events made Jim realize first-hand how painful it was to be on the receiving end of prejudice; he wanted to challenge Perkins's racist swill. But he just didn't have the spirit to do what he knew he should—at least not with an old friend who had probably cut the rent in half to accommodate Jim's ravaged finances.

"I'll let you get some rest, Coach. You look beat."

I am beat, thought Jim.

2

A note in Nick Manzello's widely-read sports column in the *Worcester Telegram* gave notice that Jim Keating was back in town. But Jim had shielded himself with an unlisted phone number so Kirk Willar, one his favorite former baseball teammates, hadn't been able to track him down. Then Willar ran into Bill Perkins at Gilrein's Pub on Main Street.

"He ain't himself, that's for sure," Perkins said.

"Think he'd want to go to the Gloves next month, Bill?"

"Here's the address, you can ask him."

A couple of days later, Willar rang Jim's apartment bell. When Jim answered the door, Willar saw the forlorn look Perkins had mentioned. Except for some flecks of white, the crew cut was familiar. But Prozac had created a puffiness that eroded the sharp features Willar remembered, and Jim hadn't shaved for a couple of days, which intensified his tired demeanor.

"Kirk Willar, Jim," he said, saving Jim from the awkwardness of not recognizing an old chum.

"I know, Kirk. God, it's good to see you. Come on in."

"Thanks, Jim, but I'm on my way to work. Saw in Nick's column you were back. Wanted to stop by to welcome you. Also, did you know the Golden Gloves are on next month?"

"Didn't know that," replied Jim in earnest.

"It's a ways away, but you might want to give some thought to comin'. We all remember your KO of Billy Carlos only a couple of weeks after you took up the sport. People still talk about that fight. Everyone'd love to see ya, Jim."

The old Jim Keating had always been outgoing, almost loquacious when trading the details of some sports event in which he participated. But now, in a lair of dashed hope, he had little interest in recalling that bout or other past exploits.

"I appreciate you thinking of me, Kirk. Let me think about it."

Jim's guarded tone made Willar think it was unlikely his former running mate would show up on fight night.

———

Jim had given Kirk Willar his unlisted phone number. Willar called several times, imploring Jim to attend the Golden Gloves.

"It's always a great night, Jim. Your bein' there'd make it even bettah," was Willar's consistent theme.

But while Jim remained non-committal, Willar could sense that his old friend appreciated the calls and that he was beginning to give serious thought to attending the event.

"There's a little more spirit in his voice," Willar said to Bill Perkins.

Now settled back in Worcester, Jim had indeed edged away from despair, although he was still a long way from optimism. His decision to return to his hometown had been a good one, for when he arrived he surely knew where he was. Admittedly, the other end of Main South had fallen victim to social decay, but his part of the neighborhood, with many of the same Irish-Catholic families of his youth still anchored there, was largely unchanged. Its familiar homes, streets, trees, and smells gave him the footing he needed to begin what he knew could be a long journey back to stability.

Jim's other source of hope was Dr. Ken Rotella, a Worcester psychologist who had been recommended by his psychiatrist in New Jersey. Jim had met with Rotella once, and the two had immediately connected. Jim liked Rotella's direct, thoughtful approach. He was especially drawn to one piece of advice: "In this first phase of our relationship, I'm going to make a recommendation: start walking every day . . . a long walk. Working on your fitness will help to revive your body and your mind."

I know that. I've just got to start doing it.

––––––

Following Dr. Rotella's counsel, Jim began to take daily walks around the neighborhood, staying within Bill Perkins's safety zone. As the psychologist had predicted, it was an activity he found therapeutic in various ways. Soon, he was up to three miles a day. Despite countless hours competing on fields and courts in his youth, Jim's knees had held up enough so that jogging was a near-term possibility. He almost joined the YMCA, but held back due to his sparse finances and reluctance to socialize.

The walks increased his comfort level with being home. Each block had its own set of distinct associations, mostly good . . . all poignant. Further up Stoneland Road was the house where the eleven-member McHale family had lived on one floor of a three-decker. Jim recalled that each Easter Sunday, all nine McHale children would proudly sport their new shoes at the 10:00 AM family Mass, a tradition many of them had carried on with their own kids. Walking down Hitchcock Road, Jim would pass the home in which a seventh-grade game of spin-the-bottle brought him his first kiss—and a mild rebuke from Mrs. McKeon, mother of Judy McKeon, the young hostess and, as it turned out, serial kisser. Jim was always certain that Mrs. McKeon had stealthily peered through the cracked kitchen door in the hope—futile as it turned out—of assuring her daughter's chastity. The memory would often prompt a smile.

Freeland Street brought to mind his boyhood friend Billy Kelleher, who, when he was eleven, saw his father forsake the parental journey in favor of another woman in Florida. Billy's anguish made Jim certain he would never abandon any of his own children. Freeland Street was but three blocks from Clark University, and Jim took note that the street had become the preserve of Clark students and young faculty.

His daily route then took him to Beaver Street and past the home he grew up in, another three-decker, where his parents rented the third-floor apartment.

Mary Keating was a doting Irish-American mother who had lost a daughter at childbirth when Jim was nine. Before the loss, she was simply a non-questioning Catholic. Afterwards, her grief drew her closer to the Church. She became a daily communicant at St. Peter's, and she was content within the comfort of her family and her religion. Mary practiced her maternal duties with unconditional love, a fact her son still reflected on with deep appreciation. With no small measure of emotion, Jim also recalled his mother's strength in the face of adversity, including the loss of her physical faculties over the course of a jagged, decade-long encounter with Parkinson's disease, which eventually took her life.

Frank Keating was a strong-willed and impassive man, a postal worker who carried the mail each day without complaint. Frank had fought in World War I, but never spoke of the experience. Years later, contemplating his father's pacific demeanor yet strident opposition to war of any sort, Jim concluded that his dad must have witnessed the most horrible of acts and likely suffered from post-traumatic stress disorder, or "shellshock," as they called it then.

One unforgettable exception to Frank's pacifism involved another Beaver Street neighbor. Mr. Casey—Jim knew him only by his surname—had also served in World War I and had been a victim of the toxic agents used in the "chemist's war," such as phosgene and chlorine. The result for Mr. Casey was not death, but, perhaps, a more dreadful outcome. With alarming frequency, Mr. Casey would be overcome with convulsive, frightening hiccup attacks of seizure-like proportions.

A favorite part of their Saturday ritual involved Frank taking his son to Louie's, the neighborhood soda shop on Main Street, for a malted milk. One morning, the young man behind the counter, Bobby O'Neil, an arrogant sort with a constant smirk on his face, was making fun of Mr. Casey to another boy, mimicking his attacks.

When they finished their malted milks, Frank took Jim outside and around the corner. "Wait here, son," he said. "And don't look into the store."

Several minutes later, Frank hastily walked back around the corner. "I did not hurt those boys, Jimmy," he said. "But I did make it clear to them what war is like . . . and what men like Mr. Casey did for our country."

On the day Jim left for basic training, his father had stayed in his bedroom until just before his son's departure. When Frank finally appeared in the kitchen to say goodbye, Jim was certain his dad had been crying. Frank looked deep into his son's eyes, reached for Mary's hand, and moved closer to their only child. He wrapped mother and boy in his arms and said softly, "Be careful, son."

Four months later, crouched in a fox hole in New Guinea, Jim's platoon sergeant handed him a telegram, which read: *The Secretary of War regrets to inform you that your father, Frank Keating, has died as a result of a car crash on November*

16, 1943. No emergency leaves were being granted to go stateside, such was the fierce intensity of the fighting. And so, at nineteen, thousands of miles from the intimacy of Main South, Jim experienced his first real loss. There would be many others.

———

With each passing day, the coach found that his daily walks strengthened the view his old neighborhood had shaped within him, values he still felt connected to: integrity, satisfaction with small pleasures, living for rewards other than money, and one that he now seemed to appreciate even more—staying close to home.

Were his reflections a concession to the fallacy of the perfect past? Perhaps to some extent. Yet, in those bygone days, for many in the neighborhood there was a special feeling about life that seemed bound to simplicity.

Well into adulthood, Jim recalled reading a passage: "You do not become happy merely by satisfying your desires. You become happy by employing a self-discipline which manages and gives coherence to your desires."

The philosophy of my old neighborhood, he thought.

3

As Jim expected, Dr. Rotella urged him to go to the Gloves. When Kirk Willar called several days before the big event to ask—once again—if Jim would turn up, Jim sounded more optimistic.

"I'd like to go, Kirk, but I'm still not sure. How 'bout we leave it that I'll try to be there."

On fight night, two hours before the opening bell, Jim fought off hesitation and made the decision to attend. As he shuffled bare-footed into the bathroom to shave, the cold marble tile floor sent chills up his body and weakened his resolve.

Keep getting ready. That's what Dr. Rotella said to do if I start to change my mind.

He dropped a dry towel under his feet and continued to shave. Then he ironed a shirt, a task he'd seldom undertaken until several years ago and one he still found difficult.

It would be Jim's first public appearance since returning to Worcester. As he ran the iron awkwardly over the shirt sleeve, he kept pushing himself to make good on his internal commitment.

The frost on the window confirmed what the weather report on *WTAG* had warned: "a cold night with temperatures falling below freezing."

Jim put on his warmest coat and Harris tweed cap and reflected on a warning from Bill Perkins—one of several the landlord had offered regarding the perils of walking alone near the neighborhood limits.

"Where you've been walkin' is fine. But there's a corner up past St. Peter's Church where all the n------s hang out. Dangerous place at night, Jim!"

But Jim Keating was now determined to go to the Golden Gloves—and just as determined to ignore Perkins's bigoted advice and walk it, two miles, right down Main Street, straight to the Ionic Ave. Boys' Club.

———

A light layer of snow covered the ground. Just as he had as a boy, Jim enjoyed seeing his footprints stamp the surface and smelling the wood smoke that permeated the cold air. Bundled with a heavy scarf, he walked by Clark University and St. Peter's Church, knowing he was about to enter "dangerous" territory.

The first few blocks had been fine, although he faltered some when he glanced at the exact spot where he had first met Edna. But when he passed St. Peter's, as Perkins had warned, the atmosphere changed. He approached the corner Perkins had described and in his view stood three black teenagers whose demeanor radiated trouble.

As a coach, Jim Keating had always prided himself on his ability to connect with young men, regardless of their race. While he did worry about what lay on the horizon, he was surely *not* worried about a bunch of kids on a corner. He threw back his shoulders and, with an athlete's grace, marched forward.

The three boys were a bit surprised to suddenly see a white man in the darkness, but the man's sure-footed stride convinced them that he was there because he could take care of himself.

"Evenin' guys," Jim said in a strong voice.

"Hey," the three said in unison. There was no hint of threat in their voices, only silent assent that they would let this older man pass without a toll.

Those kids at Jersey State—they were wrong about me, Jim thought. Feeling safe, he moved on. At the corner of Main Street and Ionic Ave., the old coach stopped and gazed up at the Club on the crest of the hill. It was just as he remembered as a boy on fight night—a beacon in darkened surroundings. As light poured from every window, a current of sensation swept down from the gym, pulling him magnetically toward it.

———

The lobby of the Boys' Club was adorned with a red, white, and blue sign: Welcome to the 1990 Golden Gloves. It also served as the setting for "Worcester's greatest all-around athlete" to greet cronies from the old neighborhood, many of whom he had not seen for more than forty years. Jim's feats as a versatile young athlete had made him a legend—Clair Bee's Chip Hilton in real life. His coaching success had even eclipsed his early heroics in basketball, baseball, football, and boxing. But now, in the company of his peers, Jim was uncomfortable, feeling as though he no longer deserved to wear this mantle of success, that it had been removed due to recent failures.

It had been some time since Jim held court, and the evening's salutations by old friends varied in length, from several greetings which jabbed and moved, to more long-spun and warmer exchanges. But all the welcomes, at least in Jim's anxious mind, were accompanied by an uncomfortable awareness of both his strained features and his failed last act. *The conquering hero? Not I.*

Jim was once a bulldozer of a man: 6'2" with a full head of close-cropped blonde hair, fetching china-blue eyes, high cheekbones, a lantern jaw, and a frame of granite. But now that powerful body was bloated. The chiseled features had surrendered to the forces of time, and ringlets of fat bulged uneasily under each blue eye. Always a bit stoop-shouldered, which, when coaching, made him appear to be prowling as he moved along the bench, Jim now simply slumped.

It finally took one man of mettle, a particularly long-standing chum named John Belanger, to bring Jim's anguish into plain sight.

"Jim, I'm very sorry about what happened to Edna . . . and that business at New Jersey State."

And there it was—in one simple, clipped sentence, a buddy from the past articulated Jim's twin problems, the two knockout blows that had put him on the canvas. A grim reliance on medication followed—a panacea that those who knew him in his early years would never have associated with a man who had once modeled self-reliance. Those blows had also caused him to seek refuge in his old hometown, the place he had left more than four decades ago when he had accepted a basketball scholarship to St. Thomas College of Philadelphia.

He had taken the scholarship in '46, after three grueling years in the South Pacific. Since then, he had only been back to Worcester on special occasions: funerals, weddings, his mom's birthday, infrequent holiday visits, and for three glorious athletic homecomings. The first of those homecomings had been in '48 when he had scorched a nationally ranked Holy Cross quintet, led by Bob Cousy, for 31 in a three-point victory at the Worcester Auditorium. Then, as head coach of St. Thomas, he had brought his teams back twice—in '59 and '63—and came out with two hard-fought wins over the

Crusaders. Now he was back for good, but under circumstances far less sanguine than he might have ever hoped . . . or thought possible.

"Hey Jim, I still remember the football game against St. John's; three TD's on Turkey Day," said Belanger, trying to dispel the darkness by casting light on one of a multitude of wondrous athletic feats Jim had performed.

In happier times, such homage would have evoked fond memories for Jim. But so savage was his sadness that the reminiscence hit flush against the vault of his emotions, caroming off without consequence.

Prior to tonight's outing, Jim's contact with the outside world since returning to Worcester had been pretty much limited to the appointments with Dr. Rotella, daily walks, trips to Glass's Market, and daily Mass at St. Peter's. He always attended the early Mass, where he would pray for the repose of his beloved Edna's soul—pray and avoid, as much as possible, contact with the locals.

But Jim knew in his heart that this evasive action was an unrealistic, even self-destructive strategy. When he finally acceded to Kirk Willar's request, he realized it might be a tottery step, for noise and crowds were a kind of quicksand since the onset of his melancholy. But the night had gone better than expected. As he concluded the last of the evening's social intercourse and headed to the door, he hoped that his old friends had not detected his abiding gloom. "Clinical depression," the psychiatrist in New Jersey had labeled it—as if this diagnosis, this antiseptic label, somehow had the power to reign in sadness and banish pain.

4

Forty minutes after his departure from the Ionic Ave. Boys' Club, and, once again, having confidently followed the route home that Bill Perkins had cautioned against, Jim arrived at his undecorated one-bedroom apartment. An 8x10 of Edna and his daughter, Sarah, was the only personal item he had put out in the bleak living quarters that were a stark reminder of the downward trajectory his life had taken. As he moved toward the couch, his thoughts slipped back two decades.

———

Jim's tattered finances trailed to a bad investment. Jim was no expert on money matters. He had put his trust in a broker, an old college friend who thought that a mall project in North Philly in the Seventies would line his own purse, and those of his investors—including his friend, the coach. When the project failed, Jim lost nearly all his savings.

A few years later, Jim experienced another series of set-backs that kept him in a financial morass. The first occurred in April of '82, when he was terminated as head coach of a pro team in Barcelona. The owner's unethical decision not to honor the last two years of Jim's contract made the firing even more painful. With no paycheck, he was forced to rely solely on a loan from his pension fund, his last cash reserve.

"The US Embassy is doing everything it can, Jim," said the Philadelphia lawyer he had hired when he returned to the States. "If you want, we can pursue it through the Spanish court system. But it'll take two to three years and will likely cost you more in legal fees than is left on your contract. Plus, the embassy told me that these guys have bankrupted a couple of their other companies to keep creditors away. Evidently, things are not going well in some of their enterprises. They're using every underhanded but, unfortunately, legal method to hold on to some of their money. In my opinion, they'll bankrupt the team if they have to. They don't sound like very nice people," the lawyer concluded with well-intended, but misplaced, irony.

But while the failed mall project and the ongoing contract dispute were taxing emotionally as well as financially, they would prove less burdensome than a critical mistake Jim Keating made when he returned to the States.

Devastated after being fired in Spain, and preoccupied with trying to claim the paychecks owed to him, Jim had overlooked the fact that the Spanish team had let his health insurance policy lapse. In July of '82, Edna, his wife and best friend of four decades, detected a lump in her breast. There would be no coverage for this illness. Partly out of compassion for her condition, and partly out of embarrassment over his foolish neglect, Jim decided not to tell Edna of his oversight.

What followed was a trying ordeal during which Edna's body was decimated and Jim's spirit nearly destroyed. Medical bills piled up as first radiation and then a mastectomy failed to stop the cancer from spreading to the lymph nodes. Only the quick sale of his house in New Jersey and his lawyer's deft maneuverings with creditors had prevented bankruptcy.

When he arrived in Worcester, his sole possessions were the '78 Chevy Malibu, his clothes, a few trophies he simply could not part with, and $1,300.

Jim's coaching career had started on a dazzling high note. Not long after graduating in 1950 from St. Thomas College of Philadelphia with a BA in Physical Education, he was named head coach at St. Pius X High School in Philly. He led that school to three straight city championships and won acclaim both for his ability as a teacher of fundamentals and as a disciplinarian. At his very first high school practice, Jim implemented a cornerstone rule: "Guys, the ability to focus is a huge separator—not just in basketball, but in life. So my first rule is this: If I see any of you not making eye contact with me when I'm talking, you're out of practice—no exceptions."

Jim brought valuable qualities to his coaching. A strong, clear voice commanded attention, a textbook knowledge of the game demanded respect, and a direct but caring approach fostered trust and loyalty among his players.

His interest in coaching was first awakened as a high school player when he found the strategies and teaching methods of basketball to be nearly as irresistible as playing the game. His hometown of Worcester was known in regional hoops circles as a hot bed of coaching excellence, and Jim's high school drillmaster, Dave O'Donahue, was among the best. "D-O-D" was ahead of his time, particularly with his use of the fast break—a strategy that was limited in the late 1930s and '40s to a very few college teams. "A Lord of Creation" was the way the *Worcester Telegram* described O'Donahue.

Inspired by O'Donahue's knowledge and innovation, as well as his influence on the lives of his players, Jim decided by his senior year at St. Peter's High that, when his playing days ended, he would become a coach. At St. Thomas College he spent summers working at basketball camps, experience that offered him graduate-level knowledge in the principles of the game. At every opportunity, he would ask questions of the coaches on the staff, all the while molding his basketball philosophy.

When he took over at St. Pius High in 1950, basketball was still a relatively new sport and was rife with opportunities for invention. Only twenty-six years old, Jim brought to the gym a well-thought-out basketball blueprint that incorporated the fast-break principles of O'Donahue and a system of changing defenses he had picked up in a late-night blackboard session with a coach from a small college in Massachusetts.

"Changin' defenses—some man-to-man, some zone, some full court pressure—will allow you to control the flow of the game," the coach had told him.

"Plus, my system is known only around New England. Philly hasn't seen it yet!" His declaration of certainty would prove true!

After winning a third Philly City high school championship, an article in the *Philadelphia Daily News* summed it up: "Keating's teams are tough to beat because they play so well at different speeds. On offense, they fast break with abandon. If nothing shows up, they take care of the ball as if they're playing on an aircraft carrier, with out of bounds being the ocean. And on defense, they utilize different levels of pressure from many different sets. On one defensive turn they might be in a frenetic full court man-to-man press with double teams in the backcourt; on the next turn they might change to a 2-2-1 three-quarter court press that lures you into the double team. The whole system allows St. Pius to dictate tempo and forces the opponents to change strategy."

Harry Litwack, the legendary Temple coach who had known Jim since his playing days at St. Thomas, was more concise: "The kid can coach."

Father Tim Cohane, the St. Thomas College president (and basketball devotee), had admired the grit Jim displayed as an undergraduate and followed his high school coaching career with keen interest. When the head slot at St. Thomas opened up in 1955, Father Cohane, confident in the accuracy of his judgment, appointed Jim, then thirty-one years old, to the position. Some members of the Athletic Board suggested that Jim might be, as one member put it, "a bit callow." Father Cohane knew better. The young coach was an immediate success: tough and streetwise, but a guy with a genuine heart. His players loved him, the sports reporters were charmed by his youthful exuberance, and the Philly and Jersey high school ranks provided him with a ceaseless source of hoop prodigies.

"St. Thomas doesn't rebuild—they reload," cracked one rival coach.

In 1969, after fourteen splendid seasons at St. Thomas, which included twelve post-season bids and two NIT championships, the school offered Jim Keating the best contract in college basketball history. It was a ten-year deal that included a radio show and camp, earning him over $50,000 per annum (in '69!). There were also yearly raises and other incentives. Of greatest appeal was an alluring annuity, paid for by the St. Thomas Booster Club. The annuity would swell to $300,000 at the end of the contract; Jim could collect on it when, and only when, he completed the ten-year commitment. "We've even looked into your own TV program. The idea is a thirty-minute show that would run during the basketball season. It might take us a year or two to get this done, but if we can do it, we'll add another eight to ten thousand dollars a year to your package," said Father Cohane.

Jim's playing career had followed the path of most who enter the coaching profession. He had been successful, but not nearly as successful as he had hoped to be. Deep in his heart (though he didn't like to think so), he knew that his drive as a coach was fueled by his unfulfilled dreams as a player.

Back in '50, the Ft. Wayne Pistons had drafted Jim in the fourth round, and Jim figured he had a reasonable shot at making the team. None of the Pistons guards were over 6'3" and none had extensive experience. He didn't get much court time in the first exhibition game, though, and was cut the next day. He took the first flight home, and by the time he grabbed his suitcase from the baggage carousel, his disappointment had turned into a resolve to succeed in a basketball pursuit over which he would have more control: coaching. He called the principal at St. Pius X to accept an offer that had been tendered to him at his college graduation.

In June of '69, a week after Father Cohane had offered him the corker contract (one unheard of in that temperate time of college athletics), those same Pistons, now relocated to Detroit, contacted Jim about their vacant coaching position.

John Ruffino, the Pistons' general manager, lost no time in coming to the point: "Four years, starting at sixty-five grand per—with a bonus that could get you up to seventy-five grand each year if you take us all the way."

Success at St. Thomas had infused in Jim a dose of hubris, which often accompanies early acclaim. Already certain he could win anywhere, he was not moved by the permanency of a ten-year contract and particularly liked the notion of coaching the only team to jilt him.

Father Cohane's final invocation would forever be etched in his memory.

"Jim, if I didn't like you so much, I wouldn't be so blunt. You're making a big mistake. With the exception of Auerbach and maybe Alex Hannum, no NBA coach lasts more than three or four years with a single team. My fear is that you're going to get on the coaching merry-go-round, bouncing around from one place to another. This is no good for your family."

But Jim felt it was time to break loose. He accepted the position—and yes, he would *always* look back.

———

Lying on the couch and staring at the darkness, the unpleasant thoughts of former times were displaced by what had happened that evening at the Gloves. Jim focused on a statement made by Bobby Duffy, one of several old acquaintances he'd not seen in more than four decades: "You left Worcester and so much has happened in your life, Jim. I stayed and not much has happened in mine."

Would Bobby have preferred the rollercoaster ride of a nomadic coach in search of acclaim—some mountain peak highs that approached heaven and some lows that cratered to the very depths of human emotion? Jim thought not. For though not much had happened in the lives of Duffy and the others Jim had encountered at the Gloves, and though many of them may not realize it, he was not certain that they were unhappier for staying behind and not certain that they would have been willing to pay the price he had paid—if they knew the true cost.

5

(1969–1976)

The Detroit Pistons had been league doormats the year before Jim arrived. In his first season, he led the team to the 1970 play-offs. In his second, the Pistons reached the NBA Championship finals, losing to the Lakers in a scintillating seven-game series.

Jim was on the fast track at full gallop when, early in his third year, his team went lame. Over the course of four short weeks, three of his five starters suffered serious injuries. Not once in the entire season did the Pistons field its normal starting five, and the team plummeted to last place in the Eastern Division. The following year the injury hex continued, and the team moved up only one notch, from last place to sixth.

Jim's demanding approach, which included an insistence on focus in both practice and games, had been embraced by the players in years one and two. But when the team began its downward spiral in year three, there were sporadic grumblings from a few malcontents. In year four, the discontent spread to the majority.

Fred Hannan, Jim's top assistant and a former NBA backup guard, summed it up on a late-season road trip in year four:

"We're fielding a team of marginally talented guys who all think they're stars. Plus, our twelfth man makes more than you."

At season's end, the general manager, Ruffino, had a frank discussion with his coach.

"Your contract's up and the buzzards are circling," Ruffino told him bluntly. "You've done one hell of a good job under tough circumstances, but the fans and the ownership are pretty unforgiving about two straight losing seasons—even if injuries played such a major role. Now, I can extend your contract for a year. But looking at our roster, we don't have much to trade. So, I'd say we're at least three good drafts away from getting back to the play-offs. We may have to stay down in the standings—get some good picks—before we can go up again."

Jim shifted in his seat and wiped his rough, suddenly clammy hands on his slacks. He was instantly aware of the direction of the conversation.

"Several ABA teams are looking for head coaches," Ruffino continued. "It's a wacky league, but I'll tell you this: They've got some players over there—the Erving kid from UMass is a good example. Hell, he's Cousy with wings."

Jim opened his mouth to speak, to tell Ruffino that he knew he could turn the team around if he was just given the chance, but Ruffino quickly continued his pitch.

"To be honest, a lot of our owners are quietly nervous about what they now know is real competition. Think it over. I'm sure you could hook on with a good contract, and I'll work behind the scenes to make it happen, if you want."

Uncomfortable silence filled the office. Jim wanted to say something, but he knew this was a one-sided discussion.

Ruffino looked Jim straight in the eye.

"Jim, I need to tell you that it might be better for you to leave on your own rather than being asked to leave." It was advice delivered with icy candor.

Jim appreciated Ruffino's frankness, but was repulsed by the unfairness of the situation.

"Two bad years, due completely to injuries, and they want to ride me out on a rail," he protested that evening to Edna. He went on to describe Ruffino's "suggestion" to move to the new league.

Edna responded with her usual patience, but not without a certain tightness in her voice. "A move would be tough for Sarah, Jim. She's starting to like it here. She's made some good friends."

Jim hesitated; he felt conflicted. "I know . . . I know," he said softly.

Edna could see that Jim was struggling with the decision and that, from a professional standpoint, the situation left little choice but a move. She rested her head on her husband's shoulder and said, "You're a great coach and a better person, James Patrick Keating. Sarah's young enough to adjust. If the ABA is the next stop, we're with you. . . . You know that."

Two weeks later, Jim signed a three-year contract with the Memphis Tams of the ABA. The family packed, sold their Detroit house short, and headed south. The Jim Keating caravan moved on, but with a tangible feeling of uncertainty.

———

Jim Keating's three-year stint in the ABA was a rocky ride filled with bad players, checks that bounced higher than the league's multi-colored balls, one last-place finish—and, in the end, a merger with the NBA that left Memphis without a team and Jim without a job.

While injuries had been at the core of the Detroit demise, a lack of capital had prevented Memphis from signing the caliber of athletes that would have kept the team competitive. And while everyone close to pro basketball knew that Jim had been hamstrung by the broken fortune of his owner, the three

NBA teams looking for head coaches showed no interest in his services.

One day, during a long talk with Edna, he analyzed the state of his career with deadeye accuracy.

"I could eventually hook on in the NBA as an assistant, hope the team does well, and then maybe get a head job. But right now, the guys who would hire me have no openings. As far as college goes, no one has called. And as I've always told you, the worst thing you can do is apply for a job. You have to be asked to apply if you expect to have any reasonable shot. . . .

"But there is something that interests me. There's a team in the Spanish pro league that's looking for an American coach. Their season starts in a couple of weeks and they want me. The money's good, it's only two games a week, and I get to come home for a week over Christmas. And frankly, Edna," he continued, with a slight but telling crack in his voice, "I think I need a job that's not a daily pressure-cooker."

————

Edna McCarthy had been a sophomore at St. Peter's High School in Worcester when Jim Keating, ace athlete and star of most girls' fantasies in Main South, had first spoken to her. She was a bright and beautiful bookworm with few friends and many pent-up dreams. Her most lofty yearning was to know this luminary who, she was certain, surely did not know her.

While Jim may have been the boy most coveted by the girls in the neighborhood, he rarely dated. He was far more interested in raising Cain or scoring points than courting young ladies. A girlfriend took up too much time!

Yet he had taken notice of Edna. She first caught his attention in the school lunch room. Jim observed that when she sat with her friends, she was the quiet one. When her friends were laughing out loud, Edna would be smiling—or reading; she always had a paperback with her. Though still a bit awkward, perhaps because of her shyness, she was without question the most beautiful girl in the school. Her hair, which hung well below her shoulders, was a light reddish brown—sorrel-like and stunning. Her eyes were a stronger reddish brown—russet in shade, striking, and a perfect match with her wealth of hair, fair skin, and full lips. Even the drab school uniform the nuns imposed on the girls could not conceal a Rita Hayworth figure.

But beyond her beauty, what attracted Jim was the way she carried herself with such quiet grace—*dignity* was the word that came to his mind.

One cold Friday in February—several hours before St. Peters' big annual home basketball game against St. John's—Jim summoned his courage. He ran up behind Edna, slowed to a walk, and approached her with caution, bereft of the confidence that was his usual companion.

"Goin' to the game tonight?" he asked shyly.

"No . . . no, I wasn't planning on it," she said.

Edna McCarthy was so absorbed in her studies that she did not even know there *was* a game—a fact she kept discreetly to herself.

Jim nodded and tried, but failed, to say something meaningful. He then headed off, leaving Edna to wonder what significance, if any, this brief encounter had.

Jim did not speak to Edna, or even approach her, until two months later. On a sunny Tuesday afternoon in April— heading to a game with his baseball uniform on—he caught up with her once more, almost in the same spot as their first meeting.

"Um . . . Edna . . ." he said coyly. "There's a prom in three weeks. You know, the Senior Prom."

Edna was stunned, but also wary that this might be some boyish prank—one that would badly hurt her feelings. Up to this point, her life had been full of books. She'd never had a date, let alone experienced the excitement of a relationship. Edna had emigrated thirteen years before from Cork with her parents, who had sheltered her to the point of near suffocation. She secretly ached for adventure—and she concluded that she must be willing to suffer some angst to find it.

"You . . . you want to go to the Senior Prom with me?" she asked incredulously.

"Well . . . yes," Jim Keating responded in a surprised tone, perplexed as to why this knockout of a girl would wonder about his request.

"Um . . . I'll have to ask my parents," she said honestly.

"No," said Patrick McCarthy when the jewel of his life asked for his permission.

"But Daddy, you don't even know who asked me."

"It's the Keating lad, Patrick," said Una McCarthy firmly, and her tone made it clear that she expected her husband to reconsider his harsh verdict.

"The athlete?" Patrick McCarthy replied.

"Himself!" Una declared.

Practical man that he was, Edna's father quickly reversed his decision. The next day, Jim found Edna, hoping for a positive response to his request. Glowing with the most radiant smile, Edna delivered the news he hoped for: "My parents said yes!"

Jim took a mental snapshot of that smile, of that entire moment. He would reflect on it many times.

Despite his popularity among females, Jim Keating had never had a steady girlfriend. And no girl had ever been close to him. That kind of platonic friendship rarely happened in Main South in those days; there was usually some romantic link. But within weeks after the senior prom, Edna McCarthy became Jim Keating's girlfriend—and his best friend.

The prom decision was easy compared to her present dilemma. Spain? If only it were so simple.

6

When Jim Keating went off to war, he and Edna McCarthy had promised each other their faithfulness. By the time he returned home three years later and accepted a basketball scholarship at St. Thomas College in Philadelphia, Edna had graduated as valedictorian of her high school class. She had then spent eighteen months working to save for college and had been awarded a partial tuition scholarship to Clark University, only two blocks from her home.

Jim and Edna both started college in September '46 and both received their degrees in June of 1950. Edna graduated magna cum laude in Art History. Jim's academic record was slightly less distinguished, but still sound, and on the basketball court he was a genius. He set school records in both scoring and assists. At commencement, he was presented the St. Thomas Scholar-Athlete Award, given to the student who "best combines academic and athletic excellence."

The couple was married in a grand Irish wedding at St. Peter's Church in Main South on July 11, 1950. Like so many other young Catholic newlyweds in the neighborhood, Jim and Edna had been certain that tampering with the sixth commandment would surely commit them to the fires of hell or, at the very least, bring a scorching rebuke in the confessional and a rosary for penance. On their wedding night, they made love for the first time and happily found another shared passion.

Edna knew that what followed marriage should be children, so she set aside her dream of a PhD in Art History. Besides, she was now "Mrs. Jim Keating," a title that was gaining stature in the Philadelphia Catholic community. But Edna's expectations and sense of purpose were shattered when she suffered two miscarriages.

After the second miscarriage, to stave off depression, Edna enrolled in a master's program in Art History at Temple and taught sixth grade at St. Paul's Elementary School in South Philly. She provided moral support to a young coach fast acquiring acclaim in his profession and steered clear of prolonged reflection on their childless state.

When Jim Keating accepted the St. Thomas job in '55, Edna soon took on several key responsibilities with the team, among them unofficial hostess and academic counselor. At home games, she organized informal receptions for boosters, and when the team traveled, she often went along. On the road trips—long before academic counseling became an integral part of athletic programs—Edna Keating would tutor players on subjects ranging from math to poetry. She was young, brilliant, beautiful, and unfailingly upbeat. The team adored her, and if some even harbored romantic fantasies about their coach's wife, she had the wit and tact to maintain propriety.

In the off-season, Edna handled the books for Jim's lucrative basketball camp. In August of each year the couple would make a trip abroad, one of the many perks Jim had in his contract with a sneaker company. Jim would conduct youth clinics and Edna would explore the local surroundings, some of which were an art historian's dream. Her life was good, if not entirely fulfilled.

Edna liked to celebrate her birthday by going out for dinner and then taking in a movie. After raising a glass to her thirty-fourth on a cold November night, she said, "Jim, let's skip the movie and have some dessert and coffee. I need to speak with you. This birthday has got me thinking."

"Fine," said Jim. "You instead of a movie is an easy choice. So what's on that beautiful mind of yours?"

Edna smiled, but her voice was firm. "Children," she said. "I met with Dr. Lahey the other day. He said there's nothing medically left to do beyond all the testing we've already done. So I think we should adopt."

The word "consider" had set the tone of their previous talks about adopting. Now she was resolved. Jim was surprised with this new direction but open to moving forward.

"It's quite a process and I'd like to be involved. The season will be over in four months. Can we begin the paperwork in March?"

"Yes," Edna beamed. "I love you, Jim Keating."

Three months later, Jim's secretary interrupted a coach's meeting. "Edna's on the phone, Coach."

"Could you tell her I'll call her right back?"

"I told her you were in a meeting. She said she just needs a minute."

Jim picked up the phone. "Hi, love. What's up?"

"Jim," said Edna, "you're not going to believe this. Dr. Lahey just called. I'm pregnant. I'm pregnant!"

Jim's throat constricted and his eyes filled up. He swiveled his chair around, and with his back to the assistant coaches, he whispered, "This is so great, Edna. We're going to make it. This time we're going to make it."

Sarah Jane Keating was born nine months later. The next seven years were the happiest of their lives. They had a daughter straight from heaven, and Jim's St. Thomas teams made seven straight post-season appearances. But then, in 1969, Jim made his ill-fated decision to accept the job with the Detroit Pistons. The decision forced the Keatings to move from their comfortable environs and begin a nomadic lifestyle that robbed Sarah of some of her childhood stability and Edna of her happy life in Philadelphia.

Though Sarah adjusted well to Detroit, Edna never quite settled into the community as she had in Philadelphia. Jim was on the road much more often and was working hard adapting to a radically different routine, including the much longer NBA season. But when he took the job with the Memphis Tams, and despite some early misgivings, Edna quickly grew fond of Memphis, with its pleasant climate and friendly neighbors. The southern city also provided Sarah with an abundant source of good friends and some semblance of roots. Both mother and daughter were happy in their new home.

Then in the summer of '76 the Tams, along with the fledgling ABA, went under. Jim had not yet heard from the pro team in Spain when he was offered a well-paying sales job with a Memphis liquor distributorship. He knew that the right thing to do would be to accept the job, get off the merry-go-round, and nourish his daughter's roots. But he was a coach, not a salesman, and he was driven to recapture that early and increasingly elusive success, which had rocketed from his grip. He thought as all coaches thought after a termination: *The job in Spain could help get me back to where I once was.*

For the first time in their marriage, Edna dug in and commandeered a course that seemed to her the best of several uninviting options.

"We both know Sarah shouldn't move again—she likes it here, she has some great teachers, and she's made good friends. And yes, Jim, I also know you're a coach, not a beer salesman."

Jim simply nodded.

"So let's enroll Sarah at St. Anne's Academy. It's both a day and a boarding school. I'll stay here at the house in Memphis, and for most of the year Sarah will be a day student. I'll visit you two or three times in Spain. When necessary, the nuns will let her board during those periods. Then, in March or April, whenever your season is over, you come home and be with us."

Despite the conviction with which Edna spoke, her voice faltered at the thought of such family disruption.

Feeling both relief and guilt, Jim hugged her and said, "We'll make it work, Edna."

Coach Jim Keating signed a four-year contract at $45,000 a year with Barcelona in the Spanish Division I League. He insisted on four years because Barcelona had not made the play-offs for the last three and he wanted ample time to build his team.

Edna went with Jim to Spain for two weeks to help him get settled. She needed to assure herself that her husband would be treated in a way that would begin to compensate for their disconnected lives.

Jim and Edna Keating found a robust and regal welcome awaiting them in Barcelona. At the time, American coaches were in great demand in Europe, and Jim was the first former NBA or ABA head coach to join the Spanish ranks.

Barcelona was fascinating—a beautiful, vibrant city with more museums than Worcester had bars. Edna was treated to a quick tour of two, but hadn't managed to get to the Picasso Museum in the heart of the old city because Catalan hospitality, overwhelming and exhausting, did not allow enough time.

"The Museu Picasso is a delicacy that deserves a full day. Save this special *un placer* for your next visit," was the advice of Andrea Lopéz, wife of the wealthiest of the three team owners. Andrea was an aficionada and rumor had it that the family owned a small collection of art treasures.

As Edna prepared to return to Memphis, the couple felt satisfied with the position. But as Jim escorted his wife to the airport, the sober reality of their first prolonged separation struck a forceful blow.

At the terminal, Jim squeezed Edna tightly. "I chose this life," he said from the pit of his stomach. "There's so much to say, but . . . I can't be looking back."

Yet as Edna's plane taxied across the runway, Father Cohane's wise warning reverberated in his mind.

My fear is that you're going to get on the coaching merry-go-round, bouncing around from one place to another. This is no good for your family.

7

(1977–1982)

Barcelona improved its record in each of the first two years of Jim Keating's leadership. Then, in years three and four, the team made the league play-offs. Jim successfully locked into place proven US tactics, such as his long reliance on switching defenses—including the match-up—as well as the fast break and a passing game offense with innumerable options, strategies not previously encountered by rival Spanish coaches. "American Coach Employs Winning Maneuvers" applauded *El Mundo Deportivo*, the major daily sports newspaper. And although his team was eliminated by Real Madrid in the semi-final round in both his third and fourth seasons, "Barca" ownership recognized Jim's tactical expertise. There was a feeling of optimism about the club's direction; its future had begun to take shape. Jim was rewarded with a four-year extension and a raise.

As planned, Edna made three visits each year: two over long weekends and an extended visit with Sarah during the February vacation. These would turn out to be some of the most joyous times of their lives. Edna had a facility with languages and gained a fluency that impressed friends and shopkeepers alike. Sarah lacked Edna's command of Spanish, especially her mastery of the Catalan accent, but she, too, delighted everyone with her willingness to try rather than depend on Edna. Sarah shared her mother's intense interest in Spanish culture and kept pace with her parents through all the museums and tourist attractions. On one trip, they spent Edna's long-awaited full day at the Museu Picasso, where the family enjoyed contemplating paintings from Picasso's blue period. Yet another afternoon was spent at Gaudi's Sagrada Familia. Edna was pleased with her husband's developing interest in art.

Of course, there was a flip side. When the trips ended, the separation saddened all three.

Although he fought off waves of loneliness during the long periods away from home, Jim came to enjoy the comfortable Catalonian climate, and he embraced the slower pace of having only two games per week. On his off-days, he directed a good deal of his energies toward invigorating the club's feeder system, which had been badly neglected prior to his arrival. He was also invited to join the steering committee that would explore the feasibility of Barcelona someday hosting the Summer Olympics. Jim's assignment was simple: Spread the word that Barcelona would be an ideal Olympic host among his friends in the international basketball community. Let people know that the country is basketball mad!

In his various meetings with the team directors, Jim emphasized a crucial difference between the American and Spanish league systems.

"In the States, college basketball acts like a farm league for the pros—it's ready-made. But here you've got no college competition. So, if you want to be competitive over the long haul, we must pay attention to our junior program. We've got to find good players around Spain, sign 'em, move 'em to Barcelona, and run 'em through the junior program. No different from what the great European soccer clubs do, Real Madrid and Manchester United as cases in point. I've also learned that the Real Madrid basketball club will soon be following the lead of its soccer club. If we're going to catch up to them in basketball, we need to be doing the same thing."

As he worked to build the foundation for a prosperous future for his club, Jim also followed Edna's advice and used some of his free time to learn more about Barcelona, to explore other regions of Spain, and to study the country's remarkable history. Jim's interest in history began with the books passed out to soldiers in the Pacific and continued with Dr. George Fetter, who made the subject come alive for him at St. Thomas. Jim was a physical education major, but ended up with more credits in history than in phys ed. Within a month of his arrival in Spain, he discovered the Universitat de Barcelona Library stocked with Spanish history books translated into English. Jim found that his Irish roots piqued an interest in the Spanish Armada, particularly stories of Spanish crew members being driven ashore in Ireland and their ensuing slaughter by the English. He also found himself enjoying Spanish novels, especially Cervantes's *Don Quixote*.

Along with his reading and research, in a comfortable Spanish-built Chrysler 180 provided by the team Jim made trips to places such as the Mezquita in Cordobà, a cathedral built in the eighth century with nearly a thousand columns extending farther than his sturdy eyes could see. Jim traveled alone. He'd made some friends, but no one he wanted to share his thoughts with on this type of trip.

Early one morning, he embarked on a long journey to the Costa da Morte, the coast of death, located at the northwest tip of Spain. After a comfortable stopover in Haro, where he had a nice luncheon and a glass of Tempranillo, he reached his destination in early evening, just in time to see the sun set over the Atlantic Ocean, the same sun that sky watchers before Columbus thought was setting at the end of the world.

Up to this point in his life, Jim had devoted himself to the pursuit of athletic excellence; he had only engaged in cultural activities at Edna's insistence. But to his surprise, he found himself absorbed in an avocation that was purely cerebral with no physical ties. *My intellectual light has finally been turned on*, he thought. His level of interest in Spanish history and culture—and the rate at which he found himself learning it—caused him to ponder how his life might have changed had he, as a student, found academic discovery to be as irresistible as his passion for basketball. Now motivated to sharpen his mind in whatever way possible, he took Edna's advice and set a goal of becoming proficient in Italian.

"It would be a nice complement to your Spanish, which is already very good," she had said.

Jim would achieve the goal in less than a year.

Jim also enjoyed the long spring and summer vacations, free from recruiting responsibilities and full of opportunities to broaden his relationship with his daughter. He wanted—and needed—to take advantage of these opportunities, and he took Sarah to any event in Memphis she was able to attend with him. Sarah enjoyed her dad's company and tried to accommodate his new demands on her time. But as both knew well, teenage girls (especially those as bright and beautiful as Jim Keating's daughter was turning out to be) had other priorities.

Sarah was popular with a wide circle of friends, but not part of any clique. Like Jim, she was tall, nearly six feet, and fit due to a daily regimen that alternated between swimming and weight training. She had also inherited her dad's blonde hair, which she wore long, halfway down her back. Her sea blue eyes set off small, delicate facial features reminiscent of Edna's. And even though her friends—both male and female—desired her company, she enjoyed being with her dad and always looked forward to their weekly father-daughter night out.

But while their outings brought them closer, they did not, in Jim's mind, make up for a career on the bench that had relegated him to a substitute's role in Sarah's upbringing.

In his fifth season in Spain, he found out, as he had in his Detroit hitch, that success in the form of making the play-offs brought higher expectations. Jim's Spanish players, reliable in the first four years, drifted to the slower side of their careers. Both a point guard and a small forward, each of whom relied on quickness, lost a half-step to age. A similar fade in skills took hold of one of the two Americans that the league allowed each team to employ.

Barcelona failed to make the play-offs and the owners, supportive of Jim but, in the end, Machiavellian men of commerce, could see that the feeder system he was crafting was still several years away from any yield. They decided to sell the team to a wealthy Spanish family with a coddled twenty-seven-year-old son in need of a new pastime.

The heir was handed the task of running the team just after he had finished driving one of the family businesses into the Mediterranean. Jim immediately pegged him as a pampered dilettante. Always known as a coach who could get along with management, he was presented with a situation to challenge that record.

Their first confrontation was over a thirty-four-year-old American player who had faltered badly in the recently concluded season.

"We need to bring in a new player. I know the guy has a year left on his contract, but we're going to have to eat it," Jim stated without equivocation.

"He's been with this team for seven years and is a favorite of the fans. Furthermore, my family will not throw $150,000 out a porthole merely on a coach's say-so," countered the new boss, Alberto Blanco.

Jim seethed, not so much about Blanco's disrespect, but about his reckless lack of reasoning.

41

"We make the play-offs and it's a guarantee of $500,000, plus more if we advance. We need a top-flight American to do that," Jim dissented. But Blanco wasn't listening.

All the calamities that Jim Keating came to dread soon arrived with blunt force. The American Keating wanted to release was indeed ineffective—more so than even the coach had guessed—and the team plunged to below .500.

"American Coach Fired by Blanco" roared the headline in the *Barcelona Times* with six games to go in Jim Keating's sixth season.

The Spanish media zealously sided with the coach, pointing to his excellent work when good players were available. They defended his innovative overhauling of the junior program and criticized his exclusion by the greenhorn general manager in the decision-making process. The media also pointed to Jim's community involvement, including his respected contribution to the Barcelona Summer Olympics Steering Committee. But as Jim knew so well, a coach's success at the professional level is bound like an umbilical cord to the competence of management.

From player injuries to administrative meddling, the season was the most difficult of Jim's career, and the jaw-breaking firing shattered his confidence. Soon after his dismissal, he free-fell into a dark thicket of despair.

Edna greeted her mauled matador at the Memphis airport and tenderly nursed him through his period of lost will. But then, only three months after his return, she discovered the lump in her breast. A hurried mammogram revealed the bad news: It was malignant. So Jim Keating tried to put his own anguish on hold to pinch-hit for his partner. There were days when he wondered if he would ever again see a shaft of life's light.

Thirty months later—an excruciating vigil for both of them—Edna's condition had deteriorated badly. Jim was still without a job and tunneling deep into whatever modest savings he had left when word came that New Jersey State, located just twenty miles from Philadelphia and the battleground of Jim's early era of prosperity, was preparing to jump from Division II to Division I. Old friend Father Cohane lobbied with his presidential counterpart at New Jersey State, and several weeks after State's arching shot at big-time basketball was made public, travel-weary Jim Keating was given a three-year contract to lead this "enterprise."

At the press conference called to announce Jim's appointment, New Jersey State President Vincent Mahon exulted: "We've hired Jim with the expectation that he'll perform the same miracles that he did at St. Thomas. We're very pleased that he has returned to his own backyard, where so many potential recruits grew up hearing about the Jim Keating legend. We fully expect to be a national contender in three or four years."

But on January 14, 1987, less than two years after that imprudent proclamation, the school issued a terse press release announcing that Jim Keating had been fired. What the press release did not report, the media did.

In a copyrighted story in the *Philadelphia Enquirer* that quickly made its way over the wires and onto national television and talk radio, three players stated that Jim Keating was racially insensitive.

8

(1985–1987)

Jim Keating's career in Jersey State imploded for many reasons, but one factor was his lost zeal. In a profession that requires uncommon energy, this was cataclysmic. While there were several reasons for the loss of that passion, Edna's cancer was by far the most formidable. It had drained her strength and diminished his willpower—at least the sort of willpower required of a Division I coach.

And the charge of being racially insensitive—devastating to Jim personally—had surely not helped matters in a professional sense.

Edna had rallied for several months after Jim's appointment, and her better health, coupled with his fresh opportunity, brought a new wick of flame to his life. But once his first season was underway, with a team of twelve Division II players with Division I egos, Edna, closing in on fifty-nine, began to falter again. Jim winced at this slippage, and he was also now acutely aware that turning State into a Division I power would be even more difficult than he had originally thought. He felt stampeded, and he made several important decisions in reaction to the pressure, even one that involved his marriage.

From the day he had wed Edna McCarthy, Jim's innermost concerns had placed Edna—and then Edna and Sarah—in first position. Yet his actions often contradicted his deepest feelings. Coaching at the college level, particularly during the season and recruiting periods, had required of him an unrelenting attention to his job. But as his wife's condition continued to deteriorate, for the first time in his career, Jim decided to focus more on her expanding needs. He would delegate some of his normal responsibilities to his assistants, one of whom had been forced on him by State President Mahon when he offered Jim the job. Jim was explaining what he expected of the coaches he wanted on his staff when Mahon interrupted him.

"I know you want to bring in your own people, but there's a young assistant from the prior regime that you must take on if we're going to get this deal done. His name is Robert Frazier and he's an African American kid. You may remember him. He was a good player here several years back, and he's been top assistant for the last two years. He's done a decent job and some of the alumni think highly of him," said Mahon. Jim noticed that the president became hesitant as the rhetoric got thicker.

"In fact, to be honest, there were a few who wanted him to get the head job, but our athletic director didn't think he was ready . . . thought he needed more time and that he'd profit from working under someone with your experience."

Finally Mahon's hands collapsed at his sides.

"I'm going to level with you," he said. "Our record for hiring minorities in the Athletic Department is not what it should be, and my affirmative action people are starting to give me a difficult time about the situation. Of the varsity athletes in our school, 65 percent are black, yet we only have four assistants in the entire department who are black, and not one head coach. I'm prepared to offer you the job, and you can make the call on your number two assistant and your graduate assistant. But Robert Frazier has to be part of the package."

Jim knew that he should insist on final say on *all* of his assistants, and he related this point to Mahon. During his career, he had consistently practiced his own form of affirmative action even before it was popular or the law. He hated prejudice unyieldingly, and he always made it a point to hire top black assistants whenever possible and prepare them to become head coaches. The result was that two such former assistants had reached the head coaching level in Division I. But all had been *his* hires, his decisions. Mahon, though, was adamant, and now Jim was going to have to go off to war with a top assistant he didn't even know.

Yet his wounds from past battles were deep, and he was in a financial bind. Jim Keating needed this job, a fact he was reminded of every time a bill came to the post office box he had opened solely for all correspondence relating to Edna's care.

———

In the 1985–86 season, Jim's first as coach and the transition year from Division II to I, State played thirteen of their twenty-six games against Division I competition. The team showed clear improvement at the end, winning four of their last eight, including two February victories over Division I opposition. State finished the season 10–16.

But to compete at the Division I level, Jim knew that he needed better talent . . . much better talent.

Two weeks after State's last game in that first season, Robert Frazier took his boss to a high school All-Star game in South Jersey to show the coach the three "blue chippers" that Frazier was certain would help turn State's fortunes around. The three all fit the profile of the majority of recruits at Division I schools. They were African Americans from urban environments, and they all looked at basketball as the best—if not the only—way out of their difficult circumstances.

Jim Keating always had an uncanny ability to judge talent. For whatever reason, he could look at a kid and generally project how good this player would be in several years. Jim knew that the three athletes Frazier had been touting were not heavily recruited by other schools. Yet he liked the fact that, as kids down at the heels, they would likely crave success. *A lot of Hall of Famers came from similar backgrounds*, he thought.

His major worry, however, was that Second Assistant Bill Laverty, whom he knew to be a sound judge of talent based on his sending more than twenty of his former high school players to Division I programs, was cool to the notion of offering scholarships to the three prospects. Laverty's doubt had caused tension in the office.

"I saw all three of these kids when they were juniors, Robert," Laverty said to Frazier in front of Jim at a mid-February staff meeting. "At the time, I didn't think they were D-I. Plus, I don't believe they're getting much interest from other Division I schools."

"They're D-I," Frazier responded stiffly. "They all have upside; they're the best we can get." His tone made it clear that he did not consider their potential to be a matter of discussion.

All of these elements concerned Jim, and so did the fact that he had not taken enough time to watch the three recruits play. He was so overwhelmed coaching his team while caring for Edna, however, that he felt he had no choice but to rely on Frazier's judgment. Ten minutes into the high school All-Star game, Jim was certain he'd made a critical mistake. At halftime, he discreetly ushered his assistant to a quiet corner of the outer lobby. At this late stage in the recruiting process, he knew he must be forthright.

"Robert, I don't think these kids can help us."

"What do you mean they can't help us?" replied an exasperated Frazier.

"Look . . . I know you've worked hard on these kids, but I don't think they're Division I players."

Frazier's reaction was not what Jim had hoped. The assistant coach was silent for the second half and then sulked on the ride home. Jim remained outwardly composed but was inwardly distressed. He also wondered if Frazier had any idea—or concern—about how his boss felt. At a meeting the next day, things got worse.

Bill Laverty had been a heavily recruited high school star in New Jersey who had chosen St. Thomas only to find, several weeks after he committed, that Jim was leaving for the Pistons. Jim had always felt guilty about not fulfilling what he perceived was an obligation to Laverty, and he had followed the young man's progress in life with interest. After a fine playing career at St. Thomas, Laverty became a successful high school coach at Archbishop Sullivan High School in Newark, New Jersey. He was known as a great tactician, and, more importantly, he had good contacts throughout the state. Sixteen years after Jim had jilted him, Laverty received a call from the head coach with an offer to become second assistant. Without hesitation, Laverty accepted the offer. He had hoped to play a key role in recruiting, but Frazier, in his capacity as top assistant and recruiting coordinator, would not have it.

As a result, there was immediate friction between Laverty and Frazier. It had brewed during the season, especially because Frazier avoided consulting Laverty on recruiting, and it boiled at the morning meeting after the All-Star game.

Bill Laverty looked at Robert Frazier as a guy with mediocre ability, someone who carried a large chip on his shoulder and who was, in his own way, a racist.

"Everything to this guy is a matter of color," Laverty had confided to his wife, Meg, while venting about Frazier's many shortcomings.

"Hell, I'd have killed for a college job at his age. It's like he thinks he's owed the position. . . . He doesn't respect me, and, as incredible as it sounds, he doesn't respect Jim. In fact, I'm pretty sure that in subtle ways, he's undermining Jim behind his back, talking to the players. A couple of the kids have made comments to me about Coach Frazier not seeing eye-to-eye with Coach Keating," he said. "And I'm supposed to have a voice in recruiting, but any time I bring a kid up, he acts as if he can shut me right off."

"Have you talked to Jim about this?" asked Meg.

"He knows I'm concerned, but he's in a tough spot. I've heard people around the Athletic Department say that Frazier was forced on Jim by the President. We've got ten black players on the team and Frazier has gotten close to most or all of them. He kisses up to the two white players, too. All twelve of 'em are decent kids, but put any kid in a losing situation and he can be vulnerable. And I've talked to enough high school coaches to be pretty sure that the three players he wants to sign aren't that good."

Laverty sighed. "You know, Meg, I've always thought of myself as fair-minded. I mean, I hate racism. But here I am, talking about this guy—and frankly thinking about this guy—as a black man instead of as a man. I know plenty of other black people who I don't think about or talk about in this way. But, damn it, this guy makes you do it."

"What about—in a nice way—approaching him about the problems?" asked Meg.

"I'd like to. I'd really like to have an open discussion with him. But to be honest, I'm afraid he'd twist things, try to make me look like a bigot."

For his part, Frazier looked at Laverty as less of a bigot and more as just another member of the old boy system, a system that still allowed white coaches to look after each other, especially when it came time to employ either head coaches or new assistants. The "Caucasian Coaching Mafia" was the term he employed.

"I get sick about hearing that Laverty is this great tactician," Frazier railed to his fiancée, Lynn Safford. "How tough was it for him to win at that Catholic high school? Look at the talent he had. Anyone could look good with that kind of talent."

He continued, "So in this program, he's the X-and-O guy and I'm the recruiter. When Keating did the assignments, I'm sure he figured that the white guy knows the game and the black guy can get the kids to play the game. Tell me that's not a racial thing!"

Lynn knew that reasoning with her partner, at least in this matter, was not an option. They had recently argued about his constant complaining over what he perceived to be injuries to his soul from growing up black.

"Look, Robert," she had said forthrightly, "I've grown up as a black woman, so I, too, have an understanding of prejudice. I also know that not every non–African American is a bigot, and I've gotten away from trying to look into every white heart to try to figure out where they really stand."

As she spoke, Frazier stared into space.

"But you . . . you dwell on it . . . constantly. You've got all this potential. So what if you didn't get the head job? You're twenty-nine for heaven's sake. Even if you don't like Bill Laverty . . . even if you don't like Jim Keating . . . you've got a good job and a great future."

Annoyed with her fiancé's lack of interest in her words, she raised her voice and said, "Robert, will you please look at me?"

Frazier turned his head in her direction, but offered only momentary eye contact.

"You know I love you, Robert, but you've got to grow up. And, by the way, in my view, you could actually learn a lot from Coach Keating, because you know what? I see the value of his 'old school' ways."

Frazier's reaction was just as Lynn assumed it would be; he didn't speak with her for several days.

During this impasse, Lynn feared that a confrontation between Frazier and Laverty and, perhaps, even Jim, was coming, probably soon. When the coaching staff gathered in Jim's office for the morning meeting, Frazier affirmed her foresight by throwing the first grenade.

"Jim," he said in an angry tone, "you've only seen these kids for one game and yet you're saying they can't play. They can play, maybe a different game from the one *you* want—or like—but they *can* play!"

Incensed at Frazier's lack of respect for the head coach, a man whom Laverty looked upon as a legend, the second assistant thundered, "Robert, the only game we *like* is winning!"

"Oh . . . is it *we*, Laverty?"

"Bullshit, Frazier," roared Laverty. "Forget the semantics crap. You know damn well what I mean. You haven't listened to me about recruits and now we've got a real problem. And Jim's the head coach. He has the final say on all recruits."

Frazier felt the crunch of a double-team, and Jim was confronted by a situation ready to explode.

"Bill, let's calm down. Both of you need to calm down," Jim said firmly.

In a conciliatory voice, the head coach continued, "Robert, these young fellas are probably great kids. But, in my opinion, they can't help us against the kind of competition we're going up against next year."

Instead of taking his head coach's words as constructive criticism and as being for the good of the program, Frazier interpreted them as questioning his ability as a recruiter and as a judge of talent. He then tossed another grenade.

"Because they're black?"

Jim and Laverty sat in their chairs, feeling electrocuted. Finally, Jim said, "Coach! Are you kidding?"

"No, I'm not kidding," raged Frazier, who then rose from his chair and stormed out of the room.

Jim and Laverty sat quietly for a moment. Their minds raced through the possible consequences of the flare-up and neither could find one with any promise.

Laverty broke the silence.

"I'm sorry, Jim . . . I blew my stack . . . I blew it."

"No need to be sorry, Bill. But we're well into March, too late for us to get involved with any real good prospects. We've obviously got a real problem here."

They both knew that the problem went well beyond the three recruits, and Jim Keating felt cornered.

9

Jim lay awake, grimly aware that the good recruiting class he needed was not on track. He was repulsed by Robert Frazier's racial accusation, yet wondered if the guilty verdict he attached to Frazier's conduct was completely fair. "Am I being racist for thinking this way?" Jim asked himself, fighting off what he hoped were not malignant sentiments.

But his record of fair treatment of minorities had been consistent and his private mindset did not permit discrimination of any kind. Upon further late-night reflection, Jim concluded what he already knew: His assistant was an immature young man who defended each of his missteps by impeaching others for their prejudice. While he abhorred white racists—and still saw plenty of them—he was also rankled by blacks who intemperately used race as a knife-edged weapon. Jim felt that such a tactic reflected selfish, if not cowardly behavior. "I'm not sure which I dislike more," he confided to Edna, "white bigots or black people who unfairly indict white people as bigots."

Jim carefully considered his options.

He could go to the athletic director, or even the president, and ask for Frazier's dismissal. After all, he had made it clear from the beginning that he wanted final say on all assistants. But he did not feel secure enough—not yet at least—to bring either of his superiors into this quandary. He also knew that neither the president nor the athletic director would allow him to discharge Frazier without reasons far more compelling than he could offer at this time.

"Why weren't you more involved in the recruiting?" would be the first question. In the hard-line world of Division I basketball, the coach would not have a satisfactory answer.

"We need the basketball program to win and win big," President Mahon had said to Jim. "We need the revenue, and we need the exposure to attract other students to this school. Don't break any rules, but get players. As long as they qualify by NCAA standards, we'll get them through."

Of course, in the same breath Mahon had demanded that Jim retain a coach who, as it turned out, would actually hinder the president's objective of achieving basketball success.

But to fire an assistant for reasons other than NCAA violations, especially a minority assistant, was extremely difficult. If the dismissal was to be based on incompetence or insubordination—or both—then the head coach needed detailed documentation, not to mention virtual unanimity of opinion among those who closely observed the assistant.

On this count, Jim had no hope for success. Aside from game stats, recruiting, and scouting, he did not keep records, and, to Jim's knowledge, Robert Frazier had broken no NCAA rules. Also, Frazier had gained the trust of most or all of the players on the team. Jim knew that members of a losing squad often bonded with an assistant. The assistant is not the guy taking them out of a game or, in most cases—including this one—disciplining them in any way. While Jim tried to be forthright with each one of his athletes about playing time and other team matters, Frazier appeared to be of the "tell them what they want to hear" school, even if that included subtle disagreement with the head coach's strategy.

Jim was sure that few, if any, players would view Frazier as incompetent, and most would probably see his politic second-guessing of his boss as evidence of his concern for the team rather than the stealth maneuver it really was.

As far as Frazier's ability as a recruiter, the three prospects had not yet been tested against college competition, and thus no objective case could be made about his capacity to judge talent. Finally, as Jim admitted to his wife, "I certainly can't prove insubordination. As you know, record keeping is just not part of my world."

He continued, "It's funny, Edna. The only resolution to this situation is that Frazier gets an offer from another school. But as we both know, coaching is a profession with a pretty lively grapevine. I'm sure our competitors realize that he had much of the say in the three recruits and that none of them can help us. I should have listened to Bill Laverty several months ago, especially when he told me that not one of the three have any other firm Division I offers.

"The irony is amazing. I've got an assistant who, while he knows the game, is not a good judge of talent, is certainly disloyal, and was forced on me. And disloyal assistants, who are also poor judges of talent, sure as heck aren't in great demand. So I have to keep him!"

Yet in making the determination that Frazier would have to stay, Jim also resolved to get personally involved with recruiting next year's class. There were many fine prospects in New York City, Jersey, and Philly. Jim would mark out a ninety-mile radius on the map and make day trips to look at recruits, thus allowing him to be home by late evening. Frazier would handle overnight scouting of players who resided out of the immediate area. And any prospect under serious consideration for a scholarship would have to be evaluated by Laverty.

Finally, because he felt he had no other choice at this belated date, Jim would authorize Frazier to sign the three recruits.

Despite the late hour, Jim called Frazier and got his answering machine.

"Robert, please come in tomorrow at 10 AM. We need to meet."

———

The next morning, sleepless and tense, Jim made coffee, then received an unexpected gift. Generally, the pain-killing pills that helped Edna sleep also brought on early-morning incoherence. But on this particular morning, she was lucid, and the timing was opportune to ask for her advice.

"You've heard most of my grumbling about Robert Frazier, love," he said. "What's your view on it?"

"Jim, you know as well as anyone that there are certain relationships when it's not 50/50. With Robert Frazier, it sounds like it's going to have to be more like 95/5. But . . . you're good at that kind of giving," she added gently.

Her eyes welled defensively, not in lament over her own state, but in a gesture of silent benediction in response to her husband's unconditional love, as reflected so tenderly in his care of her.

Edna then said, "My best advice is to approach him as a colleague rather than an opponent. And no matter what, don't lose your temper in any conversation with him."

Jim left for his office, committed to following Edna's counsel by starting the meeting with some mollifying words. But on the ride over, he found himself focusing on another weak point of Frazier's character that bothered him: Never once had Frazier asked about Edna. Jim was certainly not a man who sought sympathy, but he knew that members of a real "team" cared about those problems that trespassed upon the lives of other team members. Bill Laverty and graduate assistant Bob DiMello had consistently shown their concern over Edna's plight and the pain it caused their head coach, but Frazier had never expressed the slightest interest in the burden confronting Jim.

Jim knew that he must push these thoughts aside and be positive at the meeting. But when Frazier showed up twenty minutes late, with no apology, his tardy arrival and sullen expression quickly fired the old coach's competitive coals. While not showing any anger, Jim decided to get right to the point.

"Robert, I've been coaching for more than three decades and never—*ever*—has anyone questioned me in terms of my fairness as it relates to racial issues."

Frazier's expressionless silence chilled the office.

"We're almost into April," Jim continued directly, "and there are no other players that we're going to be able to get involved with at this late date. So you go ahead and sign those three kids and let's do the best we can with 'em."

Frazier remained silent, offering not even a nod of acknowledgement.

Jim added more force to his words.

"You'll still be in charge of recruiting, but there will have to be some changes in next year's plan."

The veteran coach paused to let his words take effect. Frazier continued to sit in silence and avoided eye contact.

Without mentioning Edna's illness, and how it related to the new plan, Jim moved to his main point.

"I'm going to work with you on kids in New Jersey, New York City, and Philly. You can handle the kids out of the region," said Jim. "Also, next year we'll have a policy that before we sign any kid, Bill will have input and I'll have the final say."

Frazier continued to withhold even the hint of a response. But while annoyed with his assistant's lack of common tact throughout the meeting, Jim tried to end the session on a positive tone by offering some genial words.

"Robert, I want you to be happy in this position. I want you to feel part of it and I want to be supportive of you. But it seems as if things aren't clicking. Tell me, what can I do to make it better for you?"

Frazier shook his head and then he stared out the window for a grating twenty seconds. Without even looking back at Jim, he finally said, "Coach, whether I'm happy or not doesn't matter. It's whether the kids are happy."

Bullshit, thought Jim. *Here's this young assistant, convincing himself that he's taking the high road by using the old ploy of "it's not my happiness, but the happiness of others that counts."*

But Jim remained composed.

"And how can I make the kids happier? I really want to do that, and I want your help."

"You have to respect them more; they're young adults."

Jim seethed, but kept his outward calm.

"And how would you suggest I respect them more?"

"Treat 'em like men, coach. Let's get rid of some of the silly rules. As I said, these are young adults, not kids."

Jim's response was reflexive and physical. He stood up and walked to the window.

College athletes need rules, he thought. *They need structure. It's not a racial thing, it's not something discovered last week, it's just a fact. My rules aren't that strict, and they certainly aren't silly. And this guy has never once questioned the rules—never even brought the damn issue up—until today!*

But Jim kept his thoughts to himself. The start of practice was seven months off; there would be ample opportunity to react to Frazier's comments. A harsh exchange at this time would serve no purpose.

He turned back toward Frazier and said, "I appreciate your points, Robert. Let me think about them. Let's talk about this again."

Frazier got up and nodded and, without saying good-bye, left the room.

Jim Keating slumped unsatisfied in his chair. His chest felt heavy, and worst-case scenarios crowded his mind.

10

Jim followed through on his resolution to take an active role in recruiting. In mid-July of '86, four months after he made this plan known to Frazier and the other staff members, the NCAA "live recruiting period" opened up. This meant that for the next four weeks, the NCAA would allow Jim and his staff to evaluate players. In Jim's case, he would remain committed to limiting his travel to a ninety-mile radius.

On those July days when there was a nearby summer league game of interest, Jim would prepare an early dinner for Edna, go down the checklist with the visiting nurse, then set out for the game, always returning before midnight.

Jim soon found that recruiting had taken a U-turn from the process he'd known in his earlier years at St. Thomas. He became fully enlightened of this transformation on a hot night in south Jersey. An assistant from another university, who had acquired a reputation as a top-flight recruiter, came over to introduce himself to Jim. The young coach spoke at a staccato pace about how, growing up, he had admired Jim, considering him to be a true leader in the profession. As Jim began to respond in a cordial manner, he noticed that the young man was looking past Jim, obviously trying to find someone else more important and losing focus on what the veteran coach had to say.

Minutes later, Jim took a seat in the stands several rows behind this same assistant, who was now regaling others with his stories of recruiting.

"We have a system that finds kids as early as the eighth grade and then we track 'em. By the time they're juniors, my 'US Postal Plan' kicks in. I send 'em somethin' in the mail every day—a postcard, letter, story from a newspaper—anything that shows 'em we're interested. By their senior year, it's my 'Fed-Ex Attack!' I overnight 'em stuff. Makes 'em feel real important."

"What about faxing, Coach?"

"Never! Any kid rich enough to own a fax isn't good enough to play for us. Now, my girlfriend, who's a real computer geek, keeps tellin' me about new technology that'll soon replace the fax and make it even easier to communicate with recruits. She's keepin' an eye on it for me, so I guess I better keep her around!"

Jim sat quietly, galled at what he was hearing. At St. Thomas, he had recruited from strength—top flight players actually sought him out because of the program's excellence. It then became a matter of several phone calls, an appointment at the young man's home to meet the family, and then a weekend visit by the player to St. Thomas—that was it. Now this: a recruiting policy named after the postal service and developing technology that Jim knew nothing about— and did not care to learn.

But despite his distaste for some of the new elements of recruiting, the summer evaluation program was successful. Jim was able to identify several "sleepers"—players who would not be recruited by the high majors, but who had the potential to really improve and thus help State. Laverty was impressed with Jim's keen eye and with the promise of the recruits. Frazier was non-committal.

Jim also used the summer months to try to enhance staff harmony and improve his own relationship with Frazier. He held several meetings with Frazier and Laverty both present to encourage the two to work more closely together. He also made it a point to take Frazier to lunch whenever their schedules allowed. But at the meetings and private luncheons, the most cooperation Frazier could muster was a polite nod at Jim's entreaties for more teamwork among the coaches. Jim knew he was making little headway with his assistant and remained wary of the potential ramifications of the poor relationship.

"Maybe when practice starts in October, he'll get caught up with what we're trying to do," he said unconvincingly to Edna.

Jim also met regularly with Athletic Director Bill Connors to keep him abreast of the program's progress, including the situation regarding Robert Frazier. When Jim had first told Connors about the potential problem with Frazier, the athletic director had stridently expressed his concern.

"This is something you *must* handle, Jim. Frazier is an alumnus . . . a number of people like him. More importantly, while I'm sure he can be difficult, the last thing the president wants to hear, especially with our record of minority hiring, is that we have a problem with a black assistant."

When practice started in October, it was well-known that State's ambitious step to Division I status forced them to play a tough schedule. The team had to book many away games for large guarantees to help pay the bills and build a formidable slate that would appeal to recruits. In Jim's second year, State's first eight games would be on the road—all for substantial guarantees and all against opponents that would, at least on paper, appear better than State.

Only two days into the pre-season practice, Jim could see that his instincts about Frazier's three recruits were correct.

One of the three, 6'2" guard Jim Atkinson, impressed Jim with his work ethic and positive attitude. But he was a marginal Division I player at best. The other two, both spidery 6'6" forwards, would need to add considerable bulk to their upper bodies to successfully compete at the Division I level. Because he needed players, red shirting these three young men was out of the question. Jim's words to the media were guarded.

"We'll be young and the schedule is challenging. I think we're at least a year or two away, but we're certainly making progress," he said.

Jim was more candid with his athletic director. "The three recruits Robert signed are borderline at best—just as I was afraid of. They're all good kids, but they're not first-rate players. The positive side, though, is that we do have some fine prospects on the line for next year."

"What about this year?" asked Connors. "Can we make .500?"

"Very doubtful . . . the talent is so poor that I'll have to include at least one of those freshmen in an eight- or nine-man rotation."

"And how about the Frazier situation—how's that coming along?"

"To be honest, it's hard to say. He's been somewhat cooperative, but it doesn't seem that he's got his heart in the program. He was upset when I took some of the recruiting away from him and, at times, it seems as if he almost doesn't care."

"What's the make-up of your team," Connors asked, frankly. "You know, how many black kids, how many white kids?"

"We have ten blacks and two whites, same as last year."

"What about the starting five, the first seven or eight?"

"We'll start five black kids. The sixth and seventh men are both white, the rest of the team are all black kids. As I mentioned, I'll probably go with an eight- or nine-man rotation."

"How does Frazier feel about all of this?"

"He seems fine about it. We've had a number of discussions about our rotation. Frazier hasn't voiced any disagreement."

"Jim, you *must* contain this Frazier thing," Connors said.

The second season began on Friday of Thanksgiving weekend on the road against the powerful University of Memphis. New Jersey State was beaten by 35 points in the opener. In the following four weeks against top-flight competition away from home, the team lost its next seven games by an average of 23 points. Morale was low, and the fingers of the players started to take aim at others on the team—and at Jim Keating. For his part, Robert Frazier grew increasingly aloof, as if he was distancing himself from the entire debacle.

The one thing that seemed to keep the team's focus was that after those first eight games, the schedule would lighten.

———

On a Friday night in early January, after eight lopsided losses and a break for exams, New Jersey State would finally play its first home game.

Better still, the opponent would be Cornell, one of the few Division I programs that did not grant full scholarships, but instead followed the Ivy League rule of awarding need-based financial aid to its student body, including its student-athletes.

Cornell was well-coached and had several fine players, but with the absence of full basketball scholarships, it lacked the overall talent of State's first eight opponents.

"A winnable game" was the way one of the local sportswriters described State's chances. Both the players and coaching staff agreed.

Due in large measure to Robert Frazier's statement about "too many rules," Jim had slightly pared down the list for this season. A standard procedure that remained, and one that was agreed upon by the team and coaching staff, including Frazier, was that players must report to practice and team meetings on time. If any player was late, it was understood the player would not start the next game and his playing time in that game would be limited.

The day before the Cornell game, with the team's state of mind already at low ebb, two starters showed up late for practice with no valid excuse. Without raising his voice, Jim told them they would be benched the following night. Starting in their places would be the squad's sixth and seventh men, the two white players. Because the rules had been made clear to the entire team, Jim gave no thought to any racial implications. In his mind, it was a simple matter: The two starters had not adhered to a guiding principal, and both subs had worked hard enough to merit the starting assignments.

When he patiently announced the changes to the team, out of the corner of his eye, Jim noticed that Frazier was shaking his head in disagreement. Jim had certainly been told of his assistant's backbiting, but until now, Frazier had never been so openly insurgent.

By showing his dissent with his head coach *in front of the team*, Frazier had committed a cardinal sin in the coaching profession. Jim was furious, and after practice he called Frazier into his office. Behind a slammed shut door, he confronted him.

"Robert, what the hell was that all about?" he asked angrily.

"I felt we should have discussed your decision," said Frazier.

"Discussed my decision!?" Jim railed. For the first time, Jim Keating was losing control in a conversation with his assistant coach. Recalling Edna's advice about the importance of composure in dealing with Frazier, Jim tried to calm himself, with little success.

"We reviewed the rules with the team in November," he continued. "All the team members signed off on the rules, including you. How the hell could you do such a thing today?"

"I don't want to discuss it," Frazier answered, contradicting his point about the need for discussion.

"Well, damn it, *I* want to discuss it!"

Frazier glared at Jim and then got up and left the room. This time, the walk-out would quick-step him to a state of severe consequence.

Athletic Director Connors was away at the NCAA annual convention. He was expected back the following night and was likely to be at the Cornell game. Jim decided he would phone Connors's secretary and schedule a meeting with him as soon as he returned.

The subject of the session would be Jim Keating's intention to fire Robert Frazier.

———

After a night of careful, albeit fretful, reflection, Jim Keating remained firm in his decision to terminate Robert Frazier. At 8:30 AM, Jim called Bill Connors's secretary, Doris Flanders, only to find that Connors had changed his travel plans.

"He called in late yesterday," Doris said. "Told me that the NCAA has appointed him to a special committee to study sports marketing trends in college athletics. He's pretty excited about it."

"When'll he be back, Doris?" Jim asked, trying to mask his sense of urgency.

"Well, the committee will meet all day today and, since it's Friday and it's Las Vegas, he's decided to stay over and fly back early tomorrow. He'll be in first thing on Monday."

"Can I get in to see him at nine on Monday?"

"I'll put you down for nine, Jim. Should be no problem."

"Will he be calling in today?"

"He normally does, but because of the time change and the tight schedule of this meeting, he wasn't sure if he'd be able to."

"Well, if he does, please have him call me. Otherwise, I'll see him Monday morning."

While Jim had made up his mind to fire Frazier, he knew that he must meet with Connors to get clearance. With the meeting likely off until Monday, he decided that any contact with Frazier would be limited to game-related matters.

The strain from losing eight in a row, dealing with the Edna's rapid decline, and now being faced with the prospect of discharging a disloyal assistant had taken a terrible toll on Jim's health and will. In each of the last four nights he had gotten no more than two or three hours sleep, and the fatigue showed in every grooved furrow on his face. Like all coaches going through a long losing streak, he did not merely hope for a win—he *craved* one.

Before heading to the gym, he made a cup of coffee and went up to the bedroom to see Edna. She managed a smile and said, "So, Coach, is it a 'W' tonight?"

"Tonight, we can do it, Edna," he intoned, as if in prayer.

Jim arrived at the gym two hours before tip-off. Thirty minutes later, when Frazier showed up, Jim said only "Hello, Robert," then quickly turned away. Frazier headed for his office and closed the door. When the players gathered in the locker room for pre-game instructions, he joined the group and stood quietly as Jim wrote instructions on the blackboard. Once Jim finished writing out the briefing, he animatedly reviewed it with his team. There was a feeling of anticipation in the locker room that had been absent since just prior to the first game.

But when the game began thirty minutes later, the anticipation evaporated and anxiety overtook the team. State missed its first eight shots, the two white players performed poorly, and Cornell went on to win by 18 points. Had the

Cornell coach not substituted so freely in the last five minutes of the game, the margin would have been even greater.

For a coach, the minutes that immediately follow a loss are occupied with a swift transformation of body chemistry. During the game, the coach is in a state of complete immersion. A wall is built between him and all thoughts other than those related to the game. Adrenaline courses through his body. When the game is over, and if the outcome is a win, the adrenaline produces a blitz of endorphins that result in a state of euphoric relaxation. But if the outcome is a loss, the transformation is a harsh sensation that Jim once described to Edna.

"It's sort of like a chill that displaces the adrenaline. As you walk off the court, you feel kind of frozen, almost as if some type of icy layer has formed around your body and also—especially—your mind. The feeling of dejection, of hopelessness, is overwhelming. You know you're going to be miserable for a day or two, or even more, depending on when your next chance is to get a win."

For Jim Keating, this particular loss not only left him with that cold and bleak feeling he so dreaded, but it also brought on the wrath of more than a few unhappy fans.

"Hang it up, Keating!" yelled one particularly vocal critic.

Within moments, he would find that the disgruntlement of the fans fell far short of what awaited him in the locker room.

11

After all games, Jim Keating's rule was that by the time he got to the locker room, the players had to be seated, waiting to listen to his post-game comments. But tonight, only a few players were in their chairs and the others were angrily removing their uniforms or talking in small groups.

Jim knew he must put his own hurt in storage and act strong. He tried by firmly ordering the entire team to take their seats. Several players refused, and the coach was faced with a direct affront to his authority. There had been a handful of times in his career when he had been challenged by individual players, but never after a nine-game losing streak—the longest losing streak in his career—and never by a faction this large.

"Hey, we're all upset, but we're not gonna throw in the towel. Now get to your seats."

The words had no impact. Several of the seated players began to look around at their rebellious teammates, wondering if they should join them. Bill Laverty tried to grab hold of the situation by imploring the group to sit, but just as he finished his appeal, Robert Frazier spoke up.

"Maybe these players have a right, yeah, a right, to be upset."

It was a statement of outright insurrection, and Jim was so distressed by it that his face literally writhed in anguish. For an excruciating moment, despair overtook this combat veteran, this coach who had fought in the NBA trenches, and he became mute. But Laverty, younger and of stronger will, quickly retaliated.

"Shut up, Robert!" he yelled.

Laverty's statement provoked a swarm of invectives by the players. Some were directed at him for rebuking Frazier; others were aimed at the team's lowly state of affairs . . . and all knifed into Jim Keating's heart. The situation had gyrated out of control.

Jim knew he had to regain some form of order, but the best he could do was to ramble a few sentences about things getting better. When the angry players refused to acknowledge his words, most either unlacing their sneakers or simply staring at the floor, Jim turned to Laverty and said quietly, "Bill, tell the team that I'd like to meet with them at noon tomorrow. Also, please handle the post-game press briefing for me."

Jim Keating was so hurt, so disoriented, he could say no more. He had to leave—*escape*—the locker room. His spirit broken, he walked into the corridor and quickly detoured away from the press room to the parking lot. When he opened the door to the outside, the cold night air roared hard into his face and made him dizzy.

Jim trudged toward his car. Only steps before he reached it, he stopped and threw up, discharging both food and pent-up emotions. After looking around to make sure that no one was watching, he got into his car and pulled it quickly to the rear of the parking lot, to the darkest area where no one would see him. The veteran coach, the old soldier, then did something that he had not done since his mother died: He wept uncontrollably.

On the way home, trying to regain his composure, he stopped at a gas station, bought a coffee, and washed his face. The nurse greeted Jim at the front door, tactfully avoided asking about the game, mentioned that Edna was asleep, and left quietly. Jim slumped in a chair and dozed off.

The following morning, he received a phone call from a campus newspaper reporter.

"Coach Keating, we've been told that at least three players are quitting the team—and that more will soon follow. One player told me you're insensitive to minorities."

"I have no comment," said Jim softly and hung up.

Insensitive to minorities.

Moments later, Jim received a call from Laverty.

"Jim, I went over to campus early this morning to see some of the players. It's not good. The co-captains, plus some other kids, are saying they're quitting. The co-captains are circulating a petition asking for your resignation. They're using race as a reason, and I'll bet that Frazier's orchestrating this whole thing."

Jim felt queasy, but he was able to speak. "Can we try to get the team together at noon?"

"I'll do the best I can, Coach."

At 11:30 AM, Jim headed for his office. On the ride over, he heard a radio news bulletin that reported on the "mutiny" of the State basketball team. The situation had advanced to a crisis.

Fifteen minutes later, Jim entered the team meeting room. Laverty and graduate assistant Bob DiMello, back from a scouting trip, were both present. Frazier was not. Five minutes later, one of the rebellious co-captains walked in and coldly presented Jim with the petition calling for his resignation. Among the points listed, the most lethal was: "Coach

Keating has lost touch with the needs of many of the minority members of the team." The petition was signed by nine of the twelve team members. The signatures of the two white players and freshman Jim Atkinson, whose grit Jim had so admired, did not appear on the document.

In some ways, Jim wished the two white players in particular had signed the petition. He deplored racial division, and their missing names would surely be construed by many as an example of that division, rather than what Jim felt to be the real case—their recognition of the injustice that Frazier had helped engineer.

Moments after the co-captain left, the three who remained loyal showed up. Each player quietly approached Jim and shook his hand. The last in the line was Atkinson, the lone African American not to sign. He stared sadly into Jim's eyes and said, "Coach, this isn't fair."

Such a declaration of support always stands out in a time of peril, especially when made by someone with the conviction to break from the peer group. In thanking Atkinson, Jim found his rickety emotions nearly melting in tears.

By early Saturday afternoon, the story was on the wires, and radio and television stations were rampant with reports of the "anarchy" on the State team. A halftime feature on the CBS College Game of the Week focused on statements of several players that referred to "Coach Keating's racial insensitivity."

Bill Connors, back from Las Vegas, left Jim a voicemail. "Jim, I need to see you today. Please come by my office at 5:00 PM."

Connors liked Jim, but he knew that he had no choice but to remove his coach from the whipping post. Jim's intended discussion about firing Robert Frazier took a 180-degree turn.

"Jim," Connors began softly, "this is about the toughest thing I've ever had to do as an administrator."

Connors had to pause for a moment. At thirty-eight, the athletic director knew he was too young to fully understand the complex emotions that overwhelmed this erstwhile legend. What he did understand was that the news he would now relay would be devastating.

"We're going to have to make a change, Jim. Robert Frazier is going to take over the team. I'm going to have to terminate you."

Jim was a veteran of firings. While not surprised with his fate, the wave of despair that accompanies such devastating news swamped his senses. His hands began to shake, physical evidence of the forlornness that now overwhelmed him.

After a brief but jarring reflection on the implications of his dismissal, including how the firing would affect him monetarily and psychologically, Jim regained enough composure to ask Connors, "What about my assistants?"

"Bob and I will have to work that out. I know there's friction, and it may be that we have to assign Coach Laverty in particular to other duties until the season ends. In any case, we'll honor the three contracts."

As Connors walked around to the front of his desk, Jim was determined to remain stoic. They shook hands. Neither said anything. In a move reminiscent of his parade ground demeanor, Jim turned and strode out of the office. In the parking lot, he instinctively looked at his watch; it was 5:25 PM, and the chilled air met the dusk.

As he walked slowly toward his car, one step ahead of the darkness, Jim thought to himself: *Nothing worse than this could ever happen to me.*

Four months later, Edna McCarthy Keating died.

II
Hope

12

Even after his lone outing to the Golden Gloves, Jim Keating still had to draw deeply from his creative resources to avoid simply going back to bed or mindlessly watching TV. Every morning, just after dawn, he would begin his one-mile walk to early Mass at St. Peter's, hoping for a brief reprieve from grief.

The Catholic Church had been Jim's lifelong companion, if not always his close friend. As with any lengthy relationship, there had been some disagreements.

Jim was firm in his belief that abortion was, in most cases, murder—"a malignancy out of control," in his words. Yet he wondered if he would be so resolute if his own daughter were raped and impregnated. He often recalled the surprise he felt when reading an article by a Catholic theologian that stated both Saint Augustine and Saint Thomas Aquinas thought prostitution immoral and yet supported its legalization. According to the author, both saints believed that "greater evils would come about if this outlet for aberrant sexual energy were outlawed." Aquinas went so far as to write that "the wise legislator would be imitating God, who tolerates certain evils lest greater evils ensue."

In making the case for legalized abortion, the author proposed that a Catholic legislator who views all abortions as immoral could still vote to keep it legal because of the problems that would occur, especially for poor women, if it were made illegal.

Yet how would Saint Augustine and Saint Thomas Aquinas really view the abortion conundrum, as opposed to prostitution? In asking himself the question, Jim could not come up with a firm answer.

Divorce, in Jim's opinion, had become a matter of convenience for too many, with little regard for its impact on children, and the Vatican was correct in standing firmly against it. And when the New York Diocese vehemently protested the notion of public schools dispensing condoms to kids, he gave this opposition his silent support. Such a misguided policy, he felt, was nothing more than a wink, with no regard for what unbridled sex does to a youngster's ultimate self-esteem.

Jim knew many priests who embodied humility. Yet he deplored the clerical arrogance that seemed so prevalent within the Catholic Church, and he also did not agree with every tenet. Priests, he thought, should be allowed to marry. This would help rid the Church of the many pedophiles that entered the priesthood to hide out from their deviancy, a deviancy that had caused irreparable harm to thousands of innocent children . . . and to the reputation of the Church. He felt outrage over his Church's shameful cover-up of these countless misdeeds.

Jim also felt that women should be granted Holy Orders and not be relegated to inconsequential positions. And he wondered why so many Catholics were so blatantly prejudiced against minorities and why the Church was not more vigilant in combating this unjust attitude. Underlying Jim's feelings about all these issues was a constant irritation at the attitude of superiority, the downright haughtiness so often displayed by some Catholics: They had the answers, and if they didn't, well, the Pope did.

In the last few weeks of Edna's life, just after he had been fired, Jim Keating's Catholicism faced its most severe challenge. Edna had been in and out of delirium. When coherent, her pain had been excruciating. Jim could not bear to see his beloved wife experience such agony, and he contemplated an option presented to him by her doctor.

"We could administer morphine; it would be very peaceful and quick. It's done all the time in these situations," said the doctor.

Before agreeing to the plan, and knowing of Edna's trust in Catholic theology, Jim consulted with the parish priest, who left no margin for interpretation.

"Jim, no matter how the doctor describes it—palliative medicine—palliative sedation—or whatever . . . it's still assisted suicide and completely against the teachings of the Catholic Church."

Jim canceled the plan and watched Edna suffer through five torturous weeks before she passed—five weeks that were, he felt, completely unnecessary. Jim still had trouble suppressing his anger over this episode; he had watched medics administer morphine to dying soldiers and looked at the act as one that would be favored by a merciful God.

While this bitter experience had caused him to seriously question his religion, and despite what he felt was the Church's fallibility on some issues in which it claimed infallibility, the jolt of spirituality from going to Mass and receiving Communion still gave Jim Keating the modicum of peace he needed to wade through this desperate time in his life. He remained a member of the flock, albeit a questioning one.

After morning Mass, Jim would stop at Alice's, a neighborhood coffee shop. Alice's husband, Paul, had been a young ref when Jim played high school ball, knew Jim's situation, and left him alone. After two over-easy with home fries, the coach would sit in the rear booth with his back to the customers, drink coffee, and read and re-read the *Worcester Telegram*. He would then take his daily walk. Back at the apartment, he would plan errands, often ones he would make up to keep busy. He always kept a book going—a biography, a book on Spanish history, or a Ludlum novel. On rare occasions, he would meet up with an old friend, but only when he felt emotionally armored. He dreaded the risk of a trusted crony witnessing one of his crying spells, which now made frequent and unwelcome visits.

His major expense these days was still his weekly visit to Dr. Rotella, who had reduced his fee by half to accommodate the coach's meager budget. Jim looked forward to his weekly consultation, for Rotella was a kind and compassionate man who clearly empathized with his client's pain.

In their first meeting, Jim remembered experiencing great difficulty in disclosing his past torment.

"Open up, Jim—you need to get in touch with your feelings," Rotella would gently prod. His entreaty evoked an atmosphere of trust and caused Jim to gradually share some important thoughts.

After several sessions, Jim had reached a point of revealing his lost hope, surprising himself with his candor and helping Rotella provide guidance.

"Jim, in your twenties and thirties, you saw yourself leaving large footprints, and the respect you generated—both self-respect and respect from others—was your oxygen. Since then, you've been hit hard with some major blows. You've lost several jobs, and this wreaked havoc on your self-esteem. It was inferred in public that you are a racist . . . and you're certainly no racist. And most importantly, you lost your most trusted friend, the one person in whom you could always confide, someone whose wisdom you fully trusted."

Jim nodded, masking a flick of sadness over the reference to Edna.

"Your career path has been different from most. You started strong in your career then encountered great difficulty. It's always hard for a person who achieves success at a young age to deal with anything short of that success at a later age. And so you think that those footprints I just mentioned have been washed away—a point of view I do not share.

"In fact, I still see a man who has much to contribute. You're healthy and, despite the depression, you're still mentally sharp, something that's not always the case with the clinically depressed. And you've even said yourself how well you remember being in great condition and, now, how much better you feel when you walk."

Dr. Rotella paused for a moment to frame his final thoughts.

"I hate to say it, Coach, but some in our profession rely too much on medication. Somehow, we've got to get you off the medication or at least reduce the dosage. Once that's been done, we need you to continue on the track to greater physical activity. Most importantly, we need to find something that will get that respect back. And Jim, I *know* there's something out there."

Dr. Rotella paused to let his words take seed and then continued, "You remember those pep talks that you gave your teams, the ones about overcoming adversity? You need to give yourself that same pep talk, because I'm certain you can still leave some more footprints."

Yet despite Rotella's entreaty, Jim could not extricate himself from the anti-depressants the New Jersey psychiatrist had prescribed for him after Edna's death. The months continued to idle by without purpose, and Jim's contact with the outside world remained limited to Mass, a stop at the coffee shop, his weekly consultation, and an occasional chat with an old friend. He harbored no amorous thoughts, enmeshed as he was in mourning and dampened by Prozac. And as for his once courted services as a molder of young men, there were no inquiries.

But then one morning, upon returning home from Alice's, he was annoyed to find his phone ringing. He tried to ignore it, but the caller was resolute and the ringing continued. He finally answered and was stunned to hear the voice of a person who had played a starring role in his wondrous Worcester youth.

"You may be the best player to ever come out of Worcester," said the caller in a prankish tone, "but I can still take you to the hoop!"

"Barry . . . Barry Sklar?" stammered Jim, utterly stunned.

Using the nickname he had bestowed on Jim some fifty years ago, Sklar said, "Yeah, General Jim, it's me, and I'm glad you answered. Christ, I've been calling for days."

Jim did not excuse his failure to answer his phone and felt a surge of excitement over hearing the voice of a guy who had been such an integral part of his boyhood.

13

Jim Keating had first met Barry Sklar in the eighth grade at St. Peter's Grammar School, an odd happenstance to begin with, for Barry and his family were Jewish, and the only other Jew with whom St. Peter's School had a relationship had died on a cross. The Sklars had wisely departed Poland four years before the Nazi invasion of '39. They had wended their way to Scotland, stopped for six months, and then spent all of their savings on a freight trip to America and a flat in Brooklyn.

While in Brooklyn, Jacob Sklar had died of cancer, and Helen Sklar, a bold-spirited and resourceful woman, decided that a smaller city would be a more suitable place to raise her children. When the Sklars arrived in Worcester, she determined that her youngest son, Barry, who excelled in the classroom, would attend a school where discipline and diligence were the norm. The sisters at St. Peter's had not only assured her of such rigor, but, while pointing out that her son would have to take part in religious training, they also promised that his faith "would be respected." Barry's older brother, Ben, was skeptical: "This may be America, but we're still Jews."

Barry enrolled in the eighth grade at St. Peter's, and despite the nuns' best intentions, Ben's misgivings proved accurate: Barry's Judaism made an impact on many in the school, especially the hooligans.

Undeterred by the nuns' frequent admonitions, a few of the roughnecks in particular savaged the "little Jew." Jim Keating, the school's phenom, was in the other eighth grade class. He had taken little notice of the new boy until one cold winter afternoon when, on his walk home, he saw two older neighborhood thugs grab Barry and thrust his face into the frigid snow. Barry fought bravely despite his small size, but the two ruffians overpowered him. Jim sensed dead-sure danger and quickly bellowed a demanding, "Let him up!" He spoke in the robust voice that would later play a considerable role in his coaching career.

The yelling startled the two muggers, one of whom looked up at the intruder and growled, "F--k off, Keating. This is none of your business."

At age fourteen, having been reared in an Irish Catholic neighborhood where few outsiders called, Jim Keating had not been forced to consider the inequities brought on by prejudice. However, he recognized that the act before him was well below the belt and quickly yanked the two bullies off Barry and administered a beating to both, which Barry told him several years later looked like a scene stolen from a Jimmy Cagney movie.

"Don't come near this kid again," was the vocal end to a message begun by fists.

Jim pulled Barry up from the snow, looked at the boy's frightened eyes, and concluded that he clearly had some experience with such terror. Jim walked the shaky, disoriented Barry home. Upon answering the door, Helen correctly assumed he had come to the aid of her son, and her appreciation was immediate. She gave Jim a glass of milk and some

cookies and quietly thanked him. As she walked him to the
door, he could see tears welling in her eyes. For the first time
in his life, he began to comprehend the pain of prejudice.

From that day on, the two boys were best friends.
Everyone in the neighborhood knew that no one could touch
Barry Sklar without reprisal from Jim Keating . . . and no one
did.

As often comes about in close friendships, the virtues of
the two soon harmonized. Barry admired Jim's athletic prowess and street-wise ways, and Jim enjoyed Barry's sophisticated and ironic sense of humor and appreciated his friend's
unswerving loyalty.

They stayed in touch through college. But after graduation, Barry enrolled in a two-year master's program at the
Fletcher School of Law and Diplomacy at Tufts and then
joined the Foreign Service. Contact between the old friends
was limited to holiday cards.

Now here was Barry on the phone, and his tone seemed
upbeat.

"A few months ago, I was reassigned to Washington after
spending the better part of thirty years in various African
and South American posts," said Barry to Jim, who was still
recovering from his surprise. "I'm calling to offer belated con-
dolences about Edna. Jim, I didn't know and I'm so sorry. . . .
She was a wonderful person."

"That she was, Barry. I miss her greatly."

"And I hope Sarah is doing well."

"Thank you. She's doing very well."

Barry made no mention of New Jersey State, and there
was an awkward pause that he quickly broke. "I know we have
to catch up on a lot of lost years, but I wanted to ask you a
favor."

Jim Keating did not consider himself capable of dispensing favors but he replied without deliberation. "Sure, Barry."

Barry then pressed to the point.

"My last African post was in a small country called Burundi. Ever hear of it?"

"I have, but only recently. Isn't that the country with all the trouble—the one next to Rwanda?"

"That's the one, and like you, most people had never heard of either Rwanda or Burundi until the last couple of months. It's a small, land-locked country—Zaire and Tanzania are the other bordering countries," said Barry, his voice beginning to resonate with excitement.

"As you've probably read," he continued, "two tribes make up most of the population in Burundi, the Hutus and the Tutsis. While the Hutus make up about 85 percent of the population, they've traditionally been in the minority as far as governance is concerned, and the Tutsis have often ruled in a very violent and oppressive manner over the centuries. About two years ago, the Hutus gained power in the country's first democratic election. Naturally, the Tutsis were not in favor of such change, and, as you've read, violence unlike most of us have ever observed anywhere in the world has broken out in the last several months."

Barry added, "While it's not as bad in Burundi as it is in Rwanda, several hundred thousand people from both tribes in Burundi are now dead and several hundred thousand more Hutus have fled to Kenya."

Jim listened intently, but was perplexed by Barry's detailed explanation of a country he knew little about.

"Jim, the point of all of this is to tell you that I've been asked to develop some programs that would, at least in some small way, help the situation and, in the process, hopefully develop better relations between America and Burundi. Our government is now concerned about what's going on over there, at least as concerned as we get about anything on that continent, which is generally not very concerned at all. But I've been pushed to come up with something—so let me tell you my thoughts.

"I may not be a great sports expert, but when I was there, I was always amazed at the natural athleticism I saw in both tribes. The Hutus are small—a big Hutu might be no more than six feet—but they're very strong and quick. The Tutsis are another story. Their average height is about six-foot-seven, and it's not unusual to see a group of seven-footers walking down the street together. What's remarkable to me is how uncannily agile many of them are. Now, here's my idea."

Barry's suspenseful pause caused Jim to press his ear closer to the phone; the diplomat had set the hook.

"The big sport is soccer, but basketball is coming along. And Jim, I've a hunch that if we organize a basketball development program, we might make some headway, however limited it might be, in bringing the two tribes together. It's heady stuff because the implications go far beyond the game. To pull it off, I need a damned good coach."

"Then you haven't followed my career lately!" said Jim. An actual laugh accompanied the statement—the first in a very long time.

"I've followed it, and I know that, in spite of all the nonsense you've been through, you're a *great* coach. And more to the point, Jim, my ass is on the line to move forward and I need the right guy. For whatever reason, the State Department is excited about this idea and I'm convinced that you're the person for this job."

Barry's offer seized Jim's mind. The coach needed a time-out to deliberate, but his old friend kept on shooting:

"It'd be one year; then we evaluate and hopefully go on with the project, but no promises at this point. The salary would be pretty good, $4,500 a month, plus the normal government benefits package, including insurance. Also, you'd stay in an apartment connected to the home of our ambassador's top assistant, so the living quarters would be fine—actually more than fine. We own several homes—mansions really—that were built in the '20s and '30s by the Belgians when they colonized Burundi.

"Jim, I'm not asking you to make a decision today, but I am asking you to give it serious thought. It's an important and noble position; probably more important, and certainly more noble, than most coaches have ever taken on, simply because the project could actually save some lives."

They continued to speak for several more minutes. Barry provided more details on Burundi. Jim tried to process the many facets of the proposal.

When the two hung up, Barry pulled from his drawer the letter that had been the real basis for the call. Another old friend from the neighborhood had written to Barry, relating the news of Edna's death, Jim's dismissal, and that "Jimmy could use some help. Here's his unlisted number."

Barry Sklar had no trouble recalling what Jim's friendship had meant to him in his beginnings. As editor of the high school yearbook, he also remembered the phrase he had made sure appeared under Jim Keating's picture, a phrase Barry had learned from his own mother:

"When a friend is in need, there is no tomorrow."

14

Jim Keating had accepted the notion that no one would ever again solicit his basketball services. But in one brief conversation, an old friend had dissolved that feeling, leaving Jim in a quandary. Barry's presentation had come at the coach like a well-executed fast break, confronting him with options with which he was not quite ready to cope.

Jim had always recognized that Edna's analytical skills surpassed his, and he had constantly sought her opinion on important decisions. In many instances during their life together, he wished he had followed her advice, particularly when he chose to leave St. Thomas for the Pistons.

Since her death, his only major decision had been to relocate to his hometown. And while his financial state played a major role in his move, he had also recalled reading a sports column in which the journalist quoted Robert Frost: "Home is a place where, if you have to go there, they have to take you in."

And Worcester *had* taken him in. The town bowed properly at his return, but also left him space to navigate the ill winds of his despair.

Jim Keating had grown comfortable in his new milieu and was thus uncomfortable with the thought of another defeat. Yet there still lingered within him a desire for greater achievement.

"What would Edna have told me to do?" he wondered to himself, quickly realizing that she would have told him to follow the path of careful analysis.

So Jim tried to follow in Edna's cautionary wake, stepping back to dissect the situation. The fact that there was a salary, and a good one at that, was no small incentive, for he was in dire need of money. But he had also gotten quite used to his apartment and, although he was at most times despondent, he felt increasingly at ease in his old neighborhood—always in sight of a good memory. Yet surely the salary would allow him to keep the apartment while away.

Jim spoke with Dr. Rotella, who was unequivocal in his advice:

"Help people through basketball? And get paid for it? This is the one—do it!"

Then there was his beloved Sarah, more strong-willed than ever. Edna's illness had brought Jim even closer to Sarah, but after Edna's death, Sarah grew concerned over her father's idleness, and Jim became upset with his daughter's recent change of address.

Due in large measure to Edna's maternal skills, especially when Jim was on his overseas sojourn, Sarah Keating had been raised with great affection and indulged by her parents to a degree just shy of spoiling. Bright and diligent, she attended the College of William and Mary, majored in English literature, and graduated *cum laude*. She then enrolled in a master's program in Creative Writing at Princeton. While there, she fell in love with a fellow graduate student.

Sarah had been devastated over the cruel, lingering demise of her mother. The searing deathwatch had prompted her to seek intimacy to hold steady. In a phone conversation several weeks after Edna's death, she drew a deep breath and then revealed to her father that she had moved in with her male companion. Since this announcement, dad and daughter, both fiercely stubborn though brimming with love for each other, had been on chilly terms. Jim knew that the time was not right for a rift with Sarah and that he needed his daughter's affection and support in this anguished period of his life. He also knew that his rigid position on her relationship was out of step with the masses. Nonetheless, he viewed her cohabitation as living in sin.

"You're too Catholic, Daddy," she had protested. "It's like Mummy used to say, 'You need doctrine, Jim. Your daughter does not.'"

"Maybe so," he had countered, "but I'm also sick of a society that takes no responsibility for its actions. And in this case, it's not about being too Catholic. You know that I love you more than anything on this planet. But the love between a man and a woman is an incremental process, Sarah. It's about going from the temporary to the permanent in steps. In my view—and I'm not alone in this view—these steps help you go from short-term desire to long-term commitment. To me, and I'm being blunt because I love you so much, by moving in with this guy, you're skipping critical steps."

In some measure, she felt that his comments were her dad's way of romanticizing the past. *Dad,* she thought to herself, *sexual relationships of people my age are not much different from what went on in your youth, and they are certainly not as promiscuous as the '60s. And by the way, that bygone era to which you are so attached had a whole lot of domestic violence and other not-so-nice activities related to marriage.*

But given Jim's state of mind, she refrained from saying these things and even admitted to herself that his words had struck a chord.

When Jim finally called his daughter to discuss Barry Sklar's offer, he decided to make no mention of her residence, and she bubbled with enthusiasm over his new opportunity.

"Daddy, you've spent your whole life helping people and you still have so much to offer. You should do this! And if you do, I want to see you before you leave."

"Me too!" said Jim.

It had been the first positive conversation between the two since Sarah had told Jim of her new living quarters. And while the thought of being thousands of miles away from her caused him great concern, he now realized that the distance might bring them closer together.

Buoyed by his conversations with his daughter and Dr. Rotella, Jim decided to go to the library to do more reading about Burundi. His research corroborated what Barry had said about the problems.

"God, this place makes Northern Ireland look peaceful," he thought.

But of greatest interest to Jim Keating was the frequent reference in his readings to the strength and agility of many Burundians. And then he viewed a remarkable picture that appeared in a dated copy of National Geographic. In the photo was a lithe and long-limbed Tutsi standing, Jim envisioned, as if he were waiting for a basketball to be placed in his hands.

At heart, Jim Keating was still a coach, and the picture of the towering boy gripped his attention. To Jim, the boy had *the look*—an insight hard to describe and one which, in Jim's view, could only be seen by an experienced coach. It was a look of confidence combined with quiet intensity, qualities that seemed requisite to success as an athlete.

He reflected on the situation for several more days, but the picture and the chance to help people in need were the clinchers. He finally called Barry and said simply, "Barry, I'm ready."

"I'm thrilled, Jim," boomed Barry. "Give me a bit of time to sort out the paperwork, including your flight, and I'll be back in touch. The next step will be for you to come down here for a briefing—about a day and half in length. It'll be a crash course on Burundi and the type of protocol that you'll have to be aware of when you get over there. Also, I'll tell you more about Cynthia Foster, our US ambassador to Burundi. She's a remarkable woman, and I'm sure you're going to like her. Believe me, she'll be very pleased to hear that you're coming."

In Washington, Barry Sklar hung up and slumped in his chair. He had put himself on the line for this job, but did so with a strong conviction that Jim would do great work in Burundi. However, pushing such an unusual appointment through the bureaucracy had not been easy. With the support of Ambassador Foster, an old and dear friend, he had succeeded by selling Jim as *the* person to hire. Due to Barry's persuasiveness, and the ambassador's backing, a massive job search that would have tied the position up interminably—and probably prevented his childhood mate from getting the job—was avoided. And when a colleague raised the issue of Jim's "racial insensitivity" from newspaper reports of his firing, Barry sat down with his fellow worker and told him about the real Jim Keating.

"When I was a kid, there was a no-holds-barred approach to abusing Jews. Somehow, Jim, unlike practically every other kid in our neighborhood, intuitively knew that this was wrong."

Barry then leaned forward and said, "In a very real sense, Jim Keating made sure that I could enjoy my childhood."

Barry Sklar's next step would be to develop the briefing session. There would be much for Jim Keating to learn before he got on the plane to a remote and troubled destination.

———

Barry kept in touch with Jim every other day or so, sent him volumes of information, and finalized the many elements of Jim's mission. Four weeks to the day his old friend gave his assent, Barry called with upbeat news.

"General Jim, everything is set. I'm sending you an airline ticket to Washington. You'll be here for a day and a half of briefings, then on to Burundi."

Jim had grown increasingly excited about his approaching adventure. Although he still topped off his Prozac with a shot of scotch before falling into a restless sleep, his waking hours slowly took up residence in future promise rather than past despair.

In their phone conversations, Barry had sensed new expectation in Jim's voice and he was determined to keep this hope fueled. He had organized a comprehensive briefing that would not only provide Jim with the necessary information for his mission, but would also emphasize the gravity of the project. The briefing would include meetings with various State Department officials, as well as a private meeting with the Burundian Ambassador to the United States.

Jim undertook all of the necessary preparation for a long absence. He issued twelve post-dated checks to his landlord, Bill Perkins, to cover his anticipated year of non-residence.

"I won't leave you in the lurch," he said to Perkins. "If I decide to stay longer, I'll let you know well in advance."

He also sent a brief and affectionate letter to his daughter, reaffirming his absolute love for her and his hope that she would soon "don the badge of responsibility." He waited several days, until he was certain she had received his note, and then called her. Sarah Keating told her father how proud she was of his new appointment.

"Are you feeling good about the project, Daddy? Because I am."

"I am, too, but I'm traveling light in case this turns out to be another disappointment," said Jim.

"It won't be a disappointment, Dad. This one is a win. . . . I'm sure. And by the way, I'm coming to Worcester to see you."

———

At 11:30 AM, two days before Jim's departure, Sarah pulled her 1984 Mustang to the curbstone of 14 Stoneland Road. Her dad was sitting on the front steps. Before she could open the car door, Jim was standing beside it, arms open and his heart bumper to bumper with love for his only child.

After this visit, they would not see each other for a very long time, so the two had already agreed to sail around the winds of contention.

"I just want to be with my Daddy, who I love so much," Sarah had said in their last phone conversation.

"You know . . . I can't wait to see you, my precious daughter," Jim had replied, a jigger of emotion intoxicating his senses.

Sarah had driven from Rochester, where she and her boyfriend were both teaching English at a public high school. Jim knew that she needed to drive back that evening, as she could only get the one day off. He planned a series of activities that would end with an early dinner, for he did not want his daughter driving too late at night—a viewpoint he had embraced the very day she got her driver's license.

The itinerary began with a tour of Jim's apartment. On the way up the stairs, he said, almost apologetically, "It's perfect for me, sweetie. Nothing fancy, but all I need."

As Sarah looked around the sparse quarters, she recalled the beautiful homes she had grown up in and felt a surge of empathy for her father's plight in life.

"It is perfect, Daddy."

Jim and Edna had uprooted from their hometown back in 1950. Their parents had all passed by the time Sarah was born, and she had only been to Worcester once as a small child. Dad and daughter began with lunch at Alice's, where owners Alice and Paul gave Sarah the royal, or as they called it, "Main South," treatment. Then they spent the afternoon touring the city, starting with a long walk around the grounds of Clark University, Edna's alma mater, followed by a car drive through the Main South neighborhood, with brief stops at both Jim and Edna's childhood homes so that Sarah could take photos. They continued on to the Worcester Art

Museum, which Sarah found to be one of the finest she had ever visited.

"I'm glad you feel that way," said Jim. "It's one of Worcester's treasures, and Mom loved this place. You know, my hometown has a lot of good things going for it," he said, with no small amount of pride.

"It sure does, Daddy. And so will Burundi."

Dinner was at the Parkway Diner, an establishment that had been open for more than fifty years . . . and the favorite Worcester restaurant of Jim and Edna.

"When I took your Mom to the St. Peter's Senior Prom— our first date—this is where we came to dinner. Just like now, it was inexpensive, and the food was great."

Sarah beamed and said, "Tell me more. I love hearing about you and Mom."

"Well, not only was the prom your Mom's first date, but it was Mom's first time in an Italian restaurant. In fact, it was her first time eating Italian food!"

"Oh my God! And Mom loved Italian food—and she cooked it so well, Daddy."

Jim smiled, shook his head, and said, "She sure did. And you know, Sarah, Mom's recipe for meatballs and marinara sauce—or 'gravy' as my Italian Worcester friends called it— well, she got it right here."

"Really! How?"

"Well, the owners of the restaurant at that time, Mr. and Mrs. Incutto, took a special interest in your mom and me. So, we invited them to our wedding. At the reception, Mrs. Incutto gave mom the secret recipe. She told mom that she was the only person outside of the Incutto family to ever receive it!"

He added, "By the way, Mom was only a sophomore and probably the youngest girl at the prom. I think you know this, but she was chosen as Prom Queen that night. To be honest, I don't think there was even a close second. But you know, Sarah, Mom was so gracious that I never detected any jealousy that night—or, for that matter, at any time—from the neighborhood girls."

From the time she was a child, whenever Sarah broached a topic she found embarrassing, she would momentarily press her palms against her forehead, smile, and then speak up.

As soon as he saw his daughter's hands move toward her forehead, Jim grinned and said, "Am I going to blush about what's coming?"

Sarah laughed hard, then clasped her hands with Jim's and said, "Daddy, Mummy once told me that at the end of that night, the best you could do was a peck on her cheek."

Sarah tilted her head back and laughed joyously.

"Now, let me defend myself," said Jim, blushing, but reveling in the conversation.

"When I walked your mom to her front door that night, guess who I saw peeking out of the curtains."

Sarah was still laughing heartily and could not answer for the moment.

"When you're ready, take a guess."

"Okay, Daddy. Hm . . . Grampa."

"Well, you're only half right. It was actually Grampa and Grandma."

Sarah paused for a second and then said wistfully, "I so wish I could have met them."

"So do I, sweetie. They were great, as were my mom and dad. You know, I got very close to your grampa and grandma. They brought the best of Ireland with them to Worcester."

Dinner wrapped up and the two headed back to Stoneland Road. There was relative silence in the car as both began to feel the onset of sadness over what was sure to be a long separation. When they arrived at Jim's home, he hugged his daughter and found that he did not want to let her go.

"Daddy," Sarah started, tears suddenly streaming down her cheeks. "I can't begin to say how much I love you." She then wiped away the tears and said, "Oh, and here is a card with a message that you can read later tonight."

Jim embraced his daughter again and held back his own tears. Moments later, he stood at the curbside, watching Sarah's Mustang make a U-turn and head toward Main Street.

When he entered his apartment, it was only 7:45 PM. But despite the early hour, he decided to prepare for bed. When he was under the covers, he reached for the card.

It was a beautiful card, set in Africa, with dazzling stars above.

He opened it and read his daughter's message:

My Dear Daddy:

There are times when I find poetry to be the best way to deliver a message. Here is my message to you:

> *There are those*
> *Who propose*
> *That to find*
> *True enlightenment*
>
> *One must descend*
> *To the*
> *nethermost depths*
> *Of human emotion.*
> *There is truth*
> *to the notion*
> *For no man*
> *Can brush*
>
> *The Comet Cloud*
>
> *Until he enters*
> *The black hole,*
> *Stares down*
> *His despair*

And cranks up
His comeback.

My beloved Father
In a
faraway land
Your comeback awaits

And so do
countless Burundians
children and adults
in need of your wisdom

And your great goodwill

All my love, Sarah

Jim turned out the light and embraced the comfort of darkness. He said his nightly prayer to St. Jude, special advocate for those in need of hope.

He then said something to himself that he had not said for a very, very long time.

I am blessed.

15

On the morning of Jim's departure for Washington, DC, he awoke troubled, not wanting to get out of bed.

Am I ready for this?

But then the phone rang—an unintended but fortuitous electric shock.

"This is your friendly wake up call," said a high-spirited Barry Sklar. "I've got a bunch of bureaucrats waiting to meet you. I'll have a driver pick you up at Washington National. Look for the placard that says 'Coach Keating.'"

The cheerful connection replaced Jim's second thoughts with brighter ones. He finished packing and headed for Worcester Airport, christened with new hope.

Jim was greeted at Washington National by a uniformed State Department driver. Such chauffeured service was generally limited to high-ranking diplomats, but Barry Sklar wanted his old friend to get VIP treatment and was able to call in a favor with the driver, whom he knew personally.

"It's only a fifteen-minute ride to Mr. Sklar's office," said the driver. "He's really looking forward to seeing you. How was your flight?"

"Good," said Jim. "DC's pretty impressive from the air." Jim was impressed during the limo ride as well. As they crossed the bridge into the city and drove by the Mall, it occurred to him, *This is the Capitol. I'm working for these people.* He liked the thought.

Barry was waiting in the lobby. After nearly forty years, the reunion was poignant for both men.

"General Jim . . . boy, it's great to see you!"

"It's great to see you too, Barry," said Jim, unable to find words that would truly reflect his feelings.

Barry beheld the influence that the march of circumstances had had on his old friend's appearance. Yet the coach's handshake was as firm as ever, and his message was well timed.

"I can't tell you how excited I am about this opportunity."

Barry was still in possession of the same engaging look of mischief that Jim had latched on to so many years ago. And Jim could see that his host had done what he always said he would—practice a fit-for-life philosophy. Barry's 5'10" frame remained notably thin. His narrow, angular face was nearly wrinkle free, and his dark eyebrows were offset by white, wavy hair and a neatly trimmed white beard. He looked like he had just stepped out of the pages of *GQ*: dark, pin-striped suit, dart collar, rep tie. His bright almond eyes seemed magnified behind oval, wire-rimmed glasses.

"Barry, you are 'squared away,' as we used to say in the Army. I'm glad I'm wearing a tie!"

"You look great, Jim—the casual coach."

As they made their way to Barry's office, Barry was further encouraged that Jim asked several pertinent questions about the Burundi materials he had been sent.

Moments later, Barry introduced Jim to his secretary, Harriet Parker, who got up and came around her desk to greet him.

"What a pleasure it is to meet you," she said with a sincerity that made Jim feel good. "I feel like I know you. Mr. Sklar's told me so many wonderful things about you, and, Lord knows, I've typed your name often enough over the past few weeks."

"Jim, okay if we eat in the office?" asked Barry. "I can have Harriet send out for pastrami on rye—what you used to like at our house. That'll give us more time to talk."

"Sounds great."

Barry and Jim played four full quarters of reminiscence, and the coach welcomed this exercise of nostalgia. He was struck by how quickly the two seemed to bond; their lost years immediately yielded to the strength of their friendship.

Barry finally steered the conversation to the cardinal point.

"Jim, today and tomorrow you'll see how important this project is. First thing you ought to know is that we've received an early morning cable stating that things have gotten worse. The streets of Bujumbura are nearly empty. The cable says it's like a ghost town. About 100,000 more Hutus have fled over the border and on into Kenya. To be honest, after we got the cable, we had a quick discussion about postponing your trip. But our embassy maintains that Americans are safe and that the violence will likely subside in the next few days. In any event, I want you to understand something."

Leaning forward and establishing firm eye contact, Barry continued, "You don't have to go *now*. We can put this thing on hold for awhile."

"Barry," Jim said gravely, "my bags are packed and I have nowhere else to go."

Barry nodded and handed Jim a copy of the itinerary.

"Your first meeting is with Roger Peterson in an hour. Pete has been with the USIA for about twenty years and much of his work has been in Burundi. He'll review the Hutu and Tutsi conflict and give you some suggestions on how to deal with the two tribes."

Jim scanned the itinerary as Barry continued his briefing.

102

"Then you'll meet with the Burundian ambassador. He's a very depressed man, a Hutu who has lost several of his family members due to the fighting, including a son and his wife...."

Barry paused for a moment, wishing he had not provided the last detail.

"The ambassador has barely heard anything from his government, what with all of the chaos. But he's glad you're going. At this stage, he'll accept any form of help.... The rest of your day will be taken up at a session with the medical people. They'll give you a lot of information, important information, on what foods to stay away from, what eating habits to adhere to. Listen to everything they say, Jim."

"I will, for sure."

"I told you about this damn dinner meeting I've got tonight, so Pete will take you to supper. Then we'll have breakfast, review everything, and I'll drive you out to Dulles."

"Everything sounds so well planned, Barry. Really thorough."

The meetings went as Barry had predicted, and the session with the ambassador was especially grim. His name was Audace Ngezeko, and his forlorn eyes belied his perfunctory smile. In clear English, he related to Jim his great hope when a fellow Hutu had been democratically elected as president with a pledge of peace displacing civil unrest. He then recounted his devastation over the violence that had engulfed his country, bringing it to a state of near anarchy.

"It has taken the blood of my family and my friends and has set our democratic process back decades. But Jim, do not let my dreary outlook affect you. What you are doing is important and could bring hope to Burundi," he said, without a trace of hope in his voice.

After his lunch, Jim received an extensive briefing from a team of Health Department officials, including a physician who provided him with a twelve-month supply of pills.

"Take two a day and you'll have a good shot of staying away from malaria," the doctor said in a monotone that Jim found irksome.

"What about your personal health; are you taking any medication?"

"Yes, my doctor has prescribed some things," Jim answered vaguely.

"Do you have enough? You won't easily be able to get prescriptions filled in Burundi," the doctor prodded.

"I'll be fine," said Jim firmly. He hoped the doctor would not continue his probe, and, surprisingly, he did not.

Jim's dinner meeting with Roger Peterson filled in many of the gaps in the briefing material about the Tutsi–Hutu conflict. Peterson emphasized the extent of US involvement and the importance of initiatives like Jim's. Early the next morning, he would call Barry to tell him he and Jim talked until midnight.

"I like this guy," Peterson told Barry. "He listens and you can tell he's got his teeth into this thing."

When Jim returned to his hotel room, he took a Prozac and fell into bed. Despite a restless sleep (he seemed to wake up every half hour thinking about some Burundi fact), he awoke energized. Another lively discussion with Barry at breakfast further hot-wired his drive.

"Are you ready?" asked Barry.

"I am, Barry," said Jim.

Barry heard an echo of the assurance he had found in his friend so many years ago when Jim added, "And I'm determined to get the job done."

The forty-five-minute drive to Dulles Airport brought forth more nostalgia and further galvanized their relationship. It also gave Barry the opportunity to tell Jim more about Ambassador Foster.

"She's a treasure, Jim. Cynthia grew up in the poorest section of Indianapolis. With as much intellect, grace, and diligence as I've seen in this business, she's become one of our most respected diplomats. And her husband, Bill, is, to use a Yiddish term my mom used to apply to you, a *mensch.* You know, they've never had children. Instead, they've mentored countless young people at every diplomatic stop. If there was ever a marital dream team, you're about to meet them in Burundi."

"Oh, and by the way," he added, "they both love basketball! And knowing that balls are pretty scarce in Burundi, I brought along eight deflated rubber balls that you can take with you."

At the airport, Barry parked his car in Short Term then helped check Jim's bags.

After Jim received his boarding pass, he looked at Barry for a long moment. He surprised himself by embracing his boyhood brother.

Playing aggressive defense against his brimming eyes, Jim pivoted and hustled off to the plane.

At the gate, Jim Keating stopped at a trash bin, opened his carry-on, and discarded his supply of antidepressants.

16

As Jim had suspected, any chance for sleep on the plane had been eliminated by his hasty, probably rash decision to discard his Prozac. The one early advantage of his impulsiveness was that the long and decidedly uncomfortable flight would give him ample time to reflect on the wagon-train life he had chosen—and on his new opportunity. The downside was that withdrawal symptoms had quickly kicked in. He remembered Dr. Rotella warning him that sudden withdrawal from Prozac could cause serious side effects ranging from nausea to panic attacks. Jim had already missed one dose amid the briefings in DC, so the drug was probably out of his system, and he was starting to sweat heavily and feel nauseous.

The flight route from Dulles would include a two-hour wait at JFK, a seven-hour flight to Brussels, an eight-hour layover, and then seven more hours in the air to Bujumbura, Burundi.

After the brief New York stopover, Jim did his best to settle his thick-set body into the unaccommodating coach-class seat. In an attempt to neutralize his distress, he recalled one of Edna's many admirable traits (and one he dearly missed): her honesty.

In fact, Edna's devotion to the truth had now and then veered toward the inflexible, which, in turn, had caused an occasional quarrel. But her scruples had also forced Jim, sometimes reluctantly, to confront the truth about his own strengths and weaknesses, making him a better person and nourishing their relationship.

A good example was a frank discussion he'd had with Edna many years earlier while at St. Thomas about his direction and the state of his profession.

"I've always felt, and still feel, that your rise in the coaching ranks has been based on your teaching ability, your concern about your players, and your work ethic," began Edna. "But lately, I've seen others in your field who aren't necessarily the best teachers. They may work hard, but they also seem more focused on fluffing up their egos and lining their purses than on the well-being of their players. It seems to me that the biggest criterion for success now is raw aggression—combined with guile."

"What's wrong with that?"

"Well, look at where college basketball is going," responded Edna. "Look at the point-shaving scandals, the recruiting violations. Jim, some coaches have abandoned whatever ethical guidelines they had in favor of their ambition. Now, I understand that, to a degree, aggressiveness in any profession can be admirable—and quite necessary—but when it dominates the overall success pattern, isn't there a real danger of it becoming an end in itself?"

Jim had given a reluctant nod and Edna continued.

"Remember when we were at the Final Four last year? I was sitting at a table where you were discussing different issues with various coaches?"

"Yeah, I sort of remember," Jim had said, somewhat defensively.

"Well, I recall an argument that two of the coaches had about the Vietnam War. The coach who seemed to gain the upper hand, and to have the last word, did it more by asserting his self-will rather than by offering any reasoned points. In fact, he knew very little about the key issues. Winning the argument seemed more important to him than reasoning through civil or logical discourse. The entire discussion centered not on who had developed a well-thought-out opinion, but who was most assertive in getting his opinion heard. To me, it was a small but telling factor about coaching—and athletics in general."

"Vietnam aside, Edna, assertiveness is important to winning, and, I might add, winning is important."

"Jim . . . now, you've said yourself that one of the great things about sports is teaching people how to deal with success and failure. If playing a sport is supposed to have educational value, then what's wrong with losing from time to time? Look at your own players. Many of your best athletes have surely not made their mark in life. In fact, I don't see that being a good player and getting ahead in a career correlate at all. So why not use the entire experience of winning and losing as teaching tools?"

"Well, we do."

"Do you, now?" asked Edna in a mocking tone softened by a smile. "Then why is it that any time a Division I coach has a losing season or two, he's fired?"

Jim stood up for a moment and massaged the back of his neck with his right hand. Then he sat back down and said, "Can we take a timeout? . . . Please?"

"No," she said, putting a hand on his arm. "Let me finish . . ."

Jim shook his head and smiled, knowing that his wife would not be deterred.

"On the matter of raw aggression and that Vietnam issue," Edna continued, "there are ethicists who propose that a person who forces an unreasoned opinion on others is unethical, simply because forcing others to follow that line of reasoning can be harmful on a whole variety of levels. There's even a further school of ethical thought that proposes that in many fields, incompetence is unethical."

"How so?"

"Well," said Edna, "certain people—because of their aggression or ego—propose that they have far more expertise than they really do. The results can be devastating. Think of politicians who've been elected based on their confidence or swagger or money, but who, in reality, lack the requisite skills to handle the complexities of the job. Think of the damage that such a politician can do to a community, if not a nation. *And* think of coaches who deliver undeveloped, half-baked opinions to kids—on issues ranging from violence to gamesmanship—and think of how harmful an effect it can have on kids."

"Then are you saying that all people in positions of influence must be smart?"

"I'm saying that all people in positions of importance must be competent—and should spend the time to develop a coherent philosophy."

After a brief pause, Edna went on. "So many decisions in coaching are made with bluster and swagger, Jim, and that approach should not be the dominating factor in a credible profession. I mean, in what other job could someone like an Al McGuire get to the absolute top by a completely seat-of-the-pants approach?"

Jim was upset that his wife should choose Marquette's old coach, whom he had always liked and thought of as a smart man, an original thinker. When he stubbornly refused to answer, she smiled and then gently offered her own reply.

"None!"

At the time, Jim had not entirely agreed with Edna about the shortcomings of his profession. But now, on a plane headed for a ravaged country where winning was more about surviving the day than playing a game, the validity of her points became even more pronounced.

Even though Jim's body felt lousy, remembering Edna's candor made him feel a bit upbeat. He was leaving behind a bad situation, flushing both the medicine and Jersey State out of his system, and heading for circumstances he hoped were clean and fresh and positive. In the midst of unimaginable violence and chaos, he might make a difference—do something positive other than simply win games.

As Jim Keating had grown older and watched people take on more intricate, multi-layered projects than coaching, he realized that careful planning, reasoned thought, civil discourse, and working with people in a team-like environment all seemed prerequisites to success. He also admitted to himself that many coaches, including some of the biggest winners, lacked some of those qualities and were not critical thinkers in the way Edna was. Rather than examining an idea from all sides and coming to a thoughtful solution, many approached predicaments by simply climbing over people and using aggressive, even childish tactics. "Few other professions would tolerate that kind of conduct—or misconduct," he recalled Edna saying.

Hours after that conversation had ended, but only moments after the heat of reconciliation had ebbed, Edna had made one of her many keen observations, one that had brought a smile to his face.

"You know, Mr. Keating, marriage is not always pretty—but it *is* profound!"

17

That vivid flashback to 1968, and the distraction of watching *Out of Africa*, helped suppress Jim's nausea and got him to Brussels, where he was to look for Frank Schwalba-Hoth at the terminal. Schwalba-Hoth was a Belgian diplomat whom Barry had asked to take Jim for a tour of the capital of the European Union during the eight-hour layover.

As Jim headed unsteadily into the arrivals area in the Brussels airport, he caught sight of a dapper man with a corona of white hair atop a smiling face who was yelling, "Coach! Coach!"

"I'm Frank Schwalba-Hoth," he said with an accent that reminded Jim of Agatha Christie's Monsieur Poirot. "And you're a tall, broad-shouldered man with a brush cut who has to be Jim Keating."

Jim smiled and nodded as they shook hands. The raccoon circles around Jim's eyes made it clear to Schwalba-Hoth that the American lacked sleep, but the diplomat had no idea of the real reason for Jim's haggard look.

"Rough trip?" he asked.

"Yes," replied Jim, without offering any hint of the reasons for his uncomfortable flight. In fact, Jim was exhausted and wobbly. Although he had at times gone off his medication in Worcester and was familiar with withdrawal symptoms, this was cold turkey. He couldn't remember feeling this bad since he'd had a severe bout with dysentery in the Pacific.

The two took a cab into Brussels and Schwalba-Hoth quickly proved to be a gracious host who, despite the predawn hour, talked enthusiastically about his home. "It's a great city—the most alive in all of Europe. As you can see, I don't own a car—don't need one because it's so easy to make your way around here." He shepherded Jim through several landmarks of the European Union capital, ending with a walk around the Grand Place with its spectacular thirteenth-century gothic town hall.

After a brief stop for breakfast, where Jim cautiously stuck to toast and tea, Schwalba-Hoth surprised his guest by purchasing two boxes of famous Belgian chocolates—a mix of pralines—at an outdoor kiosk on the Avenue Louise, a popular pedestrian street.

"I knew Ambassador Foster years ago," he explained. "As a young diplomat, she served here for about fourteen months. Loved our chocolates. One box is for you and the other for Cynthia. You'll be well received when you present it to her!"

As they continued along Avenue Louise, looking for a shop where he could buy a gift for Sarah, Jim suffered another bout of nausea and began retching violently. Schwalba-Hoth sat Jim down at an outdoor table. "As soon as you're ready, we'll get a cab to take you to the hospital."

But Jim protested, coming forth with some minimal information.

"Frank, thank you, but please don't do that. I'm trying to force myself off medication—sleeping pills and the rest," he said vaguely. "That, plus the overnight flight, has put me a bit under the weather. But I'll be okay."

Schwalba-Hoth, though, was concerned enough to hail a cab and get Jim back to the airport. Jim watched his host shift from amiable escort to efficient bureaucrat. Using his contacts with Sabena, the Belgian airline that would fly Jim from Brussels to Bujumbura, he arranged for Jim to relax in the first-class lounge and was also able to have his seat upgraded to first class.

Jim thanked Schwalba-Hoth for his kindness. The Belgian was an interesting man whom Jim would have enjoyed getting to know better. But at this stage, Jim was so nauseous that he found solitude a more appealing companion than a new and indulgent acquaintance. He kept one of the State Department briefing books on his lap to discourage conversation and opened it to "Kirundi—The Language of Burundi." Jim practiced a few words, watched a few minutes of Belgian TV off and on, and even slept for a short while.

Four hours later, he was back on a plane. While still woozy, a concoction of apple cider vinegar, ginger root, and hot water served to him in the lounge by an obliging Sabena employee had lessened the nausea.

After takeoff, now in the more comfortable surroundings of first class, Jim was trying to ward off the anxiety attacks that came with withdrawal. Dr. Rotella had warned him that he could slip into depression if he stopped taking his medication. *I'll think about the various aspects of my new job*, he decided. But it didn't work. Instead, his thoughts turned to a frequent retrospection—the fallout over his dismissal at New Jersey State. He focused on two letters he had previously blocked from memory in an attempt to sober his senses. One was from a self-described "hoop junkie" who also identified himself as an African American.

"I've followed your career, and I doubt you're a racist. Unfortunately, though, a dismissal like yours, even when it appears, on the surface at least, to be unjust, is sometimes necessary to level the field. A firing like yours tells African Americans

that, in a show-down between Blacks and Caucasians, whitey sometimes gets his, too. It's called the law of equivalent retaliation. It might seem unfair, but so is the racism that has overrun our society for hundreds of years."

Jim's initial reaction to the letter was anger, and even after he had composed himself, he'd still felt that the author was wrong. Yet now, many months after he had first read the letter, he reluctantly found himself respecting the man's forthrightness and guessing that his points were an accurate reflection of the views of some, if not most, African Americans.

On the plane, Jim also recalled a speech that Edna's frequent target of criticism, Al McGuire, had given at a coach's clinic in the late '60s. Jim's assistant, Joe Winters, a black man, had accompanied Jim to the clinic. At the time, McGuire's Marquette clubs were, in many ways, the antithesis of other predominantly African American teams. The Warriors seldom ran, they kept scores in the 50s and 60s, and their disciplined approach was the envy of the majority of college coaches—white and black.

When McGuire had finished his speech, he said to his audience, "Okay, how 'bout some Q and A?"

A young African American assistant coach raised his hand and boldly asked the question that many in the audience sought an answer to.

"How do you get black kids to play with such discipline?"

"I first let 'em know that I'm not holdin' myself responsible for what my forefathers did," McGuire began. "Then I tell 'em that the star of Marquette basketball is Al McGuire and that next in line come the seniors. The seniors are rewarded with the ball—the underclassmen have to wait their turn. I tell 'em if they want to run, they can look for a new school. But I also tell 'em that if they play within our system, they got a good shot at turnin' pro. And if an underclassman says: 'Coach—I want to go pro early,' I look in his icebox. If it's not as full as mine, I tell him to take the money!"

The typically glib reply had been a case of the tin god preaching to the converted. The coaches, including most of the handful of African Americans present, had roared with admiring laughter. But Jim noticed that his young assistant had not been similarly impressed. Jim regarded Winters as a perceptive judge of issues, especially those related to race.

"Don't you agree with Coach Al about not being responsible for past sins?"

"I'm not sure I do," Winters had replied.

"Hmm . . . what he said seemed fair enough to me," said Jim.

"Well, I guess I look at it in a different way."

Winters paused.

"Jim, Coach McGuire is basically saying that there should be no such thing as affirmative action, that we should start fresh—wipe the slate clean. But let me ask you this: If you and I were playing a Monopoly game, would it be fair if you started with two times the amount of money as me?"

More than two decades later, Jim Keating still found himself torn between the disparate views of Winters and McGuire. They both seemed right, yet they both also seemed wrong.

While the first letter had caused considerable deliberation on Jim's part, the second had brought on real anguish.

"The decline of this great country can be traced directly to the coddling of n——s and other so-called minorities. Thank God for men like you who have the courage to stand up against the left-wing welfare-staters who are running our great land into the ground. If you ever decide to sue the school, or better still, sue those n——s players who slandered you, assistance from our legal fund will be at your disposal."

The letter had been signed by the "president" of an organization called FFWA, which Jim later found out meant Freedom for White Americans. He had been sickened to think that such a perverse group would look upon him as a hero.

Though most others in the first-class section were now asleep, Jim remained wide awake, posing an all too familiar question to himself that had haunted him since the Jersey State debacle: *Is it possible that I am somehow, in some way, a racist?*

While his answer continued to be a firm "no," he hoped that if somewhere in the deep recesses of his mind he harbored a trace of those malignant sentiments, it would be absolved by the success of his pilgrimage to Burundi.

Hours into the flight, Jim was drawn from his deep thought by an announcement from the captain.

"We've hit some headwinds on our way down here. Caused us to reroute slightly and use a little extra petrol. We're going to stop for a quick refuel at the Kigali Airport in Rwanda. We'll still have you in Bujumbura within minutes of our scheduled arrival. As a precaution, and so we can refuel quickly, passengers will be asked to stay on the plane."

As the plane taxied toward a row of gasoline tanks situated about two hundred yards from the terminal, Jim's nausea resurfaced and he vomited into the air-sickness bag. When two first-class stewardesses rushed to attend to him, his discomfort was exceeded only by his embarrassment.

Moments later, the passenger hatch was opened for two crew members to disembark to sign landing papers. Needing a dose of fresh air, Jim rose from his seat and walked gingerly to the open hatch. Looking out on the runway, he wondered if the captain's order that all passengers remain on the plane had more to do with their safety than with a speedy refueling, for within fifty yards of the 727, a large group of soldiers—maybe sixty or seventy—were hunkered down in foxholes, their rifles at the ready.

During his coaching career, Jim had traveled abroad extensively, once delivering a clinic in Prague in 1968 only months after Soviet tanks had roared into Wenceslas Square. At no time in Prague, or on any other trip, had Jim Keating felt any genuine concern for his safety until *now*. Hostility itself seemed engraved on the young raven-black faces before him.

A stewardess standing directly behind the coach saw the line of riflemen and Jim's look of concern. She nervously explained that the soldiers were positioned there to guard against the violent attacks at the airport that had become commonplace during the rebel uprising against the Rwandan government.

Jim feared that the eerie scene was a grim foreshadowing of the atmosphere he would face in Burundi.

18

Jim Keating was grateful the unexpected delay in Rwanda had been brief. When the plane landed in Bujumbura, he was even more grateful that the airport was not circled by armed soldiers. Realizing his long journey was over, he felt a surge of relief that soothed his weariness. His nausea had eased, so his symptoms were now like a bad attack of the flu. He could deal with that. Drained from dysentery, huddled under a poncho, mortar fire falling as relentlessly as the rain, Jim had learned as a young soldier what deep reservoirs of resolve he could draw from. He had also coached more games than he cared to remember while fighting the flu, refusing to yield the reins to an assistant. As he was approached by a man he guessed to be a US Embassy representative, Jim was determined to mask whatever withdrawal symptoms remained.

"Welcome to Burundi, Jim," said Jesse Abbot, who looked like Pete Dawkins, the West Point football star, and who identified himself as the Deputy Chief of Mission at the US Embassy. "Sorry for the informal reception. Ambassador

Foster had planned to be here, but she was called to an urgent meeting with the Burundian president, Peter Buyoya."

"Nice to meet you, Jesse," said Jim.

Abbot appeared to be in his mid-forties and was a shade over six feet. His trim, muscular physique suggested time spent on the football field, perhaps even in a boxing ring. An upright carriage, clean-shaven face, and blonde crew-cut made Jim think that a military academy might appear on his résumé. Jim would soon learn that it was West Point, but nothing in Abbot's demeanor suggested he was the least bit stiff or regimented. Dressed in a tan linen suit, beige polo shirt, and loafers, he struck Jim as casual but confident. He smiled inwardly when Abbot shook his hand, at the same time grasping Jim's forearm with his left hand. *I think I like this guy*, Jim thought.

Abbot grabbed Jim's carry-on bags and strode, a bit more briskly than Jim might have liked, toward the airport entrance marked for VIPs, all the while reciting a list of details that challenged Jim's concentration.

"As Barry Sklar probably told you, you'll be staying in a private apartment attached to my house. You'll like it. It's clean, quiet, and there's a spectacular view of Lake Tanganyika from your front window. You'll have a domestic lady. Her name is Josiane Kakunze. She's a real treasure, a Hutu who lost her husband and several of her sons to the violence, yet who comes to work each day with a smile as big as Bujumbura."

"Josiane sounds great . . . and so does the apartment," said Jim. *Undoubtedly an improvement from the walk-up in Worcester.*

"The US Embassy employs a number of domestic workers, all of whom are assigned to the various homes of Embassy employees," explained Abbot. "Our government pays them wages which, on the surface, might appear low, but are actually far better than anything they would be paid in any other job they might be able to get here. To give you an example, a single US dollar equals 500 Burundi francs. An average worker in Burundi might make only 5,000 Burundi francs, or 10 US dollars, a month. We pay our workers 10,000 Burundi francs, or 20 dollars per month. As a result, we get the *best*—and Josiane is right at the top of the group. Also, while 20 dollars a month doesn't seem like a lot of money, it does provide a person with a reasonably comfortable lifestyle in Burundi."

He added, "By the way, Jim, any of those rumors you might have heard about how folks in the US Foreign Service have it made—they're all true!"

Jim did like Jesse Abbot. He was particularly struck by his upbeat attitude in a place Jim guessed would not bring much cheer to anyone.

"Jack Casey, our public diplomacy officer and self-appointed basketball expert, will join us in a moment. You'll like Jack, a great guy. Unfortunately, he's being reassigned to a post in Kenya next month. We'll miss him," Abbot said. "After we pick up your bags, and before we take you to the apartment, do you feel up to a quick tour and lunch?"

"Sure," replied Jim. Abbot's spirited greeting and jocular banter reminded Jim of locker rooms and gymnasiums. He was beginning to feel better.

Baggage claim was a row of tables set off in the corner of a large, modestly decorated room. Within several feet of the tables was a sizable and unevenly cut hole in the wall. Stationed behind the wall were four very tall, very lean men who began to manually remove the bags from a pushcart and carefully place them through the large hole and into the hands of three other, equally tall, men, who placed the bags onto tables directly adjacent to the hole.

"This ain't JFK," Abbot cracked as he handed his American guest a typed itinerary. While Jim reviewed it, Abbot said, "We're really excited you're here, Jim. As you'll see in the itinerary, the ambassador is hosting a big welcoming dinner in your honor tonight at the Embassy. Many of the top basketball people in the country will be there. We also invited Tutsis and Hutus who have past relationships through basketball. There haven't been many occasions of late for them to get together. So, you see, you're already a peacemaker!"

As Jim and Abbot moved forward to pick up the bags, Jack Casey joined them. Casey was dressed more formally than Abbot in a blue linen suit, white shirt, and bright red bowtie. At 5' 10", he was a stocky, solidly built man with a high forehead, receding hairline, and auburn hair. Yet his muscle-flexing look was offset by an engaging grin.

"I'm Jack Casey, Coach Keating. Welcome. Sorry I wasn't at the gate to greet you. Been on the phone with the Embassy checking on the status of the ambassador's meeting."

"Any word?" asked Abbot.

"No, she's not back yet," replied Casey.

Noticing the curious look on Jim's face, Abbot said, "No need for concern, Coach. As I'm sure you know, the last two years, and particularly the last six months, have been horrible, beyond anything we could have imagined when we were posted here a few years ago. Today's meeting relates to a massacre of 126 Hutu refugees trying to break out of a refugee camp on the northeast border—up by Rwanda. What's interesting is that the army, which of course is controlled by the Tutsis, has actually placed seven soldiers under house arrest for the slayings. Usually, the army doesn't even acknowledge these kinds of incidents, so our assumption is that these soldiers went way too far in their brutality."

Abbot went on to tell Jim that Ambassador Foster was often called to such personal meetings with President Buyoya to be updated on the violence.

"That's not just because of the force of her personality, Coach. In Third World countries, US ambassadors often take on even more prominent roles in the country's affairs than our ambassadors in more affluent nations. Here in Burundi, President Buyoya has great faith in Ambassador Foster. He relies heavily on her advice."

I can't wait to meet this woman, Jim thought to himself.

"So," Abbot continued, "like I said, don't be overly concerned. We feel safe here. We have a Marine security force, and they keep a close eye on us. In fact, there'll be two Marines out in the parking lot waiting to escort us into the city and on to your living quarters. You should know that last week's situation you were informed about has improved in Bujumbura. It was a bit scary for a few days, but the mood, at least in the city, is better now."

While Jim's apprehension was not completely eased by Abbot's words, his state of mind changed quickly with an unusual sighting. As the trio exited the airport and were met by the hot, blistering sun of Burundi, two skyscraping Burundian soldiers walked hand in hand only yards away, both smiling broadly. The sight caught Jim unawares, and his look of surprise showed it.

Jack Casey noticed Jim staring at the soldiers. "It's not uncommon to see men holding hands," said Casey. "It's merely a sign of friendship in many African countries, including Burundi."

A jeep sat parked in a cordoned-off area that had a VIP sign attached. Two sturdy-looking Marines, each of whom looked to be no more than thirty years old, stepped from the jeep and warmly greeted the American coach.

"Coach Keating, on behalf of the Marine Corps, welcome to Burundi. I'm Sergeant Clive Rush, and this is Corporal Jim Roberts. I want you to know, sir, that my dad is a high school coach in Williamstown, Kentucky. When I wrote to him to say you were coming, he wrote back right away to ask that you teach me the combination defense, which, as he said, 'Jim Keating made famous!'"

Rush's comment was like an embrace. The sergeant's effusiveness was genuine and added to a sense of well-being in Jim that was slowly replacing the anxiety that had been central to his depression. Jim responded to Rush with the enthusiasm he always brought to his lectures at hoop clinics.

"Sergeant Rush, please tell your dad how much I appreciate his thoughts. To tell you the truth, though, I first saw the combination defense when I was in college. One Christmas holiday, I was able to get home to Worcester for a couple of days. I went to a high school game to see my alma mater, St. Peter's High, play our arch rival, St. John's High. This was way back in '49, and the St. John's coach was a guy named Bob Devlin. As I watched the game, I noticed that the St. John's defense was really a combination. There was man-to-man coverage on the ball, but zone defensive principles were used away from the ball."

Jim continued, "I later heard that Devlin thought up this defense while taking a shower. Since the Shower Defense didn't have much of a ring to it, Devlin called it the Bathtub Defense! By the way, when Bob Cousy took the Boston College job in '63, he went to Devlin to ask that he help Cousy put in the Bathtub at BC. I remember there was an article in *Sports Illustrated* about this."

Rush smiled. "A great story, Coach, and I'm looking forward to more of them. If it's okay with you, I'd like to give you a brief report on security for Americans, both Embassy officials and guests."

"Sure," said Jim, and the five men quickly gathered around the hood of the jeep as Sergeant Rush unfolded a map.

"This war is between the Hutus and the Tutsis. The Marines are here, not as peacekeepers, but as security forces for American personnel. With the exception of a Peace Corps worker who was killed out in the country—right there in the Mutumba region—there's not been one attack on an

American, and we don't expect that will change. Neither side looks on the Americans as enemies, but our job, Coach, is to make sure that nothing happens to you or any other visitors. Believe me, sir, we'll make certain of that."

In a clipped, matter-of-fact tone, Rush outlined the current military situation, pointing to the map several times to show Jim danger areas.

When Rush finished, Abbot and Casey loaded Jim's bags into the back of the jeep, and the group headed for the capital.

19

The ride from the airport to Bujumbura was six miles long and only slightly more comfortable than the coach-class plane rides. But for Jim, sandwiched in the back seat between Abbot and Casey, the short trip was enlightening.

Abbot nudged Jim and pointed to a row of mud-brick dwellings on the side of the road. "About 95 percent of the people in Burundi—both Hutus and Tutsis—live in that type of house," said Abbot. Jim scanned the unusual homes, shaped like beehives with high, cone-shaped roofs made of split bamboo.

"Coach, it's just as you probably read about," continued Abbot. "No running water or electricity—and a communal outhouse. Many people can control their bowels to relieve themselves only once a day—obviously unhealthy, and just one of the many factors that contribute to an average life span of only forty or so years."

"And," added Casey, "they get their water from fountains fed by wells. There's usually one fountain for every thirty or forty huts, and when people draw water from the fountain, they must boil it right away."

"Dysentery?" asked Jim.

"Right. Dysentery is a real—and I mean *real*—problem in Burundi," replied Casey.

As Casey spoke, Jim noticed several women standing outside their huts, cooking in large cast-iron pots over an open fire. He leaned toward Abbot and motioned in their direction.

"No such thing as a stove or refrigerator," said Abbot. "Cooking's all done outdoors. But what you see on this roadside—all of these huts running one next to another—is actually unusual."

Abbot continued. "Only place you'd see this is on the outskirts of Bujumbura. Once you get out into the country, there's almost no such thing as a village or communal row of huts. Families live on hills, and they're often known, not for their village or community, but for the hill they live on. In other words, Jim, in some places it would be Jim High Hill or Lily Low Hill."

Jim looked ahead and saw two very short men holding a string across the road. Abbot broke into a wide grin.

"Each province has regions, Coach," said Abbot, chuckling. "When you cross a region within a province, you pay a fee. It's like a toll in our country, only the method of collection is a little different."

Corporal Roberts stopped the jeep and a Hutu, who appeared to be no more than 5'4", approached the Marine. Roberts cheerfully handed the toll collector five Burundi francs.

"It's about a penny. They call it a communal tax. It's used to repair roads in the region," explained Abbot.

The road continued to grind at Jim's tailbone, but though the drive was uncomfortable, he was at ease with these Embassy staffers. Jim felt he was being treated with genuine admiration. He was grateful that his hosts were giving him such special attention. It reminded him of his trip to Prague back in '68 and his early days in Spain. American basketball coaches are given near-celebrity status in many foreign countries, and Jim got the feeling that this kind of homage might well be accorded him in Burundi.

It was also clear that they simply enjoyed telling him all about his new environs. Corporal Roberts turned his head slightly toward the back seat, smiled, and said, "One thing you'll get a kick out of, Coach Keating, is that a family of ten might have ten last names."

"What?!" exclaimed Jim.

"Well, sir, you've got to understand that this is a very Christian country—about 65 percent Catholic. In certain regions of Burundi, families choose their surnames to signify their love of God. As a result, common last names are almost non-existent in those regions."

"Well, how do you tell which family is which?" asked the coach.

"Damned if we know," roared Abbot. "But somehow they figure a way."

As the jeep approached the outskirts of the city, Burundians stopped to peer at what for them was obviously an unusual sight. Their looks revealed no malice, just curiosity.

"There are very few cars in Burundi," said Abbot. "Most people walk or ride bikes. The few cars you'll see are mostly European imports, and they're generally ten or fifteen years old. This big ol' open-air jeep is one of just twelve in the country, all owned by the Marines. The combination of the jeep and our pale faces makes us quite a sideshow."

"Speak for yourself, Mr. Abbot," quipped Corporal Roberts, an African American.

Jim could see that Roberts was one very handsome kid, not unlike Muhammad Ali when he was Cassius Clay. He stood about 6'2", and his short-sleeved khaki shirt revealed muscular forearms and biceps. Roberts had an easy laugh, but Jim sensed an underlying intensity about him, perhaps related to his surroundings or, Jim thought, simply because he grew up black.

Bujumbura was unlike any city Jim had ever seen, but then everything else he had seen in the previous half hour was exceptional, too. While the main roadway was paved with asphalt, the surface of the city's side-streets was a mix of gravel and crushed stone, which caused major difficulties for motor vehicles, even the jeep. Most of the buildings were one or two stories high, made of either red brick or a white stucco-like material. The Novotel Bujumbura, an eight-story hotel located in what Abbot referred to as "the financial district"—which was really made up of only six or seven businesses—had a distinctly European look.

"It's owned by some Belgians," continued Abbot. "As you can see, they decided to spend a lot of money renovating it. Did the job several years ago. Unfortunately, when the violence broke out, business travel into this country became virtually non-existent. I don't know how they're making it. It's a damned nice place. Beautiful rooms, color TV, air conditioning—rarities in a Burundi hotel—and a new tennis court. And with its eight stories, it's Bujumbura's Empire State Building."

As Abbot spoke, Jim eyed two tall, handsome Tutsis— both at least 6'7"—standing formally in uniforms at the hotel's front door waiting for customers who were not likely to show up.

As the jeep wound through the streets, what was most striking to Jim was the dramatic variation in size among the people.

"I'm sure you've heard this stateside, Jim, but the Hutus make up about 85 percent of the population," said Casey. "Most Hutu men'll range anywhere from 5'2" to about 5'10", and the Hutu women are several inches shorter. There's a very small population of Pygmies—only about 1 or 2 percent—and they, of course, are generally less than 4 feet tall. And then the Tutsis make up about 15 percent of the population. The average height of a Tutsi male is about 6'7", and a Tutsi female about 5'11"—so they're easy to spot! If you see a man about 6 feet to 6'2" or a woman about 5'4" to 5'7" then sometimes it's as a result of a mixed marriage. Believe me, mixed marriages can cause major problems for people in this country. In fact, many murders happen as a direct result of mixed marriages."

Moments later, Corporal Roberts pulled off the main road onto a rutty side street and stopped in front of a small restaurant.

"I read on your bio sheet that pizza is one of your favorite foods," said Casey. "Well, welcome to the only pizza joint in Burundi!"

20

Corporal Roberts parked the jeep at the side of the road in a spot that would allow the group to keep an eye on the vehicle. "Coach, if we don't keep watch while we're eating, you can be certain something'll be missing when we get back to the jeep . . . if not the jeep itself," said Abbot.

The five Americans entered a tropical-like, open-air restaurant with no roof and only a gray tarp for walls. The branches of four cocoa trees—one at each corner—shaded the sitting area; the only color was provided by several yellow and white acacia plants that anchored the tarp.

"What happens if it rains?" Jim asked.

"Well," replied Abbot. "June to August is the dry season and it never, and I mean *never* rains. For the rest of the year, with the exception of the rainy season, it doesn't rain much. When it does, the cocoa trees provide pretty good cover, and people just raise the awnings at each table!"

A very short waiter poured water into small glasses, and Jim's facial expression showed concern.

"I mentioned on the ride in about dysentery from the water," said Jack Casey. "Well, it's no problem in a place like this. Restaurants in Bujumbura have to boil and disinfect the water. But if it'd make you feel better, order Coke. It's flown in from France, and it's generally thought to be the safest thing to drink."

"What about the malaria? Is it as bad as I've heard?"

"It can be," replied Abbot. "But in addition to what you received in DC, we have some very good pills at the Embassy—take one a day and you're usually fine. We've all been here for at least a year—in my case, nearly two and a half—and we haven't had any problem."

Just then, Jim looked up at the waitress approaching the table. He was nearly spellbound. Obviously a Tutsi, she was tall, slender, and statuesque. Her high cheekbones, raven-dark eyes, full, sensuous lips, and firm breasts under a loose jersey coalesced to create a vision of ethnic beauty. In DC or in Brussels, he had not seen a woman so striking.

In a soft, warm voice, she said, "*Bonjour. Puis-je prendre votre command, s'il vous plaît?* Good day, may I take your order, please?"

For the first time in longer than he cared to remember, Jim Keating felt a sudden surge of romance in his soul. She was standing right next to him so, fortunately, he couldn't stare at her. But with her hip only a hand's breadth from his head, he was certain his heart rate had spiked. He was pleasantly surprised, for antidepressants had kept a decidedly tight lid on his libido.

After the men ordered the pizza and Coca-Cola, Abbot turned to him.

"Jim," he said quietly, revealing a slight quaver in a voice that was usually strong. "Do you mind if I address a sensitive issue?"

"Of course not," Jim said, perhaps a bit too emphatically. A trace flustered that his reaction to the lovely waitress might have been rather obvious, he guessed what the subject might be.

"A man's personal life is his own business," said Abbot. "But as Barry may have told you, the Tutsi women find Americans very attractive."

"Surely not an old codger like me!"

"Well, I'm not sure I think of you as an old codger, Coach, but yeah, I'm sure the women here will be very attracted to you. You just . . . need to be careful," Abbot said.

He went on to explain the history of the AIDS virus in Burundi: how it started in the city, because most of the jobs and people are in Bujumbura, but then spread throughout the whole country. The virus, he said, was getting worse. So bad, in fact, that the situation was in danger of becoming a pandemic. Although most Tutsi women were careful—many were religious, not promiscuous—Abbot stressed how prevalent the virus was, even among those who were actively trying to avoid it.

"Now, as you just saw, many of the Tutsi women are quite beautiful. But, my *strong* advice, Jim," he said, "and you can take it for what it's worth, is that you stay away from any, shall we say, liaisons. Temptation will be there on a regular basis. Tutsi women realize that any type of a relationship with an American could get them a better quality of life."

Casey nodded in agreement with Abbot's warnings. He shared a story about a former employee who had been sent back to the United States only one month earlier with AIDS.

"We're still pretty shaken by it. Out in the country, you can go from hill to hill and literally see no one from the ages of eighteen to forty. In many regions, the virus has wiped out almost all people of that age. Just last week, President Buyoya formed a blue-ribbon commission with an alarming, but accurate, name—*Save a Generation*. You're well aware of the terrible violence here. Yet, in our judgment, the biggest safety issue for Americans is the damned AIDS virus," Casey said.

"Enough said," said Abbot. "Let's talk about other topics."

By the time the pizza arrived several minutes later, Jim's attraction to the waitress had abated—*got enough to worry about*—and Abbot was providing more facts about Burundi. He reminded Jim that the average life expectancy in the country was forty years—thirty-eight for men and forty-one for women. *Similar to what it was in the eighteenth or early-nineteenth century in the United States,* Jim thought.

Jim had read that the population was just under six million, but Abbot mentioned that the fleeing of refugees to Tanzania, Zaire, and Kenya had most likely decreased that number. Those left in Bujumbura had been dealing with a steady increase in crime ever since the outbreak of violence ten months earlier. He had to keep his eyes open in certain neighborhoods, Abbot told him, or he'd be mugged, pickpocketed, or worse.

"So many people are armed who shouldn't be, Jim," Abbot said. "Anytime you go out at night, you'll be accompanied by someone who is armed—Clive, Jim, another Marine, or me."

Abbot reached for another piece of pizza while Jim sipped his Coca-Cola. He hoped he wasn't overwhelming the coach, but the picture he was painting was accurate. And these were things Jim needed to hear.

"You know," Abbot continued, "I used to jog, but ever since one of my colleagues—an attaché from the Belgian Embassy—was mugged and robbed on a public road bordering Lake Tanganyika, I confine my jogging to the grounds of my home, which is fortunately a large area."

"Thirty loops equal three miles—I don't know how many times I've heard that," Casey cracked.

Jim laughed lightly and then cleared his throat to ask a question he'd been contemplating for a minute or so. "How do the locals view Americans? I mean, in the jeep ride, it seemed that they were more curious than anything else."

"Before the Soviet Union began to teeter," said Sergeant Rush, "the United States was essentially in competition with the USSR for the loyalty of the people here—and in many other African countries as well. But now, with the collapse of the Soviet Union near at hand, Burundians look to America as really their only potential ally—or hope."

"Amazing," said Jim.

"How so?" asked Abbot.

"Well, I don't think more than 1 percent of the entire United States population had ever even heard of Burundi until the violence broke out. Yet, you're saying, Sergeant, that they look to us as their only hope. To me, that's incredible."

"You're right. It is incredible," said Rush.

"How 'bout the Peace Corps? I read that they're mostly gone."

"True," replied Abbot. "And the ones who are still here work in agriculture. As Barry Sklar probably also told you, the vast number of employed Burundians work in agriculture as well—almost 94 percent. The rest are split up between government, industry, commerce, and services. But, as I said, the few Peace Corps people who are still here—no more than twenty or twenty-five—work on agriculture-related projects."

"What about basketball?" asked Jim. "How popular is it?"

"Very popular," replied Casey, his voice rising in excitement. "In the late '80s, an American organization sent coaches here to do clinics—one guy came over from Boston College. They also sent over a lot of equipment and even put together a Burundian National Team that traveled to the States two years ago. All of this really helped the growth of the game until the war broke out and completely stopped its progress."

"Yeah, I read about that trip," said Jim. "They actually won a game or two, although they picked up an American guard—a kid from UConn—who really helped them."

"That's true, they did better than anyone expected," said Abbot. "But, as Jack said, when the violence broke out, all of the good that had been done by putting Tutsis and Hutus together on basketball teams seemed to evaporate. That's why the ambassador thought that a guy like you coming over could have some type of, in her words, chipping effect—chipping away at the hatred that's been part of this country for centuries."

"Let me ask you something," Jim said, struggling for words. "Do . . . do the basketball players actually *hate* each other?"

"Not really. In fact, when the State Department got the idea of bringing someone like you over, the ambassador held a meeting with some of the basketball folks. They *all* thought that this could be part of a larger plan to stop the violence. They also made it clear that they—the real hoops people—*don't* hate each other. But, as I said, they really haven't been able to get together much lately, for fear of some type of violent reaction from others in their tribe."

"But Jim," continued Abbot, "let me tell you what lines the ambassador is thinking along. She's thinking about having you not only conduct clinics for kids and coaches, but also put together a national team. She's also considering how to get some funds from the Peace Corps and, possibly, the US Information Agency. She'd use these funds to host a couple of games in Bujumbura, including a big opener. As you'll see, the place you'll practice is an outdoor court. The only indoor court is at the university, and it's very small. But this outdoor court has plenty of room for people to both stand and sit. After you put the team together, her idea for the first game is to bring in a squad from Rwanda, which would also be made up of Hutus and Tutsis. Have a game!"

Sergeant Rush expanded on Abbot's points. "We Marines have often heard about a famous England–Germany soccer game played between the trenches during a World War I Christmas truce. Never got nearly as much publicity as the ping-pong diplomacy in China back in the 1970s, but it supposedly happened."

Abbot added, "Ambassador Foster thinks that a game between Burundi and Rwanda could have a very positive effect on lessening the violence—and on the way people think about each other. She also believes that forming various leagues and conducting clinics around the country would help to restore some confidence in the peace-building process and be good for the American image. Even though Burundians consider us to be their best hope, we're always mindful—here and in other African countries—of the importance of enhancing our image in whatever way possible."

"Are the Hutus athletic?" Jim asked.

"Very athletic," said Abbot. "Most of them are point-guard size at best, but they're quick. The ambassador, who, as you know, is a hoops maven, figures that they can play guard, while the Tutsis can play inside!"

The group finished their pizza, which Jim found to be delicious, no doubt because he was so hungry.

"We've got a big night planned for you, Jim," said Abbot. "How 'bout if I take you to the apartment and let you get some rest?"

21

Atop a hill on the outskirts of Bujumbura, with a breath-taking view of Lake Tanganyika, Jesse Abbot's home was as elegant as it was secure. A fifteen-foot-high cast-iron gate with spear-like rods served as an imposing bulwark.

Seated behind the gate in a small guard-house was Ntare Bagaza, a Tutsi armed with an Uzi who held the dual roles of gatekeeper and receptionist. Ntare would open the gate only for members of the Abbot family, US Embassy and Marine personnel, or individuals whose passage was cleared in advance by the Embassy. All others were turned away, and if anyone attempted a forced entry, Ntare's charge was clear: "Shoot to kill." Thus far, it was an order he had never been forced to carry out.

On sighting the Marine jeep, Ntare quickly opened the gate and approached the Americans with a wide smile. Looking at Jim, he said, "I basketball!"

Abbot roared with laughter and then said in French, "You've been practicing those two words more than your jump shot."

After Ntare vigorously shook Jim's hand, the jeep passed through the gate. "He's been waiting for you since I told him two weeks ago that you were coming. He's one of the guys selected for the National Team that went over to America. Said it was the highlight of his life. He's hoping you can get things going again, if not another American tour, then some type of revival of the National Team for inter-African play."

"Is he any good?" asked Jim.

"According to him he is, but a knee injury has slowed him down," said Abbot.

"I noticed the machine gun he was carrying," said Jim.

"Yeah," said Abbot, as if embarrassed by the need for such a security measure. "Jim, as Sergeant Rush told you earlier, we're *technically* neutral in this conflict, although behind the scenes, we support President Buyoya—simply because he supports democracy."

As the jeep edged up the long driveway, Jim leaned forward, eager to hear more.

"As you saw during the ride in from the airport, most people just look at us with curiosity. However, when extremists on either side feel that we're somehow favoring the 'enemy,' things can get pretty tense. In fact, the ambassador has had to call several emergency meetings with warlords of both sides to reconfirm our neutrality.

"But, believe me, whenever one group senses that we're favoring the other side, they make it known that our lives could be in danger. You can be sure that we take their threats seriously, to the point that all American-owned homes have some type of security guard. In fact, wait 'til you see the security at the ambassador's home—two Marines on gate duty at all times. Yet, as we said, there's never been any type of attack on US Embassy personnel."

"Are we really neutral?" asked Jim.

Abbot smiled. "Well, for the time being, yes, we're neutral."

Jim wasn't totally convinced. During his State Department briefings, he'd had a feeling that American neutrality was a complex issue that could easily change based on circumstances, and that American support was always rooted in a fidelity to democratic rule. He recalled Barry Sklar saying, "The tipping point is simple: Are those in power in favor of democracy? If they are, we support them—always."

As the jeep approached the white stucco home, Jim was struck by the geometrical balance of the grounds. The putting-green lawn was surrounded by a symmetric French-style formal garden with a galaxy of blooming flowers. The brilliant display of crimson bougainvillea, pink hibiscus, blood-red roses, and orange leonatis arrayed against bordering palm, eucalyptus, and acacia trees was in sharp contrast with the dusty, trash-filled streets and gray buildings Jim had seen on his way to Abbot's house. When the jeep came to a stop, two very small men came running from the garden.

"That's Albert and Anatole—they'll collect your bags," Abbot said.

After warm greetings were extended to Jim in French by the two gardeners, Abbot ushered him through the main house to the veranda.

"It's a bit empty now, Jim. Because of the spread of violence, I decided to send my wife, Elizabeth, and ten-year-old daughter, Karen, back stateside about four months ago. I'll be going home to see them within the next few months."

He didn't need to add that their absence was a cause of profound loneliness; his sad expression, while fleeting, delivered that message—one Jim understood.

Out on the veranda, Jim exclaimed, "Jesse, it's like being in a park!"

"Yeah, it's quite a place. While the pay in Foreign Service is modest, and being so far from home can be difficult for various reasons, housing for a US diplomat is generally pretty damned spectacular. This is especially true in African countries, where the US government can purchase these homes dirt cheap."

"If you don't mind my asking," said Jim, "how much would a home like this go for in Burundi?"

"Today, about 40,000 US dollars."

"It'd be ten times that much in the States."

"Maybe only ten times in Worcester!" kidded Abbot. "In a place like Westchester County, it'd be more like thirty times!"

"You're right," smiled Jim.

A fourth servant appeared, Josiane Kakunze, the Hutu domestic Abbot had told Jim about. No more than four feet tall, her smooth, sable skin was lit up by a radiant smile. Dressed in a traditional wraparound *pagnes* with lime green and umber flowers, she was very pretty and probably in her mid-forties. Somehow, her personal losses in life did not smother her spirit.

Jim made certain he didn't stare as he had at the restaurant, but he did notice her hair fixed in tight ringlets, her deep-set eyes, and her full lips. *Another lovely Burundian woman*, he thought.

Josiane greeted Jim warmly in near-perfect English. "*Salama*, Mister Jim Keating. Welcome to Burundi. We wish you peace and happy stay. Please excuse to make iced tea."

"*Salama* and thank you." Jim bent slightly at the waist.

When she had left the room, Jim turned to Abbot and asked, "Um . . . how many domestic workers do you have?" asked Jim diplomatically.

"We have eight, Jim—four Hutus and four Tutsis. Before the outbreak of violence, we had five, and Ntare's job was not as an armed gatekeeper, but as my driver. . . . Also, before the violence exploded, we didn't pay any attention to our Burundi Affirmative Action Policy, as we call it. But we sure do now. If it got out that we were employing a majority of one side or the other, it could cause us problems."

Abbot added, "And, as I mentioned at the airport, by Burundi's standards, we pay well—very well. 'Heavy lettuce,' as Ntare says. The result is that we get *great* people."

"Do they get along, the four Hutus and the four Tutsis?" Jim asked.

"They do. In fact, Burundian society has been, and is, to a large extent, quite fluid. Many, if not most, Burundians don't sympathize with the insurgent groups. And, of course, they want to keep their jobs. I don't mean to say that they socialize after hours, but yes, they get along fine."

As Jesse spoke, Jim found himself increasingly curious about his new living quarters.

"Tell me about this home," said Jim, who by now felt completely comfortable with Abbot. "I bet it has quite a history."

"Sure does!" said Abbot. "It was owned by a Belgian industrialist who purchased a cattle farm here in the early 1950s and built this home in '54. Now, understand, when this was a Belgian colony, if you take into account the tax advantages he received, a guy like that could build it for practically nothing. It was like a little paradise for him, and, as legend has it, he had a rather large appetite for the Tutsi women. In fact, the apartment you'll stay in was supposedly built for his mistress. He'd come down here for a month and then go back to stay for a month with his wife and three kids in Brussels."

Jim felt his usual Catholic unease about a discussion involving sexual matters, particularly with someone he just met.

Abbot continued, "Anyway, one summer he was down here on one of his so-called business trips. His wife, who had never been here before, decided to surprise him."

"And I guess it was quite a surprise," said Jim, forcing a smile.

"Sure was. As I heard the story, the wife made him sell the house and plantation to another Belgian. Then, in '62, when the Belgians gave independence to Burundi, the Swiss

Embassy purchased the home. When they downsized their diplomatic corps several years ago, we bought it for the princely sum of 25,000 US dollars. So now that you have all of the prurient details of this hideaway, let me show it to you."

As Abbot escorted Jim into his new home, Jim's delight with his surroundings was tempered by sudden pangs of guilt. The apartment's graceful elegance was in sharp contrast to the conditions, only several miles away, where human beings were living in what Jim imagined might rival the worst of thirteenth-century serfdom. But his concern receded somewhat as his host ushered him around the apartment, which had surely been built with someone of consequence in mind—in this case, a mistress. It was a small jewel, with the kitchen, living room, bedroom, and veranda all having spectacular views of the gardens, Lake Tanganyika, and the hills beyond. Soon, Jim's feelings of guilt melted away, overridden by his appreciation for such nice quarters.

"Jesse, this place is *great*."

"I'm glad you like it, Jim. Now, it's 1:45, and the reception starts at 7:30. I'm sure you're exhausted. Why don't you get some sleep, and I'll knock on your door about six."

"Sounds good."

After Abbot closed the door, Jim surveyed his new quarters more closely. Jim would never pretend to be an expert in interior decoration, but after so many moves with Edna, he'd gained some sense of what created comfort and harmony and what didn't. It wasn't roomy, but it was exquisitely furnished, each piece having been carefully chosen and arranged. Jim would later learn that the dressers and writing table, both beautifully carved mahogany, were brought by the Dutch in the early 1900s. The lilac shades in the bedroom opened onto the spectacular view, but Jim soon drew the shades and slumped into the soft feather bed.

Throughout the trip, the withdrawal from the Prozac had prevented Jim from sleep, save a few winks. When he landed, his adrenaline kept him moving. Now he was so completely weary that he drifted off immediately. When Abbot knocked on the door at six, Jim awoke refreshed, reminding himself that, for the last decade, he had not required more than four or five hours of sleep a night.

"Did you sleep okay?" asked Abbot.

"Slept great," said Jim.

"Well, the ambassador would like us to get there by about 7:00 so that she can greet you personally before the other guests arrive. Sergeant Rush will pick us up at 6:45."

"I'll take a quick shower and shave," said Jim. Retrieving a shirt and a tie, he turned to Abbot and smiled. "I haven't worn a tie very much lately, but I think I can remember how it goes on. I'll be ready, Jesse."

Underneath his shirts, Jim saw his picture of Edna and Sarah. He put it on the dresser.

"That's a very pretty pair, Jim."

"Thanks. Edna was a great traveler. She had a special love of Spain. Visited there many times when I was coaching in Barcelona." Jim was relieved that he was remembering good times. He was definitely getting better. "Sarah likes to travel, too. Maybe I can get her over here if things ever calm down."

"That would be great, Jim, on both accounts—getting her here and having things calm down," said Jesse. "I'll let you get ready, Coach."

The shower was low and the pressure was less than Jim was accustomed to in Worcester. But it felt good, and he might have wanted to luxuriate awhile if not for his greater desire to meet Ambassador Foster and begin this challenge in earnest.

The ambassador's residence was about two miles from Abbot's, in the Kiriri district, by far the most exclusive neighborhood in Burundi, consisting of twenty mansions, all built by the

Belgians in the 1940s and '50s. While none of the homes had a view of Lake Tanganyika, they were all magnificent, including the ambassador's—a twenty-two-room palatial estate built by another wealthy Belgian whose background Jim would soon discover.

When the jeep arrived at the gate, Abbot stated the obvious: "Heavy security tonight, Jim." Four Marines, two more than usual, were on gate duty, and after each one greeted Jim, the jeep passed through into a large parking lot off the side of the house.

"Jim Keating! Welcome to Bujumbura!"

The strong, clear, and cheerful voice came from a side door, out of which walked a woman dressed in a beige safari suit. Ambassador Cynthia Foster had taken on late middle age with grace. She was of medium height and slightly overweight, but not excessively so. "The traditional build of mature African women," Jim would later hear her say in a bantering tone. Her hair was black and braided, her face clear skinned and worldly, and her eyes conveyed a kindness that immediately made Jim feel comfortable. He saw a lady who was attractive, not so much because of her physical beauty, but because of her intelligence, warmth, and natural personality. When she smiled, she glowed, and her presence was compelling without being domineering.

"I can't tell you how glad I am you're here!" she said.

"Ambassador Foster, I can't tell you how glad *I am* to be here," said Jim, who, up until that point, had been uncertain how to react, but now was ready to discard his wariness.

The ambassador invited him into the house. Holding his arm as they walked, she said, "Jim, I can sense you're a little bit concerned, but I honestly think you're going to like Burundi."

III

Uncommon Surprises

22

"Glass of iced tea, Jim?" Ambassador Foster asked.

"No—no thanks."

"Well then, shall we take a tour?"

"Love to."

Ambassador Foster was obviously comfortable taking the lead, and she did it with an ease that Jim found appealing, if not disarming. As the two walked from room to room, Jim marveled at the grandeur of the home. He had seen some magnificent dwellings in his travels. Colonial mansions in New England, antebellum estates in the South, and the haciendas outside of Barcelona had all been imposing. This home, though, was majestic. Yet, once again, an image of mud-brick and thatched huts flashed in the coach's mind.

"Did Jesse tell you about all the rich Belgians who built these houses?" Ambassador Foster asked.

"He did."

"Well, the unusual thing about this particular home is that it was built by a woman—an industrialist who, unlike most of the Belgians who built here, had a humanitarian side.

She started a successful literacy program out in the country. When we moved here, the history of this home was related to me by our chef, and I became interested in her work. I did what I would call modest research on the results of her literacy program and found that more than 1,000 adults can now read because of her efforts."

"Is she still alive?" asked Jim.

"Oh, no. She died in '59, at age forty-six. She was in northwest Burundi working on her program and was caught on a country road in a battle between the two warring tribes. She was killed by a machete, although we are not certain which side did it."

Pausing, the ambassador appeared to be momentarily unsettled.

"You've heard the old saying, Jim, Oscar Wilde maybe, that no good deed shall go unpunished? Well, Odette Racouille—that was her name—she embodied that expression. And if my understanding of the Belgian contribution to Burundi is correct, her humanitarian initiative was remarkable, perhaps without equal. Fact is, Jim, Belgians were essentially absentee landlords who left most of the administrative and supervisory jobs to the Tutsis."

As Ambassador Foster spoke, Jim could sense her kindred tie to this woman, and he was struck by the way it seemed to suggest Cynthia Foster's humanist sensibilities. But the coach was eager to shift the conversation to more immediate matters.

"Madam Ambassador, thank you for the tour. This just may be the finest home I've ever been in. It's certainly a long way from a triple-decker in Worcester, Mass."

As Jim spoke, the door leading to the library swung open, and a tall, lean, and graceful man appeared.

"Jim, this is my husband Bill, who, I might add, played basketball at Indiana State!"

"We weren't quite as good as the Larry Bird teams," Bill Foster said quickly. "Coach, this is an honor. I've really been looking forward to your arrival. Welcome aboard."

Foster had ramrod-straight posture and a thoughtful, intelligent face that seemed to transmit an aura of contentment. His white hair sharply contrasted with his swarthy skin, and his eyes were dark brown with small flecks of green. They were kind eyes. Jim noticed that he carried himself with the unmistakable bearing of a life-long athlete.

"Bill, I was just saying to Ambassador Foster that this may simply be the most magnificent home I've ever been in."

"Yeah," replied Bill, "just like the one where I grew up in Indianapolis. Only difference was that there were twelve other families in my house!"

Bill delivered this ironic memory in a droll tone, but, at the same time, Jim observed that it was said in a low-key, unpretentious way. As he watched him drift over to Cynthia and throw an arm over her shoulders, he also guessed that Foster had no discomfort with being called "the husband of." Jim got the feeling that he was going to like Bill Foster. And since he expected that Bill would play some role in this basketball peacekeeping enterprise, liking him would be important.

"Jim, if it's all right with you, I've got to shift gears shortly from guide to ambassador," said Cynthia. "We've got about twenty minutes before our guests arrive. How about if you and I have a brief chat?"

On cue, Bill politely excused himself, and the ambassador ushered Jim into her home office.

"Sure you wouldn't like some iced tea?"

"No, I'm fine," Jim replied, anxious to move right into the conversation. Besides, he wasn't so much thirsty as he was hungry. A good sign, he thought.

"Well, Jim," she said earnestly, "I'm too old to think I'm going to solve the problems of the world. But I think we have a special opportunity here. When Jesse and I put the finishing touches on this project with your friend Barry Sklar—who, you should know, is one of my very favorite people—we realized that a basketball program was surely not going to put a stop to centuries of violence and ethnic hatred. That's naïve. But, being from Indiana . . . by the way, what Bill and I didn't mention was that our high school was the actual one beaten in the finals of the movie *Hoosiers*!"

Jim's face broke into a broad grin and, borrowing an old childhood expression, exulted, "For real?"

"For real," she smiled. "Bill was on that team a few years earlier. In fact, we're probably about the only two people who loved every part of the movie except the end!"

She paused, changing directions again. "But back to the point. Because Bill played—and the two of us have been such fans—well, we think that when you're a Hoosier, you can tell what a basketball player looks like."

Leaning over and softening her voice as if she were about to tell a secret, the ambassador said, "Jim, while the basketball players don't get together that much, Bill and I have seen them play several times. We've watched athletes here, 6'8"—6"10"—even 7 feet and taller, who, while not refined, are *very* natural. I watch my ESPN tapes that we get each week in the diplomatic pouch from Washington. I know that you coaches look for players who, in your jargon, 'can run the floor.' Well, Coach, some of these young men—these Tutsis—are like gazelles!"

Jim was not used to talking with a woman so knowledgeable and enthusiastic about his game. He found it enjoyable, albeit a little unnerving.

"Ambassador, your goal, as I understand it, is to use basketball as sort of a unifying force?"

"That's exactly my goal. Although, as I said, I'm aware that there are limits to any singular project like this."

"Well," said Jim, his coaching hat now firmly in place, "the Hutus . . . can they play?"

She smiled. "A true coach! And to answer your question, yes. I believe you'll find they *can* play. As a rule, they're stronger physically than the Tutsis. They're very athletic; very quick. Again, they're not refined in their game, but I bet you'll be able to develop some excellent Hutu guards! Now, did Jesse speak with you about our thinking on the overall concept?" she asked.

"Well, he mentioned that you'd like to see the National Team brought back together. Also, he said that you'd like to host some type of a big game against Rwanda."

"Yes, that's part of it. I'd also like to get youth programs going—in Bujumbura and out in the country. Like the ones I remember back in Indiana."

She stopped for a moment, as if to restrain her enthusiasm.

"But Jim, I want you to know you're in charge. I'd like to use the game to, in a small way, help bring the two sides a little closer together. But you're the boss of this project. And," she said with a grin, "despite what people might think, I can take orders as well as give them.

"One last thing," she added. "I followed your career closely, and Barry sent me many clippings, including those regarding the situation at New Jersey State. When we get to know each other better, I'll give you my views about racial discrimination and all things related. I'd like to hear your views, as well. But for now, I want you to know that I admire you—I know what a gifted coach you are—and I'm absolutely thrilled that you're here."

Her sincerity was evident. There was no doubt in Jim's mind that this woman was not only a leader, but also a very genuine person. He found himself giving fleeting but potent thought to what such a race-themed conversation with a woman of color would be like.

"Ambassador Foster, I'm truly thrilled to be here," he said, doing his best to keep his excitement in check.

"Well," she said with a twinkle in her eye, "before we go out and meet our guests, we've got to come up with a name for this program. Now, being from Indianapolis, how about the name Project Oscar?"

"For the Big O?"

"For the Big O!" echoed the ambassador.

"Then Project Oscar it is," said Jim Keating, recalling the many times he saw Oscar Robertson make the improbable seem the norm.

———

Ambassador Foster had invited thirty-five people—seventeen Hutus, seventeen Tutsis, and one Pygmy—to the welcoming dinner in Jim Keating's honor. These were an assemblage of basketball players, coaches, and administrators.

Due to the significance of the dinner, the ambassador, along with two representatives of Burundi basketball (whose importance Jim would soon come to know), had spent considerable time developing the invitation list. Special care was given to identifying people who could help move Project Oscar forward. All thirty-five accepted the invitation.

While most of the invitees lived in or near Bujumbura, eight had traveled from outlying regions. Because night travel was severely restricted, Ambassador Foster asked all eight to stay over at the Embassy. No US ambassador had ever extended this kind of hospitality. Yet in Ambassador Foster's humanitarian term of service, the practice had become commonplace, and was both well known and appreciated by many Burundians.

Following diplomatic protocol, Ambassador Foster decided that the cuisine would be a combination of American and Burundian food. With Thanksgiving coming soon, the ambassador had arranged for ten frozen turkeys to be flown in from Brussels. Before introducing Project Oscar to the guests, she would use the turkeys to offer a brief history lesson about American Thanksgiving. The Burundian food would be rice and cassava and a banana-and-bean stew, which were regularly eaten by both tribes and thus were considered, in the words of Audace Bugaza, the ambassador's Hutu chef, "safe choices."

Ambassador and Bill Foster, Jim, and Jesse Abbot formed the reception line and greeted the guests. Jim took note that they were all male.

A moment later, Ambassador Foster seemed to have read Jim's mind. She leaned toward him and whispered, "One of my goals is to introduce the game to women. But tradition at a dinner like this calls for only men to be invited. I'm not too happy about the tradition, but one battle at a time. I promise, Coach, I'm not losing sight of my goal of getting women involved in Project Oscar."

During a brief break in the line, Jim noted that while some of the Hutus were dressed in the Western attire of shirt and tie, none wore sport coats. Abbot nodded, "Few people in Burundi can afford such a luxury." The other Hutus, and all the Tutsis, wore colorful, toga-style garb that hung loosely from their shoulders.

At first, Jim thought that many of the guests seemed intimidated by the grandeur of the affair. One man was so nervous that he perspired profusely as he walked through the reception line. But Ambassador Foster's friendly demeanor quickly made this man, as well as the other guests, feel at ease. Most importantly, she let each person know his presence was vital to the success of the mission.

After most of the guests had been greeted, Jim saw two distinguished men, both well into their sixties, arrive together. One was a Hutu, the other a Tutsi. Ambassador Foster greeted them warmly and, in their presence, said to Jim, "Mathias Bizimana and Terrence Ndayisaba have been friends for many years. They are the founding fathers of basketball in this country. Despite many obstacles, the game has kept their friendship alive. They helped me assemble tonight's invitation list, Jim. Both will be key contributors to our work."

The two men, both of whom spoke clear English, smiled at Jim. "We are glad to be here, Coach Keating," said Terrence, the Hutu. "We plan to be your most loyal supporters."

After the two friends headed off for hors d'oeuvres, Ambassador Foster said quietly, "They are the most respected men in basketball in this country. What I just said in front of them is true—they will be crucial to the success of this project."

The dinner, a four-course extravaganza that concluded with a pineapple trifle made specially by the chef, was a big hit with all the guests, most of whom had never dined in such splendor—nor eaten turkey.

As coffee was being served, the ambassador gently tapped her glass. In flawless French, she began with brief remarks about the history of Thanksgiving in the United States and "the role of poor Tom Turkey." She then addressed the main point of the gathering.

"How many of you have ever heard the name Oscar Robertson?"

Five of the thirty-five Burundian guests, including Mathias and Terrence, raised their hands.

"Well, my husband, Bill, and I grew up in Indianapolis, Indiana, right in the middle of the United States and a hotbed of basketball. We both had the chance—indeed the pleasure—to watch one of the greatest basketball players in history develop: Oscar Robertson. We followed his career as a youngster, through his time at Crispus Attucks High School in Indianapolis, then on to the University of Cincinnati in Ohio, then to the 1960 Olympics, and then to the NBA. And was it ever a thrill!"

She continued, "What Oscar did for Bill and me—and so many others of our generation—was unite us in our love for this game. Because Oscar was such an inspiration—he was so smart, so disciplined, such a great player—well, if it's alright with everyone here, we'd like to name the program in his honor."

"A grand idea," said Mathias Bizimana, and the others all nodded in accord.

"Wonderful," said the ambassador. "I know that Oscar would feel very good about this. . . . Gentlemen, my husband Bill, Jesse, Jack Casey, and I, along with a great American coach—who will address you in just a moment—feel that there may be some potentially outstanding players right here in Burundi. More importantly, we feel that a love of basketball is one thing that *everyone* in this room shares. We'd like to use that common thread to weave friendships and to create, in a small way, a sports quilt, if you will, to counteract violence. And we've asked you here tonight because we believe that you can help us braid that quilt.

"Now, I'm going to call on a man who is a great coach—a man who is here to help us start braiding that quilt. As you know from my letter of invitation, this man came all the way from America. His background includes coaching at the high school, college, and professional levels—both in the NBA and in the European League. He has a well-deserved reputation as a brilliant teacher of the game. Fellow lovers of basketball, it is my pleasure to introduce Coach Jim Keating."

In his days as a coach, Jim had delivered hundreds of speeches, yet none since his dismissal from New Jersey State. Abbot had told him at the airport, "Be ready to say a few words tonight." Despite being forewarned, as he began his address, he felt nervous, especially because he planned to add something untried. Having a translator—Jesse Abbot, in this case—added to his stage-fright. He stopped-started awkwardly, until he and Abbot eventually achieved a kind of cross-rhythm of English and French. Yet once he was several sentences into his speech, he felt a semblance of his old eloquence returning—and an overpowering sense of meaning in his words.

"As Ambassador Foster said, we're all here because we believe in the power of basketball as a force of goodwill. My job is to simply ask for your help. I need your help in identifying the right players to be on the National Team, because a good national team is one of our objectives. We'd like to put this National Team together and train for a period of several months. Then, due to Ambassador Foster's great vision, we'd like to host a game against Rwanda. And, if all goes well, we'd like to continue with the development of the team, possibly working it into the African Championships—even another trip to America.

"We'd like to develop a youth program, and I'll need your help there, too. You'll need to show me where the best athletes are. Also, we want the game to be open to young players who are not necessarily great, but who would enjoy the participation. Earlier today, Jesse Abbot quoted to me the words of Ambassador Foster: 'Let's use basketball as a chipping effect.'

"Well, I like that—I really like that. So let's develop Project Oscar to, in a small way, chip away at the violence, at the hatred.

"Ambassador Foster and gentlemen, it's no different in my country. I've coached this game for four decades." Jim leaned forward and added with emphasis, "At its very best, the sport of basketball can be a bridge, a source of great friendships, a profound learning process among people, a wellspring of lessons, of teamwork, of fair play—not to mention an appreciation for people's differences. In my best days as a coach, I would see, in a pregame meeting, the hands of a black player, a white player, a Catholic, a Protestant, and a Jew all come together as one. On the court, I would see a black player pass to a white player, or an Asian American set a pick for an Italian American. That is the essence of the game—brotherhood and teamwork.

"Let me read a short poem written by an American coach. I believe this poem catches the essence of Project Oscar."

Here goes, thought Jim, as he readied to embark on untrodden oratorical turf.

"When we put our hands together

Before the game, in prayer
Black hands, white hands, Christians, Jews
United by how much we care
Our coach would bellow
'We are one,
And there is room for every fellow.'"

The coach looked out into the eager faces of his audience as Abbot finished the translation. "Gentlemen," Jim said, his voice rising, "I'd like to use the concepts of this poem—of teamwork and brotherhood—to make a difference here. And I'll need your help. Today is Monday. As I understand it, our first practice is Friday. So please get the word out. On Friday, *tuzopina intango nzizo*—we'll get off to a great start."

When Jim was finished, there was a spontaneous burst of applause that quickly gave rise to a standing ovation—his first in a long time. The coach felt buoyed and wished the Friday practice could come sooner.

Ambassador Foster leaned over to her husband and whispered, "I'm glad Barry Sklar pushed so hard for this. And he even likes poetry!"

23

Next morning, Jim Keating and Jesse Abbot sat on Jesse's veranda, sipped hot red bush tea, and began to set the game plan. They agreed that the Friday gathering of the Burundi National Team, the first such get-together in many months, would be as much a tryout as a practice.

"Jim," said Jesse, "some of the players who went to America are now in their late twenties or early thirties. So the ambassador and I felt that the fairest thing to do would be to open this first session to that group, as well as to younger guys who would like to try out."

Knowing that less than 1 percent of the population had phone service, Jim raised an important issue. "At last night's dinner, I encouraged the guests to get the word out. Then it dawned on me just how difficult that might be."

"Don't worry, Coach," Abbot assured him. "First, most of the guys who play basketball are from the Bujumbura area. So, we're relying on word of mouth from those at the dinner. In this country, that kind of communication is generally effective, although it takes several days to plan something. Also,

Sergeant Rush and five other Marines will head out to the country today."

Handing Jim a copy of a flyer, Abbot continued. "They'll post these on bulletin boards and hand them out to anyone who looks like a player. By giving, several days' notice, we feel it'll be plenty of time for the word to spread."

"My guess is that no one has done much playing lately," said Jim.

"You're right," replied Abbot. "Because of the violence, all sports have really suffered. But based on the great reaction at the dinner—thanks, by the way, to two fine speeches—we're optimistic about a good turnout. Now, bear in mind, the younger players who attend will have had virtually no coaching."

"How many of the players will know any English?"

"Very few." The response caused Jim to decide on the first phase of his foreign language program.

"Barry told me that he thought all of the players would know French. Correct?"

"Yes."

"Then there are certain words, certain phrases, I'm going to need to learn. Certain things every coach says to his team, like 'move the ball,' 'box out,' 'good pass'—you know, things that players need to hear."

"I know what you mean. Good point."

"So, I'm going to make a list. I'm wondering if you'll help me with the French translation."

"Absolutely!"

"Now, you're sure that French will be okay, as opposed to Kirundi?"

"Definitely okay," replied Abbot.

Jim made his list, included every phrase he could think of that related to teaching the game, and presented it to Abbot.

"Phew . . . that's quite an undertaking for you before Friday!"

"Well, I'm not going to say that I can learn all of them, but I'll learn most of them. I became proficient in Spanish and Italian when I coached in Barcelona. In the coming months, I plan to become well versed in French and learn as much Kirundi as I can. Plus," Jim said with a smile, "we can bring a sheet of paper with the translations, can't we?"

"Sure," said Abbot, returning the smile.

When Jim received the translations from Abbot, he sequestered himself in his apartment. With the sliding glass door open to the majestic view of Lake Tanganyika and a chorus of chirping birds, he worked without interruption for the better part of two days. On both evenings, he was joined on the veranda by Abbot, who quizzed him and helped him with accents. Josiane supplied Jim with her special blend of lemonade. She also kept a bowl filled with French fries. Jim had laughed when Josiane asked if he wanted some chips and then put down the bowl of fries. *I should have known—fish 'n' chips!*

As Jim found during his experience in Spain, where he had intensified his love of knowledge, his pace of learning accelerated dramatically when he was motivated.

"Coach, you're a regular Berlitz course!" marveled Abbot as Jim rattled off translation after correct translation.

"By the way, the ambassador is going to stop by tonight. She's got an idea that I think you'll like."

Thirty minutes later, Sergeant Rush's jeep pulled through the gates with Ambassador Foster looking very much at ease in the front seat.

When Jim and Abbot approached the jeep, she hooked her arm over the back of the seat. "Now, gentlemen, I hope I'm not interrupting you. But my reason for stopping by is that, as I'm sure you agree, an important part of Project Oscar will be to develop good coaches. So, how would you feel about two assistants—a Hutu and a Tutsi? Both are passionate about basketball and both speak near-fluent English!"

"I'd love to have 'em!" Jim said enthusiastically.

"I thought you would," she said. "They were hand-picked by Mathias and Terrence, and, as I said, they have a love affair with the game. They're both former players who, despite the violence, have tried to develop basketball programs in their communities. Déo Ndvwayo is a Hutu who lives about twenty miles out of Bujumbura, and Gilbert Hatungimana is a Tutsi who lives on the outskirts of the city. Both men were at the dinner and both are anxious to get involved."

"How will Déo get here?"

"Same as many of the players," said the ambassador. "He has a bicycle. He'll cycle in."

Jim nodded and smiled, "Thanks, Ambassador. Much appreciated. I look forward to meeting both of them."

Jim remembered the last time an assistant coach was assigned to him. He had a sense, a hope anyway, that this experience would be far different.

———

On Friday evening, the night of the first practice, Ambassador Foster invited Jim Keating and Jesse Abbot to an early dinner, after which she and her husband would accompany Jim and Abbot to the workout. When he and Abbot arrived, Jim was pleased to see the ambassador and Bill decked out in Indiana State warm-ups.

"We're ready, Coach!" she said with an adventurous air. Cynthia Foster's enthusiasm was infectious. On the way over, Jim and Abbot had talked intensely about the practice. Jim was a bit anxious, but as he walked into the house, whatever concerns he might have had dissolved at the sight of a US Ambassador dressed for dinner in the sky blue of the ISU Sycamores.

During a delicious meal of stir-fried vegetables, wild rice, braised chicken, and an avocado and banana salad, along with a Bordeaux wine flown in from Belgium—which the coach politely passed on—Jim explained his practice agenda.

"It's a bit hard to develop a complete plan when I'm not sure how many guys will show up. But I thought I'd check out each player's skills and conditioning. As part of this, I'll show them some skill development drills they can practice on their own. We'll scrimmage at the end, and I'll probably put in a simple passing game offense so that we have some structure."

"I love that offense," said Bill. "Saw Bobby Knight lecture on it once at a clinic in Indianapolis."

"Bobby is a master at teaching it, as is Larry Brown," said Jim. "And, as you know, Bill, there's a lot of nuance to the passing game. For tonight, though, we'll just teach the basics."

"Jim, one slight problem about the drills, which Barry may have told you about," said the ambassador. "Basketballs, and other equipment, are in very short supply here. I'd be surprised if any player actually owns a ball, and we'll have but four balls at the practice."

Jim nodded. "Four balls will be fine for tonight. Plus, Barry gave me eight rubber balls. I thought we'd give them out a few at a time to the players who seem most serious, especially if one ball can be shared by several players in a certain area."

"Great! And through the Peace Corps, I've requested that some other balls be flown in, but the request is still tied up on someone's desk. Also, there aren't many hoops in Burundi. We've succeeded in getting four half-moon backboards with rims flown in from Brussels. I was able to get a Belgian company that still owns a small plant here to donate them. Just like your plan with the balls, perhaps we can use the hoops out in the country in areas where there are none. But as far as players working on their skills on off days, it might not be that easy."

"Barry had mentioned a general lack of equipment, Ambassador. I've got a plan for that," said Jim.

"Oh? Tell us!"

"Well, Barry thought that if we could get equipment donated in the States, we could perhaps ship it here through the daily Embassy mail out of DC. Is that a possibility?"

The ambassador actually pumped her fist in the air and said, "It's more than a possibility. It can be done!"

"Then what I'll do is survey the equipment needs—not only with the National Team, but with the younger kids in Bujumbura and out in the country. If you can get me some secretarial help, I'll prepare a letter to every college coach in the States. Barry said that if we ship the letters to him, he'll get them mailed from his department."

Jim continued, "You may know this, but most every coach, especially the Division I's, have all kinds of stuff lying around their offices. Balls, sneakers, nets—you name it!"

"How so?" asked Abbot.

"Because the sneaker contracts that many of these coaches have gives them access to a whole lot of equipment of various sorts. Heck, stuff they toss or give away could be used here."

"Jim, it sounds like a terrific idea and we'll definitely provide the secretarial help. But do you think it will work?" the ambassador asked.

"To what extent, I can't tell. But yeah, most college coaches are pretty good about this kind of thing."

When dinner ended, and using Jesse as his translator, Jim made sure to thank Audace the chef for "a tremendous meal . . . totally delicious."

Audace's expression confirmed how much the compliment meant to him.

On the ride over to the workout, Jim fidgeted in his seat. He felt nervous—and excited. It had been more than two years since he'd run a practice and part of his trepidation was that he had absolutely no idea what to expect.

The asphalt surface on which the Burundi National Team tryout would take place was called Nimbona Court. In the heart of Bujumbura, only a five-minute drive from the ambas-sador's home, it was named in honor of Gospard Nimbona, a National Team player who had traveled to the States as part of the historic tour and then died of AIDS nine months later.

Awaiting the arrival of the American contingent were a group of twenty-two players and a gaggle of chickens owned by a family whose mud hut rested fifty meters from the court. A group of onlookers was also present, there out of curi-osity more than any real interest in the game. Mathias and Terrence, the Hutu and Tutsi founders of Burundian basket-ball, walked over to welcome Jim's group.

"A good turnout, Coach Keating," said Mathias. "And I know of others who are coming today and will be a bit late."

The court surface was cracked in various places, and the court had white wooden backboards at both ends. The top of each backboard carried an unusual sign, inscribed in black: "NE SMASHANT!"

"We have a scarcity of hoops and backboards," said Terrence. "Even though many players love the dunk, it bends the rims and sometimes even breaks the backboards, which, you will note, are wooden and not very strong. Thus, the 'no dunking' sign."

Jim also noticed that neither rim had a net, a situation the coach would quickly address with Barry.

The court was parallel to several sections of bleacher seats on the north side and plenty of space for spectators to stand.

"This is where I'd like to play my dream game," the ambas-sador said. "I can envision people lined up on the hills." As she spoke, she motioned to a knoll shaped like a theater-in-the-round, which sloped down on three of the four sides of the court.

"As you can see, Jim, there are no lights. But because it doesn't get dark until ten or so, we can play the game in the early evening—around six—and finish in plenty of time. Also, we can accommodate several thousand spectators."

"Ambassador, I think you may be a sports promoter at heart!"

"She is!" agreed Bill. "Stay tuned, Coach."

Jim had done some reading about another sports entrepreneur, Pierre de Coubertin, founder of the modern Olympic Games. Coubertin's principal goal was to use sport as a global unifying force—a dream the Frenchman had successfully executed in Athens back in 1896. Ever since the first phone call from Barry Sklar, the coach had found inspiration in the vision of bringing the two sides together, using basketball as the magnet—a vision similar to, albeit more modest than, Coubertin's.

"Coach Keating," said Mathias, "meet Déo Ndvwayo and Gilbert Hatungimana, your two new assistants."

Gilbert, the Tutsi, stood 6'7". He had the reed-like frame of a marathoner and a gaunt, thoughtful countenance intensified by his shaved head. But his seemingly doleful appearance was brightened by hazel eyes, a wide smile, and a boisterous laugh. Déo, the Hutu, was about 5'8". He, too, had a shaved head—which rested atop a strong, fullback-like build—and a finely chiseled face full of strength—full lips, large ink-black eyes, and a ready smile that revealed ivory-white teeth, a common trait in Burundi. He reminded Jim of Marvelous Marvin Hagler, the middleweight champion from Brockton, Mass.

Both greeted Jim warmly, shaking hands, but—to Jim's relief—foregoing the French "three cheek kiss" he had seen them exchange with Cynthia and Bill. Jim had never been a hugger and kisser when greeting people. In heavily accented but near-perfect English, Déo said, "Thank you for letting us to work with you. We are your trusted aides!"

Jim had an immediate sense that the loyalty problem he'd experienced with Robert Frazier back at New Jersey State would not exist in Bujumbura, Burundi.

After welcoming the two assistants, Jim looked out at the court and saw many examples of the equipment problem addressed earlier by Ambassador Foster. The four rubber balls appeared to be the only thing new on the hot asphalt surface. More than half the players wore sandals strapped tightly around their ankles, two wore sneakers that were old and tattered, and six were barefoot. Jim wondered how many American coaches ever imagined running a practice with athletes who had no footwear.

As the players nervously warmed up in front of this American they knew nothing about, Jim followed a common practice among basketball coaches by first taking note of the tallest men in the group. He was immediately struck by their grace and agility, and he also noticed that the Tutsis seemed to commune easily with the Hutus. Had he not been so aware of the strife between the two tribes, he would have never thought that a problem existed.

"Anyone have an air pin to deflate the balls a bit?" Jim asked.

"There's probably one back at the Marine headquarters," replied Sergeant Rush.

"Possible to get it, Sarge? These balls have too much air. They're what we used to call Spaldeens—which means they bounce too high. Be hard for the players to dribble 'em, plus the balls will get ruined if they're not deflated."

"You got it, Coach," said Rush, impressed with the detail that Jim picked up on right away. "I'll be back in a few minutes."

The head coach turned to his two assistants. "As soon as Sergeant Rush gets back with the pin, I'm going to call the players over. But before I do, I want you both to know that I'll be asking you to help teach specific skills. I always try to make good use of my assistants. So, after I introduce each skill, I'll ask both of you to work with a small group of players to reinforce what I've taught. Sound okay?"

"Sounds a-okay," replied Gilbert with a grin.

Jim knew that one of the most critical elements of the team concept was to put the assistants to work and not have them be mere onlookers. He also wanted to develop Déo and Gilbert as coaches.

Despite the obvious athleticism of several of the Hutus and Tutsis, Jim could readily see that all the players had poor shooting technique. He also noticed something far more important, which caused him to think back many years.

In his high school coaching days and also during his early success at St. Thomas, Jim Keating's wit had played a considerable role in his overall coaching approach. But in the latter stages of his career, faced with the unnerving pressure to merely hold on to his job, the burden to win had overshadowed his humorous side.

Yet on this weather-beaten asphalt court, a continent away from his home—and with the help of Mathias's expert translation—Jim could see by the players' exuberance that this break from the acrimony that enveloped their lives was cathartic. He would not dampen their high spirits by being too rigid. Instead, he would make sure these players got a full dose of his humor ... and his humanity.

Rush's jeep fishtailed into the dirt parking area, scattering chickens amid clouds of dust. As soon as the four balls were deflated to the proper weight, Jim blew his whistle. The players, a few of whom he guessed must have engaged in acts of violence, all trotted eagerly in his direction, and Ambassador Foster emerged from the stands to formally introduce the new coach.

In fluent French, she began, "We've decided to name this basketball program in honor of one of the greatest players of all time. Oscar Robertson is a name that many of you have probably never heard. The Big O, as we called him, grew up in my American hometown of Indianapolis in the State of Indiana. My husband, Bill, that handsome man sitting right over there ...," she stopped, smiled broadly, and motioned in

Bill's direction. He raised his hand and the players all laughed and applauded.

"I'll hear about this when we get home," she said. "But seriously, Bill and I had the pleasure of watching The Big O from the time he was in junior high right up through his brilliant career in the NBA. As we move forward, you'll all learn more about the great Oscar Robertson. For now, please know that he was one of the best players of all time. He also had a love for the game that I believe some of you already have, and, hopefully, some others in this group will develop."

She continued, "You see, I believe that a love of the game will also bring about a love of the teamwork so essential to good basketball. And as passionate as I am about the sport, I am even more passionate in my hope that Project Oscar, as we will call it, will have—in some small way—a positive impact on ending the violence and creating friendships."

She paused, then said, "Ending the violence that has taken so many lives and caused so much pain."

The ambassador spoke with the eloquence of a seasoned politician and the intense sincerity of a missionary, and her message visibly affected the players.

"We want to use basketball as a means to promote friendship," she continued. "And we are fortunate that an outstanding coach has traveled all the way from America to be with us. He was a very successful coach at the high school, college, and professional levels. This man is a highly respected teacher of the game, and he is the perfect person to lead this important project."

She extended her hand out to Jim and motioned him to take her spot in front of the group. "Gentlemen," she said, "it is my great pleasure to introduce Coach Jim Keating."

24

Ambassador Foster's introduction evoked spontaneous applause from the players, and their reaction pleased Jim. Encouraged by their response, he went straight to his gym bag and pulled out several gifts.

With Mathias at his side, Jim began. "Okay, before we start the workout, I brought a few things from the States, including this Chicago Bulls World Championship hat."

As Jim waved the hat, the facial expressions of the players left no doubt about their designs on it.

"Let's find out who the real basketball historian is in this group! I'm going to name certain famous players and coaches from the United States. If you know which team they're with, raise your hand. If you give me a wrong answer, you're out. First guy to give three correct answers wins the hat. I'll do my best to see whose hand goes up first. . . . Ready?"

The players all nodded.

"Which team does Phil Jackson coach?"

Five hands went up, and Jim pointed to the one he felt was the first.

"Chicago Bulls!" said a slender, shoeless Tutsi.

"You've got one point!" said Jim. "Okay . . . who does Larry Bird play for?"

About twice as many hands were raised, and Jim pointed to a Hutu.

"The Celtics!"

"You've got a point," he told the Hutu. "Okay, who did Bill Russell play for?"

Not one hand went up, and Jim laughed heartily.

"My heavens, you know about the famous players around now. But not one of you guys knows the man who's probably the greatest team player of all time. Bill Russell played for the Boston Celtics. In his thirteen-year career, he led the Celtics to eleven world titles!"

The players all nodded at this new morsel of basketball history and then laughed when Gervais Bagaza, a 5'11" Hutu guard, said loudly, "*Billl Rooosell!*"

Pleased with the enthusiastic reaction, Jim continued, "Okay, this one is a matter of opinion, but I'll ask it anyway. As of today, who's the best coach in the NBA?"

"Phil Jackson!" yelled a Tutsi.

"Close, but not yet," roared Jim.

"Larry Brown," said another Tutsi.

"Brilliant, but he needs to stay in one place a bit longer," said Jim.

"Pat Riley," a Hutu blurted out without raising his hand.

"Okay, I'm with you. You get a point."

The lighthearted interchange went on for about five minutes, until finally Venuste Nsabimana, a Hutu, won the hat by correctly stating that Bobby Knight was the coach of Indiana. As Jim hoped, the contest did create humor and camaraderie between the players and the American, to whom they took an immediate liking.

Jim then spoke from the heart.

"Gentlemen, I'm a coach, and I'm your friend. I'm here for a couple of reasons, and one is to help you guys have some fun. I know it's hard for some of you to make each practice, so my first rule is that practice is optional. You come when you can, and it'll be my job to make it an enjoyable experience so that you'll want to come back."

As he spoke, Jim noticed that his call for brotherhood was returned by the players through their expressions of accord. He also detected in their innocent eyes a trust in their new mentor, even after only a few minutes with him.

"Another reason I'm here is that basketball, in its best form, does not discriminate. Before and after each practice and game, we'll put our hands together as one. And every hand, Hutu or Tutsi, is welcome. So let's do that now. Let's come together before we actually start practice, with our hands as one. And then let's go out and have a good workout."

Everyone, players and coaches alike, moved quickly into the huddle, all reaching toward Jim's hands. They echoed Jim's shout of "TEAM!" Then the players eagerly broke out of the huddle in groups of two or three. Standing next to Jim, Bill Foster said, "You've got 'em, Jim. They're excited."

Jim nodded slowly. The veteran coach felt ready to run his first practice in Burundi, Africa.

———

After two years in coaching hibernation, Jim Keating stretched his vocal cords and found himself teaching this simple game with a fire he'd not felt since his days as a young high school coach. He taught fundamental after fundamental, encouraged his two assistants to reinforce each point, and reveled in watching the players absorb his every tip. And when a player did something wrong, the coach often used humor to make his case.

"Good thing the backboard is there, or that ball would be in Rwanda," he cracked after a powerfully built Hutu had launched a jumper that nearly broke the sound barrier. Upon hearing Mathias's translation, even the errant shooter joined in the laughter, and Jim seized on the missed shot to talk about acquiring a soft touch.

"Shooting is about rhythm and follow-through. It all starts with bending the knees and keeping your elbows in and your hands positioned properly. Now, in the last few minutes, I've noticed that many of you are holding the ball incorrectly. Starting today, and over the next few weeks, I'd like to meet with each of you near where you live and just work on your shot."

"But Coach Keating, many of us don't have hoops where we live," a player said through Mathias.

"No worries. Ambassador Foster has gotten us several hoops that we plan to put up at convenient places out in the country. Besides, in the early stages we won't need a hoop anyway. Matter of fact, it's sometimes better to learn to shoot without a hoop—to get rid of the hoop as a distraction and get the proper technique down," he said. "So, for those of you who live within a few miles of this court, we'll meet here. For those of you who live out in the country, I'll travel there. Is that okay, Ambassador Foster?"

The ambassador and Bill were sitting in the front row of the bleachers, able to hear every word.

"Sure is!" she beamed.

Jim broke the group into layup lines, which he used to introduce simple concepts like pick and roll ("Hey big guy, set that pick on an angle and make your body wide") and back door ("It's simple, when you're overplayed you reverse cut to the basket—that's what we mean by back door"). He could see they didn't understand the fundamentals, but the layup lines reinforced his earlier observation that there were some remarkable athletes on the Nimbona Court.

"Okay, enough of the layup line. Now let's work on some ball-handling skills. The way I'll teach 'em is to break each skill into its parts. And when I teach you some of these skills, I'll also tell you about the players who popularized them. Ever hear of Earl Monroe?"

Silence. Then Terrence, the Hutu who helped introduce and establish the game in Burundi, said from his front-row bleacher seat: "The Pearl!"

"You win a hat!" shouted Jim. He then turned to the players.

"Gentlemen," the coach continued, "Earl 'The Pearl' Monroe came up with this move called the spin dribble back in 1966 or '67, when he was playing at Winston State College down in North Carolina in the United States. At first, the referees called him for palming the ball. But when the refs began to realize the ball control required to execute the move, they stopped calling it a palm. And when rival coaches saw how The Pearl was beating their defenders off the dribble, they began to figure out how to teach the move."

Jim was impressed by Mathias's translation, guessing that his skill matched any simultaneous translation at the United Nations. His basketball savvy also allowed him to mimic Jim's demonstrations, like palming.

"Now, let's put the balls down and break the spin dribble into its parts. First, in order to do it properly, you have to learn the footwork. As we go forward, you'll find that the essence of a great player is footwork. This is especially so for the tallest players. More on this later."

Jim showed the players the proper footwork, including the pivot, an essential element in the change of direction required to execute the move. After the group got the footwork down, and still without using the ball, Jim walked the players through the hand movements of the skill.

"Okay, now we're going to go to three stations. The first station will be to review the footwork, including the pivot.

Déo will run that station. The second station will be to review the hand movements, and Gilbert'll run that station. I'll be at the third station, where we'll put everything together."

He turned to the bleachers and said, "Bill and Ambassador, would you like to come out and help with the stations?"

While the two Americans were initially surprised by the invitation, within seconds they were eagerly heading to their new assignments.

"You have to hook the ball like The Pearl did," Jim yelled, and then showed them what he meant. He had not touched a basketball since his final days at New Jersey State. But when he was a coach he had practiced this move to teach it properly to his own team, as well as at summer camps and coaches' clinics. At sixty-six, he could still execute it, and when he did, his timeless know-how impressed the players and observers—including Ambassador Foster.

For her part, the ambassador completely deferred to Jim's leadership. This was his domain, and her role was to act as a supporting team member. And while it was an unusual part for Cynthia Foster to play, it was one she found herself enjoying.

———

After thirty minutes of work on the spin dribble, with every player making progress, and several executing the move with surprising control, Jim called the group to center court.

With Mathias translating, the coach said, "That was good—very good. At each practice, I'll try to teach you four or five skills. On the days in-between practices, I hope you'll find the time to work on these skills. Now, I realize that a problem we have is a lack of basketballs and hoops. Leave it with me for now. I'll be working on that."

174

Jim then organized a shooting contest. "Winners get Chicago Bulls hats and some New Jersey State basketball camp t-shirts. I have plenty!"

The shirts were left over from the camp Jim never ran in the summer following his dismissal. Until now, he'd been unable to bring himself to speak publicly about anything related to New Jersey State. The wry comment about his surplus of camp t-shirts was, he knew, a small but important step in dealing with the dismissal—and moving on.

"Best out of ten from the foul line!" he yelled. "Take five shots at a time, then go to the end of the line and wait your turn for five more. Déo and Gilbert, you work at each hoop. Guys, keep your own score—you're all on the honor system. Meanwhile, I'm going to call some of you over to work on shot technique."

Jim had found that the honor system was an effective way of promoting responsible behavior among team members. Letting his players know that he trusted them sent an important message.

"Okay, how 'bout if Venuste, Albert, Richard, and Claude come over with me!" he said.

As the four players—two Hutus and two Tutsis—jogged purposefully toward Jim, Ambassador Foster leaned over to Bill and said, "I'm still wondering how he's going to teach shooting without a hoop?"

"For a camp t-shirt," Jim said to the four players, "anyone know who the coach of the University of North Carolina is? Hint: As of now, he's won more games than any coach in the history of college basketball."

After several moments of silence, Bill Foster could not hold his tongue.

"Dean Smith!"

"Sycamores are ineligible!" roared Jim and turned back to his players.

"Bill is right; Dean Smith is his name, and, like I said, he's won more college basketball games than anyone in history. What's important for you to know is that Coach Smith has always taught that corrective work on a player's shot is best accomplished without a hoop. Remove the hoop and you remove an important distraction."

Working patiently with the four players, Jim first showed them the proper stance. "Balance is very important in any athletic skill. In shooting, balance means getting into a comfortable position, with your feet about shoulder-width apart. If you're a right-handed shooter, your right foot should be slightly in front of your left." After Jim demonstrated the correct stance, he walked in a stooped position from player to player—at times even resting one knee on the asphalt surface— to adjust their feet.

The coach then focused on the upper body. "Elbows in. Right handers—tuck that right elbow into your rib cage; left handers—tuck the left elbow into your rib cage. Remember, shooting is all about fundamentals. You guys not using the right fundamentals would be like me trying to speak to you in French without using nouns and verbs."

The moment Mathias translated, the four players laughed and clapped, and Jim continued.

"Now, imagine a ball in your hands, bend your knees and make believe you're shooting. Okay, follow me."

Placing his left hand behind the imaginary ball, he said, "This is your guide hand." He bent his knees and, from his crouched position, raised his body and fluidly arched his right hand into the air, finishing with a cupping motion of his right hand to demonstrate proper follow-through.

"Let's get the rhythm of the shot down," he kept saying. Soon, the players—two small and two tall—were executing the imaginary shot with good, if not perfect, form.

"Okay, now we're going to put a ball in your hands. Along with the proper positioning of your feet, there are six other things I'm looking for—elbows in, knees bent, arc, back spin, follow-through, and rhythm. When I say rhythm, make the shot look pretty! Let me show you."

While his body was slightly stiff with early-stage arthritis, he still had the smooth, sure-handed skill of a premier athlete. As his hoop-less shot was lofted high in the air, the seams of the ball spiraled inversely in perfect back-spin. The ball hit the ground several feet in front of Jim and, with the back spin taking effect, bounced straight back into his hands. The four players, along with Ambassador Foster and Bill, all applauded the graceful agility of the veteran instructor.

"Okay, everyone," the coach bellowed, "let's hold on the shot contest for a moment and pay attention over here."

With all eyes trained on him, Jim continued, "At my camp back home in the United States, we developed what we called 'the shot equation.' It's a simple but fun equation all of you can learn. So, here's my question: Who's good at math?"

Only one player, Mats Coulibaly, a Tutsi, raised his hand—and everyone looked at him with broad smiles.

"Okay, Mats, here's the Project Oscar shot equation: arc, plus back spin, plus follow-through, equals . . . what?" At this point, Jim placed his right hand at his ear and, grinning, leaned forward toward Mats.

When Mats did not answer, Jim roared "*SWISH!*" The coach's cry was greeted by hearty applause and laughter, with Mats displaying particular glee.

"The shot equation," repeated Didier Kwizera, a Hutu. "We will all remember . . . including Mats!" The young men again broke up in laughter, and Ambassador Foster smiled with delight at this small demonstration of Hutu–Tutsi bonding.

One by one, Jim adjusted the hands of each player on the ball. "Remember, your left hand is your guide hand." In years past, he would have drawn the analogy of the left hand or guide hand as the one that would hold a rifle, and the right hand or shooting hand as the one that would pull the trigger. But in Bujumbura, Burundi, that analogy seemed inappropriate.

Jim finished his shot instruction by calling the four players over to one of the hoops and asking everyone else to gather and observe. "These guys will now demonstrate good shooting fundamentals for you."

At first, they were a bit timid trying their newly learned techniques at a hoop. But Jim patiently reviewed each step, then demonstrated his own soft one-hander—this time with a target.

"Automatic!" Bill Foster hollered as the coach nailed a foul shot.

The four pupils each took their turn. Two of them, one Hutu and one Tutsi, actually "got it," a fact not unnoticed by the clapping onlookers and appreciated by Jim. And while the other two showed good progress, Jim knew that breaking old habits would take time.

"Okay, let's scrimmage!" he yelled.

There was a look of puzzlement on the faces of most players. Even Mathias seemed unsure of the correct translation.

"You know, let's play full court!"

Mathias grinned as he translated. As recognition graced their faces, excited chatter hummed through the group. The players then smiled and clapped—their standard response to things they understood and that made them happy.

"I was going to show you an offense called the passing game. But because it's a bit late, we'll do that at our next practice. For this first full-court game, just try to push the ball up the court and play good defense and also . . ."

He paused for a moment.

"Hold on here, let me check my notes."

Jim pulled from his pocket his written translations.

"Oh yeah—let's also *transmettre à l'homme libre*—pass to the open man."

The players burst into laughter at the sight of Jim's crib notes, a reaction welcomed by Jim. In most of his years as a coach, he'd felt such intense pressure to win that he seldom was able to laugh at himself. But seeing the response to his crib notes, Jim found himself chuckling as well.

Assigning Déo and Gilbert to shuffle guys in and out and give everyone an equal chance, Jim used the next twenty minutes to survey his talent. What he observed, even more vividly than in the drills, was a complete lack of fundamentals. Yet he also saw five or six Tutsis, and at least two Hutus, who were clearly Division I college athletes—not real basketball players yet, but surely young men with top-notch athletic ability. Most of all, he observed a group of players who were enjoying themselves and who, to a man, took to heart any suggestions he made.

"No attitudes on this court, Ambassador Foster," he said.

"Not a one!" she agreed.

When the scrimmage ended, Jim called the team to center court.

"I've had fun today, and let me tell you, there's some real potential here. Now, as I mentioned at the beginning, we'll have one full group practice every Friday at 6:00 PM. Remember now, the practice is optional, but I hope you'll keep coming because I think we can learn from each other."

...because I think we can learn from each other. Ambassador Foster was touched by the statement.

"Now, I'll also be here on Monday and Tuesday at 6:00 PM for any of you Bujumbura-area players who'd like to work on skills. On Wednesday and Thursday, I'll head out into the country, and Déo and Gilbert will accompany me. On that issue, those of you who travel in from a distance, please stay for a few minutes after practice. Mathias, Terrence, and Sergeant

Rush will discuss where you live. We'll pick out some places we can meet up that won't be too far for you," he said. "Okay, everyone get a hand in."

Twenty-nine hands—twenty-eight black and one white—some Hutu, some Tutsi, some Catholic, and some Muslim, all clasped as one.

Moments later, Jim Keating walked off the court, keenly aware of the worth of his mission. It was the best feeling a coach could have.

25

Nine players remained after practice to arrange for private shooting sessions with Jim. With the help of a map, Déo, Gilbert, and Jim picked out the locations for the following Wednesday and Thursday clinics. After the players left, Mathias approached Jim.

"Coach Jim, in your speech at the dinner, you asked us to help you find players."

"That's right, Mathias."

"Well, for the last forty years, I have lived in Bujumbura—mostly because I feel it is safer for my family. But before that, I lived here."

Mathias pointed to a place on the map called Kayanza, which appeared to be at least forty kilometers from Bujumbura—and twenty kilometers beyond Bukeye, the furthest point the group would travel to the next week.

"As you see, Kayanza is near the Rwandan border. It is known as a region of high violence, and I have not been back to my home for many years." His voice trailing off in sadness, he said, "I lost two brothers to brutal murders. . . . But when I lived in the Kayanza region, there was a group of families—all linked by marriage and heredity—that were the finest physical specimens I have ever seen. The fathers and grandfathers will probably all be dead now. Most had been Tutsi warriors—so fearless and powerful that everyone stood in awe of them."

He continued, "Since I learned about Project Oscar, I wondered if I should go back there, to my old home, to see about the children or grandchildren of that large extended family joining in this basketball movement of peace. And just now, as we looked at the map, I was thinking that when we travel to Bukeye, since we will be under the protection of the Marines, perhaps we should travel out further to see if any of those family members are still around."

Jim nodded. "Mathias, it's a good idea, but let me run it by Sergeant Rush and Jesse first."

Jim was honestly intrigued, but he knew the closer they got to the border, the more likely they might encounter roving militia. His briefings on the civil war and accusations of genocide made him wary, to say the least.

———

Monday night, when Jim showed up at the Nimbona Court to work on individual skills, he was pleasantly surprised. Word of his coaching savvy had spread in Burundian basketball circles, and thirty-two players were waiting, already working on spin moves and shooting. When the number increased to thirty-six on Tuesday night, Jim decided that all future individual instructional workouts would be offered in two shifts: 5:30–7 PM and 7–8:30 PM. To his delight, Jim would soon find that some players participated in both sessions.

Despite the limited equipment, Jim felt both sessions were successful. Before the workouts, he had held extensive meetings with Déo, Gilbert, and Mathias to review the fundamentals he'd teach. The three men caught on quickly, and Déo and Gilbert worked well at the instructional stations. And while Ambassador Foster could only make the Monday session, Bill Foster attended both workouts. At Jim's request, he helped at the stations and did so with enthusiasm and surprising skill.

During a break, Jim approached him. "For someone who's never coached, you're a real natural."

"Thanks, Jim. By the way, I'd like to come out to the country with you on Wednesday, if it's okay."

"Be fine," said Jim. He was pleased; he enjoyed Foster's company, and, aside from his basketball acumen, Bill spoke some French and a bit of Kirundi.

On Wednesday morning, before setting out, Jim, Mathias, Terrence, and Bill met with Sergeant Rush.

"Even though it stays light 'til nine-thirty or ten, we don't feel it's safe to be driving after dark," said Rush. "Coach, you really got into it the last two nights and kept going 'til nearly nine. If that's the case tonight and tomorrow, it'll mean driving home in the dark. So, first question—do you think you'll go as late?"

"Would you prefer that I not?"

"Up to you. But if you feel you're gonna go much past eight, our option is to bring along some tents and camp out in the public campground. Ever since the violence broke out, with the exception of certain border areas, the campgrounds have been pretty safe. Also, Corporal Roberts and I will alternate on night watch," Rush said. "The other option is to finish by eight, which will get us to the outskirts of Bujumbura before dark."

"Well," said Jim, "I don't want to cause everybody a lot of hassle . . . but if it's okay with everyone, how 'bout if we bring the tents along and decide at the end of practice?"

The group agreed, then Jim said, "On a related matter, Mathias mentioned that he wanted to head out further—

twenty or so kilometers further—to a place where he feels there might be some great athletes. Right, Mathias?"

"Right, Coach Jim,"

"What do you think, Sarge?" Jim asked.

"Yeah, I heard about this from Jesse," said Rush, "and I must say it sounds pretty interesting. I've checked with our patrol up there and it should be safe. Might be another good reason to maybe camp out tonight, since we'll be that much closer to Kayanza."

"Sounds good to me," said Jim.

"Me, too," said Mathias. "You know, I really think the extra trip could be worthwhile."

Looking over at Bill Foster, Rush said, "Hey Bill, any problem sleeping under the African stars?"

"Are you kidding? Hell, I was a boy scout in Indianapolis, although the farthest I got on a camping trip was my backyard." The men laughed.

"On a serious note," said Rush, "there's some pretty wild animals in that region. But I'm sure that if Corporal Roberts and I are both armed, we'll be okay. And, besides, it's our only choice. You won't find any Marriott Hotels in the rural sections of Burundi!"

Underneath Rush's occasional quips, Jim knew there was solid confidence based on extensive military experience. If the Sarge felt things were safe, that was good enough for the Coach.

———

On the ride to Gitega, Jim pulled out some note cards and was practicing several basic Kirundi phrases when Mathias clapped him on the shoulder. "Jim, you haven't seen this yet. Take a quick sighting."

Jim looked up to see a group of nine or ten young people, probably in their teens, walking about a hundred yards in front of the jeep. They carried on their heads large baskets shaped like the spinning tops Jim remembered playing with as a child. A couple of them were holding the baskets, but most of the kids had their arms at their sides, walking in a rhythmic gait. As they came alongside the group, Mathias said, "*Bwakeye.*"

Jim understood *bwakeye* as Kirundi for "hello," so he waved as they passed and echoed Mathias's greeting. The kids smiled and waved, and one of the girls said loudly in English, "Good day."

Jim continued to memorize Kirundi phrases, but kept his gaze on the surrounding countryside as they traveled a bumpy, dusty, red clay road. The shrubs close to the road were covered with red road dust, and the roadside was littered with the usual trash. But beyond the side of the road, the vistas were often striking. Lush green vegetable fields gave way to rolling hills covered with stretches of acacia trees and patches of fig trees.

They had taken the northern route to Gitega, and as the road took them close to the southern boundary of the Kibira National Park, Jim said, "Robbie, please pull over for a minute, will you?" He had spotted through an opening in the trees a waterfall cascading over granite rocks, a sight as pretty as anything the coach had seen in his travels through the Adirondacks.

However, as they approached the outskirts of Gitega, the sights became less attractive. They passed the hulls of several burned out pickup trucks and a ramshackle bicycle repair shop. Jim saw a boy with a couple of dead chickens hanging from his handle bars wearing a jersey with the number 33 on the back. Jim's mind snapped back to the reason they were going to Gitega, and some slight anxiety began to crowd his otherwise upbeat thoughts. Despite the large turnout the previous two evenings in Bujumbura, he wondered aloud if the six players—four Tutsis and two Hutus—scheduled to attend tonight's session would turn up.

"They all live within 10 k's of where we agreed to meet 'em," said Rush. "I'll bet they'll all be there—might even bring an extra player or two."

When they arrived at the meeting place—a soccer field abutted by a smooth dirt area that would serve as the court— the six players were waiting along with a surprise guest.

"Looks like I'm a prophet," said Rush. "Though I wasn't expecting the extra player to be quite so pretty."

Upon spotting their visitors, the players began to jog toward the jeeps. Immediately, Jim was struck by the grace of the young girl. She was tall, lithe, lean, and eager. As she ran, her head was up as if scanning the horizon; her shoulders were level, low, and loose; and her arms flowed forward and back. Her fluid forward motion was aided by a long, efficient stride.

"Looks like she is quite athletic," said Jim to no one in particular.

The girl turned out to be the fourteen-year-old sister of Alain Kurabitu, one of the four Tutsi players. Omella accompanied her older brother, ostensibly to watch the session. She was certainly close to six feet tall and indeed quite pretty. Her hair was braided in corn rows, and she had a long neck and high cheek bones that reminded Jim of the bust of Nefertiti he had seen on display at a Barcelona museum.

After greeting the six boys, Jim turned to Omella.

"Would you like to learn?"

She glanced shyly at Alain for guidance. Without hesitation, he said, "She would, sir. Thank you."

In welcoming Omella's participation, Jim knew that any attempt to launch women's basketball in Burundi would present its own set of problems. The culture of both Hutu and Tutsi dictated that a woman's physical activities should be confined to bearing and raising children as well as working in the planting and harvesting seasons.

Not much different than how we looked at it in the States years ago, Jim thought.

"I'm glad you brought Omella," Jim said to Alain.

"I am glad you will let her play, sir."

As Jim and Mathias walked with the group toward the dirt "court," a basketball joined at each man's hand and hip, the coach whispered, "Mathias, if she plays, will this cause her a problem?"

"I don't believe so. I imagine her brother brought her here today for that very reason, although I wonder if he gained permission of their parents. But even if he didn't, I don't think that merely playing with us today will be a problem. For the long term though. . ."

When Mathias's voice trailed off, Jim decided to provide a bit of American sports history.

"You know, Mathias, it took the NCAA, the organization that rules over college sports in our country, until 1979 or '80 to figure out that they ought to embrace women's sports."

"Why was that?"

"Well," replied Jim, "a law was passed by our Congress in the early 1970s called Title Nine that demanded equality for women in sports, including college sports. Up until that point, women's sports at the college level was governed by an organization called AIAW—and don't ask me what those letters stand for."

He continued, "But after that law came in, the NCAA, over a period of five or six years, gradually recognized that women's sports was becoming a very important business. So, like many big corporations in our country, they decided to push AIAW aside and take over governance of women's sports."

"Hmm, why didn't they realize women's sports were a big deal before that law?" asked Mathias.

"Well, first of all, until Title Nine came around, it *wasn't* a big deal, with the exception of a certain few colleges. And to be honest, very few men, myself included, noticed that women were taking a greater interest in sports, both as play-ers and as fans."

What Jim did not say was that his prominence in the coaching field had placed him in a position to help the wom-en's sports movement in its embryonic stage. But, like virtu-ally every other well-respected male coach at that time, his indifference, and, frankly, his wariness of the agendas of some of the movement's early leaders, had held him back from mak-ing any meaningful contribution.

"Bunch of lesbians who are using basketball as a lever," he recalled a fellow coach saying. His silence had been a vote of neutrality, if not agreement.

Jim regretted lacking the foresight to see beyond the spe-cious thinking that prevailed among the male coaches of that era. He had also become an admirer of those early pioneers, no matter their sexual orientation, realizing that their goals were far more noble—and visionary—than he, and many of his colleagues, had ever given them credit for.

And so while his job description in Burundi did not include introducing basketball to women, Jim would, with an open heart and mind, provide as much opportunity as he could for this girl—and any other young women who wished to play.

"Okay, come on over so we can get started!" he yelled to the seven players.

The smooth dirt area was shaded by several large oak trees. Rush and Roberts busily measured ten feet up the tall-est and straightest of the trees. Within minutes, the two were nailing the half-moon backboard into the tree. For poster-ity, Mathias took a photo of the two Marines while Jim was addressing the athletes.

"I'm glad you're all here, including you, Omella. Today, we're going to focus on shot technique. And even though we've just put up the first hoop in Gitega, we're not going to worry about the hoop just yet. For now, we're going to work on proper fundamentals."

As he had done the previous two evenings, Jim patiently reviewed the points he'd covered in last week's session, "Feet shoulder-width apart, knees bent, elbows in, arc, back-spin, proper follow-through, and rhythm."

The players, including Omella, gave Jim their full attention. And while Jim found their natural athleticism and appetite to learn to be great aids, the poor shooting habits the six young men had developed would take time to undo. On the other hand, Omella, as athletic as she was spirited, had never shot a basketball. As a result, she did not manifest any of the poor fundamentals of her counterparts.

"Okay, let's work at the hoop," said Jim. "Now, remember what we just worked on. I'm looking for good technique, ending with good follow-through."

The six males varied in their success at the newly installed target. Omella was another story. Jim was amazed at her grace and fluid technique—this after touching her first basketball only thirty minutes earlier. When she swished six straight ten-footers with perfect form, Jim said to Bill Foster, "God, she could be a real player. I have one deflated rubber women's basketball in my bag that I brought from the States. When practice is over, let's blow up it up and give it to her."

———

It was 8:45 by the time the jeep pulled out of the parking lot in Gitega. A couple of the kids, including Omella and Alain, were still playing and waved goodbye.

"Gents," said Rush, "we've only got about an hour and a quarter of daylight. I don't think it's a good idea to go back to Bujumbura tonight. Looking at the map, I'd say the Mutumba camp is only a thirty-minute drive and, according to our reports, quite safe. Still okay if we camp out tonight?"

Jim heard less of a question than a strong suggestion. Besides, he was weary. During the demonstrations and the drills, he was always moving and didn't think about being tired. Now, he'd rather risk a night in a sleeping bag than take the long jeep ride back to Bujumbura.

"I'm okay with camping out, Sarge," said Jim. "But what about the rest of you guys?"

Bill Foster gave a thumbs up, and the others nodded their agreement.

"Then," said Rush, "we'll need to get the tent pitched by ten. Burundi nights are dark—real dark. First things first, though."

He trotted back to the trailer containing all the provisions he'd packed for what he glibly called The African Experience. Lifting a corner of the tarp, he pulled out a large pill bottle and tossed it to Jim.

"Here ya go, Coach. Take two of these and pass it around. They're extra malaria pills and you'll need to take two a day on this trip; where we're going is a very—and I mean *very*—high-risk area for malaria. I also brought along mosquito nets to put over our heads when we hit the sleepin' bags. The open fire going through the night will help, too."

Rush got behind the wheel. "Hold tight, folks. Here we go."

Jim settled back and closed his eyes. He found himself in a quiet state of euphoria over the enthusiasm of the six young men . . . and the remarkable potential of Omella. *This could work*, he thought.

Thanks to Rush's sense of direction and camping skills, the large tent was pitched just before dark, the night watch for wild animals and militia was manned by Corporal Roberts, and the rest of the group was huddled next to an open fire. All except Jim were holding mugs of hot coffee. The coach drank disinfected water instead, knowing that caffeine this late would wreak havoc on his system, which, while getting better, was still unsteady.

Jim had not been camping since his youth. While concerned about the threat of wild animals and other intruders, he felt good in the company of the six men.

"You know," said Bill Foster, "my adventurous wife was dying to come on this trip, but Wednesday night is her poetry group, and she never, and I mean *never*, misses that."

"She writes poetry?" asked Jim.

"Oh yeah," replied Bill. "She loves it, and I don't mind bragging that she's very good. Had three poems published in different poetry journals. Her big goal is to get one in *The New Yorker*. By the way, she was very impressed with the poem you read at the opening dinner. And so was I."

"Amazing," said Jim. "She's an amazing woman."

"Won't argue with that," said Foster.

"Neither will I," said Sergeant Rush. "In fact, I'm convinced the ambassador could someday be the first woman president of the United States. But guys, I've gotta trade places with Robbie at 3:00 AM, so how 'bout if we get some shut-eye?"

"Yeah," said Foster. "If Mathias is right, we might find the next Hakeem Olajuwon tomorrow. I want to be ready for it."

So as not to put a damper on Bill Foster's statement, Mathias kept his own thought to himself: *I hope they have not killed each other off.*

26

By 7:00 AM, the group had consumed a breakfast of bananas, pineapple, bread, fried eggs, and coffee, had broken camp, and were bouncing along the treacherous stone roads leading to Kayanza.

"It's only about twenty kilometers away, but it'll take us a good two hours," said Mathias, who had taken on the role of navigator and was riding in the front seat of the lead jeep.

"You must be looking forward to this, Mathias," said Jim.

After a moment's hesitation, Mathias responded so quietly that Jim had to lean forward.

"A long time and many changes, Coach Jim," he said, his words barely audible.

For Mathias, the trip produced a conflicting set of flashbacks. Judging by his dour expression, Jim guessed his diverse memories were more bitter than sweet.

Jim was thinking they were making pretty good time when Mathias announced, "We'll be coming to a village soon—I believe just beyond that hill. If it's still there, it's the only one in this region, as most people live up in the hills without the aid of any community."

Fifteen minutes later, when the jeep rolled through the small, rather grim village, Mathias drew Jim's attention to a distressing view.

"Look—do you see anyone except kids and old people?" asked Mathias rhetorically.

"The AIDS virus," said Sergeant Rush in a somber tone. "It's wiping out an entire generation in rural areas like this."

"You know," said Jim to no one in particular, trying to blunt the unease in his voice, "the majority of Americans have no idea of this horror. And I'll bet that those few politicians who do don't much care."

"You're right, Coach," said Rush. "But you know, it can't be easy for a congressman whose district is in dire financial straits to worry about a country that seems a world away."

"Might not be easy, but that doesn't make it right," said Bill Foster.

The depressing sight, and Foster's frank words, made Jim reflect on a disturbing fact: *The overwhelming poverty and disease these people face make the problems we complain about seem trivial.*

The beginning of the dry season had turned the smaller roads from mud to ruts. The turbulence caused by the bumpy route interrupted Jim's thoughts, and he joined the other passengers in tightening his seat belt.

"We're not too far," Mathias said.

Twenty minutes later, as the jeep passed by a veiled crescent of overhanging brush, Mathias's memory was jarred. "Stop!" he yelled. "You see that archway? The brush is very dense. Well, behind that brush is the road, I am almost certain."

Rush pulled the jeep into reverse and then began to maneuver through the brush. Jim thought of the archway as akin to a discrete door of a restaurant or hotel, but, in this case, providing entry to less of a road than a long and foreboding passageway.

———

As the jeep wended its way to an uncertain destination, Jim noticed that Corporal Roberts had placed his rifle at the ready.

"Looks like you're leaning forward a bit, Robbie," said Jim.

"Just bein' careful," Roberts said quietly—as if he needed to say it at all.

While the rutted stone road challenged Clive Rush's driving skills, Jim took in the spectacular views of green fields, wild flowers, and mountains in the distance. All the while, though, he wondered if some machete-wielding warriors lurked in the brush, priming themselves for attack.

"Are you sure this is the way, Mathias?" Rush asked, seemingly more wary of unseen hazards than of the treachery of the road.

"I am not totally certain," the Tutsi replied. "But I believe we are on the right course."

After twenty muscle-bruising minutes, a fear of what might be concealed in the forest pervaded those in the jeep. Yet for Jim Keating, the specter of danger was neutralized by the more positive possibilities that might lie ahead. When Rush suggested, strongly, "We might want to think about heading back to the main road," Jim said gently, "Just a bit further."

Fifteen minutes later, when the bumps of the road turned to yet deeper ruts, a compromise was reached.

"If I am not mistaken—though please understand that it's been many years—I believe that beyond that ridge is where the families live."

"Okay," said Rush firmly. "How 'bout if we go as far as the ridge and then turn back if we don't see anything?"

Everyone nodded, some a bit more slowly than others.

Ten minutes later, the jeep pulled to the crest of the ridge. Below, on a level grass field, a group of tall, barefoot boys were playing soccer.

"This is it!" said Mathias.

———

For fourteen young Tutsis, the strange sight at the top of the ridge stopped play, as though someone had blown a whistle. Not one of the young men had ever seen a jeep before or, for that matter, a human face that wasn't black.

"Do not worry," Mathias yelled to them in Kirundi. "I grew up here many years ago, played in these fields as you are playing now. We are fans of sport and we would like to watch your football game. Please, continue to play."

Despite Mathias's entreaty, the anxious lull persisted for several moments, until the tallest of the group, obviously intent on finishing the game, uttered something, and play continued.

The visitors perched on a set of large rocks to watch. The view from the ridge was not unlike being seated at midfield in a stadium with a perfect line of sight. Within minutes, each observer could see why the tallest boy was so intent on resuming the action.

"We're looking at a real athlete," commented Bill, expressing Jim's exact thoughts.

For the first few minutes, this boy played goalkeeper and expertly stopped several high-velocity shots. But in a creative twist of the rules, the goalkeeper in this informal game was allowed to play the field after a missed shot. When the switch occurred, another player simply rotated back into goal. After a near-miraculous save, the tallest boy employed the change of position rule, dropped the ball to the ground, kicked it out to a wing man, and received a return pass.

Jim didn't need to be a soccer coach to appreciate what happened next.

The boy took the pass and dribbled several steps to his left. With a head fake and a shimmy of his shoulders, he exploded by the first defender. From that point it was, for Jim, like watching Michael Jordan maneuver through a core of Utah Jazz defenders. The difference was that this boy was zigzagging past the opposition while controlling a soccer ball.

After rendering a string of defenders hamstrung with his quickness and ball-control skills, the young giant blasted a bull's-eye shot to the far corner of a makeshift goal of bamboo and rope.

"My lord," gasped Sergeant Rush. "Did you see that?"

Even the coach, who had a practiced eye for impressive athletic exploits, was astounded by the feat, especially because the kid was so tall.

"He looks to be at least six-ten," said Jim. "But Mathias, how old would he be?"

"If he's out on this field playing football, and not in the Tutsi army, I'll bet he's only fourteen or fifteen."

"Can we meet him?"

"Let's find out. . . . Young men!" he hollered. "As I said earlier, we are sport fans and we are enjoying watching you play. May we come down to meet you?"

The boys looked to their leader, the goal-scorer.

"Yes," the boy shouted back in Kirundi.

———

Ever the coach, Jim Keating grabbed a couple of basketballs from the jeep and tossed one to Bill, and the group scrambled down from the ridge to the field below. In the middle of their descent, four of the boys, fearful of these intruders, two of whom were carrying rifles, disappeared into the woods. But the rest, including the boy Jim was anxious to meet, stayed on.

By not taking flight with the others, they were disobeying the orders of their elders, who would have told them, firmly, to run fast and far from any strangers. But it was obvious that the man who had yelled from the top of the hill was a Tutsi—one of them. They were also transfixed by the sight of white men.

As the strangers approached, the boys shifted a bit closer to one another, causing Mathias to say gently, "Please do not be frightened. We are here as sportsmen to talk to you about a game. It's a game that most of you, perhaps even all of you, have never seen. Do any of you know of the game of basketball?"

Blank stares met Mathias's question. Still perplexed, they didn't even shake their heads.

"Well, this man here," he said, pointing to Jim. "He is a great teacher of basketball. He has come to our country from the United States on an important mission—to use this game as a means of friendship. . . . You know when I told you that I lived here—many years ago? Well, I remember the strong men of this region, warriors like Myo Hatungimana and Natare Nizigama."

Jim noticed the boys looking at one another. He also recalled Mathias explaining that in Kayanza, unlike certain other regions, they did use surnames due to the proud heritage of the various warrior families.

Mathias continued, "I told this man that I was sure that some of the sons and grandsons of these great warriors could become good basketball players!"

The barefoot boys smiled timidly at the thought of playing a game they had never seen or heard of.

"Young men, let me have this man from America, whose name is Jim Keating, talk to you about this game called basketball."

Jim moved alongside Mathias. "Use the same tone I use, okay? I'm going to start gently."

Mathias nodded, and Jim began.

"I enjoyed watching you play football—or soccer, as we call it in America. Do any of you know anything about America?"

The white man's words did nothing to lessen the boys' shyness, still somewhat rooted in fear. When they didn't respond, Jim continued.

"Well, as Mathias said, I came from America to teach this game to young people like you. It's really a simple game. What you do is throw this ball through a hoop."

The boys looked puzzled. "Do you know what I mean when I say 'hoop'?"

"No," several of the boys replied in Kirundi, and Jim decided right then to make an investment.

"Sarge, we have one half-moon backboard left, and I'd say put it on that tall cocoa tree over there." He pointed. "Where the grass is beaten down."

"You're on, Coach," said Rush. He slung his M-16 across his back and hollered to Corporal Roberts. "Robbie, gimmie a hand!"

As Rush and Roberts made their way to the jeep, Jim could no longer contain his curiosity. He turned to the prodigy—the boy who had displayed such dexterity in scoring the goal. With Mathias still at his side, the coach asked, "What is your name, son?"

"Leonard," replied the boy. "Leonard Tangishaka."

"Leonard, would you like to try something with this ball?"

"Yes," responded Leonard, his enthusiasm causing his companions to giggle.

As the young man stepped forward from the group, Jim realized that his visual measurement from the ridge had been conservative. Leonard Tangishaka was at least seven feet tall, with massive hands, and arms that reached well below his knee-caps—physical traits not unusual among Tutsi men. What was unusual were his sturdy calves and strong upper body. Since Jim had arrived in Burundi, he had encountered few Tutsis with such remarkable muscular definition.

What would six months in a weight room do for this kid?

Jim's interest in Leonard's physical attributes nearly caused him to overlook the boy's strikingly handsome face. His complexion was dark brown (*Edna would have said sable*, thought Jim), his eyes deep-set and lucid, and his teeth ivory white. He had that look of clear-skinned health that often comes from living a largely outdoor life.

"Leonard, I'm gonna throw this ball *very* high into the air. As the ball begins its descent, I'd like you to jump into the air and catch it. Have you ever done anything like this?" Jim asked.

"No."

"Okay, then let's try it. Now keep your eyes focused on the ball and time your jump to catch it just as it's on the way down." Mathias imitated Jim's movements as he translated.

Jim Keating hurled the basketball high into the arid Burundian air. With total concentration, Leonard did as the coach told him—he eyed the ball on its upward flight. At the split second it began to drop, he soared, snaring the ball with hands so large as to obscure it from view.

The remarkable sight gave free rein to Coach Jim Keating's imagination.

27

From their vantage point at the crest of the ridge, Rush and Roberts had a clear view of Leonard's prodigious vertical jump.

"Did you see that, Robbie? The kid's amazing."

The Marines scurried back down the hill, half-moon backboard and small ladder in tow.

While they nailed the backboard to the cocoa tree, Jim and Mathias learned the names of the other boys. Ever since his days as a high school coach, Jim had always made sure he knew everyone's first and last name—and how to pronounce both. He also expected his assistants to follow his lead. In Barcelona, he even learned how to roll the R's in names like Rodriguez. But he'd never been challenged with reeling off surnames like Nzikobanyanka, Ndimurwanko, or Bandyambona, so he decided to memorize first names only.

"Ready, Coach!" yelled Rush.

The boys had been glancing at Rush and Roberts mounting the backboard. Yet there was no hesitation when they heard Jim, having just gotten a Kirundi translation from Mathias, say "tugende," ("let's go") and motioned for the ten young giants to move under what was the first hoop in the Kayanza region of Burundi.

"Ingo, ingo, come close, come close," said Mathias.

"Now, gentlemen," began the coach, "one of the great advantages you all bring to this game is your height. Question: Do any of you know the name Hakeem Olajuwon?"

"No," was the unanimous response.

"How 'bout Dikembe Mutombo?"

"No."

"Well, both of these men have some things in common with each of you. They're both from African countries, Mutombo from Zaire and Olajuwon from Nigeria. Like all of you, they're both very tall. Also, they both played soccer as young boys and developed their footwork. And, like all of you, neither Olajuwon nor Mutombo was introduced to basketball until they were about your age. Last, but not least," Jim said with a bit of a lilt, "they're now world-famous basketball players in what is called the National Basketball Association in the United States—and they're *very* rich!"

Jim chuckled, causing the ten young men to join him in laughter, even though none of the boys understood the meaning of the word *rich*. And when, in his translation, Mathias mimed Jim's buoyant tone and his emphasis on "very rich," the kids laughed even more.

"They're relaxing. He's getting their trust," said Mathias quietly to Bill Foster.

Mathias had been anxious about how the boys would react to Jim. Now, he was pleased, if not relieved, with the lively atmosphere created by the American coach.

Jim decided to hold shot technique until later in the session and focus instead on a skill required of all forwards and centers, one that these soccer players might have fun practicing. "I'd like to teach you a simple move near the basket called the drop step. Now, when I say 'basket,' I mean that iron hoop up there."

He pointed to the hoop nailed into the tree. "Bill, would you come out and help demonstrate the drop-step?"

Bill Foster quickly positioned himself with his back to the basket. With Jim talking and Bill performing, the two patiently—and expertly—worked through each move of the drop-step, starting with the footwork and finishing with the actual lay-up.

Still spry even at sixty-one, Foster was the perfect demonstrator; the old Indiana State star had the drop-step down.

As Jim and Foster broke the skill into parts, the coach couldn't help but notice Leonard's look of fascination with this simple move.

"Remember, guys, basketball is like your game of football—you must learn offensive moves to get by the defender.... Robbie, come on out and cover Bill."

By calling out Corporal Roberts, Jim Keating used an old coaching trick: *In a demonstration lecture, always choose a defender who is unlikely to cause the offensive player much difficulty.*

While thirty-plus years younger than Foster, Roberts was also a few inches shorter and devoid of basketball skills. Using his size and expert footwork, Foster easily scored three straight lay-ups.

"Yesss!" Bill chortled after the third shot dropped in. "Tickling the twine. The first six points ever scored in the Kayanza region!"

While not knowing what he said, the boys joined in laughter at the black American's enthusiasm.

"Leonard," said Jim. "Would you like to give it a try?"

Leonard nodded eagerly, and this was followed by a reminder from Jim.

"Now, as I said few moments ago, before any player can execute this move, like Bill just did, we have to break it down into its parts."

With Foster's help, Jim once again reviewed the elements of the drop-step move. Because of Leonard's soccer skills, the footwork came easily to him. But blending the various elements of the move—catching the ball, chinning it up for ball protection and examining the options, faking, utilizing the proper footwork, turning to the basket, and laying the ball in the hoop—required Jim's patience and Leonard's full attention.

"Catch, chin it up, fake, step, and turn," Jim repeated metronomically, and Mathias expertly imitated Jim's tone and message.

Jim knew this experiment would take time. Not wishing to offend the other boys, he assigned Déo, Gilbert, and Bill to work with them in groups of three on the footwork. He wanted Mathias with him, for he didn't want one word to be dropped between him and this remarkably talented kid.

"Gentlemen, eventually I'm going to spend a good amount of time with all of you," said Jim. "But for today, I'm just going to instruct Leonard. And until I come back again, I'm going to ask that he assist each of you with these moves."

Without letting Leonard shoot the ball at the basket, Jim coached him on the components of the drop-step. At first, the boy had difficulty synchronizing the parts, but his eagerness to learn and his remarkable athleticism were as obvious as they were impressive.

Thirty minutes later, when it finally appeared that he had gained command of the different aspects of the move, Jim said, "Okay, now let's put it all together, Leonard. First, I'm gonna pass you the ball. Now, as we just worked on, when you catch it, spread your elbows and chin the ball up. Remember, this'll help you protect the ball and, by glancing over your shoulder, see the positioning of the defenders. Give a little head fake, just as you do in soccer. Then, using your drop-step, turn and lay the ball in the basket."

Hearing Jim's words, Déo stopped his instruction, sensing he was about to witness something special. Bill and Gilbert noticed and followed suit, as did Rush and Roberts, who had moved back to the ridge for surveillance.

Jim passed the ball to Leonard Tangishaka. On cue, Leonard chinned the ball up, head faked, drop-stepped, and, using his remarkable vertical jump, deposited the ball softly through the hoop as effortlessly as a veteran star, soaring so high his head was almost parallel to the rim.

As the jaws of the other visitors literally dropped, Bill Foster looked quickly at Jim Keating, whose usual veil of indifference to such feats was nowhere to be seen.

Meanwhile, the four boys who had disappeared into the woods had headed to the hut of Leonard Tangishaka, where they told his mother, Consolaté, about these strangers. The boys quietly escorted her to a cluster of trees 150 meters from the action.

Out of sight of the group's view, Consolaté watched intently as the first white man she had ever seen taught her son a strange game also new to her eyes.

———

Like many good teachers, Jim spent the last twenty minutes of his first lesson preparing the students to train without his supervision.

"We'll be back next Thursday—same time. Until then, I'm going to give you a series of things to practice. Sound okay?"

"Okay," was the robust response of the group, now enjoying use of their newly learned English word.

"First thing will be for all of you to work on the drop-step. Now, it seems to me that each of you has done a good job learning the various elements of this move. So, for the next week, help each other. Best way to do it—at first—is to assign one player to be the passer. Rest of you get in a line under the hoop—like so."

Jim called on Leonard to be the passer and positioned the other boys in a straight line underneath the basket.

"Simply come out one at a time, execute the move, then go to the rear of the line. If a player does something wrong, you other boys should point out the mistake. If you can, spend about twenty to thirty minutes each day on this drill as a group."

As he heard himself say "minutes," the coach wondered how the boys measured time. He decided to ask Mathias about this on the way home.

"All right, let's try it!" he bellowed, then pointed to a boy who looked to be among the youngest in the group, but stood at least 6'5". "Claude, c'mon out, and Leonard, pass him the ball."

When Claude's large, soft hands easily embraced the pass, Jim said, "Good catch."

After he'd made an imperfect move to the hoop, Jim added, "Good effort, Claude." Turning to the group, the coach asked, "But what did he do wrong?"

Mathias translated and Leonard Tangishaka responded quickly.

"He drop-stepped too far. Ended up under the hoop. Out of position to shoot."

"Exactly!" said Jim, gratified, but not surprised with Leonard's grasp of the move.

Another boy called out minor mistakes and helped Claude correct them. As Claude trotted back to the end of the line, Jim saw a couple of other boys gesturing to him to fake before taking the drop-step. *The beginnings of teamwork.*

"Okay, within a week or two, our goal should be that everyone in line will be able to execute the move properly, so that there's virtually no stoppage in action. As I said before, let's see how close all of you can come to reaching the goal by practicing this line drill every day until next Thursday. Okay?"

"Okay!" roared the players.

Jim finished up the workout with a brief session on proper shot technique, using Bill as his demonstrator.

"Now that you've learned these simple pointers about shooting, help each other on proper shot technique, as well. Remember, good shooters have good form. If you see someone taking the shot without elbows in, proper arc, follow-through, or backspin, or if their feet are not positioned properly—or if you see anything else that they're not doing correctly, tell 'em. Okay?"

"Okay!"

"Now, I'm going to leave two balls. Please take good care of 'em. Work on these drills and have fun! I'll see you all next Thursday morning right here. Okay?"

"Okay!"

Watching from behind her shelter, Consolaté Tangishaka was struck by the goodwill of the white man, obviously the leader of this group of visitors. It was clear to her that Leonard, and the other boys, were enjoying themselves.

As a young girl, Consolaté's grandfather had warned her about the sinful ways of the white man—especially with Tutsi women. Yet this leader's gentle but firm manner had nearly hypnotized his new pupils. Somehow, she was certain that he was not corrupt in the way her grandfather had described men of his color.

In the last fifteen years, Consolaté had lost her father, her husband, and two sons to the brutal violence. Leonard was her last born—the most kind, intelligent, wonderful son a mother could ever hope for. His physical development had spawned great interest among the tribal warriors. Before long, they would attempt to recruit him for their deadly battles. And while Consolaté had done her best to protect Leonard from this seemingly inevitable fate, only an act of God would spare her son from following in the bloody wake of his male kin.

Each morning and evening, Consolaté had prayed for such a miracle. Now, shrouded by the cover of the brush, she dared to wonder if God had answered her many appeals.

———

Before heading home, Leonard Tangishaka and his friends followed their normal routine after playing football or, in this case, the new game they'd just learned. They walked through the woods toward a spring-fed *nyanza*, where they would cool their sweat-lathered bodies. Along the way, Leonard found himself adrift in his thoughts, pondering the many implications of the last ninety minutes—the most extraordinary experience of his young life.

From the time, several years ago, when he realized God had equipped him with exceptional physical gifts, he'd assumed he'd use these gifts to follow his father and brothers into the unceasing war with the Hutus. Yet, unlike his dead brothers and father, and many of his friends, he silently looked on this inevitable service as an unwelcome demand—not a calling.

His mother's non-violent views, compounded by the deaths in her life, had caused her last-born son to see, clearly, what most other Tutsi males his age did not see: The violence was nothing more than a waste of lives. But Leonard knew that he could not discuss this heretical view with anyone but Consolaté.

"The Tutsi warlords will not hear of such talk; they might kill you," she warned her son in a hushed tone.

And so, on the walk through the woods, while his friends spoke animatedly about the fun they'd just had learning this new game, Leonard focused on something the white man had said to him. Translated into Kirundi by Mathias, Leonard took it to mean: "If you practice this game, it might give you the chance to travel to many places, including, perhaps, America."

The thought was so thrilling that he stopped, put his hands on his knees, bent over, and closed his eyes. *America. America.* He simply could not bring an image into focus.

Leonard's knowledge of other countries was mostly limited to Rwanda, the country not far from Kayanza that had been in conflict with Burundi for as long as he could remember. And because he knew few facts, he used his imagination to make up the rest of the world. He heard the Tutsi warriors speak of foreign places like South Africa, Tanzania, and Zaire. And lately, the place called America, where this white man came from, had been mentioned to him on occasion.

"You look like an American," some older wise people would say, admiring his powerful physique and implying that such strength was typical among boys and men in this faraway land.

And then there were the two missionaries, a husband and wife who referred to themselves as African Americans and who had come from America to spread the Word of God. They had visited the Kayanza region just after the deaths of Leonard's father and two brothers. Their message of faith and love had brought comfort to Consolaté and Leonard. Their message of non-violence had reinforced Consolaté's view of the futility of war. The missionaries had also provided other gifts: They had taught mother and son to read French and left behind several French books, as well as an American magazine called *Time.*

While unable to read English, the pictures in the American magazine had sparked Leonard's curiosity about this faraway land that somehow now seemed closer because of today's visitors.

Would this new game, which he found so enjoyable, become an important part of his life—perhaps even offering him the chance to travel to the places of his dreams? More immediately, would it provide him with the means to avoid his dreaded obligation to *kwica*—to kill?

While Leonard realized that his opponents in war would be the same people—the Hutus—who had murdered his brothers and father, he also knew that these people were responding to centuries of cruel acts inflicted on them by his own tribe. He knew this because his mother, his brave and honest mother, had told him so.

Responding to the shouts of his friends, Leonard joined them for a swim, then headed to his home, a mud-floor hut on the side of a large hill that overlooked a valley full of eucalyptus trees. His mother was not home yet, but awaiting his arrival was Charlé Tinyabokwe, the most fearsome of Kayanza's Tutsi warriors.

Leonard had deep but unspoken contempt for Charlé. Since his father's murder, Charlé had used his power promiscuously, taking liberties with Leonard's beloved mother and other Tutsi widows of war. For Consolaté's part, she knew that if she did not accede to Charlé's demands for sex, his abuse might extend to a violent act on her only remaining son. She knew this because another widow had rebuffed Charlé, and her son had suffered the consequences—a terrible beating that left the boy blind in one eye.

Because she feared for her son's safety, Consolaté had relented, praying silently to Jesus for forgiveness during each unwanted *gusambana*, all the while harboring a fervent hope that a Hutu bullet might soon find Charlé's evil heart.

Charlé's sullen expression made it clear to Leonard that today's visit had nothing to do with his sexual desires.

———

After silently watching Leonard and his friends head off to swim, Consolaté decided to remain for a while in her shelter behind the trees. She had to make a decision, one that only those in the grip of the violent Tutsi warlords could understand. If she allowed her son to join the brigade of butchers, as she thought of them, Leonard would either be killed or forced to discard his Christian instincts and become a killer himself.

The alternative was one she was not certain would work. And if it did, it would surely have serious consequences for her.

When Consolaté had peeked from behind the cluster of trees, watching this white man enlighten and excite her son, she felt certain this man must surely be some type of godsend. His good-natured approach was unlike the intimidating tactics the Tutsi warriors used on young boys of Leonard's age. They would force foolish tests of machismo, telling them that successful completion would mean their passage to manhood. For her son and other young soldiers, she also knew that the final rite would be to kill a Hutu. By some tangled twist of reasoning, these men—cowards dressed up as warriors—convinced themselves that this type of act was a sure route to heroism.

As for her late husband and his role in this violence, she often reflected on the early years of their marriage, a time of transient peace in Burundi. Evariste was a good provider and, unlike many other Tutsi warriors, showed reasonable interest in his offspring. But Evariste was also the son of Olivier, among the most fearsome Tutsi warlords of his time. When the Hutu–Tutsi fighting spilled over into Burundi, Evariste, as his father's son, felt it was his duty—and the duty of *his* sons—to fight off the Hutu uprising. He was called upon to be head warlord.

During the conflict, in his brief forays home, Consolaté noticed a distinct change in her husband. No doubt because of the horrors he faced each day, Evariste grew detached from his wife. The change also included his near indifference to Leonard, who was too young to enter the battle.

Over a period of eight genocidal months, Evariste and Consolaté's two older sons, Didace and Simon, were killed.

Now a bereft widow, she was fair game for the new head warlord, Charlé, who had always envied her late husband for being on the martial side of a fearsome ancestral line. She dreaded this man's carnal ways as much as his cruelty. Because of his insatiable lust, it was, she feared, only a matter of time before he contracted the deadly virus that had killed so many of her generation. She also knew that Charlé's envy of her late husband was shared by several other warlords, who joined him in treating Leonard with disdain, frequently chastising the boy for not joining in the war.

By contrast, this white man Consolaté had just observed took a far different approach with her son. He was firm, but kind. And while she knew nothing of the peculiar activity he was teaching her son, she could readily see that he had great knowledge of this game. It was also apparent that he enjoyed instructing Leonard and that her son took to the game quickly.

Consolaté still harbored a deep fear of white men, leery of their supposed treachery and loose morals. Yet she realized that those who spread these tales included not only her own father and grandfather, but other Tutsi warlords, who were hardly examples of chivalry themselves.

Of all the boys in the region, Consolaté also knew that Leonard was the prize for the Tutsi civilian army. He had his father's height and his grandfather's strength—the most perfect physical specimen anyone in the Kayanza region had ever seen. And now it would be time for others to take advantage of her son's God-given gifts. The warriors Consolaté had come to loathe would soon take her son and place him in the cauldron of this senseless war.

She could not allow this to happen. But Consolaté's alternatives were few—and unappealing. She and her son might steal off in the middle of the night and head over the border into Rwanda, perhaps finding temporary sanctuary in a refugee camp. But from all that she had heard, the refugee camps were full of the virus she dreaded and run by the same type of men who made her life so wretched.

The other possibility was one she'd pondered from her brush-covered stakeout. She heard the white man tell the boys that, although he lived many hours away in the capital city, he would return on this day next week. When the white man and his companions had left the grounds and Leonard and his friends headed off to swim, Consolaté followed the advice of the missionaries and asked God for His Divine Guidance.

After a short period, she felt reasonably certain she'd found His answer within herself. Next week, when the white man returned to Kayanza, Consolaté would approach him. She would need the old Tutsi who accompanied the white man to be present to translate her urgent request. She would also need to make sure this meeting was conducted out of sight of Charlé and the other warriors.

Please, she would say, *please take my son back to Bujumbura with you.*

She would explain the alternatives and hope—pray— that this man was as kind and as interested in her son as he appeared to be.

What Consolaté would not explain to him is that once Leonard was gone and Charlé learned of his absence, his reaction would be harsh. He might even kill her.

Still somewhat uncertain of the blessedness of this plan, Consolaté headed home. As she approached her hut, she heard Charlé's threatening voice chastising her son for not joining in the *in-tumbara*—the war.

God's message was clear.

28

Just past midnight, Corporal Roberts dropped Jim off at his apartment. The long ride home had been tiring. The group made one last late-afternoon stop where four players turned up. But the coach was in high spirits. In answer to his concern about time, Mathias told Jim that the boys would have an intuitive concept of minutes and hours.

"They'll be there next week at the time you set, Coach."

It was far too early to judge Leonard Tangishaka as a basketball player, yet Jim was impressed enough by his extraordinary physical gifts to compare the athlete to another young phenom he had encountered many years earlier.

In the summer just before his senior year at St. Thomas College, Jim had been invited to play for a college all-star team at Kutsher's Resort in the Catskills, a summer haven for exceptional players. When he arrived, word was already buzzing about a teenaged giant working as a bellhop, one of several high school basketball stars chosen for the coveted Kutsher's assignment. The job allowed the young standout plenty of free time to sharpen his already considerable skills against top-flight competition. While Jim had heard about him from a number of basketball enthusiasts, he'd never seen the boy play.

The Kutsher's College All-Star Team had two days of workouts before their game against a group of NBA players, and they invited the hot prospect to scrimmage. At sixteen, and already 6'11", he had point-guard agility, which later, in his storied NBA career, would give way to Herculean strength.

On a steamy June night, at that remote Catskill location, in front of no more than twenty-five onlookers, the sixteen-year-old dominated a highly acclaimed college all-star group in a forty-minute scrimmage. After the scrimmage, Jim, his coaching instincts already developing, passed up a visit to the local tavern with the other college stars. Instead, he stayed at the court with the prodigy, working with him on inside moves until well past midnight. Later on, he lay awake in his cabin, certain he had just worked with a player destined to change the course of the game.

Leonard Tangishaka was clearly a different case, the grand sum of his basketball experience the ninety minutes spent with Jim. Yet at fourteen, not only was he an inch or two taller than the slightly older American had been, but in the relatively brief work-out, he seemed even more agile, more graceful, more athletic than the future NBA superstar had seemed those many years ago.

Jim kept reminding himself to be realistic about whatever basketball exploits might lay in the young man's future. He also knew that Leonard's improvement would require that he eventually leave Kayanza to benefit from regular coaching and good competition. On the ride home, he asked Mathias about the possibility of such a move.

"From what I could gather in a brief conversation with two of the other boys," Mathias began, "Leonard's father and two brothers were killed. By the way, I have a vague recollection of a man I think was his grandfather. Olivier was his name, and he was a mammoth man. But back to the boy, even though it is likely that his mother wants to keep him out of the war, I am sure that the Tutsi warlords in Kayanza have big plans for young Leonard Tangishaka. I'm also sure that those plans do not include basketball."

He added, "Jim, in other words, it will be a real struggle—and perhaps a dangerous one."

Yet despite impediments that seemed nearly insurmountable, Jim felt as if he were back at Kutsher's. He remembered the sleepless night following the workout, when he decided that coaching would definitely be in his future.

The difference now was that if the Burundian boy decided to devote his energies to basketball, it would most likely be Jim Keating who would spend long hours molding Leonard Tangishaka's skills, rather than that one-time interlude with a young Wilton Norman Chamberlain.

———

When he awoke, Jim Keating's first thought was the same one that had occupied his mind before he finally fell into a restless sleep: *Leonard Tangishaka must move to Bujumbura in order to develop his basketball skills.*

Moments later, Jim got a phone call from an ally.

"Jim, I was up half the night thinking about Leonard," said Bill Foster. "I've never seen anyone like him—ever. I talked with Cynthia first thing this morning. Told her that we must find a way to develop the kid's ability—that we've got to move him to Bujumbura."

"What'd she say?"

"She agreed, but wants to meet with you to discuss the details. If he does move here, she wants to make sure we don't cause a lot of problems for the boy, or his mother. Okay if Robbie comes over to get you?"

"Just need to shave. Give me twenty minutes."

When Jim arrived at the ambassador's residence, the enthusiastic diplomat and her husband had coffee, banana bread, and fresh cut melon waiting for him.

"Jim," said Ambassador Foster, "I've never seen Bill more excited about a player. And that includes, and I *never* thought I'd say this, the first time he saw Oscar play when The Big O was but a seventh grader. . . . So tell me, Coach, is Leonard Tangishaka that good?"

Jim related the story of a callow Wilt Chamberlain at Kutsher's. "Ambassador, you can't measure a kid's heart or desire, but Leonard's athleticism is unbelievable. In fact, and I'm obviously not talking about him as a basketball player yet, but as an athlete, he's at Wilt's level—maybe even more gifted than Wilt at that age!"

Jim hesitated, shaking his head slightly.

"With proper training, I'm betting he might well put Burundi on the international basketball map."

"Then let's talk about how we can best help this young man," said the ambassador. "I'm certain the Tutsi warlords in that region have designs on the boy. We'll have to be careful about that; we don't want to cause a violent reaction."

The ambassador paused for a moment to gather her thoughts.

"But . . . I think the first thing we need to worry about is the mother's reaction. Bill, you mentioned this morning that it's just the boy and his mother, that the father and brothers have been killed?"

"That's what Mathias heard," Bill confirmed.

"Well," said the ambassador, "speaking as a mother, and taking into account all that I've heard in the last several months from Tutsi women sick of the bloodshed, I'm guessing that Leonard's mother would be receptive to anything that would keep her son out of the war."

"My view as well," said Jim. "So, let's assume that Leonard's mother agrees to let her son move to Bujumbura. Where would he stay, and are there funds for this sort of thing?"

"As far as a place to stay goes, as much as Bill and I would love to have him stay here, US diplomatic policy will not allow us to host a native for any more than a brief period. So, after Bill called you this morning, I asked Clive Rush to go by Mathias's home and bring him here. Mathias lives alone and he has very nice quarters. I bet he'd love to have Leonard stay with him."

Looking down at his plate, Jim realized he hadn't touched his breakfast. He was too anxious, distracted. *Gotta make this happen*, he thought.

"On the matter of expenses," Cynthia continued, "I have some discretionary funds I can use to pay for food and clothing. Also, I'm sure that Jesse can enroll Leonard in a local school run by Irish missionaries. That will be good for him, because in most of the war-torn regions like Kayanza, the violence has dramatically cut educational opportunities for young people. Plus, if he turns out to be an elite player, acquiring a fluency in English will be of great help to him."

"You're right, Ambassador," said Jim. "And you've laid out a terrific plan. But now we're back to the mother. I told Leonard and the other boys that we'd return next Thursday. I guess I'll seek her out and speak with her."

"Jim, as a mother myself, I'd like to come along. Would you mind?" asked the ambassador.

"Not at all. I'd love to have you come!"

———

It was not long before Sergeant Rush arrived with Mathias Bizimana. Ambassador Foster presented the proposal, including her contribution of food and clothing. Without hesitation, Mathias said, "It would be my honor to host young Leonard."

"Thank you, Mathias," said the ambassador. "Now, let's hope Leonard's mother agrees to the plan."

Jim Keating added his own words of caution. "At this week's practice sessions, how 'bout if we hold off on telling the players about Leonard. As the ambassador said, we need to make sure he's moving to Bujumbura. Plus, I'd rather that he arrive without any fanfare."

They all glanced at Cynthia Foster, who was nodding her approval.

"Before tonight's practice," Jim continued, "I'll tell the others who traveled with us to Kayanza to keep quiet about him."

The practice sessions that week at the Nimbona Court went better than Jim had hoped. He saw marked improvement in several of the players, and four new athletes turned up who looked good in the drills.

"It's obvious that some of you guys are practicing the skills on your own. It shows. Some of you are getting better. Good job!" Jim bellowed.

During a shower back at the apartment, Jim decided to call Jesse.

"Jesse, I was enthusiastic about Cynthia going to Bukeye and Kayanza with us, but now I'm wondering if that's a good idea. I mean, it's one thing for a gnarly old hoop coach to venture into the boonies, but the US ambassador?"

Abbott's response was serious and measured. "Jim, as soon as you showed no hesitation, I got on the horn to the province chief in Muramvya where Bukeye is located to ask for the latest updates. He said things have been quiet for the last two months. Mathias's contacts said the same about Kayanza. It'll be safe, Coach."

"Okay, Jesse. Now I can concentrate on who's going to be our point guard!"

———

On Wednesday, Cynthia passed on her cherished poetry session to join the travel party. Upon arrival in Bukeye, the group was met with disappointment.

Though Jim's thoughts were primarily focused on Leonard Tangishaka, he had told Ambassador Foster about the considerable potential of Omella Kurabitu. She was anxious to meet the young lady and to watch her work out. In her heart, Cynthia Foster fervently hoped that Project Oscar would be a gateway to basketball opportunities for Burundian women.

Maybe Omella will be the first beneficiary, she thought.

But when the jeep pulled into the makeshift dirt basketball court, the forlorn face of Omella's brother, Alain, signaled a problem. "Omella will not be here. Our father has decided she will not learn basketball," he told them.

It was obvious from Alain's rueful tone that he disagreed with the decision. But as Ambassador Foster knew well, changing the deeply rooted Tutsi traditions took time, and any attempt often ended in disappointment.

"Perhaps your father might reconsider if I spoke with him," the ambassador said.

"I'm sorry, but I do not think this will happen," said Alain.

So, much to his disappointment, Jim ran an all-male practice in Bukeye. At the end of the session, after telling the players he would be back next week, he approached Alain.

"Omella has fine potential, and I'd really like to work with her. I hope your father will someday change his mind."

Alain looked down and repeated what he said to Ambassador Foster: "I'm sorry, but I do not think this will happen."

On the journey to the campsite in Kibira National Park, near Leonard's home, Jim began to consider ways he might approach Omella's father. Similar thoughts ran through Ambassador Foster's mind. Even Alain began to formulate his own plan.

———

Once the tents were pitched, Corporal Roberts stood lookout. The rest of the travel party nestled close to the campfire in quiet conversation.

"Cynthia," said Bill Foster, "since you missed tonight's poetry session, would you be willing to read some of your poetry to us?"

Before she could answer, Mathias exclaimed, "Oh! Would that be a grand treat!"

Bill knew that even when his wife traveled she brought along her spiral notebook full of poems. Each morning, no matter where she was, she would spend twenty to thirty minutes on her beloved hobby.

Without hesitation, she warmly assented. "But with a big day ahead tomorrow, how about if I read just two?"

Flipping through the notebook, she said, "I'll start with one called 'The Curse of the Iron Maiden.'"

The poem was one of Bill Foster's favorites. He looked around and saw five other men listening intently as Cynthia recited in graphic, riveting detail a story about her experiences with Burundian women and the enormous heartache the violence had brought them. Bill had to wonder, *Are these guys simply being polite?*

The answer was reflected in enthusiastic applause, but especially in Mathias's quiet comment, "I like this poem, Madam Ambassador. I like it very much."

"Thank you, Mathias," said the ambassador. "Now this second poem has special meaning to Bill and me. In some ways, the theme of the poem is the reason we're all gathered around this campfire. It's called 'Oscar's Gift.'"

The title piqued interest. As Cynthia began, and in unplanned unison, the men all edged a bit closer to her.

"Before the triple double
Or the many valiant advances
To the altar of triumph,
Only to be rejected
By a goateed Zen master.

AN AFRICAN REBOUND

Before the gold medal
Or backing an overmatched NBA guard
Down low
And lofting home a soft one hander
Making mastery seem effortless.

Long before his greatest assist,
The life saving pass:
A kidney from his perfect body
To his daughter.

Or feeling the need
To remind us
That whatever Michael could do
So, too, could he.
But a dust mote
Of difference in skill—if that.

Before he was discovered
By the world

He was ours

Our link to honor roll status

Memphis had Elvis
Latrobe had Arnie
Harlem had Sugar Ray.

At Crispus Attucks,
We had Oscar

And when he rose
With photogenic form

Higher and higher
The perfect release coming
At the very peak of his jump
We all rose with him
Braided by
Our unfettered pride
In a young man's
Fluid skill."

As he listened intently, Jim Keating reflected that, until now, he had never been present at a poetry reading. In fact, he knew almost nothing about "the supreme fiction," as the ambassador, quoting Wallace Stevens, had described it.

Yet on a peaceful night in Kibira, by a warm fire, embraced by the light of a full moon and inspired by the thought of being in what surely seemed to be a holy place, the veteran coach was transfixed by the emollient effect of his new friend's verse.

I wish I could do that, he thought.

29

At 7:00 am on the dot, the group broke camp. En route to Kayanza, as they drove slowly through the small village ravaged by AIDS, Cynthia Foster experienced a similar range of emotions as those felt by the others the previous week. She was horrified but not surprised; she had seen the same devastation in other regions of Burundi. Her sense of despair remained as the jeeps lurched down the stone road leading to the soccer field, where Leonard and his friends would, Jim hoped, be waiting.

At the rendezvous point, though, she felt reassured by the sight of the half-moon hoop and the gaggle of towering young boys.

Jim noticed immediately that the group's number had grown back to fourteen; the four boys who had scurried into the woods one week earlier had rejoined the gathering. After warm greetings were exchanged, Mathias asked the boys for their attention.

"Young men," he said in Kirundi, "I am pleased to introduce you to a great friend of our country. She is also the person most responsible for this basketball project, and she is the United States ambassador to Burundi. This means that she is the official representative of her country here in our country. I want you to know that she is also a great supporter of anything that will help end the violence. Plus, she is extremely excited to meet all of you. Her name is Ambassador Cynthia Foster."

Not one of the young men had any knowledge of what an ambassador did. Yet all sensed that this woman was very important—like a queen. Following Leonard's lead, they all bowed solemnly in deference.

"Thank you Mathias, and thank you young men—not only for your kind welcome, but for your willingness to learn this new game from such a great coach."

Motioning to Jim to join her, Ambassador Foster said, "As you know, Coach Keating is also from America, and he's just as excited as I am about this basketball project, which we call Project Oscar after a very famous American basketball player who you will learn more about."

Stepping forward, Jim said, "Thank you Ambassador, and, yes, I am very excited. So let's get started, let's learn some more basketball today, and, most importantly, let's have some fun!"

"Okay?" bellowed Jim.

"Okay!" roared fourteen boys.

Despite the constraints of a court with one hoop and a dirt surface, Ambassador Foster could easily see why the men were so energized about young Leonard. He was as fluid as he was powerful, and she also noticed that he gave the coach his *full* attention.

For his part, Jim was again struck by the boy's focus, not to mention how much he had improved in only seven days.

"Bill," he said in a low voice to Bill Foster, "it's obvious the kid's been working on his skills. And he seems to have some other great attributes. He's certainly bright, in the way he picks things up, and he sure has leadership qualities."

Jim's words rang true. Mathias had approached two of the boys and asked about their practices. They said that in each of the last six days, Leonard had led the group in a lengthy session, diligently practicing the exact moves the coach had taught in the first practice, as well as the drop-step rotation line Jim had asked them to work on.

"So, young men, do you and the other boys like the game?" Mathais had asked.

Both boys had nodded, and one said eagerly, "We love the game. We love being able to use our hands and we love jumping in the air!"

"A good answer," Mathias had replied, wondering how all of the boys would feel once they learned that Hutus were included in Project Oscar.

"Now," said Jim to the group, "I'm going to teach you a new shot called the jump hook. And when I teach you a new shot, I'm also going to tell you about the great players who made these shots famous. Okay?"

"Okay!"

"About the jump hook: There was great player by the name of Dave Cowens, who played a position called center. For now, think of the center as generally the guy who's the tallest man on his team, and the man who plays closest to the basket," he said. "Anyway, even though Dave Cowens was a center, he was a little bit shorter than many of the other centers he played against. So, he developed a jump hook so he could score points against the taller centers he faced."

He continued, "Even though all of you guys are very tall, this is a great shot to learn because, as those players who tried to guard Cowens found out, it's a *very* hard shot to block. Also, teaching this hook will make it easier for you to learn the other shot—called the regular hook shot—that I'm going to teach you later on."

Jim looked around at the other adults, all basketball enthusiasts in their own right and all familiar with the story he told. "Bill," he said, "please line up in the low post."

Bill Foster took his position, and Jim continued, "First thing you need to know, guys, is that the drop-step is an important part of this jump hook move. The only difference from what I taught you last week is that instead of laying the ball in the basket, you're pulling up a little short and taking a jump hook. Now, watch."

Jim passed the basketball to Foster, who drop-stepped. Using his body and left forearm to shield the ball, he lofted a soft jump hook through the net.

"Okay, Leonard, come on out and try to guard Bill," said Jim.

By calling on Leonard Tangishaka, Jim knew that he might well be abandoning his normal practice of choosing a defender who would not cause the offensive player much trouble. But Leonard had *never* played any defense in his life, and Foster, while seven inches shorter, was an expert practitioner of the move.

Jim made the entry pass, and Bill Foster did everything by the book. He head-faked Leonard out of defensive position, he drop-stepped to gain an even better angle to the hoop, he used his body and forearm to protect the ball, and he let go with a perfect jump hook.

There was only one problem: After being faked out by Foster, Leonard recovered his defensive position with remarkable quickness, and, as Foster released his shot, the young man timed his jump perfectly.

The ball was swatted thirty-five feet—onto the soccer field!

The other boys roared with delight, and Jim smiled at the grim-faced shooter. "Well, Bill, maybe I should have chosen Sergeant Rush to demonstrate."

Knowing that her husband had considerable pride in his offensive repertoire, Cynthia Foster turned away to hide her irreverent smile. Then, looking out into the woods, her eyes unexpectedly met those of a tall, handsome woman. While half hidden behind a cluster of bushes, it was evident this woman wanted the ambassador to see her.

Though she couldn't be certain, Cynthia guessed she might be the mother of Leonard Tangishaka.

———

From behind her cover of Olea bushes, Consolaté Tangishaka had watched the black woman arrive in the strange vehicle. Consolaté had never met, nor even seen, any woman who possessed such a commanding presence. Yet it was obvious from the manner in which this woman was treated by the men who accompanied her that she was a *umuzungu-kaikuru* . . . a powerful woman. And, like the white teacher Consolaté wished to meet, this woman had a kind, bright face, a sign perhaps that she was a person of wisdom and goodwill sent by God.

As she squatted quietly in her hideout, Consolaté thought she heard God tell her that this special woman was here for an important reason and that she, Consolaté, must meet her. So, when the woman gazed out into the woods, Consolaté bravely moved from behind the shrubs and into her field of vision. As their eyes met, Consolaté felt a strange and powerful bond with the *umuzungukaikuru.*

"Mathias," Ambassador Foster whispered, "I have just seen a lady out there in the woods. Is it safe for me to go and meet her?"

"I will come with you, Madam Ambassador," replied Mathias.

"You know, somehow I feel certain she is Leonard's mother."

After making eye contact with the powerful woman, Consolaté took cover behind the bushes, only to see the woman and a Tutsi man walking cautiously in her direction. Fear momentarily overtook Consolaté. At the same time, though, she felt a strange kinship with this woman. Her fear was further allayed by the calming words of the Tutsi man: "We come in peace. May we speak with you?"

"*Ego*," said Consolaté in Kirundi, as she took a small step away from the bushes.

"I am originally from this region," he continued, "and this is Cynthia Foster, the United States Ambassador to Burundi."

Like the boys, Consolaté did not know the word *ambassador*, though she was certain it carried great importance.

"What is your name?" asked Mathias.

"Consolaté."

Cynthia hadn't mastered the accent, but she had a good facility with basic Kirundian. She decided now was the time to use it. Smiling warmly, the ambassador bent slightly at the waist and said, "I am Cynthia and I am honored to know you."

Consolaté nodded. Feeling much more at ease, she returned Cynthia's smile.

As Consolaté relaxed and stood more erect, Cynthia was suddenly struck by her compelling demeanor. She was at least six feet tall and very attractive. *Good Lord*, thought the ambassador, *she looks like Lena Horne*. The only marks that marred her face were two scars, one on her chin and the other on her left cheekbone, both no doubt the perverse legacy of a cruel man. Yet Cynthia would later write in her diary that Consolaté was so attractive that the scars might just as well have been beauty marks.

"Are you the mother of one of these boys?"

"Yes," she said.

"And which boy is your son?"

"The tallest boy—the strongest boy!"

The pride of a mother's statement brought an even broader smile to the ambassador's face which, in turn, caused Consolaté's fear to completely subside.

"Your son—he is very gifted, very special," said the ambassador. "Tell me, do you know anything about the game he is playing?"

"No."

Inexplicably, Consolaté found herself momentarily wondering if Charlé might be spying on this meeting. Anxiety beclouded her face, and Ambassador Foster sensed that Consolaté's concern had nothing to do with the conversation. She decided to take a bold step.

"Do you fear for your son?"

The question took Consolaté by surprise; she was not quite ready to expose her veiled emotions about the issue. But within moments, and disregarding the possibility of Charle's surveillance, she allowed her deep-rooted feelings to surface and broke down in tears.

"Why don't we go sit on those rocks," said the ambassador. She pointed to a few flat rocks among a pile of volcanic rubble.

Sensing that he should not be part of this conversation, Mathias said, "I will remain here to ensure your privacy."

Once the two were seated, Ambassador Foster placed her hand on Consolaté's shoulder and asked, "And why do you fear for your son?"

Although she had met her only minutes earlier, Consolaté felt that she could trust Cynthia, at least up to a point. She also knew that she really had no choice, considering the alternatives.

"I have watched my husband and two oldest sons go off to war to have their courage tested. All three are now dead. I do not want this fate for Leonard, who is my youngest son . . . my only family member left on this earth."

"Have you any ways of preventing young Leonard from entering the war?"

Consolaté grew silent, her unsettled expression making it clear that she would be uncomfortable revealing her ambitious solution.

"There may be a way, Consolaté," the ambassador said. "But it would mean a major change for Leonard—and for you."

Consolaté's heart raced, and Ambassador Foster continued.

"The man who is teaching Leonard this game, which is called basketball, is an expert. He feels that Leonard could become a great player of basketball. But in order for your son to develop his skills, he would have to leave Kayanza and move to Bujumbura."

The ambassador intended to finish her proposal by suggesting that if such a move were to endanger Consolaté, arrangements would be made for her to move to Bujumbura as well. But before she could offer this alternative, Consolaté, her eyes welling again with tears, embraced Cynthia Foster and said, "Yes, this is what I have prayed for."

"But what about you, Consolaté? Will you be safe here? Because if not, you too may move to Bujumbura—I can arrange that."

"Oh, no. You are most kind. But no, I would not leave the graves of my husband and sons so soon after their deaths. No, I must stay here."

As Ambassador Foster knew, this was another of the traditions the Tutsi culture still embraced. And while pleased that young Leonard would move to Bujumbura, she was concerned for the well-being of this fine woman with whom she had so quickly connected and for whom she felt instant—and vast—empathy.

As Cynthia Foster arose, Consolaté Tangishaka placed a hand on her forearm and posed a surprising question.

"Would it be possible for Leonard to go with you today?"

The request caught the Ambassador off guard. In her mind, Leonard's move would involve at least several days of preparations. He would need to get his belongings together and say his good-byes.

"I . . . I hadn't thought about bringing Leonard today. Is there some reason for the urgency?"

"There is, Madam," said Consolaté. "You see, since I saw the white man teach my son this game seven days ago, I was overcome by a strange and wonderful feeling that he had been sent to us by God. Before I saw you today, I planned to approach the white man."

She continued, "Madam, I was going to ask him to do exactly what you have so kindly offered—to take my son to Bujumbura. As for making this request of you today, it is because Leonard will soon be taken by the soldiers. I am sure of this."

"How soon?" the ambassador asked.

"Very soon. Weeks, maybe even days. And surely, if anyone has seen me talking to you, they'll tell the warlords. These men—evil men—will think it strange for me to be talking to an American queen. If they suspect that Leonard is moving to Bujumbura, they will surely act to prevent this."

"And their way of preventing it would be to force Leonard into the army," the ambassador thought aloud.

"*Ego.*"

The ambassador looked away for a moment, and then turned back to Consolaté. "I'll be right back," she said, placing an assuring hand on her forearm before walking away.

She walked over to Mathias, spoke with him briefly, and Mathias nodded. She returned to Consolaté and said, "Yes, it can be done today, and Mathias, the man with whom I just spoke, has offered to host Leonard in his home. But because we must depart soon, Mathias suggests that he quietly tell your son to leave the practice session and go straight home to see you."

Once again, Consolaté hugged Ambassador Foster.

"I will go to our home and wait for Leonard."

Fifteen minutes later, Leonard Tangishaka entered the mud-floored hut, only to find his mother weeping softly.

30

"You will love your children so much that their lives will become more important to you than your own."

Solange Irakoze had said these words to her daughter Consolaté only hours before Consolaté's marriage to Leonidas Tangashika. At the time, Consolaté wondered about the accuracy of this seemingly extreme statement, but her doubt had disappeared after she bore her three sons.

The death of a husband and two sons burdened Consolaté's soul with unbearable grief, intensified by having to yield to Charlé's sexual demands. Her only source of hope—of strength—was Leonard, whose strong body and mind were matched by the might of his devotion to his mother.

Consolaté selflessly returned the devotion. She would not diminish the happiness Leonard drew from good times with his many young friends, so she internalized her grief. And to ensure her son's safety, she consented to Charlé's lust.

Now she would complete her cycle of self-sacrifice. She would set her only living son free, knowing that their reunions would likely be few and that—perhaps forever—there would be a distance between them.

"Mother, what is the matter?"

Before answering her son's question, Consolaté sank into Leonard's muscular arms, her gentle crying intensifying to sobs. Leonard could recall only one other time when his embrace had released such powerful feelings in his mother. It was moments after she had learned of the deaths of his father and brothers—together, all three had been hurled into the quagmire of tribal hatred and together all three had perished in a brutal encounter with the Hutus.

Despite his powerful physical appearance, Leonard's emotional make-up was still that of a fourteen-year-old. Without knowing the reason for his mother's reaction, he joined her in a flood of tears.

When Consolaté was finally able to regain her composure, she escorted her son to one of the two wooden chairs in the hut. Looking deep into his trusting eyes, she spoke in a tone that expressed both affection and regret. "My son, God has sent these people to save your life. I am as sure of this as I am of my love for you. Without your knowledge, I have watched you learn this new game."

"How so?" asked Leonard.

"I have hidden behind the bushes in the forest. And while I know nothing of this game, I do know that the white man who has taught you is a good man. Leonard, I am sure that God has sent this man here so that you will not have to follow your father and brothers into the terrible war."

"But how could this be so?" he asked.

"This man, my son, and the people with him are going to take you today to the capital city, where you will be safe. You will stay in the home of the Tutsi man—the kind man who just sent you to me—and you will learn about this game from the white man. And by doing this, Leonard, I believe great things will happen for you."

"But mother, what about you? Surely you will come with me?"

"In time, I will, son. But not now. Not so soon after the deaths of your father and brothers. You see, I cannot leave their graves—not just yet."

"Then I cannot go without you, mother," Leonard insisted. "I cannot leave you here alone."

Out of respect for Consolaté, Leonard did not mention the real reason for his reluctance. In his heart, he knew that a move to Bujumbura might place his mother's safety at risk. Leonard knew that Charlé had beaten several other widows he had sexually abused.

One revealing encounter had convinced Leonard that his presence prevented such abuse. Late one evening, Charlé had approached the hut. Consolaté was ill, and, at her request, Leonard told Charlé of her condition. A muscular, wiry man with a vicious temperament, Charlé showed no sympathy and instead tried to brush the boy aside and enter the hut. While only fourteen, Leonard was already bigger than Charlé. Although fearful of this evil man, Leonard concealed his fright and blocked the entrance. To Leonard's surprise, not only did Charlé withdraw, but in his eyes the boy detected a strange and surprising fear. At the time, Leonard had the feeling that he had intimidated a demon who could someday return to harm him.

Consolaté interrupted her son's recollection of Charlé. "My son, you have been a most obedient boy, and you must now do as I say. I know of your concern for me, but, for the present at least, I must stay and you must go."

In the end, Leonard Tangishaka knew that he must obey his mother. He hugged her hard, leaving Consolaté almost breathless. In silence, they packed Leonard's modest belongings.

———

Leonard had slipped off quietly, before his friends could ask questions. When he departed, Mathias whispered the new plan to Jim, and the coach felt equal measures of surprise and exhilaration.

After Leonard left, Jim wrapped up his lesson on inside defense: "Basketball is a game that requires you to outthink and outwork your opponent. This is especially true when you're defending a player in the low post. Guys, if you relax down low—mentally or physically—even for just a split second, it'll likely cost your team a basket. . . . Okay, line up, gentlemen. Time for the shooting contest."

As usual, there was no hesitation. Whoops, hollers, and clapping followed almost every shot. One of the boys, Emery, won for the first time and jumped up and down waving his prize New Jersey State camp t-shirt over his head. Clovis, the other winner, was already wearing a shirt he'd won earlier. He laughed as he pulled his new prize over the first.

Jim smiled. He walked over to Bill. "Bet he wears 'em both to bed."

"Guaranteed," laughed Bill.

"I'll be back next week," Jim shouted, knowing the plan could change with an increase in the violence and wondering how he could get word to the boys, should such an outbreak prevent his travel.

As the players headed through the woods for a swim, Ambassador Foster asked Mathias, "How long would you guess Leonard will spend with his mother before he returns?"

"From what I can gather," Mathias replied, "his hut is a fifteen-minute walk. He probably has only a few belongings to pack, but I'll bet he'll need a good deal of time to say good-bye—as will his mother."

As Ambassador Foster and Mathias discussed their reaction to the swiftness of Leonard's move to Bujumbura, Jim Keating's attention wandered back to the early '60s, to a recurring dream, one well remembered. In the dream, he discovered in a remote Pennsylvania town a young giant, fifteen,

6'9", powerfully built, blessed with fine athletic talent, and unschooled in the fundamentals of basketball.

As the dream evolved, Jim decided to teach this great prospect to copy the skills of the most proficient big men in the game. The boy would learn the George Mikan hook shot, the Wilt Chamberlain finger roll, the Clyde Lovellette short jumper, and, naturally, Bill Russell's techniques of defense and rebounding.

Of course, the exhilarating experience of developing the boy ended when Jim awoke, but one result of the dream was that Jim always thought such an approach with a young phenom had merit. As the group continued their wait for Leonard, Jim told Bill Foster about his fantasy and about a strategic teaching plan for Leonard.

"In other words," said Foster, "you'll decide which center had the best jump shot and teach Leonard that shot. Same with the hook shot, power move, outlet pass—the whole package!"

"That's it," said Jim.

"I love it."

"Well then," said Jim, "while we're waiting for Leonard, let's talk about it. Let's start with the jumper. From among the great centers, which jump shot do you like the best?"

"You know," replied Foster, "if you look at the best centers, Russell and Chamberlain being the most obvious, a lot of the great ones were not good jump shooters. But I guess the five who come to mind right away would be Robert Parish, Willis Reed, Bill Walton, Patrick Ewing, and David Robinson."

Jim Keating was pleased that Bill's suggestions were also at the top of his own list.

"So, which jumper would you choose for young Leonard?" asked Jim.

"Well, because of Leonard's long arms, I guess I'd teach him the Parish jump shot. As you know, Jim, because of his arm extension and arc, Parish's jumper is difficult to block.

This kid—with his long arms and all—could develop one that would be damned near impossible to get at."

"I agree, so we'll go with a Parish jumper. Okay, how 'bout the hook shot?" asked Jim.

"Well, with deference to George Mikan and even Russell, that's a no-brainer!"

"Kareem?"

"Absolutely!" said Foster.

As the two continued to wait for Leonard, they had a wonderful time choosing the premier practitioners of the various big-man moves. In making their choices, they not only considered the highly-skilled players, but also paid attention to the particular physical attributes of those players—and matched them up to Leonard's.

"Walton—he was the best passer," said Jim. "Kevin McHale, even though he was mostly a power forward, had the best inside drop-step move. By the way, I don't think we should teach the kid McHale's up-and-under move, simply because Leonard will be too tall to go under anyone."

"You're right on that," Bill agreed.

"And on defense," Keating continued, "I'd like to get some films of Russell. There's a famous one called *Block Art*. The film does a good job of not only showing the way he blocked shots, but also the way he positioned himself. Also, the way he'd psych out his opponents by blocking a shot and then timing his next block to always keep the opposition thinking."

"And it would be great if we could get some of the books that Russell wrote," said Foster. "Perhaps part of Leonard's instruction in English could be to read Russell's books, especially the ones about his defensive philosophy."

"Right on target, Bill," Jim said, then suddenly found himself ducking under an errant pass thrown by an apologetic boy.

"Still got the quick reflexes, Coach," said Bill. "But let's head over to safety!"

As the two moved away from the spirited young players, the coach continued. "Now, as far as rebounding is concerned, how 'bout if we have him watch films—if we can get them here. We'd have him watch Walton on the offensive board, and Olajawon, Kareem, and Russell on the defensive board. You know, John Wooden taught his players to go right to the ball on the defensive board instead of boxing out."

"I remember," said Foster. "He also taught them to *always* have their hands above their shoulders. In fact, I don't think I've ever seen a picture of Kareem or Walton near the hoop without their hands well above their shoulders."

While her husband and Jim discussed strategy, Ambassador Foster took pleasure in their unbridled enthusiasm. Finally, she couldn't resist yelling over to them, "It's like the two of you are thirty years old again!"

As she spoke, Leonard Tangishaka and his mother came into view. Watching mother and son holding hands, Bill placed his arm around Jim's shoulder.

"Here he comes, Jim . . . our special project."

"What a privilege!" said the coach.

———

Each September, Jim made it a point to greet his freshman recruits when they were dropped off at orientation by their parents. It was an important rite of passage—for both parent and child—and Jim recalled many poignant, often surprising, acts of tenderness by boys hiding in men's bodies. In one such case, back in the early '60s, Jim remembered a tough, burly 6'8" player breaking down in the arms of his 4'11" mother.

But, of course, at no time in his life had Jim Keating ever been part of such a unique and complex convocation as Leonard Tangishaka's departure for Bujumbura. Clearly, this move was not only one of uncommon adventure for the boy, but also one that might likely imperil the safety of his mother.

"When he leaves, there will be no one to protect her," was the somber comment by Mathias.

As Consolaté and Leonard walked toward the makeshift basketball court, each carrying a small satchel full of Leonard's belongings, Jim knew he must carry out the same function he had performed so many times as a college coach. He must offer gentle words of encouragement to the boy and, perhaps more importantly, words of reassurance to the mother.

Ambassador Foster had similar thoughts. After greeting mother and son, she asked Consolaté to join her in quiet conversation. Jim, in turn, asked Mathias to translate his message to Leonard.

With Mathias at his side, Jim looked into Leonard's trusting eyes and began, "Young man, I know this is a difficult move for you. To be honest, you will probably find yourself missing your mother and your friends a great deal. Sometimes you'll miss them so much that you'll want to turn back. But please trust me, for what I am about to tell you is the truth."

He continued, "I've heard it said, Leonard, that the loneliness that comes from leaving home is very much the companion of learning, of growing, and of growing up. Your mother knows this move is right for you, and so do I. In time, and please believe me on this, you will know it, too. But for now, I want you to be assured that Mathias and I will treat you as if you were our own son."

As the coach spoke, Leonard listened intently. When Jim was done, the boy extended his hand and said, "*Urakoze.* Thank you."

Meanwhile, the ambassador conferred with Consolaté. She offered Leonard's mother a place in Bujumbura "when you are ready."

Consolaté's appreciation of this important woman's goodwill was heartfelt. Handing Ambassador Foster a folded piece of paper bound by a piece of string and covered with a small patch of yellow cloth, Consolaté said, "Since I have learned to read, I have come to love the deep meaning of certain words. When you return to your home later today, please look at a beautiful prayer I read in a book."

The ambassador took the paper and embraced her new sister. "I will read the prayer. And I want you to know that until you come, I will look after your son—not as well as you—but with the love of a mother."

When he was certain the ambassador and Consolaté were finished with their conversation, Jim gently approached Leonard's mother and, with Mathias's aid, told her a story.

"When I was a young coach many years ago, I had a boy on my team who was very difficult to work with. The boy broke several rules, and I decided to ask him to leave the team. After the season, the boy's father came to see me. Early in our conversation, I realized that the father was a good man. To be sure, he had spoiled his son, and admitted as much. But he also told me how much my decision had hurt the boy—and had hurt him."

Jim paused, took a deep breath, and continued his story. "And then he said something that I wish someone had said to me before I began my coaching career. He said, 'I only hope that you treated my son the way that you would want your own son to be treated.' In truth, I knew I had not treated that boy as I would have liked my own son to be treated. While he was difficult to work with, had I been a more mature coach, I would have found a way to work with him, to somehow keep him on the team."

He waited for Mathias to finish translating and then added, "Ever since the meeting with that boy's father, I have tried very hard to treat each young man under my direction the way I would want my own child to be treated. I haven't always been successful, but believe me, that has been my goal. Ma'am, you have my assurance that I will treat Leonard as if he were my own son."

To Jim's surprise, as he concluded his words, Consolaté Tangishaka embraced him.

Moments later, as the jeep began to navigate the treacherous, rutted stone road, Charlé Tinyabokwe, hiding in the woodland, watched Leonard Tangishaka leave Kayanza with a group of intruders he found easy to loathe.

———

Just shy of midnight, Ambassador Foster reached her study. She pulled from her pocket the folded paper, carefully removed the string and yellow cloth, put on her glasses, and read:

A Mother's Prayer

I pray you will be my eyes and watch him where he goes.
And help me to be wise.
Help me to let him go.

31

Master teacher that he was, Jim Keating developed a comprehensive lesson plan for the basketball education of Leonard Tangishaka. With the help of Jesse Abbot, who was fluent in Kirundi and a wizard at the computer, a print-out of the two-month plan was ready within three days of Leonard's arrival in Bujumbura. The plan would provide the young man with instruction in every phase of basketball—as well as other details of the game's history.

As soon as Jesse delivered the plan, Jim approached Bill after lunch one day.

"If you've got some time right now, I'm anxious to have you look at this material we've put together for Leonard. I asked Jesse to search the internet for the bios of Russell, Walton, Chamberlain, and other great ones. Before I give this to Leonard, I'd like your feedback."

Bill nodded and took some time to review the material. "Looks great. My only thought is that we add Paul Silas to the offensive rebounding category. Also, the big Russian—Sabonis—in the High Post/Low Post passing category."

Bill's suggestions triggered more discussion, after which they agreed on the following Post Player Models:

- Jump Shot—Robert Parish
- Turnaround Jump Shot from Low Post—Jack Sikma
- Hook Shot
  - Sky Hook—Kareem Abdul Jabbar
  - Regular Hook Shot—George Mikan
  - Jump Hook—Dave Cowans
- Outlet Pass—Bill Walton
- High Post/Low Post passing—Arvydas Sabonis
- Running the Floor—Robert Parish
- Shot Blocking—Bill Russell
- Defensive Strategy—Bill Russell
- Offensive Rebounding—Paul Silas
- Defensive Rebounding—Hakeem Olajuwon
- Aggressiveness—Dave Cowans
- Footwork — Hakeem Olajuwon
- Drop-Step—Kevin McHale

While Foster took the bios and outline to the typing pool, Jim called Barry Sklar to tell him about Leonard and to ask a favor.

"Hey, ol' friend, I really wanted to talk with Harriet; by the way, please give her my best."

Barry laughed. "Will do, Coach. And it's good to hear your voice. Tell me, how's it going?"

"It's going great, Barry. Since the last time we talked, we've discovered a kid—make that a seven-foot, fourteen-year-old kid—who is simply phenomenal."

Jim gave Barry the particulars, including where they found Leonard and his move to Bujumbura. He also reviewed Leonard's physique, his athleticism, and his rapid and remarkable grasp of basketball skills.

"So, General Jim, let me get this straight. You're actually saying that he could be better than Russell, Jabbar, Chamberlain, and Hakeem!" exclaimed Barry.

"I am, Barry, and speaking of those guys, I'm wondering if you can get me some films on them—as well as on George Mikan, Bill Walton, Robert Parish, Dave Cowans, Paul Silas, Jack Sikma, Kevin McHale, and Sabonis, the Big Russian?"

"Tell me where to go, Coach," said Barry, pleased with his old friend's emotional health, which was obvious from the vitality in his voice.

"NBA Properties, a division of the NBA, as well as the Basketball Hall of Fame in Springfield, both have lots of old films," said Jim. "I'm sure they'll cooperate. And the Portland Trail Blazers have the draft rights to Sabonis. I'll bet they have plenty of film on him. And Barry, for now, please don't tell anyone about Leonard. I don't want any college recruiters or pro scouts here just yet."

"Understood," said Barry.

Within an hour after the conversation ended, Barry found out that two US senators were tied to family ownership of two NBA teams. Barry placed calls to the staffers of both senators. One week later, a collection of films, including footage of Sabonis, as well as a bonus gift of more equipment from both teams, was on the way to Bujumbura, Burundi.

———

During his first week in Bujumbura, Leonard Tangishaka was clearly burdened by a concern for his beloved mother. The distance that set them apart would, he feared, increase the depths of Charlé's lechery. And then there was the dreaded virus. Leonard did not fully comprehend the vast expanse of its terrible reach. But he did know of the virus's steely tie to *gusambana*, and he prayed hard that it would never infect his mother.

Because of her own fear of AIDS, Consolaté had warned her son to refrain from any sexual union with the young girls of Kayanza.

"They will see you as a god, and you must be strong in your resistance," she had said.

In recent months, before he left his home, Leonard had found himself increasingly attracted to the *abukobga*—the girls. And though he had been in Bujumbura for just a few days, the young ladies in the capital city were even prettier than those from Kayanza. But despite the hormones surging through his fourteen-year-old body, Leonard would follow his mother's wishes.

As time began to alleviate the pain of Leonard's separation from his mother and his home, he became adjusted to his new surroundings. An important addition to this life—and one he enjoyed—was daily school. In Kayanza, schooling in times of peace was sporadic at best; in times of war it was non-existent.

Leonard's favorite course was English. His teacher, a Catholic missionary from Ireland, was so impressed with her new pupil's progress that she told Mathias, "He is already my best student."

But despite finding a measure of happiness in his new surroundings, Leonard's concern for Consolaté never wavered. And while he often thought about visiting his mother and friends, he was too shy to raise the matter with his host, who was so kind to him.

Mathias had lost his wife and only child, a daughter, at childbirth many years before, and he treated Leonard like the son he wished he had. Each morning before classes, he made the boy breakfast of *matoke*, a small banana, and *ugali*, a flour paste that Leonard ate with a piece of French bread. In rural Burundi, people routinely skipped breakfast and returned at noon for a large meal. So this was a new, but welcome, experience—especially the French bread. When Leonard returned after school, and prior to his daily basketball workout, Mathias had snacks of sugar cane and nuts waiting.

For dinner, Mathias would make delicious dishes of red kidney beans, cabbage, or sweet potatoes. Of course, Leonard was familiar with these kinds of food, but Mathias added spices and cooked with a French flair that made the meals particularly enjoyable. Though they were in short supply, Mathias was also able, through his friends in Bujumbura, to obtain chicken and meat, which they enjoyed at least twice a week. After the evening meal, he would help Leonard with his homework, marveling at the boy's diligence and aptitude for learning. Before retiring, the two would discuss the great players who appeared in Leonard's Basketball Digest, the impressive compendium of hoops history and skills development techniques so carefully prepared by Coach Keating.

And if Mathias acted as surrogate father to young Leonard, Jim took on the role of teacher, mentor, and trusted friend. Each afternoon, Leonard received private lessons on the fundamentals and history of basketball. Jim handled the sessions for five days. The other two workouts were delegated to Gilbert, Déo, and Bill Foster so the coach could make his weekly treks out into the country.

Since Leonard's arrival in Bujumbura, Jim had been unable to include Kayanza in his travel itinerary, for the Marines had reported increased violence in that region so near the Rwandan border. Through the Marines, Jim had gotten word to the other thirteen boys that he fully intended to return. He had also asked the Marines to bring along additional equipment, but they couldn't be sure the boys would be able to use it for fear of reprisal by Charlé and his warriors.

After five weeks of intensive instruction, which included viewing the video tapes sent by Barry, Leonard's progress surprised even Jim Keating. The coach decided it was time for the next step.

"Bill, he's already much better than the guys trying out for the National Team. I say we let him join the group."

"I agree," said Foster. "You've done a masterful job, Jim. You've taught him the fundamentals as well as I've ever seen them taught. Plus, and this is a big plus, you've made him believe in himself. The Pygmalion Effect right here in Burundi!"

As usual, Jim felt uncomfortable with the compliment. "You're too kind, Bill. But you know, I sure understand how Mathias feels—I, too, love the kid like a son."

———

An average of thirty-six players—slightly more Tutsis than Hutus—were regularly attending the National Team practices. The youngest was nineteen, and most of the athletes were in their mid to late twenties.

On occasion during the five weeks of private workouts, the coach had invited Dieudonne Kinshaba, a schoolteacher and National Team candidate, to work against Leonard in the drills. At the last private session before joining the National Team practice, Jim assigned the 6'9" Dieudonne to guard Leonard in a shot test from ten to twelve feet out. Leonard devoured the defender, scoring on 17 of 25 attempts, causing Bill Foster to refer to the young man's newly constructed jumper as "impossible to block and Robert Parish water-soft."

Later in that session, Jim began to teach Leonard the Paul Silas method of rolling off the back of the defensive rebounder to get better offensive rebounding position. After fifteen minutes of instruction on this rarely used technique, Jim asked Dieudonne to "box Leonard out."

Dieudonne girded his body and aggressively fixed his buttocks to Leonard's upper thighs in proper box-out position. Leonard began his roll, and Jim's intentionally errant shot caromed off the rim and high into the air.

Dan Doyle

With perfect timing, and slightly better rebounding position due to his effective "roll," Leonard ascended a full two feet above the reach of Dieudonne. He snatched the ball with his mammoth right hand and smashed it through the hoop in one fluid and powerful motion. Jim was so amazed that he momentarily forgot the no dunk rule

Bill Foster did not. "Jim," Foster whispered to the coach, out of earshot of Leonard. "We'd best enforce the rule with this kid, or we'll have no hoops!"

Prior to Leonard's joining the group for practice, Jim said to the team, "We have a young man who will join us on Tuesday night. His name is Leonard Tangishaka, and I know that you've all heard about him from Dieudonne. In two weeks, he's turning fifteen years old, and he is now 7'1" and still growing. A little over a month ago, we discovered Leonard in the Kayanza region. Because of the violence there, and the fact that he's a boy with special basketball potential, we helped him move to Bujumbura, where he is staying with Mathias."

He continued. "Since he arrived, we've been working with Leonard on his skills. We feel it's time he practiced with this group. Gentlemen, this boy has the potential to make a real impact on basketball in this country. I'd like all of you to treat him as if he was your younger brother."

"Seven-one and still fourteen?" shouted Egide Nashambi, one of the team's best shooters, and most assuredly the team comic. "Coach Keating, he can definitely be my brother."

The group's laughter made Jim comfortable that the team would welcome Leonard into their ranks.

———

Even though Jim had told Leonard Tangishaka to "relax and enjoy your first practice with the National Team," Leonard was noticeably nervous when he arrived at the Nimbona Court.

Jim, on the other hand, was not at all concerned about how Leonard would fare. Even in this rudimentary stage of his basketball development, the boy was far ahead of the other National Team hopefuls. His strength, quickness, and overall athleticism were superior—and the rate at which he mastered skills was astounding.

While Dieudonne was the only National Team member to have seen Leonard play, he had told his teammates plenty about the "wunderkind," as he had nicknamed Leonard. An eruption of interest, if not intense curiosity, awaited Leonard's arrival at the practice.

Jim introduced the newcomer to the team, and their warm reaction pleased the coach—and the young player. The favorable response and a five minute warm-up in the lay-up line relaxed Leonard.

"Okay, let's get into the full-court drills," yelled Jim. "How 'bout if we start with the five-on-three fast-break drill we worked on at the last practice."

The fast-break drill called for the rebounder to take the position of "trailer." The trailer was to remain behind the other four players until the three defenders were pulled out of position due to a crisp series of passes. At this point, the trailer's job was to cut hard to the hoop. If open, he would be fed the ball for an easy lay-up.

In Leonard's first attempt at the drill, he did something Jim had grown fond of in the boy. Because of his energy—and diligence—he knew, in Jim's words, "only full speed ahead."

When he grabbed the rebound, Leonard pitched the ball out to a wing-man and then bolted down the court, outrunning the other four members of his team, plus the three defenders. He received a lead pass from the ball handler and slammed home a thunderous dunk, causing Déo to yell, "Leonard—please remember the dunk rule!"

Jim had a more measured reaction. "Well," he whispered to Bill Foster, "I guess we ought to refine the fast-break pattern to take advantage of the kid's speed!"

Bill turned and winked at Jim. "I'd say you're right on that one, Coach."

The practice ended up with two 12-minute scrimmages. Leonard played 18 of the 24 minutes. He scored 22 points, grabbed 13 rebounds, and blocked 7 shots. So remarkable was his performance that the players actually cheered several of his more astounding feats.

"Not only do they like him, but they realize what he can do for the game here," observed Mathias.

When practice was over, Jim was exultant. After he dismissed the team, he spent an extra fifteen minutes with Leonard, reviewing the boy's play and offering pointers for improvement, such as, "When you get double-teamed in the low post, don't be afraid to pass it back out to a teammate for an open three-pointer."

"Yes, sir," said Leonard—his standard response to any instruction.

"Before you head off with Mathias," said Jim, "I'd like to talk to you for a moment. How 'bout if we go over to the bleachers?"

Once seated, Jim said, "Leonard, Ambassador Foster has received word that the fighting has moved out of the Kayanza region and over the border into Rwanda. She feels that it's safe for me to go back to Kayanza and resume teaching the game to your friends."

He continued, "While you have never told me that you are homesick, I know you would like to accompany me there—to visit your mother and your friends. But the ambassador thinks that it's best for Bill and me to go first. We'll be accompanied by Mathias, Sergeant Rush, and Corporal Roberts, as well as two other Marines. We'll seek out your friends, and your mother, and find out how safe it would be for you to travel there. If our Marines feel it is safe, and Ambassador Foster agrees, perhaps we can arrange for you to visit. But . . . not just yet, Leonard."

"Yes, sir," said Leonard, his stoic expression belying his disappointment.

32

"Even though the fighting's supposedly crossed over the border into Rwanda, this'll be a two-jeep, four-marine trip," Sergeant Rush said to Jim as Corporal Roberts loaded supplies, including two M-16 rifles, into the trailer.

Along with Rush, Roberts, and Jim, the group of seven traveling to Kayanza included Mathias, Bill Foster, and the two other Marines.

"Gentlemen, we're in good hands. Meet Private Smyth and Private Francis."

Jim shook hands with the two soldiers, both of whom looked like they had just stepped out of a Marine recruiting poster.

"Thanks, fellas. Glad to have you along."

Happily, the trip to Kayanza was uneventful, and when the jeep arrived at the ridge overlooking the lush green field, the men were pleased to see the boys playing soccer below.

But ten minutes later, Mathias offered a bleak translation of his conversation with the young men. "It is not good. The boys told me Charlé was furious about Leonard's move, which he called an escape. He told them if they attempt to leave, he will kill them all. He also said that as soon as he returns from the fighting in Rwanda, they all must join the army. They are not too young to realize that this could be a death sentence."

"Do they want to work out?" asked Jim.

"They want to very much, but they are afraid to," replied Mathias. "I am sure they would be reluctant even to be seen with us."

"Then, can we see Leonard's mother?"

"Yes. One of the boys has volunteered to take us to her, although our arrangement is for him to walk a good distance in front of us and leave a trail of broken branches."

Fifteen minutes later, the group arrived at Consolaté's home, a conical thatch hut, a *rugo*, similar to those Jim had seen in other regions. Outside the hut, a wood and peat fire burned below a large kettle. As the group approached the open fire, Consolaté drew back the curtain that served as entryway to her home.

When she saw that the group did not include her son, she panicked, recalling another visit when she had been informed by a company of warriors that her husband and two of her sons had been killed. The memory was wrenchingly painful, and she eyed these visitors warily.

Taking note of her anxiety, Mathias said gently, "Do not worry. Leonard is fine. We were not sure if bringing him here would be safe, so we left him behind in Bujumbura with the ambassador—the American queen."

Consolaté closed her eyes and nodded. "I am so glad you came," she said. "Please . . . please come in."

Amid the haste and intensity of their previous conversation, Jim had not taken much note of Consolaté's physical characteristics. That all changed today.

He remembered seeing the scars on her chin and cheekbone, but now he was struck by her astonishing beauty. An azure blue scarf framed her high cheekbones, dark eyes, and full lips—features similar to those of her son. Not surprisingly, she was very tall, about six feet. Dressed in a *pagnes* of blue and yellow vertical stripes that accentuated the soft curve of her firm breasts and slender waist, Consolaté was simply captivating.

As the group passed by the open curtain, Jim was immediately impressed with the hut's neatness. There was a wooden table, two wooden chairs, two straw beds—one much longer than the other—and a hutch for dry foods, such as cornmeal and flour. The hard-packed dirt floor was covered by mats and a goat skin. Most striking were the beautiful watercolor portraits of four males, one of whom Jim easily recognized, the other three he assumed, correctly, to be her dead husband and sons.

Jim posed a question: "May I ask who painted these?"

"I did," Consolaté replied modestly.

"They are beautiful—just beautiful," said the coach, moved in particular by the lifelike portrait of Leonard.

"I am sorry that I cannot offer all of you a chair." As she spoke, Consolaté carefully laid a large, handmade red and blue patchwork quilt over the mats on the floor.

When she began to ease down onto the quilt, Mathias insisted that Consolaté take one of the chairs. Jim suggested Mathias take the other chair "because you need to translate."

Once the group was seated, Consolaté looked at Jim, and then at Mathias, and asked, "How is my son?"

"Your son is just fine, but there is more—and it is good. You see, ma'am, your Leonard has been blessed with extraordinary gifts. I have worked with basketball players for nearly fifty years. Over this time, I have seen all the great players in this game."

From his Indian-style seated position, Jim paused for a moment, then leaned forward, ready to emphasize the full import of his message.

"While it is still too early to tell exactly how much Leonard will achieve in basketball, I can tell you today that, in my opinion, he will be among the greatest players ever. He has that much potential."

Having no idea of the implications of Jim's statement, Consolaté asked, "What will this mean for my son?"

"What it means, ma'am, is that your son will become very famous—and very rich."

Realizing that Consolaté might not have any concept of wealth, Jim added, "He will have a great deal of money to buy himself—and you—whatever you both want."

"Will he live in Bujumbura?"

"No. For Leonard to achieve the fame and wealth I speak of, he will have to move to another country—likely America."

"And when would this move occur?"

"Not right away." Jim paused. "Probably in a year or two."

Consolaté realized that the information the white man had just delivered was good. But it was also overwhelming, and she needed several moments to process the facts. Not yet ready to delve further into the subject, she changed the course of the discussion.

"It is best that you did not bring Leonard here today," she said.

"We heard this," responded Mathias. "But tell us more. Will his life be in danger? And you—are you in danger?"

Consolaté looked down at the quilt for a long moment. "I am in no more danger than any other woman in Kayanza. And they could kill him, yes. But more likely, they would simply force him to join the army, as they will force his other young friends to. So you must, at least for now, keep Leonard away."

"And you—what about you?" Mathias asked again. "Your son wants to see you very much."

"And I want to see him very much. But not here, not now, anyway. If the war ends—or even if there is a truce that we have heard about—then Leonard can come home. But not now."

"Well, then, would you like to come to Bujumbura?" asked Bill Foster.

"Because I want to see my son so much, at some point I will come to Bujumbura. But not just yet."

Jim momentarily thought it odd that Consolaté would not simply pack up and go off with the group. But he recalled the words of Mathias on the matter: "In the Tutsi culture, it is the widow's duty to stay near the graves of her dead. The length of this period of mourning is usually about a year."

Sensitive to this unusual tradition, Mathias said to Consolaté, "Leonard misses you as much as I know you miss him. If there is a truce, or if the fighting continues to remain over the border and away from here, these Marines will bring him here to see you. I know that he would like that very much."

"As would I," said Consolaté. "But the militia, the machetes, are everywhere."

Looking straight into Jim eyes, she asked one more question.

"This fame and money that my son will soon have—will it be good for him?"

At first, Jim was startled by the question. But after a moment, he said, "What you ask is important. Let me try to answer it as best I can."

He cleared his throat. "As you know, ma'am, we all have to face change in our lives. In Leonard's case, the fame and fortune he will soon encounter will be a powerful force. As this force confronts him, it will be up to all of us to help guide him through the challenges. Many good people have fallen prey to the evil side of wealth and fame. There is a saying we use in America: 'Be careful not to get discovered too early.' This relates to the problems that early fame can bring. But we will all act as Leonard's guardians to ensure that this discovery is incremental . . . that it does not happen all at once."

Jim looked at Mathias, who was about to begin to translate Jim's words. The old man had folded his arms across his chest, pursed his lips and furrowed his brow. Leaning toward Consolaté, he slowly and kindly translated Jim's explanation.

Consolaté nodded, and Jim continued.

"Leonard is a special person, and you have grounded him well in good habits. As I said, I'm sure that there will be some challenging times, as there are for all human beings. But in answer to your question: Overall, the wealth and fame will be good for your son. And because he is such a fine person, I am certain that he will use his position to help others."

"Thank you, sir. You have made me feel very settled," said Consolaté.

Mathias smiled as he translated. "'Settled' is a good word, Coach Keating. It covers much. You have done well."

After the men left, Consolaté slumped in her chair. She had just listened to news that would dramatically alter the course of her son's life. In an hour's time, she would officially learn more news. In that case, the news concerned her own fate, delivered by the Red Cross volunteer who had taken samples of her blood.

IV
The Game

33

Project Oscar was only one of several initiatives Cynthia Foster had conceived to "get the Hutus and Tutsis talking." Her skilled diplomacy not only drew praise from as far away as the White House, but also began to attract the notice of the media.

Finbar Finnegan was a CNN correspondent assigned to cover the Hutu–Tutsi conflict in Rwanda and Burundi. Finnegan had grown up in Athy, Ireland, a small town in County Kildare forty miles west of Dublin. A brilliant student, he had been awarded a full scholarship to Trinity College, where he graduated with honors as a double major in English literature and international relations.

Upon graduation, Finnegan took a job as a fact-checker in the *International Herald Tribune* London office. Three promotions later, at only twenty-seven years old, he found himself the youngest senior correspondent on the *Tribune* staff. His assignment was to cover the on again–off again peace talks in Northern Ireland. While in Belfast, he befriended Sandra Boland, a CNN correspondent.

Finnegan was a solid reporter, and he was disarmingly handsome. At 6'3", he had a chiseled frame, which resulted from the weight training he'd undertaken to tone his body for successful participation in Irish basketball. His brown, curly hair rested atop a face of well-favored harmony. Most striking of his facial characteristics were his deep blue eyes; "Paul Newman-like" was a common observation among women.

"Finbar," said Sandra one morning over breakfast in the Europa Hotel located in downtown Belfast. "Have you ever thought about working on the telly?"

At forty-nine and twice divorced, Sandra Boland knew that a romantic relationship with someone as young and attractive as Finbar was unrealistic. But beyond his charm and roguish good looks, she saw a young man with the eloquence and grit to go far in her field. Like most others in TV journalism, she looked upon those on the small screen as "the elect," and she felt that Finbar was worthy of such a "promotion" from what she perceived to be the mundane world of newspaper reporting.

Finnegan had always been fascinated with television journalism, and he made no attempt to hide his interest.

"I'd say I've more than thought about it, Sandra."

"Well, we have an opening in our African division. I can arrange for an audition if you'd like."

Two weeks to the day of their Belfast breakfast, Finnegan flew to London. An hour after his audition, Sandra Boland received a call from Eleanor Pardy, the CNN producer who conducted the try-out.

"He was brilliant—absolutely brilliant. It's as if he and the camera were old friends. Before he came in, I checked with the *Herald Tribune* bureau chief. While he was a bit annoyed that Finbar was thinking of moving over to our side, he told me that his journalistic skills are as impressive as his gorgeous face. Well, he didn't say gorgeous—that's me talking," Pardy said, excitement in her voice. "I'm going to hire him, Sandra. Send him to our Johannesburg office."

After just two months in South Africa covering the affairs of Nelson Mandela and State President Frederik Willem de Klerk, Finnegan was transferred to Bujumbura to cover the heightened violence in the region. Within days of his arrival, he could see that Cynthia Foster was playing a major role in the peace initiative.

"More so than most ambassadors," he was told by a high-level Burundian official.

Finnegan was fascinated with The Regal One, as she was referred to by the official.

Having read up on the plight of minorities in America, Finbar found it remarkable that an African American—*who was also a woman*—could have advanced to such a position in the staid, male-dominated world of American diplomacy. He found it equally notable that leaders from both the Tutsi and the Hutu sides held her in such high regard.

Finnegan decided to explore the possibility of a piece on the work of Cynthia Foster for CNN Worldwide News. He arranged a preliminary meeting with Jesse Abbot, who handled all media inquiries.

At the US Embassy security gate, Finnegan saw one of the guards wearing a t-shirt that featured the words *Project Oscar* and a likeness of one of his favorite basketball players, Oscar Robertson, holding a basketball. Guessing Ambassador Foster had something to do with the t-shirt, Finbar decided to raise the issue with Abbot, which he did the moment the two sat down in Abbot's office.

"What's this Project Oscar?"

Abbot knew that it would be unwise to withhold information. "Okay, on this one—for now at least—we're off the record."

"Hmmm, sounds even more interesting," said Finnegan with a wide grin. "Okay, we're off the record."

When Abbot finished a brief description, Finnegan exclaimed, "Using sport to bridge the divide . . . and naming it for The Big O . . . what a grand idea!"

He continued, "When I was in Northern Ireland, there was a similar initiative called Belfast United. Brought equal numbers of Catholic and Protestant youth together on sports teams. It was quite successful in breaking down barriers."

"That's exactly what the ambassador and Jim Keating, the American coach we brought over, are trying to do here," said Abbot.

Finnegan nodded, then, with a glimmer in those striking blue eyes, leaned forward and said, "Jesse, I played a bit of baskets myself back in Ireland. Don't mind tellin' ya I was more than a fair baller . . . made the Irish National Team, in fact. . . . Tell me something. Do you think this Coach Keating would mind if I worked out with the team some night? Might help me to develop the story angle better. Plus, I'd die for the odd run—and sweat."

Jesse was still hesitant to match the Irishman's enthusiasm. He came on a little strong, but he had to admit Finnegan's idea had merit. The diplomat rose from his chair, walked around his uncluttered desk, opened a closet door, retrieved a Project Oscar t-shirt from the upper shelf, and tossed it to Finnegan.

"Let me find out," Abbot replied evenly. "In the meantime, add this Project Oscar t-shirt to your wardrobe. Ambassador Foster got a friend from the States to send over a hundred for free."

Next morning, Abbot called Finnegan. "The team is practicing tonight. Our American coach, Jim Keating, the one I told you about yesterday, said you're welcome to join in on one condition."

"What's that?"

"No story yet," said Jesse.

Finnegan asked, "Why so secretive?" His curiosity was now thoroughly piqued.

"You'll see tonight," said Abbot.

———

As a follower of the European basketball circuit, Finbar Finnegan vaguely recalled reading about Jim Keating's stint in Spain, including the favorable publicity Jim received when he was terminated. Finnegan's conversation with Jesse Abbot filled in some gaps and increased the reporter's curiosity about the coach. Finally, a call to his bureau in South Africa produced a twenty-page fax full of clips on Jim's dismissal at New Jersey State.

As the reporter headed off to the Nimbona Court for a workout with the National Team, he was looking forward to meeting Jim.

"Coach, I'm Finbar Finnegan," he said upon arrival at the court, his right hand extended. "Sure it's okay for me to work-out with the lads?"

"Long as you take it easy on 'em, Finbar," said Jim, amused at Finnegan's kelly-green Irish National Team uniform and black high-cut Converse sneakers. "By the way, last time I saw those Chuck Taylor high-cuts, Bob Cousy was wearin' 'em."

Finnegan was surprised with Jim's easy and humorous demeanor, but he enjoyed the ribbing and took an immediate liking to the coach.

"Back in style, Coach," said Finnegan. "Though only for a select few—all of us pre-approved by the Cooz!"

Jim chuckled and then said, "We're about to start, so let me introduce you to the team."

After quick introductions and cordial greetings by the players and coaching staff, Finnegan joined the lay-up line. He was immediately impressed with Jim's use of the line to teach such fundamentals as back-door cuts and pick and

roll. He also took note of a young giant with muscle definition unusual for a Tutsi in Burundi. Finnegan was struck,
too, by the young man's complete attention to his coach's
instructions.

"Okay, let's do some three-on-three, one dribble only,
so you're working on passing and movement away from the
ball," hollered Jim. "Coaches, you make up the teams. Winners
out, first team to score three hoops wins. Then, another team
comes out to play the winners. Remember: one dribble!"

Jim's assistants knew to move quickly on the head coach's
command. Within in a couple of minutes, the three-on-
three teams were set, and Jim reminded the players, "When
you pass, you must screen away. Don't go behind the guy
you passed to. We're lookin' for back-door cuts; good, hard
screens away from the ball; and good, crisp passes. The one-
dribble rule will help this!"

Though a bit rusty, Finnegan had extensive experience in
basketball and was a fundamentally sound player. He easily
picked up on Jim's call for back-door cuts, scoring two quick
lay-ups off bounce passes from a Hutu guard named Dama
Ndikuriyo. Moments later, when Finnegan hit a short jumper
to bring his team the win, Bill Foster chortled, "Hey, we got
a ringer."

Leonard Tangishaka's team took the court to play Finnegan's
group of three. Once again, Finnegan broke free on a back-door
cut, received a pass, and elevated toward the hoop. But this time
Leonard was waiting. The youngster vaulted, his right arm
extending to just below the top of the backboard. Following
Jim's instruction about how Bill Russell would not only block
a shot, but keep it in play, Leonard directed the ball straight
into the waiting hands of a teammate. Once in possession of
the ball, Leonard's team went on to score three easy hoops. The
last bucket was made by Leonard, who, off a switch, posted up
Finnegan and lofted a soft jumper off the backboard and down
through the net.

"Okay, shell drill on defense. Let's focus on weak-side help," shouted Jim.

The twenty-minute shell drill was followed by work on rebounding and ball handling, after which Jim said, "Now, we'll go five-on-five full court for about twenty minutes. Play straight man-to-man on D. On offense, we'll use the passing game, and let's get more ball movement today."

Jim assigned Finnegan to Leonard's team. During the scrimmage, the reporter gained an even greater appreciation of the boy's potential.

Leonard controlled the action at both ends of the court, scoring at will, blocking shot after shot, and running the floor with remarkable speed. So superior was his play that Finnegan found himself joining the others in what was becoming an almost standard routine at practice: stopping to applaud when Leonard would perform an amazing feat.

Ten minutes into the scrimmage, Jim gave Finnegan a much-needed rest.

"Too much Guinness, Finbar?" the coach cracked.

Finbar laughed and trotted over to Jim. Bending over and out of breath, he said, "Coach, I played on the Irish National Team that went to the States a few years back. We got trounced by some top-flight D-I teams with some great pivot men. Two of them are still in the pros. This young kid may have some rough edges—not many, mind you—but he has the potential to be far superior than any of the blokes I played against." Finnegan smiled, shook his head, and walked toward the bleachers.

When practice was over, Finnegan again approached Jim. "Coach, back to the big lad . . . amazing. Could I ask you about him?"

"Let's go back over to the stands," said Jim.

Jim was intent on protecting Leonard's basketball education, and, at this early stage, the coach was wary of any publicity.

"Finbar, as you just saw, this young man has a brilliant future in the game. But there are issues—not only relating to his own need to take this learning process one step at a time—but also important to his mother's safety. So, are you okay that we stay completely off the record?"

"If that's what all of you want, Coach, then yes," said Finnegan. "But from what I've just observed, it won't be a secret for long. Can we agree that when the time is right, you'll give me first shot at the story?"

"I'm not sure I can promise that because I don't know the US Embassy's position on these matters," said Jim.

Standing a few feet away, Bill Foster overheard the conversation. "Gentlemen, I don't mean to be eavesdropping, but Finbar, I think Cynthia and Jesse will be receptive to you breaking the story—as long as we agree on the timing."

"Sounds good," said Finnegan, pulling out his notebook and pen. "Now . . . you know, Coach, even someone from Athy, Ireland, can spot a hoops prodigy. How old is he?"

"He just turned fifteen," said Jim. Bill nodded, concurring.

"Well, along with that trip to the States, I played against most of the European National Teams. Never have gone against a player who could touch this kid," said Finnegan.

"Don't doubt it," said Jim.

"Next question: How long has the kid been playing the game?"

"About eight weeks," replied the coach.

Finnegan gasped. "Eight weeks? Impossible! How could he have gotten so good in eight weeks?"

Before Jim could answer, Bill pointed at Jim and said, "You are looking at one of the biggest reasons."

Jim shook his head slightly and changed the subject back to Leonard.

"Finbar, let me break it down for you. First the obvious—Leonard has great size; huge, soft hands and great natural strength. But five other physical qualities would place him at the very top of anyone who ever picked up the game. There are also some special intangibles."

He continued, "On the physical side, the five are remarkable hand-eye coordination, an equally remarkable vertical leap, tremendous quickness, lightning straightaway speed, and uncanny footwork—from playing soccer."

"And the intangibles?" asked Finbar.

"What you just observed. He's a team player who's a sponge for learning and knows nothing less than 100 percent," said Jim.

"In other words," said Finnegan, "the perfect basketball machine."

"Well said," responded Foster.

"So, gentlemen, how good will Leonard Tangishaka be?"

Jim paused for a moment and then said, "Again, off the record, I've been around basketball for fifty-plus years, and I've never seen any player, college or professional, who is this kid's equal in terms of potential."

"Bill?" asked Finnegan.

"Same view, Finbar."

"Well," said Finnegan, "What about the timing? What would make the two of you—and Ambassador Foster—comfortable with me doing a piece on CNN?"

"More time," said Jim. "We need to bring Leonard along slowly—and protect his mother. Still off the record, we have concerns about his mother's safety that we'll get into with you later."

Pausing yet again, the coach carefully considered his words. "Finbar, it's not that I'm against a story at some point. It's just that this kid arrived here only several weeks ago, and I feel that he needs to acclimate himself a bit more before the world of basketball discovers him."

Finnegan's journalistic instincts were competing against what he was sure was Jim's proper concern over the young giant's maturation process. The reporter went straight to the point.

"Coach and Bill, I appreciate everything that's been said. But I have a job to do, and Project Oscar is a fascinating story that should be told. So, Bill, if you would clear it with Ambassador Foster, I'd like permission to begin the process of planning the story. Per Jim's point, the timing would be subject to the approval of both of you and the ambassador."

"Sounds reasonable," said Foster, and Jim nodded.

As the conversation concluded, Jim knew he needed to reflect on his own motives for keeping a lid on Leonard's public introduction. The coach wanted to make sure that the reasons were not selfish.

34

An early-morning knock woke Jim from a deep sleep. As soon as he opened the door, a smiling, excited Jesse Abbot grabbed Jim's arm.

"The ambassador just called me. Got to her office early— as always. Awaiting her arrival was a fax from Washington. We've got the go-ahead for a game against Rwanda!"

The news yanked Jim from his drowsiness. "Great! When will it happen?"

"Well, the next step is a call with my American counter- part in Rwanda. Mark Newlen, our ambassador to Rwanda, has already talked to the Rwandan basketball people and they're agreeable. So the call is simply to sort out the date, who'll ref, things like that," said Abbot.

"What about the site?" asked Jim.

"You know the ambassador," said Abbot. "She told Ambassador Newlen that since it was her idea, she wanted the game played here."

"What did he say?"

Abbot chuckled. "He knows the ambassador, too. He said yes!"

———

Jesse Abbot was well aware of the importance of nurturing good relationships with the press. This was especially true in his Burundi posting where, because of the violence, outsized media attention was focused on the small African nation.

He joined the ambassador, Bill, and Jim at breakfast. Even before "Good Morning" was out of his mouth, Jesse asked, "Now that we have approval for the game, can I inform Finbar Finnegan, including a time frame for his interview with Leonard?"

Ambassador Foster turned to Jim and asked, "What do you think, coach?"

"Well, I like Finbar, and I like the fact that he knows the game. Plus, I can tell from his comments that he sees the value of Project Oscar," he said. "You know, Madam Ambassador, Finbar feels that sports actually helped bring the Catholics and Protestants together in Northern Ireland."

The ambassador raised her eyebrows, seemingly impressed. "I did not know that."

"Yeah, he spoke about a program called Belfast United that had goals similar to what we're doing. So, he's a believer in the concept, which I think bodes well for a positive story. Plus, and correct me if I'm wrong about this, Jesse, I don't think we have much choice!"

"You're not wrong, Coach," said Abbot.

The ambassador glanced at Bill, who gave her a quick, firm nod.

"Okay, then," she said. "Jesse, go ahead and contact Mr. Finnegan. I have a feeling this is going to be a big story— make that a very big story. Let's all hope for the best."

As though on cue, they all leaned back in their chairs, except Jesse, who was already halfway to the door. He called Finnegan as soon as he got to his office. "Finbar, we've made arrangements with Rwanda for a game! It'll be played in about six weeks."

"Now there's some real news," said Finnegan. "Will this mean you'll be making Leonard available for an interview?"

"Yes, though we'd like it to be in two to three weeks so we can get him a bit more acclimated." Abbot went on to explain the grand plan of the game, concluding with, "The State Department has signed off and we're ready to move forward."

Finnegan immediately made an excited call to Johannesburg. The young reporter was not surprised that his veteran bureau chief's first response was to trivialize the idea. "Show Me Sid," as Sidney Hawkins was known among CNN field correspondents, was a world-class devil's advocate. And while his first line of response was generally as cynical as it was predictable, Finbar knew that it was Hawkins's way of forcing his reporters to flesh out a story before approaching him.

"I don't know, Finbar," said Hawkins in his cement-mixer voice, the result of inhaling too many Camels. "I'm not sure a piece on some fifteen-year-old basketball player will fly."

"But the story goes far beyond the boy," replied Finnegan, who by now had risen from his chair and was pacing about. "This is also a story about an ambassador's dream, the rebirth of a broken down coach, and the novel use—at least in this part of the world—of sport as peacemaker."

"Now Finbar, isn't that stretchin' it a bit?"

"Not at all," replied Finnegan, ready to play his trump card. "You see, as part of Project Oscar, Ambassador Foster has arranged for a game between Burundi and Rwanda."

"A basketball game?" asked Hawkins, his interest now roused.

"That's right! And the game will be the first formal inter-action between the two countries since the fighting broke out."

Hawkins knew that since the centuries-old Hutu–Tutsi animosity had recently exploded—first in Rwanda, then in Burundi—there had been a diplomatic chill between the two small nations. The chill had turned to frost bite when Hutu Rwandan President Juvenal Habyarimana's private Falcon 50 jet, which carried Burundian President Cyprien Ntaryamira, also a Hutu, was shot down in a rocket attack near Kigali International Airport in Rwanda. The offshoot was a slaugh-terous spree by extremists from the majority Hutus against rival Tutsis. Within three months, the Rwandan Genocide had taken the lives of more than 500,000 Rwandans, and the violence had spread over the border into Burundi. Since the plane crash, the grim wall of mistrust between the two countries had elevated to perilous heights.

Hawkins realized Finnegan had proposed an important story, and the bureau chief wasn't surprised. In truth, the Irishman had become his best field correspondent. "He has the nostrils of a bloody Basset," Hawkins would say, though not to Finnegan; the bureau chief did not want his young ace's head to swell in this early stage of his career.

"Am I sensing that you're looking at a twofer, Finbar?"

"I am, Sid. The initial piece will review the background of Project Oscar. I'll get the ambassador and Keating on camera—and the kid, too."

"Does the kid speak English?"

"He's learning the language and he knows enough for us to get a good answer or two out of him. But," Finnegan continued, "Leonard's major role in this first piece will be to show the world that he might someday rewrite the NBA record book. And I'll make sure that we get some shots of him doing his stuff."

"And the second piece? Some clips of the game—and the historical significance of the competition?"

"That's right."

"And what's the timing of all of this?" As he posed the question, Hawkins reached across his desk for a pack of cigarettes.

"Well, my embassy contact thinks the game will be played in about six weeks. It'll be an outdoor game, and they don't want to risk running into the rainy season, which will start in about eight weeks."

"Why will it take six weeks, then, to put the game together?" asked Hawkins, lighting up.

"First, both teams want plenty of training time. Plus, Ambassador Foster and her people really want to hype the game. With Hutus and Tutsis playing with each other on the two teams, the ambassador hopes the game can be a good first step in getting the two sides to begin talking again," he explained. "So, to answer your question, Sid, I'd like to run the first piece in about three weeks—introduce our viewers to this interesting plan by a US ambassador, to Coach Keating, and to Leonard Tangishaka. Then we'll go with the second piece on game night."

"How can an Irishman be so damned sure this kid is so good? I mean, what if he chokes up in the game?" barked Hawkins, his final protest.

"I scrimmaged with the team, Sid. Trust me. The first piece will send a buzz through the basketball world, if not the diplomatic community. As for the game, he'll dominate. Wait and see!"

Hawkins inhaled and then let a few more seconds go by. He didn't want Finnegan to follow the lead of some other correspondents who were often—too often, he felt—motivated by a scoop mentality. But Finbar had him hooked.

"Well . . . all right . . . sounds like it has legs. We'll go with it," said Hawkins, satisfied that Project Oscar was a major story, but unwilling to share his view with his cub reporter.

Finnegan smiled as he hung up the phone and spoke to himself in his native tongue. *Did I actually detect a wee note of enthusiasm?*

———

After getting the go-ahead from Sid Hawkins, Finnegan called Abbot.

"I've got the okay for two pieces. The first will focus on Project Oscar, and my boss wants it to run in about three weeks. We'll start with the ambassador explaining her vision of Project Oscar and the game against Rwanda, then we pick it up with Coach Keating, who'll lead us into an interview with Leonard, where we cut back and forth between him and clips of his scrimmages," he explained.

"And the second piece?" asked Abbot.

"About the game itself, and it will air within twenty-four hours after the final buzzer. So, for the first piece, we'd like to film a practice. We'd start at seven sharp on a Wednesday— three weeks from today—with an interview with the ambassador. The piece will then run the next night. Would that work for her schedule?"

"No problem," replied Abbot, well aware of what a piece on *The World* could do for his boss's career, and pleased the ambassador would not have to be late for her 8:00 PM poetry session.

———

Three weeks later, Finnegan—wearing his Project Oscar t-shirt—and his crew arrived early at the Nimbona Court. Twenty minutes before the start of the workout, they were fully set up.

"Remember our deal, Finbar," Jim said upon spotting the correspondent.

The deal involved the crew filming the entire practice so Jim could use it as a teaching tool, especially with Leonard, who had never seen himself play on video.

"You got it, Coach!"

By 6:50 PM, all the players had arrived, and a buzz ran through the court over the presence of the CNN camera crew. At 7:00 sharp, with the players moving through the lay-up line in the background, Finnegan interviewed Cynthia Foster. The ambassador eloquently addressed the "chipping effect" that Project Oscar would hopefully have on the violence.

Jim was next. Finnegan began his series of questions by asking, "What's it like for a sixty-something American coach to 're-up' in Burundi?"

"Great! I feel like I'm in my first job again."

With the camera focused on Leonard Tangishaka, Finnegan asked Jim, "How did you find this young man?"

In detail that Finnegan knew must be edited, Jim reviewed the process: the suggestion of Mathias to travel to Kayanza, the first sighting of Leonard, and the wondrous first session on the makeshift soccer field. When the coach concluded, Finnegan popped the important question, "How good is he?"

In analyzing young stars, most coaches follow a time-honored practice of temperance—using rote clichés to avoid heaping too much praise on a player of promise. Jim employed one such favorite: "Well, with a lot of hard work, Leonard has a chance to be a good one."

Finnegan smiled at Jim's non-answer. After this failed attempt to draw a candid opinion from the coach, Finbar decided to let the camera tell the story. The crew filmed Leonard's every move, and the boy unwittingly cooperated, demonstrating extraordinary athletic prowess and skills that were remarkably refined. In the twenty-minute scrimmage that wrapped up the practice, Leonard, as usual, dominated both ends of the court, hitting jumper after soft jumper, blocking shots with abandon, and showing remarkable speed—mastery that the camera easily embraced.

When the scrimmage was over, Finnegan joked to Jim, "Coach, even to a casual fan, I'd say that Leonard's 'chance to be a good one' is a bettin' man's wage!"

Finnegan wrapped up the filming by interviewing Leonard. In a pre-rehearsed question-and-answer session, the reporter asked, "What do you hope to be doing in five years?"

"To play in the NBA," responded the youngster, smiling broadly.

When the shoot was done, Finnegan and his crew returned to the CNN office, a two-room storefront adjacent to the Novotel Bujumbura. For the next three hours, the group edited the footage down to a slick four and a half-minute piece. Finnegan's diverse knowledge of basketball streamlined the editing process and made for a tight, especially engaging story that expertly captured the mission of Project Oscar, the eloquence of Cynthia Foster, the avuncular wisdom of Jim Keating, and the vast potential of Leonard Tangishaka.

Twenty-four hours later, the piece aired on *The World*. Forty-eight million people in 110 countries watched the clip, and Finnegan's earlier prediction to Sid Hawkins proved accurate.

The diplomatic community was interested in the project; the international basketball community was abuzz over one Leonard Tangishaka.

35

Jesse Abbot was short of breath as he slowed from a sprint to a walk alongside Cynthia Foster. He had important information to share.

"Well, Ambassador," he gasped, "the good news is that since the piece ran last night, millions of people know about Project Oscar. The bad news is that the group includes every NBA, European, and college basketball scout on this planet. And they all want to visit Burundi!"

Even Ambassador Foster, wise to the power of the media, was caught off guard by the reaction of the CNN report—especially from the international basketball community.

"We've only been open for three hours, and we've already had sixty-one calls and another forty-six faxes from basketball people wanting to come here," continued Abbot. "And most of them want to speak with Jim."

The phone lines were constantly busy, so Jim had not yet spoken with anyone at the Embassy and wasn't aware of the reaction. However, unlike Ambassador Foster, Jim had expected the flood of responses. He had watched the piece in Abbot's living room the night before. Finnegan and his crew had done an excellent job portraying Leonard Tangishaka's enormous potential. So much so that the coach was worried.

"I know about recruiting, Jesse," he had said after watching the clip. "Believe me, some people will try anything to get this kid."

"Colleges?" asked Abbot.

"Colleges, the European league, Israel—you name it. If this thing just aired throughout the world, you can bet we're going to be presented with some potent challenges in protecting Leonard's interests."

As Jim knew so well, the intense recruiting of a young star often robbed the prospect of many of the enjoyable experiences of growing up. Recruiters would dangle every form of bait before the player's eyes—money, sex, cars, even jobs for family members. And for a once-in-a-generation player like Leonard Tangishaka—an athlete whose skills could mean millions to a college or professional team—the inducements could descend on him like an avalanche. As a result, the courtship of a young prodigy often produced an abrupt transformation from innocence to arrogance.

Yet as Jim considered ways to protect Leonard from the swarm of vultures that would soon circle, he also continued to wonder if his wariness was tied to self-interest. In their lust to recruit Leonard for their team, recruiters would tell him that he would be better off leaving Burundi right away— for America . . . or Italy . . . or Israel . . . wherever—to learn the game in "more suitable conditions." And while Jim knew that such a move would be necessary at some point, he was also convinced it was premature. By the time Leonard left Burundi, Jim wanted him to know all the fundamentals of the game, and he wanted him to learn them in an environment that would protect his youth and his innocence. Despite occasional pangs of conscience, the coach also wanted to be the person to teach those fundamentals. For Jim Keating knew that no one—not anyone—could do it better.

As he considered these issues, a startling realization suddenly came over him. The depression that had so engulfed his life was gone—banished by his purposeful work and the presence of Leonard Tangishaka.

The realization was interrupted when his phone rang.

"Jim," said Jesse Abbot. "The reaction has been unbelievable. The ambassador would like to meet with you."

———

By the time Jim arrived, the Embassy had logged in nineteen more inquiries about Leonard Tangishaka. Jim took a seat across from the ambassador in her office, a setting he had become familiar with over the last few months.

"They all want to speak with you, Jim, and some even asked to speak directly with Leonard," said Ambassador Foster. "I guess my first question is—do you want to speak with them?"

Cynthia posed the question half jokingly, but Jim was dead serious in his response.

"Frankly, Ambassador, I don't want to speak with them. It's because I know what some of these people will do to entice Leonard to join their teams. I'm not saying that everyone in the business is bad, but some, if not many, are. And Leonard's still developing—not only as a player but also as a person. I'm convinced that exposing him to the craziness of recruiting will be harmful. And I'm sure a number of questionable characters are among the callers."

Leaning forward, the coach continued, "What we all have to understand is that Leonard is *so* good that some guys will do just about anything to get him."

The ambassador paused for a moment. "So you feel that letting these recruiters come to Burundi would not be in Leonard's best interests?"

"That's exactly how I feel."

Cynthia Foster was not unwilling to employ the power of her position. She was also passionately interested in the well-being of Leonard Tangishaka. After reflecting for a moment, she said to Jim, "There's not much I can do about the media entering Burundi. But I sense you're not as concerned about the media."

"No, not really," Jim confirmed. "The mistake would be to let the recruiters come in."

The ambassador turned her attention to Jesse Abbot, seated next to Jim. "Jesse, call Paul Corcoran at State. Tell him that for the next two months we are restricting American visas to Burundi to the media and diplomatic missions only."

"And if he asks why?" said Abbot.

"Tell him security concerns—he'll be fine with that." She turned back to Jim. "Jim, I would imagine that pro teams from places like Spain, Italy, Israel, or Australia would be interested in Leonard as well."

He nodded. "Without a doubt."

"Okay . . . Jesse, you and Coach work up a list of countries and let's see if our diplomatic friends will follow suit on this restriction." She paused. "Jim, it's possible that some of these recruiters with political clout, from the United States and other countries, might be able to get around this restriction. But for the most part, we'll keep the predators away—at least for the time being. This will allow you to coach the young man and get the team ready for Rwanda."

Once again, Jim was struck by Cynthia Foster's resolve.

———

Few people in Burundi had television sets; most who did had watched the CNN report about Project Oscar. The day after the report aired, the *Bujumbura Gazette* ran a front-page story with the headline, "Burundian Basketball Gains World

Attention." The sub-head declared "Fifteen-year-old Leonard Tangishaka is a future star."

A Reuter's story that ran throughout Africa confirmed that the CNN piece was seen in 110 countries. Minister of Sport, Claude Ntahombaye, was quoted in the article as saying, "At last the world has seen Burundi in a favorable light. Leonard Tangishaka could become an invaluable resource for our nation."

The media buzz made the upcoming basketball game against Rwanda a lively topic of conversation among Burundians. Not only was basketball now a close second to soccer in popularity, but the Rwanda game also had implications far beyond the Nimbona Court.

The level of interest in the game became tangible. More than five hundred spectators turned up at the first practice after the CNN report to watch the wunderkind, the nickname that had now spread far beyond the team. The hubbub stirred Jim Keating's coaching instincts.

"You know," he said to Bill Foster as the two stood at center court. "I'm happy with all the people showing up. But this commotion will make it tough to get the team ready for Rwanda. We may need to think about closing the practices."

As Bill surveyed the swelling crowd of both Hutus and Tutsis, he responded. "True. . . . But, on the other hand, Jim, we're seeing the fruits of Project Oscar come to bear tonight. Think about a plan that'll get us some privacy but also foster this kind of mingling of the tribes."

Jim was embarrassed that he had not considered the big picture. "You're right, but there's still one element of the crowd that concerns me."

Jim jerked his head toward the pack of young ladies whose eyes were trained on Leonard Tangishaka. While Leonard seemed nearly oblivious of his appeal to the opposite sex, the coach decided to approach Mathias after practice and raise his concerns.

"You know, Mathias," he started, "in our country, the birds and the bees talk, as we call it, is the talk a father or a mother gives a son about sexual activity—and generally not very well. Because Leonard lost his dad at such a young age, it struck me that he may never have had such a talk. And with all the attention he's getting from young ladies, and with the AIDS virus so common, well . . . "

Before he could finish his thought, Mathias said calmly, "Jim, in Burundi we also call it the birds and the bees talk. And you can relax because I have already given it to Leonard. I think he understands the dangers of sexual intercourse, but even so, I plan to monitor his activities very closely. What is good is that he is a very obedient boy who desperately wants to please his mother—and all of us."

While Jim had great faith in Mathias, he was determined to watch the situation with a father's care. Regarding spectator interest in the team's practice sessions, Jim had made a decision that he related to Foster.

"We need more time together," he told Bill as they left the court together later that night. "So, as a result of our conversation, my thought is to work out five times a week instead of three. We'll close three practices to the public. That'll give us the privacy we need—plus hopefully satisfy the public's interest in us."

"Sounds like a plan. I'll work with Cynthia and Jesse to make it happen."

Through his wife, Foster arranged for the Bujumbura Garda to cordon off the area for the three closed practices. Abbot had the *Bujumbura Gazette* run a story which, in making note of the importance of the game, implored basketball fans to "respect Coach Keating's desire for three nights of closed practice."

Jim was pleasantly surprised when the public actually cooperated.

As for his concern about recruiters invading the life of Leonard Tangishaka, Ambassador Foster prepared to relate good news as the two, once again, sat across from each other in her office. When Jesse joined them a moment later, he sat to Jim's left, unbuttoning his suit jacket as he took his seat.

"Jim, not only is the United States limiting visas to government officials, medical personnel, and the media, but Canada, all of Europe, Australia, and Israel have agreed to do the same. Unfortunately, other nations will be able to send recruiters, but at least we have the cooperation of most of the key countries," she told him.

She added, "We're getting a number of media requests, though, especially for interviews with you and Leonard. *Sports Illustrated* is sending a reporter. So is *The New York Times* and several of the large European newspapers. How do you want to handle those requests?"

Jim clasped his hands behind his head and nodded slowly. Just before he began to answer, Abbot, the media expert, spoke up. "Jim, can I make a suggestion?"

Jim nodded, and Jesse went on to suggest they set an afternoon aside a day or two before the game for a single general session followed by thirty-minute one-on-ones with *Sports Illustrated* and *The Times*. From the looks on their faces, Jesse could tell that both the ambassador and the coach approved of the idea.

"The whole plan sounds fine to me, Jesse," Jim said. The ambassador nodded in agreement.

"Then I'll arrange it—and you can focus on getting the team ready."

"That sounds even better," said the coach.

———

As Jesse and Jim arrived home, Josiane greeted them at the front door. She bore a smile flushed with joy, and there was an energy in her twinkling eyes as she spoke.

"Mr. Coach, the Embassy just tried to patch a call through to you from your daughter in America. She saw the report on

American television and she is thrilled—and very eager to talk with you. I believe she will be calling the Embassy back any minute, and they will be patching the call through to your apartment."

"Thank you, Josiane," said Jim, as he moved quickly toward the door. Moments later, he heard his favorite voice come through in a surprisingly clear connection.

"Daddy, oh my God, this is so incredible," Sarah gushed.

"It is incredible, and I'm so happy to hear from you. You know, I tried to call you earlier but couldn't get through to the overseas operator. We're being inundated with calls about the CNN piece."

"I don't doubt it, Daddy. In fact, I've gotten a bunch of calls here and . . . I mean, Leonard—he looks so great. On our last call, I sort of got that impression, but wasn't sure. Is he that good?"

"Sarah, he's even better! And you're right, I didn't want to say too much on our last call. I wanted to be sure myself. But now I'm sure."

"You know, Daddy, it's so strange . . . but somehow . . . well . . . I knew something great like this was going to happen in Burundi."

Since less than one percent of the population in Burundi had phones, the country's telecommunications system resembled what Jim recalled in his youth in America. And during the current strife, all overseas calls, except those that were official government business, were limited to five minutes.

Mindful of the time constraints, father and daughter quickly and lovingly caught up on details of each other's lives. Jim then said, "This call . . . hearing your voice . . . you know, it means so much to me."

"Me too, Daddy."

When the two hung up, Jim looked at a note from a US Embassy staffer who had done him a favor.

"Coach, I checked out your request about the distance between Bujumbura and Rochester, New York, where your daughter lives. It's approximately 7,114 miles."

A long way, thought Jim. Yet he had never felt closer to Sarah Jane Keating.

36

Spared the burden of dealing with recruiters, Jim devoted his full attention to preparing for the Rwanda game. With three weeks to get ready, his first job was to cut the team down to twelve players, never an easy task—and one certain to hurt feelings. But an idea by Bill Foster eased the difficulty.

"We've got thirty-six guys regularly showing up for practice at the various courts. If you keep twelve for the Rwanda game, we could split the remaining twenty-four into two teams—play a prelim before the big game."

"Great thought," said Jim, "But how do you think the players who don't make the big squad will react—especially the older ones?"

"They'll be disappointed, Jim, but they believe in you and they believe in Project Oscar. As you've said to all of them, their role in the future can be as coaches—working with younger players. So, even though some will be disappointed, I'll bet they'll all remain in the program—play the prelim and stay with Oscar in the future—as players and, in many cases, as youth coaches."

"I know my top twelve right now, and I'd like to meet with each guy we cut," said Jim. "Tell each guy about the preliminary game, and let 'em all know that we want 'em to stick with Project Oscar."

"Well," said Foster, "We've got a day and a half before the next practice. I'm sure we can find all of them before then, but it's going to mean a lot of time in the jeep."

"True. But as you said, Bill, all of the players who are cut will be let down. This way, we can show we care about 'em and that we really want 'em to be part of the program."

Often jolted and bounced over rutted, rocky roads, Jim and Bill, along with Rush, Roberts, Déo, and Gilbert, found every player who was to be cut. And while all expressed varying degrees of disappointment (two even broke into tears), each man recognized the special effort Jim had made to bear the bad news. Many were quite moved when their coach related his own disappointment at being cut by the Pistons decades earlier and by his message that such disappointment can often produce new and meaningful opportunities.

"I bet I wouldn't be here today if I had made the NBA as a player. And if that had been the case, I would have missed out on a wonderful experience, including getting to know you."

Jim was gratified when Gilbert would often translate a genuine, "and I would have missed knowing you, Coach."

In explaining the preliminary game idea to each player, Jim said, "One team will be called the Celtics and be coached by Déo. The other team will be called the Bulls and be coached by Gilbert."

Jim ended each session with an upbeat message: "We'll have special practices for both teams. Plus, the Celtics and Bulls will be able to work out against the National Team on a pretty regular basis."

All twenty-four players committed to remain in Project Oscar, and Jim vowed he would attend every practice of the two newly formed teams.

———

"We've got size and speed," Jim said to Déo and Gilbert at a strategy session at his apartment. "So we'll fast break at every opportunity and run the passing game when nothing shows up on the break. If Rwanda zones us, we'll attack the seams in the zone. And in both our man-to-man and zone offenses, we'll get the ball to Leonard down low."

"How about on defense?" asked Déo.

"We'll pressure full court but we'll change up—sometimes straight man-to-man pressure, sometimes zone pressure. In Spain, I found that most of our opponents weren't used to changing defenses. It confused them and often allowed us to dictate the tempo of the game. I'm betting that the same will be true against Rwanda."

Jim paused while the other men scribbled down quick notes. Then he revealed another strategic decision—a real thunderbolt.

"I'm not going to start Leonard," he said. Two heads turned his way, concern or confusion on the assistants' faces. Jim smiled and said, "Not to worry, guys. You see, instead, I'll bring him in at the seventeen-minute mark of the first half. For those first three minutes of the game, I want the two of you to sit next to him and help him relax and observe what's going on. And by the way, there's a bit of history to this strategy."

Jim's two assistants enjoyed hearing the coach link his tactics to something from his deep reservoir of basketball lore.

"What history?" asked Déo.

"Well, Bill Russell did not play his first game for the Boston Celtics until December 22, 1956, ten games into that season. Russell had captained the US gold medal team in Melbourne, Australia, and the Olympic competition did not wrap up until November," he told them.

He continued. "Anyway, in his first game, which was nationally televised, a rarity in those days, his coach, Red Auerbach, decided to bring him in after three or four minutes, figuring that a few minutes on the bench would allow Russell to observe and mentally prepare."

"And what happened?" asked Gilbert.

Jim smiled again. "He was prepared all right. The Celtics won, and he shut down Bob Pettit of the Saint Louis Hawks, one of the greatest players of that era. Russell went on to lead the Celtics to eleven world championships in his thirteen-year career. . . . So, I think this same approach will make things better for Leonard, especially because it'll be his first real game. And he's only fifteen! Watching for the first few minutes will hopefully drain off some of the nervousness."

————

Over the period of weeks that Jim prepared his team, it became increasingly apparent that many Burundians had not only developed an interest in the "friendly competition," as the US Embassies in both countries called the game, but were focusing intently on the outcome. Ambassador Foster met with Jim to discuss the fan interest. Both were aware that their meetings in her office had gone beyond formal; they'd become good friends through Project Oscar and were comfortable in both conversation and moments of silence.

"On the one hand, Jim," she began, "it's great to see the Tutsis and the Hutus actually bonding in their desire to beat Rwanda. On the other hand, it would be disastrous if the level of interest caused some type of violence to break out—either among the players or the fans."

"Do you expect many people from Rwanda?" asked Jim.

"Jesse Abbot and the Marines scoped out the space around the Nimbona Court. They figure about 3,000 people can comfortably watch the game. Ambassador Mark Newlen, my counterpart in Rwanda, feels that roughly 250 Rwandans will want to attend. With the help of the Peace Corps and Rwandan government, Amdassador Newlen has organized special train transportation for the Rwandan fans, as well as easy clearance at the border. As part of this plan, he's insisting that both Hutus and Tutsis travel together on the train. By the way, he's also staffing the train with heavy security, to ensure no problems," she said. "In any case, I've already talked with Jesse about cordoning off a special seating area for the Rwandan fans."

"What if we get more than three thousand?" asked Jim.

"Well," replied the ambassador, her promotional instincts coming to the fore, "let me run this idea by you!"

She grinned and shifted in her seat. "Before we realized the huge interest in the game, I thought it best to not charge any admission. Now, because of the crowd control issue, we'll give the 250 complimentary tickets to Ambassador Newlen because that's what he requested. We already have more than eighty media requests for credentials, so we'll honor all those requests and seat the media at courtside.

"We'll give away five hundred or so comps to local schools. This leaves us room for about twenty-one hundred more spectators. We'll sell those tickets on a first-come, first-served basis for one centime. Anyone who wants to attend can afford that. Plus, by selling the tickets, it will keep us from having to turn a lot of fans away. Oh, and the proceeds will benefit Project Oscar."

"Will we sell that many tickets?"

"From what I can gather, it shouldn't be a problem. If the tickets don't sell the way we expect, we'll simply give more away to local schools."

"Let's say we do sell all of the tickets," continued Jim. "Will the word get out so that people know not to show up without a ticket?"

"Good question. We spoke with the Burundian Football Federation people. Before the violence broke out, they had many sold-out games. According to the federation president, as long as the *Bujumbura Gazette* publicizes the sellout, and we put up notices around the region with the same message, people will get the word. And, as we've already found out with Project Oscar, it's amazing how fast word spreads."

After a moment's hesitation, Ambassador Foster continued. "Jim, going back to the crowd control issue, let's talk a bit about the objectives of the game." Jim detected a bit of an edge in her voice. The conversation shifted from friendly and comfortable back to business—very no-nonsense.

"I know how competitive you are and that you want to win this game. Believe me, so do I. But as we can all see, there's an even higher purpose to the game that would be shattered by any outbreak of violence. So what I'm asking—and this is a very important request—is that you get the team ready to play its best, but also impress upon them the importance—the absolute importance—of good sportsmanship."

She continued, "From what I've observed, the crowd will often follow the lead of their team and coach in this area. If the coach is harping on the officials—or if a player argues a call—this could send the crowd into a frenzy and could compromise—even destroy—our goals."

Cynthia Foster leaned over, put her hand on Jim's forearm, and looked straight into his blue eyes.

"Coach," she said gently, "We need to employ that John Havlicek 'don't punch back, play harder' credo that you told me about."

Jim knew that her points were not simply a request, but an order.

"You know," he responded, "with all of the hoopla surrounding the game, I guess I hadn't given the issue of sportsmanship much thought. But you're absolutely right. Rest assured I'll make certain that all of us—myself included—conduct ourselves with what I've always called 'competitive self-restraint.'"

As Jim rose from his chair, he turned to the ambassador. With a broad grin, the coach asked, "Just so I'm sure, who's reffing the game?"

"Sergeant Rush—and a Marine stationed in Rwanda," responded the ambassador. "They've both reffed at the high school level," she said, returning his smile.

——

I want my players to approach winning and losing with equal measures of effort and sportsmanship. I also want them to treat either outcome with the same quiet dignity.

Jim Keating had read these words in an obscure athletic journal many years earlier. The writer was a high school coach from a small Connecticut town, and the two sentences struck a chord with him. But because the coach had a sub-.500 record, Jim doubted that others in his profession would pay much attention to the article; high-profile opinion forums were reserved for coaches with outstanding records. He even guessed that most of those who read the piece would dismiss the man as a pious loser. For his own part, Jim was always under such pressure to win that he had filed the message in the deep recesses of his mind.

But as he reflected on his conversation with the ambassador, Jim knew that a key objective in the forthcoming game was for the team—head coach and players alike—to display the highest standards of on-court behavior. As for handling victory and defeat with the same quiet dignity, the coach admitted a desire to display such dignity—but as a winner.

"If we're going to win," he said to his assistants, Déo and Gilbert, "we'd better find out as much as we can about the Rwandan team."

"Mathias will know, or he'll know where to find out," said Déo. "He knows almost everything about African basketball."

Later that day at the Nimbona Court, as the players warmed up, Mathias told the coach, "Throughout the years, they would almost always beat us. We really didn't have a national program, and they had a reputation of always trying to bring in 'guests.' Ringers, as you call them."

"Where would they get them?"

"Just over the border in Zaire. . . . We would play two or three times a year," Mathias recalled. "One game would be a 'friendly' and the ringers would never show up for that game. But whenever the game was for standing in the African basketball community—well, we always knew to expect some new faces."

"What about now?" asked Jim. "How can we find out about the team that will play us?"

"I have a schoolteacher friend," said Mathias. "He's a basketball man who lives just outside of Kigali—a Tutsi who used to coach the Rwandan sixteen-and-under boys. I've not spoken with him in several years. I know that he was pushed off of the Rwandan Basketball Board when the new Hutu regime came into power. They took over everything, including sports. But I'll bet he knows about the team."

"Okay. But will he tell what he knows?"

"I bet he will, and I believe I can reach him at his school."

"Then please go about contacting him, and I'll speak with Ambassador Foster about this guest issue," said Jim.

"A good idea," said Mathias, who paused then said, "And Jim, I also bet the Rwandans will bring a very good team."

———

Later that night, Mathias's scouting report confirmed his earlier prediction.

"My friend says the Rwandans are treating this game quite seriously. The Hutu regime has recruited the best Tutsi players from Rwanda, along with several Hutu ball handlers. Plus, they saw the CNN report about Leonard," he told Jim.

Jim leaned back in his chair, placed both hands behind his head, and stared out beyond the space of the veranda. He let out a long, steady breath while Mathias continued.

"He also says two big men originally from Zaire will play. The Rwandans will defend this because so many Tutsis are constantly relocating due to the violence in Rwanda and Zaire. Both players from Zaire recently fled that country and are living in Rwanda, near the Zaire border. So, I don't know how much of a protest you can make."

"That's exactly Ambassador Foster's opinion," said Jim. "Ambassador Newlen called her about the two guys. He explained that if he tried to convince the Rwandan basketball officials that the two should not play, it would jeopardize the game. We agreed to drop the matter and focus on getting our players ready."

"One other thing, Jim," said Mathias. "The Rwandans have imported Billy Banda from South Africa to coach their team. They feel that if an American is coaching the Burundi team, then they have the right to import a top coach as well."

Through a conversation with Finbar Finnegan, Jim was familiar with Banda. The Irishman had observed him while on assignment in South Africa. "Since an NBA All-Star Team visited South Africa several years ago, and brought along some superstars like Patrick Ewing and David Robinson, basketball has really caught on," Finnegan had told Jim. "They have a pro league now. In fact, one of the teams is owned by Sam Vincent, the former Celtics player."

Finnegan had told Jim that Banda was the best coach in the league. The South African Basketball Federation paid his way to attend several clinics in the States. And when the South African National Team had toured the States last year, Banda was appointed head coach.

Jim had recognized the name and the appointment as soon as Finnegan mentioned Banda. He was a disciple of John Chaney at Temple—disciplined offense, tough zone defense.

"I wonder if he's a firebrand like Chaney," Jim thought aloud, reflecting on the information from both Finnegan and Mathias.

"Don't know," Mathias said. "But I do know that he's originally from the Chiawelo section of Soweto. I heard that he battled prejudice and actually received a degree in physical education at the University of Pretoria. He's quite a man—and a very good technical coach."

Jim was genuinely invigorated by the scouting information, and the next day his players could hear in his voice the relish with which he approached this game. "Gentlemen, I've got good news. Rwanda is a very fine team with an excellent coach. I wouldn't want it any other way, and you guys should feel the same. It'll be a real test of our progress, but that's what's so great about this game."

As he spoke, Jim could not help but notice that Leonard Tangishaka seemed visibly energized by the spunk of his words.

"Guys," the coach concluded, "only eight days 'til tip off. Let's work real hard."

37

The Rwandan National Team arrived two days before the game. With her customary entrepreneurial savvy, Ambassador Foster arranged for the team to receive complimentary rooms at the Novetal Bujumbura in exchange for fifty free tickets in a special VIP area at courtside. She further arranged for the VIP section to be catered throughout the game with hors d'oeuvres and soft drinks. It would be the first such in-game entertainment in Burundian sports history.

At a reception the ambassador hosted at her home in honor of both teams, Jim got his first look at the Rwandans. Most of the players were dressed in the traditional toga with the blue, yellow, and green colors of Rwanda. Many looked to be as tall as and physically stronger than Jim's athletes—with the notable exception of Leonard Tangishaka.

Through embassy friends in Belgium, including Frank Schwalba-Hoth—the supplier of her favorite chocolates, which Jim had presented to her on his first night in Burundi—Ambassador Foster had organized a shipment of navy blue blazers for the Burundian team, including the coaches. She had made sure to have the Burundian coat of arms sewed on the breast pocket. A yellow lion head on a red background, it stood out sharply against the navy blue coat. Many of the players had never worn a suit coat and proudly sported their new gift at the reception.

Mathias had explained the significance of the coat of arms, which included three crossed spears behind the lion head and a banner with the words "Unity—Work—Progress" in French. No one looked more resplendent than Leonard, whose jacket fit perfectly on his well-sculpted body. In fact, when he entered the reception with Mathias, every eye turned his way, including those of the Rwandans. They had viewed the CNN clip and were anxious to see the wunderkind in person.

At the reception, Jim was introduced to Coach Billy Banda. Banda appeared to be in his mid-thirties, and his bearing reflected the intensity and focus Jim had observed in many successful coaches. In Banda's case, he also possessed a pleasing measure of good manners.

"I have a powerful respect for the great American coaches such as John Chaney, Dean Smith, and you, Coach Keating. I have an article you wrote on changing defenses that I review quite often."

While taking an immediate liking to Banda, Jim was certain this young coach had drilled his team on the various methods of countering the changing defensive system. *So much for my surprise!* He was also keenly aware that Banda's comment was perhaps more rooted in gamesmanship than flattery.

Moments after the two head coaches finished their brief conversation, Jesse Abbot approached Jim. "That guy is taking this game seriously. As soon as he got here, he requested a closed practice at Nimbona Court for tomorrow morning. Wanted our assurances that no one other than the Garda would be present."

Jim had always been amused at the universal paranoia of those in his profession; this time was no exception.

At Ambassador Foster's request, the athletes shook hands with their opponents. While the Burundians could easily see that the Rwandans were an imposing group, they also realized that none of the players had any physical advantage over their young star. As for Leonard, he was not the least bit intimidated by meeting the opposition—most of whom were more than a decade his senior.

After the handshakes and some genuine words of welcome by Ambassador Foster, Billy Banda politely excused himself and his team, pointing to the need for a good sleep after the long journey.

"He sure is all business," Cynthia whispered to Jim.

Jim just smiled, nodded, and thought: *So young, so ambitious. How well I remember!*

———

The day before the game, Jim put his team through a brisk ninety-minute workout. After the workout, he took Jesse Abbot's advice and convened those members of the media who wanted to talk with Leonard Tangishaka.

While Leonard seemed to enjoy the attention, he carefully followed his coach's guidance by answering all questions with politeness and modesty. Asked to name his favorite player, he drew smiles from the thirty-odd journalists. "I have five: Parish the jump-shooter, Hakeem the rebounder, Walton the passer, Kareem the sky-hooker, and Russell the defender and shot-blocker."

The reporters were as charmed by young Leonard as they were skeptical of a statement made by Finbar Finnegan at the conclusion of the press briefing: "He'll be better than all of them!"

After the briefing and one-on-ones with the *Times* and *Sports Illustrated*, Jim and Leonard joined the rest of the team at Ambassador Foster's home. Cynthia had offered the full use of her "palace"—as the players quietly dubbed it—for the entire weekend.

"Staying here will allow the young men who live out in the country to avoid having to make their way into Bujumbura on Sunday," she said to Jim. "Since we sold tickets in the rural communities, as well as in the city, I've got a feeling that the trains will be quite full on Sunday. I don't imagine you want any one of your players being forced to cycle twenty miles on game day!"

At dinner that evening—a buffet of vegetable soup, ugali, kidney beans, sweet potatoes, roasted lamb, and fruit—Ambassador Foster proudly announced to the players what Jim already knew. "We've sold every ticket to tomorrow night's game!"

Well-publicized in the *Bujumbura Gazette* and posted on bulletin boards within a thirty-mile radius of Bujumbura, the ambassador's sales plan worked to perfection. Phase One had been successfully executed at the last two open practices. Ambassador Foster had ordered that ticket outlets be placed at the Nimbona Court. "This will take care of the basketball loyalists," she had predicted to Sergeant Rush, who, along with Private Roberts and five other Marines, would man the outlets.

Her prediction proved accurate—more than fourteen hundred tickets were sold on the two nights of practice.

"We have seven hundred left," the ambassador had said to Rush. "We'll sell them on market day."

Saturday was market day in Burundi, and every Saturday morning, even during the rainy season, people gathered at outdoor markets in Bujumbura and in the countryside to purchase their supplies for the upcoming week. The ambassador positioned Marines and embassy personnel with blocks of tickets at makeshift ticket outlets at every market within a thirty-mile radius of Bujumbura. The remaining seven hundred tickets were sold by noon.

"You know, Cynthia, you may have chosen the wrong profession," kidded her husband.

That evening, the *Bujumbura Gazette* ran a special game edition with the headline: "No Tickets Left." Large posters repeated the same message, pre-printed by the confident ambassador and distributed in and around Bujumbura.

Sundays were generally quiet on the streets of the capital city. With their fidelity to the Catholic faith, even the two warring sides generally rested on the Lord's Day. But by 11:00 AM on Game Day Sunday, large crowds congregated in the city's business district.

Jim's team had a light breakfast at the Embassy, followed by a private Mass in the chapel on the third floor of Ambassador Foster's spacious home. After Mass, the team was driven to the Nimbona Court for a thirty-minute shoot-around. When word reached city center that the team was practicing, a crowd of more than six hundred converged on the court. Jim felt the unmistakable buzz that surrounds a big game.

The coach was well aware that none of his athletes had ever played in any game of such importance. "And my best player has never played in any formal game at all!" he said to Bill Foster on the van ride back to the Embassy.

Mindful of the importance of relaxation for his inexperienced crew, Jim had arranged a special treat at Ambassador Foster's home.

"How many of you have ever seen the movie *Rocky?*" Jim asked his team.

Not one player raised his hand, and Jim turned to assistant Déo and said, "Coach Déo, lead the group into the library. Then hit the light switch."

When the violence had escalated, the only movie theater in Burundi, a sixty-seat amphitheater in the Bujumbura business district that showed second-run films from Belgium, had closed down. Watching the French-dubbed *Rocky* on Ambassador Foster's forty-six-inch color television was a special treat, and the players became thoroughly engrossed in the movie. While unable to understand much of the translation,

Jim found himself amused at Rocky Balboa giving voice to French phrases like *bon soir* and *a bientot* in low, guttural tones.

Leonard Tangishaka had never seen a movie before, and for him the experience was thrilling. By the thirteenth round of the white underdog's valiant effort against the dark-skinned champion, Leonard and his black teammates were cheering every one of Rocky's punches. The emotion in the library grew so intense that Jim wondered if he had made a mistake. "Hope it doesn't sap their energy," he whispered to Bill, as Rocky received between-round instructions from Mickey Goldmill, played by Burgess Meredith. But at the pre-game meal of pasta and beef, the players seemed completely relaxed—and ready.

As two domestics—one Hutu and one Tutsi—cleared the dinner table, Ambassador Foster entered the dining room. "Play hard tonight—and play as sportsmen," she said. "Win or lose, you have made Project Oscar a success."

As the coach nodded in agreement, he once again thought to himself that winning would make Project Oscar an even bigger success.

It had been a long time since Jim Keating had felt the butterflies of a big game, and he found himself actually reveling in his state of anxiety. It struck him that he had not been this close to a team since his days at St. Thomas, nor had his mindset brimmed with such confidence—coaching to win as opposed to the corrosive fear of losing that had been so prevalent at New Jersey State.

"Gentlemen, it's now 3:45 PM. Head back to your rooms for an hour of rest, and let's gather back here at 5:00 PM sharp. The vans will be here to take us to the Nimbona Court."

38

When two Marine vans pulled into the dirt parking area adjacent to the Nimbona Court, the sellout crowd—early to arrive and aroused—turned their attention from the preliminary game to the grand entrance of the Burundi National Team. As the players made their way from the vans to their makeshift locker rooms, a thunderous cheer erupted.

To assure some privacy for both teams, Ambassador Foster had asked the Marines to pitch two large tents on opposite sides of the court. Clive Rush, in a ref's jersey and shorts, led Jim and the team up the hill. As they approached the home team tent, Jim said, "Looks good, Sarge. Looks about the same as what we used to call a squad tent."

"About the same," said Rush. "But this one's a bit bigger—figure about three Leonards wide and five Leonards long. Take a look inside."

Jim pulled aside the flap and walked into the tent. He smiled and shook his head. The Marine contingent had outdone themselves. The tent was replete with folding chairs, a cooler full of Gatorade and water bottles, and a metal rack with hangers.

"First class, Clive. I've been so fixated on basketball that none of this entered my mind."

"We enjoyed doing it, Coach. And by the way, the Rwandan tent is the same."

Several minutes after the Burundi team had settled inside the tent, the Rwandan squad—which had just walked the 300 meters from the Novotel Bujumbura almost in formation—entered the grounds and was met by the other Marine referee. The applause from their 250 fans, while spirited, was inaudible in comparison to the clamorous welcome just accorded the Burundians.

"Ain't no doubt whose got the home court advantage," laughed Corporal Roberts, who was overseeing game security.

Roberts and his fellow Marines, along with Jesse Abbot (titled Event Manager by Ambassador Foster), had done a splendid job attending to the many details required by what was "clearly the most historic game in any sport ever played in Burundi," as described by the *Bujumbura Gazette*. Special yellow and blue tickets allowed access to the catered, courtside VIP section cordoned off for "corporate supporters," such as the owners of the Novatel Bujumbura, and dignitaries such as Burundian President Peter Buyoya. Responding to the recent popularity of Greek food in Bujumbura, Ambassador Foster's staff served up moussaka and tzatziki along with Burundi's famous Chapati bread and Urwara wine.

"This kind of event hospitality is so new to us," raved Burundian Minister of Sport, Claude Ntahombaye. "Seeing how it is done will help us run events in a proper manner in the future."

Eighty-six credentialed media were seated courtside. Abbot had even arranged for a computer hookup for reporters to file their stories immediately after the game—a convenience unheard of at any prior Burundian athletic event.

The security was tight, but friendly, the weather was seventy degrees with a slight breeze ("perfect," as Mathias said), and the fried plantain and sombé from the vendors situated throughout the grounds produced a wonderful aroma.

Cynthia and Bill Foster walked toward their seats next to the Burundian President. The ambassador was dressed in a tan skirt and an ensemble of red linen jacket, white cotton blouse, and light green silk scarf that merged the colors of the Burundian flag. She walked with a measured gait befitting her position, but she was brimming with excitement. She turned to Bill and, almost bursting with enthusiasm, said, "It's electric."

Bill, attired in a navy blue team jacket and khaki slacks, said, "Indeed, it is. You've done a terrific job, my love. But you'd better hang on to me or I'll be joining Jim on the bench!"

Halfway up the hill, the Burundian National Team's tent was situated in a perfect spot to watch the preliminary game between the "Celtics" and the "Bulls." As fans roared their approval over each move in the prelim, their reaction—and the enjoyment of the participating players—prompted Jim to approach Bill Foster.

"Making up the two extra teams was a great idea on your part," said the coach. "You can join me at halftime, right?"

Bill nodded.

"Send him to the right tent, Madam Ambassador," said Jim.

"I promise, Coach."

With ten minutes remaining in the preliminary game, Jim directed Déo to drop the sides of the tent. "Okay, gentlemen," the coach called out. "Time to get ready for business!"

Jim went on to review the strategy: "We'll start in full-court man-to-man pressure—to get the blood flowing. Then we'll change our defense throughout the game—but everything will be based on pressure. On offense, we're looking to run when the opportunity presents itself. When

304

it's not there, we want to take good care of the basketball. Remember guys, this game is one of percentages—take high percentage shots—and also remember *that the ball is gold!*"

As soon as the prelim ended, the Burundian National Team made their way down the side of the hill. As they jogged onto the court, a booming roar erupted. Walking behind the team, Jim Keating felt the chills of a big game—but he remained focused and full of positive energy.

"It doesn't get any better than this," he said to his assistants Déo and Gilbert.

Both assistants smiled. Over the months of practice and travel, they had become infused with Jim's passion. Two men—a Hutu and a Tutsi—who once simply enjoyed basketball had, because of Jim's influence, come to love the game.

Mathias remained behind in the tent for a few moments and scanned the huge crowd. His eye was caught by a Mediterranean-looking man who was mixing in with the other spectators, yet appeared to be alone. "Must be a coach from the Middle East," Mathias thought, realizing that the ban on visas did not extend to a number of countries.

————

A palpable electric surge ran through the crowd, a frisson of energy and excitement few of the spectators had ever experienced. Jim, Mathias, Déo, and Gilbert—they could all feel it. First of all, attendees had the clear sense that they were part of something historic. Several in the diplomatic community even believed that the name of the visionary diplomat who conceived of the game and nurtured the idea might well appear one day in history books for the impact of her humanitarian ways.

Then there was the notion of this public spectacle serving as a catalyst to bringing warring tribes and competing nations together in an event the likes of which no Burundian had ever seen. Mathias had called Jim to relate the gist of a story in the French daily, *Le Renouveau*. "This article was on the front page, Coach. As you Americans say, 'above the fold.' I'm sure my translation is correct. They called the game 'a cathartic force.'"

Jim smiled, pleased with the news. "I like your translation."

The presence of credentialed media and the specter of television cameras and bright lights added yet more drama and importance to the event. And, of course, there was the wunderkind, whose grace and power were evident, even during the usually predictable routine of a lay-up line.

"I've been to a couple of Final Fours—the college championships in our country," said Bill Foster to President Buyoya, sitting in the VIP section of the bleachers. "But I've never experienced anything quite like this. The combination of history, competition, expectations—what drama!"

"I know of your Final Four, so that is quite a statement," responded Buyoya, his eyes skimming over the players on the court and settling on Leonard Tangishaka.

In what was Leonard's first-ever pre-game warm-up, he thought back to a Jim Keating lesson: *The warm-up is generally twenty minutes, Leonard.*

First, you want to loosen up your muscles. You do this by breaking into a light sweat. Don't do anything too physically strenuous in warm-ups. It's more a half-speed approach to get loose.

Next, loosen your mind. You always want to enter a game with a clear mind, a state of what I call relaxed focus. The idea is to block out any negative thoughts and get into that area of untroubled confidence. Think positive thoughts during the warm- ups, Leonard. Imagine great success. Know that you are the best player on the court.

By the time the warm-ups ended, Leonard Tangishaka found himself in a zone of self-assurance. He could not wait for each step of the game to unfold—from the first minutes on the bench observing to his entry into what would surely be a new and more civilized type of pitched battle than the violent sort from which his mother had protected him.

The thunderous noise that pervaded the grounds abated to respectful silence when two pairs of singers—first a Hutu and Tutsi from Rwanda, then a Hutu and Tutsi from Burundi—walked to center court to sing their respective national anthems. When the Burundian anthem concluded, Eric Nicumbura, a sixty-two-year-old Tutsi who, before the onslaught of violence, had gained some acclaim as a stadium announcer at soccer games, strode to the microphone.

On a stanchion, the mic was a bulky hexagon, and Jim had to smile. *Looks like the one Sister Angelita used during Friday afternoon assembly at St. Peter's Elementary School.*

Snatching the mic and leaning it first left, then right, Nicumbura, with great relish, announced the Rwandan starting five to raucous cheers from the 250 Rwandans in attendance and polite applause from the rest of the crowd.

As the last of the Rwandan starters jogged onto the court, Jim edged next to his young star and asked, "How are you feeling?"

Manifesting an assuring combination of focused intensity and serenity, Leonard said with quiet conviction, "I am feeling great. I will be ready whenever you say, Coach Keating."

"AAAND NOWWW," roared Nicumbura, "Forrr the hoOOmmmme teeeeAM!"

Nicumbura followed with a sonorous introduction of the Burundian starting five that caused a cacophonous combination of cheers, clapping hands, shouts, and screeches. The din was punctuated by the use of a *djembe*, the goblet-shaped drum covered by African goat skin and used for the famous African drum calls. Brought to the game by a Hutu who had never seen basketball played, the call, in this case, was to exhort Burundian fans to cheer on their team.

After the introductions, the rumbling combination of drum and crowd noise continued, causing Rush to blow his whistle at fourth octave, signaling both coaches to wrap up final instructions and send their teams onto the court.

"Okay, it's game time, gents," referee Rush bellowed to Coaches Keating and Banda.

Ten perspiring players broke from their teams' huddles and walked to center court amid an atmosphere of charged anticipation.

39

Rwanda controlled the opening tap, and a 5'9" Hutu guard was short on a baseline jumper. But 6'8" Burundian Venuste Nsadimana, as nervous as he was inexperienced, missed a box-out assignment, and Mutara Boshoso, the bullish 6'11" Rwandan team center and one of the two players from Zaire, muscled Nsadimana and converted an offensive rebound.

After the basket, Rwanda employed full-court man-to-man pressure. Jim was pleased that Albert Obadele, his 5'10" Hutu point guard, advanced the ball into forecourt with little difficulty.

On their first offensive possession, the Burundian team ran the passing game well. After six "touches," Obadele curled off a down screen and missed an easy eight-footer.

"Good execution!" yelled Jim, surprised that Rwanda had opened in man-man defense.

But moments later, there was more trouble on the defensive backboard. After a Rwandan guard missed a three-point attempt, Boshoso, once again maneuvered by Nsadimana, grabbed the offensive rebound and scored.

Rwanda 4–Burundi 0.

Burundi scored on its next possession, a fifteen-foot jumper by a sinewy 6'8" forward, Adolphe Bagaza. But over the next four minutes, Boshoso continued to pound the offensive board, scoring on three more put-backs. And while the Rwandans seemed slightly off balance in their attack of Jim's changing defenses, they moved the ball well and took judicious shots. At the Rwandan defensive end, Jim could see Temple Coach John Chaney's influence on Billy Banda. After the first Burundi possession, Rwanda had set up in a tight, aggressive 2-3 match-up zone.

"It's definitely Chaney's Temple Zone," Jim remarked to Déo. "And this guy can coach it."

After five minutes of play, Jim knew that he was as challenged by Banda as his team was challenged by the opposing players. His starters needed help; it was time. "Leonard—check in!"

———

In December 1956, Jim Keating was in his first season as head coach at St. Thomas and married to the perfect woman. His alma mater had gotten off to a strong start; 5-1 with an upset victory over Harry Litwack's Temple Owls in the Palestra. The college basketball world was fast taking note of this savvy, soaring young mentor.

It was seven years earlier when Jim had first met Bob Cousy. The two had played against each other in the Worcester Auditorium in '49, and St. Thomas had come away with a surprising victory. Even in '49, Cousy was already established as the most exciting player the fledgling game had ever seen. Jim had taken an immediate liking to the Cooz, whom he found to be a thoughtful person without pretense. "He's one of the boys," was Jim's common description of the budding superstar known as "the Houdini of the Hardwood."

During Cousy's first years with the Celtics, the two stayed in touch. Despite the press of coaching duties, Jim would always attend several Celtics home games as Cousy's guest, making the drive to Boston. Jim loved to watch Cousy display his Monet-like creativity on the court. The way Edna once described it was "French Impressionism at its best." The young coach was proud of their friendship and grateful for Cousy's public praise of Jim's early success.

By the mid-1950s, Cousy had become the top box office attraction in the NBA and, along with Bill Sharman, formed the league's top backcourt. But Jim knew that his friend was frustrated over the Celtics' lack of a big man, the one missing component that seemed to keep "The Green" from scaling the NBA summit.

"But Arnold has a plan," Cousy confided to Jim in the summer of '55, referring to his coach, Arnold "Red" Auerbach. "Can't give you the details, but if he can pull it off, it's a strategy that could take us to the top."

For the next nine months, Jim kept wondering what Auerbach had in mind. On draft day, April 30, 1956, he found out.

A series of moves that would ignite the greatest dynasty in NBA history, and elevate Auerbach to basketball mensa status, began by virtue of the league's territorial draft rule. Implemented purely for gate reasons, the rule permitted a team to pick a local star. Holy Cross, Cousy's school, was in Worcester, only fifty miles from Boston and well within the team's territorial region. The geography allowed the Celtics to select Crusader All-American Tom Heinsohn, a 6'7" scoring machine. In the second round of the regular draft, the club took San Francisco All-American K.C. Jones, a defensive stopper.

But it was a daring pre-draft day trade Cousy had foreshadowed that sealed the master plan. Auerbach sent two future Hall of Famers, Ed Macauley and Cliff Hagan, to the St. Louis Hawks for the draft rights to 6'9" Bill Russell, Jones's All-American teammate at San Francisco.

The trio of rookies—Russell, Heinsohn, and Jones—would all go on to Hall of Fame status and help lead the Celtics to unprecedented basketball success: eleven NBA titles in Russell's thirteen years as a player.

On December 19, 1956, three days before Russell's much-anticipated debut, Edna answered a phone call and heard a familiar voice at the other end of the line. "Tell James that if the two of you would like to witness what I think might be a historic game, I'll leave two tickets at Will Call."

At 6:00 AM on December 22, Jim and Edna departed Philadelphia for the Boston Garden. That afternoon, 13,909 fans jammed into every seat, and the game was nationally tel-evised—the full house and national TV audience both rari-ties in those days. Thanks to Cousy, Jim and Edna sat in the sixth row, center court.

Auerbach followed his plan of holding Russell on the bench for the first few minutes to allow the rookie some time to compose himself and observe the flow of action. Jim recalled the anticipation that permeated the Garden and Auerbach's role in stirring the emotional embers of the fans. Several times, the coach glanced in Russell's direction; each glance caused an agitation in the crowd like a gust of wind through trees.

Four endless minutes into the game, Auerbach—the director—finally motioned to his new leading man. Jim Keating would never forget the sequence that followed, one that would be a deep-dye in the fabric of basketball lore.

When the rookie stood up from the bench, the crowd—one and all—stood with him and began to cheer. When he walked toward the scorer's table to check in, the crowd's roar exploded, literally shaking the foundation of the old build-ing. What happened next would become one of Jim's favorite basketball memories.

When Bill Russell walked onto the parquet floor, every player on the court—teammates and opponents alike—literally stopped to watch him. It was as if they were observing a crown prince entering their midst.

After the game, the ever gracious Cousy met up with Jim and Edna outside the Garden press room.

"I think this kid is going to make Arnold a genius," said the Cooz, adding, "and I think he's going to change my life."

———

As Leonard Tangishaka trotted onto the court with his team trailing 14–6, there was a reaction eerily similar to that which Jim recalled occurring back in 1956 when Bill Russell entered his first game for the Boston Celtics. On the court, the players stood stationary for a moment, eyes trained on the entry of the young giant. The Burundian players smiled; the Rwandan players feigned disinterest, though Jim was sure he could detect a look of concern.

As for the fans, Leonard's entry was greeted by a momentary hush, which quickly erupted into a joyous roar that resounded throughout the grounds. For a moment, Clive Rush held the basketball. He wanted to let the crowd noise subside so his whistle might be heard before he handed the ball to the player waiting to make the inbounds pass. Rush would later confide to Jim that his hesitation was in part due to his fascination with the spectators' reactions.

Jim glanced at the Burundian fans. The keeper of the *djembe* pounded hard on the goat-skin cover. The Burundians, many attired in their rainbow colors, rose up to cheer, clapping and waving their arms. Some of the women twirled their vivid umbrellas, brought to the game as sunshades. The effect was kaleidoscopic. As the coach turned his attention back to the court, he couldn't help thinking, *I hope we have a picture of this.*

313

Sensing the angst of his players, Coach Billy Banda vaulted from the bench. His trumpet voice alley-ooped the crowd bedlam. "Boshoso," he yelled to the 6'11" center from Zaire, "you've got *him*."

For Mutara Boshoso, there was no need to parse the sentence. His assignment had been made clear by his coach ever since word of the young phenom had been beamed worldwide on CNN. Jim sensed—correctly—that "got him" had double the normal meaning. Usually the term referred only to a defensive player's assignment. But in this case it encompassed intimidation at both ends of the court. Within the Rwandan matchup zone, Boshoso shadowed Leonard, creating double teams and muscling the prodigy at every step. At the offensive end, he utilized his elbows as weapons.

"Side front him, Leonard!" yelled Jim.

Leonard wrapped his left leg around Boshoso's and positioned his left arm in a direct line between the ball handler and Boshoso's outstretched hands.

Boshoso was experienced in the cunning of low-post play. When the ball was quickly reversed to the weak side, both referees followed its flight. With swift stealth, and out of sight of the refs, he uncorked a forearm shiver deep into Leonard's chest.

Three thousand people—less two with whistles—seemed to observe the preemptive strike, and the Burundi fans roared in dissent.

For Boshoso's part, the attack was calculated, intended to provoke a response from Leonard that the officials *would* see. Jim's first reaction was to leap from the bench in protest. But before he could express his complaint, he not only recalled Ambassador Perry's appeal for sportsmanship, but was also struck by the icy composure of his protégé.

Leonard's reaction was in direct contrast to the crowd's response; it was smart, it was mature, it was everything Jim had taught his young star about what he called "competitive self-restraint."

"When an opponent tries something dirty, it's better to be tough and smart than tough and dumb," he had told Leonard.

Leonard also thought back to the time he had stood up to Charlé Tinyabokwe to protect his mother.

If I did not back down from Charlé, who might have killed me, then I surely will not let this player frighten me.

Despite Boshoso's forearm to low-post freedom, his teammate traveled and Burundi took possession. A fifteen-foot jumper by Hutu point guard Albert Obadele was long. When the shot was released, Leonard had been boxed out by Boshoso. But he used the Paul Silas roll, the offensive rebounding ploy that Jim had taught him so well. Leonard rolled off Boshoso's back and vaulted above the rim to tip the ball into the basket.

The crowd cheered wildly and adrenaline flowed freely through Leonard's body. Jim was exhilarated. The boy's energy seemed visible, like an aura. The coach allowed himself a quick smile. *This kid is the real deal.*

In Burundi's man-to-man defense, Leonard's assignment was to guard the 6'11" Boshoso. When the ball was passed to him in the low post, Boshoso made a half-turn toward the basket, and up-faked once, twice, then three times. None of his fakes caused Leonard to react. Out of frustration, he pivoted away from the fifteen-year-old and attempted a hook shot. With perfect timing, Leonard soared, and swatted the ball into the hands of Obadele, who quick-stepped up the court for an easy layup.

Rwanda 14–Burundi 10!

In the remaining minutes until halftime, Boshoso was made to regret his foul play. Leonard Tangishaka took over the game in a manner that, in the words of Jesse Abbot, "gave the crowd more than their centime's worth."

315

Over those 15 minutes, Leonard scored 19 points, grabbed 14 rebounds, blocked 6 shots, and dished out 5 assists. Moreover, he played with a ferocious intensity that surprised even Jim Keating.

Bill Foster described the performance to the dignitaries seated near him as "No dirty play—just good, aggressive basketball."

But it was at the end of the half that the overflow crowd was treated to an extraordinary athletic feat, one that caused Jim to revisit the memory of what many thought to be the singularly greatest play in basketball history.

With only ten seconds remaining, Leonard received an entry pass, drop-stepped by Boshoso, and laid the ball in. His momentum carried him two feet over the end line.

The moment the ball went through the net, a Rwandan player grabbed it and looked to half court, where he spotted a 6'9" teammate all alone. He hurled the ball to his teammate, who took off toward the opposite-end basket.

Leonard looked up, only to see that the two Burundian teammates closest to the tall Rwandan were both Hutu guards, neither of whom could stop the opponent. Despite trailing the player by a full fifty feet, Leonard put his head down and sprinted toward the other basket, nintey-two feet away.

Just as the 6'9" Rwandan began his elevation toward the hoop, from seemingly out of nowhere, and with equal measures of speed and resolve, Leonard tracked down his prey. As the player elevated, the fifteen-year-old leaped into midair and blocked the shot as the buzzer sounded.

Amid the crowd delirium, Jim walked off the court, transfixed. *The Bill Russell–Jack Coleman play from the '57 playoffs. Never would I believe I would see that play again.*

Burundi took a 46–33 half-time lead. Cynthia Foster's enthusiasm overflowed with the sound of the buzzer and she grabbed President Buyoya's arm. "Mr. President, we have just seen the debut of a superstar."

"And that last play," said the president, shaking his head slowly in disbelief. "It was astonishing. My God, astonishing!"

During intermission, Finbar Finnegan called his office in Johannesburg. "Sid," he said to his bureau chief, "it's only halftime, but you should have seen the kid. He was better than even I imagined. Wait 'til you see the footage! Wait 'til you see what he did just before halftime!!"

In the thick of jubilation that pervaded the tent, Jim cautioned, "Guys, you did a great job, but 13 points is not a big lead against a good team like Rwanda."

Yet even as he offered these customary words of caution, the coach knew that no one was about to hold back his protégé.

Leonard scored the first 8 points of the second half. With five minutes to go, and Burundi leading 75–41, Keating removed him from the game to a thunderous ovation.

The final score was Burundi 85, Rwanda 54. In his first formal competition, and in only thirty minutes of play, Leonard's numbers were astounding: 36 points, 24 rebounds, 10 blocked shots, 10 assists. A quadruple double!

The post-game plan called for a reception at Ambassador Foster's home for the two teams and VIPs. At halftime, Mathias asked Ambassador Foster for her permission to invite the Angolan coach, who was present at the game.

"I've also seen two or three others who I assume to be coaches as well."

"Invite them all," said the ambassador.

But when Mathias went to the area where he had seen the Mediterranean-looking man, who he had assumed to be a scout or a coach, he could not find him. He asked several people if they knew the man's whereabouts.

"I saw him leave just before halftime," said one fan.

Now that is quite strange, Mathias thought.

———

As soon as the game was over, Ambassador Foster, awash with delight, was escorted to her car by Bill and two Marines. She politely asked for a few minutes of privacy so that she could write a brief letter to Consolaté, telling her of Leonard's great play. She wrote, "You should be so very proud of your wonderful son, my sister. You have raised him well!"

The letter would be hand-delivered to Consolaté by a group of Marines the next day.

40

The two Marine security guards outside Ambassador Foster's home were never so challenged.

"Bet there's at least 250 people in there," said Sergeant Matt Kocay of Auburn, Maine.

"Yup, more'n I've ever seen, but I feel good we've checked 'em all careful," added Private Mark Epstein of Clemson, South Carolina.

The post-game reception, originally planned for "approximately one hundred" per Ambassador Foster's directive to her chef, Audace Bugaza, had swelled amid the high spirits of victory. Fortunately, Bugaza had had an inkling that the original estimate was conservative. He responded to the challenge by preparing extra helpings of Burundi specialties like spiced carrots mixed with mustard seeds and chili peppers, and *bamabara*, a traditional rice porridge flavored with sugar and peanut butter.

The gathering was testament to the remarkable success of Project Oscar. Hutu and Tutsi mingled easily, all sharing a sense of pride in Burundi's win.

Victorino Cunha, the Angolan coach who was clearly there to scout, sought out Jim. It was obvious that the American coach was still in a state of euphoria.

"Coach, your team was well prepared, and you will be a force to be reckoned within the FIBA African Tournament. You probably know that the winner goes to the Olympics."

Jim had been so engrossed in preparing his team for the Rwandan game that he had never considered the possibility of qualifying for the Olympics. After his sojourn in Spain, Jim was well versed in the structure of international and Olympic basketball, but he figured a refresher about the Olympics from an African perspective couldn't hurt.

"I actually didn't know that," Jim admitted. "Tell me about the process."

"Well, as you know, only twelve countries actually make it to the Olympic Games in Men's Basketball, and only one team from Africa."

"How many times have you been to the Olympics?"

"Oh, just once. We came in tenth, but played good basketball. Just making the 'terrific twelve,' to echo your famous 'sweet sixteen' phrase, is a great honor for many countries. And after watching your team tonight, my guess is that you will have a very good chance as well. But it all comes down to the winner of the FIBA African championship."

Cunha smiled and added, "That kid in the pivot is a force, to be sure, but I still hope we both make it to the finals. While we've been fortunate to win it, we've never faced a player like your Tangishaka."

Jim was struck by Cunha's sincerity. As the two coaches were wrapping up their conversation, Mathias approached them and extended a hand to the Angolan.

"I've been eavesdropping," Mathias said. "Coach, I know your reputation well. You are a great strategist and we are honored that you attended this game. . . . I also overheard you mentioning the Olympics. At the game, I did notice one fellow, a Mediterranean-looking man. I thought he must be a coach from somewhere in the Middle East or perhaps Morocco. But he left at halftime."

"I did not notice him," said Cunha. "But he surely must not be a coach, for no real coach would leave at halftime of the historical debut of Leonard Tangishaka!"

"Very true," said Mathias, again giving momentary thought to the curious early departure.

As the center of interest at the reception, Leonard inwardly took pride at the attention accorded him. But he also acted as a gentleman, even offering a friendly handshake to Mutara Boshoso, the powerful center who tried to intimidate him—and whom he had "devoured," as the *Bujumbura Gazette* would report the next day.

As Jim watched his protégé soak up praise that bordered on reverence, the coach felt button-popping pride over the boy's performance on the court—and his courteous manner at the reception. And Jim knew something that the player most likely did not—that this night, at the very genesis of his career, would be one that Leonard Tangishaka would forever treasure.

Jim also knew that information that had been given to him just hours before the game by Ambassador Foster would have a profound effect on Leonard. In the northwest section of Rwanda, just over the border from Burundi, a Hutu priest had offered sanctuary in his church to a band of Tutsi warriors who had been engaged in fierce fighting with their Hutu foes. The Tutsis were in dire need of a night of rest in a safe place. The priest had offered it "in the name of the Savior."

As the men lay asleep on wooden pews, fifteen Hutu guerrillas were quietly let into the church. Once in position for their attack, the church lights were switched on. Within minutes, the unsuspecting Tutsi warriors were all dead.

The person who let the guerrillas in—the Hutu priest—had conspired with them in the whole barbarous plan. He had done so because he viewed their mission as one inspired by God.

"You must remove the bodies and their blood" had been his only condition.

Among those slaughtered was Charlé Tinyabokwe.

———

When the reception was over, Jim Keating and Ambassador Foster decided to meet with Leonard Tangishaka to inform him of Charlé's murder. As his coach led the way to Cynthia Foster's study, Leonard sensed that the meeting was one of consequence. Moments later, as the news of Charlé's death was related to him, the boy sat stoically and felt not one grain of remorse. Charlé Tinyabokwe was an evil man and Kayanza was well rid of him.

"Leonard," said the ambassador, "we learned of the massacre from a Hutu nun who was mortified that a priest was part of the conspiracy. From what we can gather, Tutsi guerrillas in and around Kayanza have also learned of the priest's role. They have banded together and crossed the border to Rwanda in search of the killers—including the priest."

"Would my friends have been taken into the group of Tutsi fighters?" Leonard asked.

"I wish I could tell you. We simply don't know," the ambassador said. "But because all the fighting is now over the border in Rwanda, what we do know is that it may be safe—at least for the time being—to travel to Kayanza."

The moment she finished her thought, Leonard said in earnest, "Then I must go—to see my mother."

"I know that is your wish. But Leonard, before we can agree to take you there, I have asked the Marines to survey the Kayanza area to make sure it is as safe as we have been told. We should hear back from them in a day or two."

Jim's initial reaction to Leonard's request had been one of concern for the boy's safety. After hearing the ambassador's security plan, he felt somewhat relieved.

The following evening, Sergeant Rush reported to Ambassador Foster that two Marine Fire Teams, a total of eight men, had spent the entire day patrolling the Kayanza area. "From what they observed, there are no armed fighters from either side in the region. All the warriors seem to be engaged in the battle across the border."

"But the fact that there are no Tutsi warriors in the region to defend women and children—wouldn't that open the way for a Hutu attack on Kayanza?" she asked.

"Not likely," said Rush. "First, the Hutus have all they can handle defending themselves over the border in Rwanda. Second, the Tutsi women and children in the Kayanza region are so spread out that the Hutu warriors would probably not think it worth their while to attack."

Ambassador Foster called a meeting to confer on Sergeant Rush's estimate of the situation. Present were Rush, Jim Keating, Mathias Bizimana, Terrence Ndayisiba, Jesse Abbot, and her husband, Bill. After thirty minutes of discussion, it was agreed that Leonard Tangishaka could visit his mother for Christmas, which was only eight days away.

The boy would be transported by Marines. To ensure his safety, the Marines would remain in the Kayanza region on patrol. They would also bring along more balls and hoops, in the hope that Leonard's friends would somehow find the means to continue their interest in basketball.

"And at the end of Leonard's Christmas visit," said Ambassador Foster, "I will travel to Kayanza with a Marine guard to try to convince Consolaté to return to Bujumbura with her son."

The ambassador began to gather her notes. "Thank you all. If you need me, I'll be in the office for the rest of the day."

Jim didn't get up to leave, but swung around and gazed outside. He was still slightly uneasy about Leonard going home. But because of the boy's intense desire to see his mother, coupled with the protection of a Marine patrol, he agreed with the plan.

Plus, Jim was discovering that the Christmas season was a very special time in Burundi, hopefully a time when all Burundians would reflect on the merits of a truce.

———

For three days prior to the Burundi–Rwanda game, CNN had aired a short promo to boost ratings for the feature that would run within hours after the final buzzer. The promo began with snippets of the widely viewed piece that had been shown several weeks earlier and concluded with Finbar Finnegan on camera at Nimbona Court: "We'll see if Project Oscar—and the career of young Leonard Tangishaka— will take flight on Sunday evening. This is Finbar Finnegan reporting from Bujumbura, Burundi."

The discovery of a superstar, in a sport or the arts, always generates lively interest. Yet in this case, the Leonard Tangishaka story, with so many fascinating sidebars, stirred uncommon curiosity that extended beyond the sports world.

"This has all the elements of high drama. A strife-ridden region whose plight might be lifted by the genius of a diplomatic plan—and the emergence of an athletic prodigy who may change the face of the sport," trumpeted the *International Herald Tribune*.

"The fond hope of the organizers is that Leonard Tangishaka will go far beyond being merely the face of Burundian basketball and be thought of as a force for peace," read the AP wire story dispatched to over one hundred countries.

In response to the widespread hype, Sid Hawkins, Finnegan's boss at CNN, decided to pull out all stops; Show Me Sid was now a believer. The plan would make full use of the Irishman's considerable journalistic skills, as well as clever camera work, and, thankfully, the cooperation of Leonard Tangishaka in the form of some dramatic plays.

The feature began with a shot of the crowd, including the *djembe* drummer, and the hypnotic excitement that enveloped the Nimbona Court. It then focused on Leonard and his striking skills. The final segment was television at its best. Thanks to a Jim Keating comment to Finbar Finnegan after the game about the storied but largely forgotten Bill Russell–Jack Coleman play in the 1957 NBA Championship game, CNN tracked down footage of Russell's tour de force. The CNN piece concluded with the Russell play and then Leonard Tangishaka replicating it.

CNN went so far as to convince legendary Celtics coach Red Auerbach to appear at the station live. Even Auerbach, whose praise was generally confined to players wearing green uniforms, was persuaded.

"I never thought I'd see anyone do that again. I mean, when Russell did it, it brought together so many of his qualities—his speed, timing, vertical jump and, mostly, his heart."

With his customary glibness, and drawing on an ever-present cigar, Auerbach continued: "Now, what the kid did can't compare to Russell's play; I mean my guy did it in the seventh game of a world championship series. But, I must say, I'm damned impressed. He looks like a hell of a prospect."

The seven-minute feature received the highest ratings in CNN history in the "features category." The piece was viewed by 50 million people in more than 125 countries, and the reaction was so strong that CNN decided to air it over four consecutive days at various hours.

In his first game in a sport he had picked up less than three months earlier, Leonard Tangishaka was quickly becoming a household name. As Jim watched the clip alone in his apartment, his concern about Leonard being discovered too early was somewhat neutralized by a real possibility that, only weeks earlier, would have been nearly unthinkable: This young man could well be the greatest of all time.

———

Leonard had watched the CNN piece with Mathias.

"He enjoyed it, Coach," Mathias told Jim on an early morning phone call. "Yet I certainly did not see any swelling of his head. Your lessons about modesty and focus have surely sunk in. But I'll tell you, he is certainly looking forward to today's trip home. The Marines are picking us up in about an hour. Leonard wants to say goodbye to you—and wish you a Merry Christmas. We'll stop by on our way out of Bujumbura."

"Thanks, Mathias. I'll be waiting out front."

After Leonard related his excitement over his approaching reunion with his mother and friends, Jim said in a quiet, fatherly tone, "Leonard, please give my best Christmas wishes to your mom and those boys. And *please* be careful."

Strong from the outset, the bond between the two had coalesced like many such devoted coach/player relationships—and then some. Leonard's early admiration for Jim had evolved into a love that a son, in the best of family ties, accorded a father. As he prepared to leave, and without hesitation, Leonard bent down and hugged his coach hard. "A very Merry Christmas, sir. I will see you next week." Jim simply smiled and nodded. He couldn't speak, for if he opened his mouth, he feared he'd break down.

As the jeep departed, Jim heard the phone ringing in his apartment.

"Good morning, Coach," said Ambassador Foster. "Did Leonard stop by yet?"

"He did . . . just left. What a terrific kid. I miss him already."

"Oh, I don't doubt that for a minute. He's a special gift to all of us," she said. Without missing a beat, she continued. "Jim, since we have a bit of a break, I'm calling with a thought. When you first arrived in Burundi, I mentioned that it might be good for us to discuss some issues related to race. You know, I've never really had what I would call a deep, penetrating conversation with a white person about race relations. What do you think?"

Even though Jim was struck by the slightly forbidding sound of a "deep, penetrating conversation," he quickly responded, "I'd love to, Ambassador. No doubt I can learn from you."

"And I from you, Coach. How about if we start tomorrow at my home? If it's okay with you, I thought we could focus on some things that I'd like to share . . . things that I have been storing up for years . . . things that might give you a better perspective of how I, and many other people of color, feel about certain issues."

"That would be great," said Jim.

"Would 10 AM work?"

"Perfect."

41

When Jim arrived the next morning, he was still a bit on edge at the thought of a discussion on race with a woman of color. But his nerves abated when he was greeted warmly by the ambassador.

"I'm looking forward to this, Coach."

"So am I."

"Then let's get started!"

As the ambassador ushered Jim toward her private office, the coach was struck by the dazzling panoply of Christmas adornments that brightened each room.

"Your decorations are beautiful."

"Some of the ornaments and other decorations are from Indianapolis. Many of the others are ones I've collected over the years in my various diplomatic postings. I've had assignments in six different countries and they're all represented. But the tree decorations are strictly Burundian!"

Jim marveled at the variety of the decorations hanging radiantly from a very tall tree taken from a stand of spruce planted by the Belgians. He felt a twinge of nostalgia looking at the vivid mix of colorful glass, cookies, ribbons and lights, especially two large ornaments near the top: the flags of Burundi and the United States. Jim's dad always put a small American flag near the angel at the top of their tree. In memory of Frank Keating, Jim, Edna, and Sarah did the same each Christmas Eve. The placement of the flag, always done by Sarah from the time she was old enough, was followed by Jim sharing a story or two about his late father.

As they entered the ambassador's private office, Jim once again took note of her personal library. The array of books, all neatly stacked on three oak bookshelves, was marked by section including Africa, women, race, international relations, poetry, and, to Jim's delight, basketball.

"You know, as I mentioned yesterday, I'd like to have this conversation serve to help you gain a greater perspective from a black point of view. If it's okay with you, let me begin with a story from my youth."

"Sounds great."

"There was an incident, Jim, one that I've only spoken about to my sister, Carolyn, who was with me at the time, and to Bill. Growing up black in Indianapolis in the thirties was not easy, but my mother did all she could to raise my sister and I to be people of goodwill. When this incident occurred, I was eight and Carolyn was ten. Daddy had passed five years earlier, so my mother had the double duty of raising two daughters and working as a domestic for a family in the Golden Hills section of Indianapolis, a job she took after Daddy died and kept until my sister and I finished college," she said.

"That must have been tough for your mother. I can't even imagine trying to raise Sarah without Edna at that age," Jim said. The ambassador nodded in agreement and continued.

"There was an ice cream shop, Jim, about ten blocks from our home in a white neighborhood. For many years, there was a 'No Coloreds Allowed' sign in the window. Then, a new family purchased the shop and removed the sign. This was cause for great joy in our neighborhood. A mark of progress. And so, one Saturday morning, my mother dressed my sister and me in matching outfits. Since we had no car, we walked the ten blocks to the ice cream shop. Even as a little girl, I knew how much hope this small step forward brought my mother.

"'Things are changing, girls,' she said to us on the walk. 'Slowly, but for the better, things are changing.'"

The ambassador picked up a paperweight shaped like half a basketball from her desk and ran her fingers along the grooves as she spoke.

"When we first walked into the ice cream shop, I felt such a rush of joy. I remember there were colorful posters of famous people on the walls, including one of Clark Gable. A moment later, I saw a group of white men sitting off in a corner booth. Right away, their presence made me uncomfortable. As soon as they saw us, one of them let out a large groan and then said loudly, 'Let's hope they got plenty of chocolate ice cream today.' The other men laughed.

"My mother ignored the comment and quietly ushered us to the other side of the shop to an empty booth. She asked each of us what we would like. As she spoke, I could see the hurt in her eyes, and I found myself fighting back tears."

Jim examined the ambassador as she spoke and noticed that even though she was physically present at that very moment, her mind was back in the 1940s at the ice cream shop. He knew from the distant look in her eyes that she was replaying the memory as she told him the story.

"Then, one of the cruelest acts I've ever seen occurred. Even to this day, it's hard for me to think about what happened, let alone talk about it."

Cynthia stopped for a moment—distress visible in a deep frown.

"Jim, my mother was a large woman and quite overweight. As she walked to the counter to place her order, that same belligerent man said, even more loudly, 'Bet the husband—if there even was one—cut 'n' run. Can't blame him. Can you imagine f--king that heifer?'

"Now, I had heard the f-word in our neighborhood, but I didn't know what it meant. Only that it was a forbidden word in our house, as was the n-word."

The ambassador paused, taking a deep breath to gather herself. For the first time in their relationship, Jim thought that he detected a trace of bitterness in her eyes. A moment later, she continued.

"It was following that remark that I would see the great-est example of courage and restraint in my life, a reaction by my mother so extraordinary, so admirable, that it has stayed with me to this day."

The ambassador paused again to sip her ice water, and Jim felt himself leaning forward.

"My mother brought our ice cream sundaes to the booth. Her face now reflected, not anger, but a look of ineffable sad-ness and despair. 'Eat your sundaes, girls,' she said softly, and we did, but with no pleasure, certainly no joy. . . . As we were leaving, that same dreadful man could not resist another cruel taunt. Emboldened by no fear of consequences for his actions, he said, 'Surprise she's not getting a second helping,' causing another burst of laughter from his friends.

"Once we were outside, my mother put one arm around my sister and the other around me. 'We will talk about this when we get home, girls,' she said.

"As soon as we arrived at our apartment, Mother hugged both of us and asked us to sit with her at the kitchen table, her favorite place for important discussions.

"What she then said has forever shaped my life. 'Cynthia and Carolyn, what you just saw was the worst of human behavior. But I want both of you to promise me that you will never judge an entire race or religion based on the ignorance of certain people of that race or religion.'

"So my first point: I have kept that promise, Jim. It hasn't always been easy, but I have kept that promise."

After yet another pause, she said, "How about if we take a hot tea break?"

"A good idea," said Jim, for it was clear that this revelation had stirred deep-felt emotions in his friend, who rose and headed for the kitchen.

When tea was finished, Jim spoke up, "Ambassador, I've never heard anything more moving. I can see how it shaped your life."

"Well, Coach, it surely did, and I appreciate your reaction. I felt I had to tell you about it because I thought that as we continue our discussions over time, this might give you a glimpse of what I call the 'Black Experience.' But now, I'd like to share a more positive example."

She sat back and smiled. "Let me tell you something about African Americans you may not know, something that might surprise you. We know who the good guys are!"

Jim furrowed his brow. "I'm not sure what you mean, Ambassador."

"Well, as a case in point, we knew that your friend Bob Cousy was a good guy, that he once took an overnight train with his black Celtics teammate, Chuck Cooper, when a southern hotel wouldn't let Cooper stay with the rest of the Celtics. That was the kind of information that spread quickly through the black communities—and still does. Did you know the Cousy-Cooper story, Jim?"

"Yes." Jim smiled, pleased at the ambassador's reference to Cousy, a man he admired.

"Well here's one you may not know about; one that was a key to Bill attending Indiana State. You see, before our school was called Indiana State, it was called Indiana State Teachers College. In 1946 and 1947, the school had a future legend as its coach."

"John Wooden!"

"Yes. And I'm not surprised you know that Coach Wooden was at our school just before he went to UCLA. But let me tell you what John Wooden did. In his first year, the team had an 17-8 record, good enough to be invited to the NAIA National Tournament in Kansas City. But the NAIA had a no colored rule, and the team had but one player of color on the roster by the name of Clarence Walker.

"Well, Jim, Coach Wooden refused the invitation, pointing out the unfairness of the rule. By the way, Clarence Walker was one of the last players on the bench, but that didn't matter to the coach.

"And so, the school's basketball program became known in the black community as one of fairness, which is why Bill chose to play there.

"The larger point I'm making is that there is a great deal of discussion among blacks about who the good guys are, and who the bad guys are."

Jim nodded in fascination. He had never heard this point of view.

"For example, Boston was a frequent topic of discussion and a real paradox. We knew the Celtics and their Coach Red Auerbach were color-blind. Yet when I was a girl, and even through college, we thought of the Red Sox as racist."

"Which they probably were," said Jim. "I heard that many times about that era."

"I'm not surprised. You know, Jim, there was a story around our neighborhood about the former Red Sox owner, whose name slips my mind."

"Tom Yawkey."

"Exactly. Anyway, as the story goes, when Jackie Robinson was among several African Americans trying out for the Red Sox, Yawkey allegedly ran out of the dugout yelling 'get those n——s off the field.' We also heard that not only did Jackie try out for the Red Sox, but so did Willie Mays. Can you imagine being so racist as to not want Willie Mays on your team?"

"I cannot. But, and this is interesting, Ambassador, I once read an article about Yawkey which suggested that, in the later stages of his life, he changed his views. Growing up in Worcester, I was a Red Sox fan, so I knew quite a bit about Yawkey, including the rumors that he was a racist. Yet this article, which was written after he died, pointed out that Yawkey and his family set up a charitable foundation, which, to this day, helps kids from at-risk neighborhoods."

"Now, that *is* interesting, Jim. And to be honest, I never heard that about Yawkey, and I'm glad to hear it now. I believe, strongly believe, that many inherently good people are in this category. You know, I remember a college philosophy professor saying to our class that many of us have false beliefs, and that when we see the truth it's up to all of us to change our beliefs. Now, bear in mind, this was a white professor at Indiana State in the '50s. There were several African Americans in the class, and we all wondered if he was directing his comments toward white people and race. And you know what? The very next class I summoned my courage and asked him if this was his intention. And, Jim, in front of the whole class, the professor said, 'That's exactly what I intended!'"

Jim smiled again, and said, "You've always had courage."

"Not always, but I appreciate the compliment."

And then, with a look of mischief and vitality in her voice, the ambassador said, "Jim, guess who my favorite baseball player was?"

"Willie?"

"Nope."

"Jackie?"

"Nope."

"Then I give up!"

"Teddy!"

"Ted Williams?"

"Ted Williams!" she confirmed. "You know, Coach, I will never forget the first time I saw Ted swing the bat. It was the summer before I went off to college and I was at a friend's home who had a television. Her dad was watching what I believe was called the Game of the Week, the Red Sox against the Yankees. I was mesmerized by his swing. It was flawless, the most beautiful execution of a sports skill I'd ever seen, and that even included Oscar's jump shot. About a month later, I read an article about Ted in *The Sporting News*. He was so authentic, so much himself."

"I agree with that, Ambassador. As a young man, other than the Cooz, Ted was my favorite player."

Jim shifted forward and put his hands on the arms of his chair, feeling like their conversation may be coming to an end.

However, the ambassador spoke up. "Coach, before you go, I have one final story about the racial lens, a personal experience that had a lot of meaning for me."

"I'd love to hear it; I want to hear more!" said Jim.

"Well, when I was a sophomore at Indiana State, I took an introduction to poetry class, which changed my life in a variety of ways. The professor was white and wonderful. Her name was Dr. Wilma Sheehan, and she had a particular love of Emily Dickinson. By the way, Professor Sheehan always called the poet Miss Emily. Our text contained a number of Miss Emily's poems, including one of her greatest, 'I Measure Every Grief I Meet.'"

The ambassador continued, "Professor Sheehan assigned our class to read the poem and produce a paper that provided analysis and interpretation. The analysis, of course, involved our thoughts on syntax, imagery, and the like. But, as I mentioned, we also had to offer our interpretation of the poem.

"Well, there were twenty students in the class, eighteen of whom were white, my friend, Marilyn Nixon, and I being the only two students of color. I found the poem to be both extraordinary and very sad. My God, Jim, it is so beautiful, and it so poignantly reveals the kind of courage and strength that those who grieve must possess in order to get through life. By the way, it was clear that much of the poem was written based on the personal experience of Miss Emily. I'll make sure to get you a copy."

"I would like that."

"But here's the point! In the interpretation part of our papers, all eighteen white students saw the poem as relating primarily to the loss a loved one through death. But independent of each other, Marilyn and I both saw the poem as one related to race as much as or more so than to death. In other words, we connected grief to the racial hurts inflicted on people of color. So, eighteen whites see it one way, the two African Americans see it in a completely different way."

"Now that, too, is interesting!" said Jim, at once absorbed and motionless.

"It surely is. And for me, it made the case that virtually all people of color, myself included, most definitely see things through a racial lens. A lot of white people ask about those deep thoughts that go back generations. The truth is, because people of color so often see things through a racial lens, we are, at least in my view, several generations away from removing that lens. But, Coach, on the other hand, we simply can't let our lens shade our views of all things white. I hope in my case, my lens has been one of brightness rather than one of darkness."

"Madam Ambassador, you radiate brightness."

The ambassador smiled, then looked at her watch. "You know about my 11 o'clock meeting. And I realize I've done all the talking. But I hope that this at least gets us off to a good start."

"It sure does," said Jim. "Thank you for such a great conversation."

"A pleasure. And I'm looking forward to seeing you on Christmas Eve."

"Can't wait," said Jim.

"Coach, may I conclude with one final message?"

"Sure."

"When you arrived in Burundi, and throughout your stay, I've sensed that you need to purge from your mind the doubts, the troublesome thoughts, caused by the Robert Frazier incident."

"You're right on, Ambassador."

"Well, do me a big favor. Please leave this meeting knowing that you are no racist. In fact, you're just the opposite, both in your words and, most importantly, in your spirit. So, if I may borrow from the Bible, go in peace, Jim, for you deserve peace."

As Jim prepared to depart, he thought to himself, *I must reach out to Robert Frazier.*

The two good friends stood, embraced, and felt the fruits of mutual respect.

After he left, the ambassador sat down and leaned back in her chair. *Now, why didn't I tell him more about Ted Williams?* she wondered.

42

Christmas Eve

It would be Jim's first Christmas in a foreign country. Even during his stint in Spain, he was always able to make it home for Christmas Day, an improvement over his intercollegiate coaching experience. The travel schedule required to compete in Division-I holiday tournaments often precluded spending December 25 with family, an ill-advised practice he never liked.

Though Jim had saved enough money to get to Worcester for the holidays, the decision to remain in Bujumbura had been an easy one. He was immersed in his job, and he felt anxiety about returning to a place where his life had careened into clinical depression. Even if he went back, where would he go? Sarah had made plans to spend Christmas with her boyfriend's family in Chicago, and Jim did not think it fair to ask her to cancel the trip. He'd kept his apartment in Worcester, but the notion of staying there alone was not appealing. Plus, life was on the upswing in Burundi, and he knew that his daughter was saving to visit him.

Christmas in Burundi turned out to be better than Jim could ever have imagined. The Christian culture of the country included a variety of traditions that Jim enjoyed, especially the presence of drummers and tambourine dancers, both of which raised the festivities far above the "Silent Night" level he was used to. But the primary source of Yuletide cheer came from Ambassador Foster, who did her utmost to make the Christmas season a joyous experience for everyone around her.

This was especially so on Christmas Eve.

Years earlier, Ambassador Foster had served as Cultural Attaché at the American Embassy in Rome. While in Italy, one of her friends had invited the Foster family to a Christmas Eve *cena* at which the friend introduced the Fosters to a lovely Italian tradition that Cynthia had replicated on each Christmas Eve since—the Italian "7 Fish" dinner.

The hostess, Juliana Coppola, had explained the tradition. "The reason behind it, Cynthia, is that Christmas Eve in Italy was always part of the *Vigilia Di Magro*, a day of abstinence in which the Catholic Church prohibits the consumption of meat. Please understand that, over time, as the stricture became less observed, the tradition has continued . . . even flourished."

The ambassador had been taken by the elegance of that night, not to mention the savory taste of the slithery eels, bowls of heaping shellfish, and other delicacies served by Juliana. Cynthia decided to make it her own annual Christmas rite, and Juliana had surprised her by eagerly offering her various Christmas Eve recipes, which had been passed down by Juliana's family over many generations.

In her posting in Burundi, Cynthia always planned Christmas Eve dinner well in advance, including flying in seven kinds of frozen fish.

The night of December 24, Bill Foster rang a small ornamental bell he'd retrieved from the Christmas tree, and the guests, including all embassy personnel as well as Mathias and Terrance, dined on broccoli rabe, a choice of vermicelli *aglio e olio* (or vermicelli with garlic and olive oil), and a seven-fish main course that included roasted eel. Cynthia had chosen wines from the Piedmont region, a Pinot Grigio and a Cortese.

The ambassador wrapped up the meal with a *caponata di pesce*, a delicious fish salad, followed by desserts, tiramisu— Jim's favorite—and Amaretto truffles.

On the way out that evening, the ambassador approached Jim and said, "I hope you enjoyed yourself, Coach."

"It was wonderful, Ambassador . . . wonderful."

"By the way, Jim, this came to our office." The ambassador handed Jim what was clearly a Christmas card from Sarah. Later that evening, surrounded by darkness and no small measure of loneliness, Jim felt comfort from a beautiful message written by his daughter that concluded: *You are the most important person in my life, Daddy. And I just knew that Burundi was the perfect place for you! I love you so much.*

He missed Sarah dearly. He also admitted to himself that he missed the comfort of female companionship. He looked much better; the Burundian air and sun, daily exercise regimen, and a low-fat diet had resulted in a twenty-five-pound weight loss—and a healthy, outdoor mien.

But any thought of a new relationship was tempered by an old question: Could any other woman arouse the feelings of warmth and excitement he still felt for Edna?

His thoughts then turned to their final moments together.

———

"Can you hear me, love?"

Edna's eyes flickered, and she squeezed his hand tightly.

Of the thousands of messages he had imparted to Edna since their first brief meeting on a cold winter February in 1941, and knowing she was but breaths away from passing, Jim wanted to get this last one right.

Leaning closer, he whispered, "I remember reading something, Edna—a quotation from one of your favorites, the sculptor Saint Gaudens: *'Don't come down from the high place I hold you in my heart.'*"

Edging yet closer, he kissed his beloved wife on her forehead and said, "And you never have, my love . . . ever."

Edna mustered one last gentle squeeze of her husband's hand . . . and then departed.

———

She was so strong. How can I not be? And she would surely want me to be happy.

43

Two evenings later, the first soft knock went unheeded. One product of Jim Keating's renewed state of contentment was deep and restful sleep. The second knock, more intense, caused Jim to adjust his pillow and assume that the vague intrusion of sound must be part of a dream. The third knock, loud and insistent, startled Jim, and he fully awoke.

The old coach abruptly rose from his bed and looked at the clock. 2:11.

Jim's first reaction was concern for his personal safety. While no American had been attacked within the confines of Bujumbura, Jim knew that such aggression was conceivable. As he stepped cautiously toward the back door, he grabbed a large knife from the kitchen counter. In a robust voice that camouflaged his fear, he asked, "Who is it?"

"It's me, Jim," said Jesse Abbot, in an ominously spiritless tone.

Jim set down the knife, switched on the light, and opened the door. Abbot stood before him, his face twisted in stark despair.

"It's horrible news, Jim. Horrible . . . horrible."

As Jesse Abbot's words succumbed to a fit of tears, Jim's mind raced through the dreadful possibilities. Within seconds, Abbot regained enough composure to confirm the most heartbreaking option Jim had considered.

"It's Leonard, Jim. He's dead." Holding back another sob, Jesse said, "And so is his mother . . . his wonderful mother."

The news rendered Jim helpless. Instinctively, he wanted more facts, but his grief was so immediate, so powerful, that he could not speak. For several moments, the two men faced each other, both crippled with anguish. Finally, the one who would carry the heaviest weight of sorrow, the one whose once-shattered spirit was remarkably sanguine again here in this African land, somehow summoned his self-control.

"Jesse, we must sit down."

A sip of water helped Jesse Abbot regain enough composure to tell Jim all he knew. "Ambassador Foster called me half an hour ago. The Marine patrol returned at about midnight and went straight to her home."

Agitated, Jim covered his face with his hands. "But I thought they were on patrol to protect Leonard?"

"They were, but fighting broke out near the border, about fifteen miles from where Leonard lived. They went up there to check on the situation, primarily to make sure that those involved were not heading toward Leonard's region. When they showed up, they were fired on and pinned down."

Abbot paused to sip more water. He took a deep breath and let it out slowly. He went on to tell Jim what the ambassador had shared with him: After taking intermittent fire for several hours, things suddenly got quiet and the Marines realized that their attackers had fled. But before they took off, they managed to disable the Marine jeeps—shot the tires out. The Marines radioed for help. Six hours later, a UN peacekeeping force showed up. The UN people immediately brought the Marines to Leonard's area. By the time they got there, Leonard and Consolaté had been murdered.

"That's all I know, Jim," Abbot said. "But the Ambassador and Bill are on their way over here. She'll give us more details."

For a moment, the two men sat in silence, which Abbot finally broke. "Jim, I'm *so* sorry."

For Jim, the terrible implications of the two deaths were now in clear focus. Jesse's despair and the Fosters' impending arrival caused Jim to withdraw into a Spartan stoicism.

I won't break down.

Yet despite this façade, Jim knew that the tragedy might force him, once again, into the depths of severe depression. As he held his emotional ground, there was a gentle knock at the door.

———

As soon as the Fosters entered the apartment, they broke down in tears, which set to rest Jim Keating's plan to stifle his own grief. Jim, who had changed from his sleeping clothes, hugged the two and wept himself.

When the long embrace drew to a close, Ambassador Foster spoke in a near whisper: "I was just on the phone with President Buyayo. He is concerned about what the reaction will be over the murders. He feels, and I agree with him, that when the Tutsis learn of the deaths, they might react violently."

"Ambassador," said Jim, "I may be completely naïve about this, but at the Rwanda game, it seemed that the Hutus were every bit as proud of Leonard as were the Tutsis."

"You're right, Jim. In fact, on the way over, Bill and I talked about that, as well as about the way these murders should be revealed to the public. At Bill's suggestion, I'm going to encourage President Buyayo to hold a press conference with a number of Hutu and Tutsi present—all of whom will be asked to forcefully express their complete revulsion over the murders. And

I'm also going to suggest to the president that he state what is fact—that Leonard and Consolaté Tangishaka ..."

Cynthia Foster harbored great affection for Consolaté. She paused to gather herself.

"Sorry, gentlemen. As I was saying, we hope the president will remind everyone that the lives of Leonard and Consolaté were about the rejection of violence. We hope he will challenge people to follow their lead. We hope this terrible tragedy will unite the people in their denouncement of killing."

As she spoke, the ambassador became so intense and moving that it almost appeared as if she were delivering the speech herself.

Jesse Abbot felt the full force of Cynthia Foster's eloquence and acute emotion. His diplomatic instincts made him realize that his boss must play a prominent role in announcing the circumstances of the deaths.

Jim offered his own perspective. "You know, you're right, Ambassador. That's exactly what Leonard and Consolaté stood for. One evening during dinner at Mathias's home, Leonard told us at length about his mother's insistence that he shun all forms of violence—even words of incitement. . . . Speaking of Mathias, we must tell him."

"I agree," said the ambassador. "We'll go there together. But first, let's talk about the next twenty-four hours. There are certain people like Mathias, as well as all team members, who must be told personally. In fact, as a show of unity, the players and Mathias are among the group who should be present at President Buyayo's announcement.

"Then there is the matter of the funeral or memorial service. The Marines said they considered trying to bring the bodies back to Bujumbura. However, a Tutsi warrior, evidently wounded trying to help Leonard and Consolaté, insisted that the bodies remain in Kayanza because Tutsi burial tradition calls for the bodies to be buried near the hut of residence."

For a moment, a slight expression of hope crossed through Jim's face. "So there has been no positive identification of their bodies?"

"Actually, there has," the ambassador replied with a sad sigh. "The Marines took photos of the bodies, and I personally viewed them. I'm sorry, Jim, but there is no doubt about the identities."

After a solemn lull, Jesse said, "Something just occurred to me—I thought all the adult warriors in that region were in Rwanda fighting?"

"So did we," said the ambassador. "But both warriors supposedly returned for several days to check on their families and to offer protection to the other families in the region.... Anyway, it is the Tutsi tradition to bury their dead right away—and literally within yards of their hut. But despite this, after we sort things out with President Buyayo's office, I plan to work with the president to send a group of Marines and Burundi National Defense Force officers to Kayanza, along with a doctor, to conduct an autopsy."

The men nodded, agreeing that an autopsy was needed.

"Also, if Leonard and Consolaté are to be buried in Kayanza, then I think that we should arrange for a memorial Mass in Bujumbura as soon as possible. This will give all of us, including teammates and fans, the opportunity to pay our respects. Plus, a memorial Mass will hopefully prompt people to temper their anger.... Oh, and one other important matter: Until we find all the team members and gather them for President Buyayo's announcement, we must keep this information from the general public."

"We'll do that," said Abbot.

Cynthia moved a step closer to her husband. She put her hand on his shoulder and Bill put his arm around her waist. She closed her eyes for a moment.

"Now," she said, "I think we should all go to Mathias's home."

As the group moved slowly toward the door, Bill Foster felt a measure of relief, knowing that a minor but important step had just been taken amidst the catastrophe. When his wife had learned the devastating news, she had gently dismissed the Marines, returned to their bedroom, and wept uncontrollably, her body shaking in a fit of convulsive rage. Amid the guttural wails were the words: "It is my fault. I let him go home and look what happened."

As the man behind the woman, Bill would do as he had always done; he would extend his unconditional love to his partner. And in this case, as much as ever before, he would keep watch over Cynthia, who, to him, was a hero—a person who had always defied the odds—a person who had always defined courage and leadership.

This tragedy will present Cynthia with the most severe test of her life. This to someone whom I have seen pass test after daunting test and never turn back . . . never give quarter to what should be.

———

It was just before 3 AM when the four anguished and exhausted comrades arrived at Mathias's home. As they approached his door, Cynthia said to the three men, "He will surely see in our faces that tragedy has struck. So I will tell him as soon as he greets us. . . . I will not make him wait."

Needing to control her own emotions, she was gentle and direct when Mathias opened the door. "Mathias, I am so very sorry to bring terrible news. Leonard and Consolaté have been killed. We don't have all of the details yet, but the deaths have been confirmed."

Stunned, Mathias stared at her for a moment, motioned for the four to enter, and then turned away. Jim stepped closer and rested a hand on his shoulder. Mathias put a hand over his mouth and groaned deeply. It was almost a growl. His face was eerily impassive, but his words sounded forced from his throat.

"When my wife and son died, I thought I could never again feel such grief. But this boy . . . this boy—he was a son. I don't know how it will be to live without him."

Everyone remained silent. Mathias closed his eyes, bent his head back, breathed deeply, and let out a long sigh. He then faced his visitors. "I am grateful that all of you came to tell me. Please . . . please do sit down."

Intuitively, the old man knew that he must choke back his grief and project a strong, stable demeanor in the hours and days to come. He spoke slowly, as though he were translating.

"This terrible situation could go one of two ways: Either the murders will cause an outbreak of violence by Tutsi and Hutus or, if we handle it carefully and we are lucky, perhaps people from both sides will finally see how this violence is poisoning our lives. . . . Ambassador, I will work in the Tutsi community to try to prevent a violent reaction. In my opinion, our next step should be to visit Terrence Ndayisiba, for he can help in the Hutu community."

The relationship between Mathias and Terrence, the founding fathers of Burundian basketball, spanned more than three decades and was as devoted as it was enduring. Terrence reacted as Mathias knew he would, his sorrow exceeded only by his commitment to rally his fellow Hutus in outrage over the senseless act.

"I know where every Hutu player lives, and I will go with all of you to tell each one," he said.

With the aid of a four-man Marine detail, Ambassador Foster and the men spent the next hours making their middle of the night and early morning duty visits—first to team members in Bujumbura and then, at first light, to the players in the country.

Every athlete reacted with the same shock and sadness, and all agreed to Ambassador Foster's two requests: "Please keep the murders completely quiet and please come to my home at noon."

It was 10:45 when the group finally returned to the capital city. Ambassador Foster immediately called President Buyoya to relate the tragic news. The president agreed to her suggestion of a formal announcement with both Tutsi and Hutu present. The announcement would take place at 2:00 that afternoon at the president's office.

By noon, every player had arrived. Joining the team were several prominent Hutu and Tutsi citizens, each of whom had been hand-picked by Mathias and Terrence to attend the announcement. After a light lunch of sandwiches and soft drinks, Ambassador Foster called the group together.

"Our Deputy Chief of Mission, Jesse Abbot, is now calling the media to inform them of the press conference. We have asked all of you to be present at the announcement to show a united front. All of you who knew Leonard are aware that he was opposed to the civil war that has torn this country apart. What you might not know is that it was his dear mother, Consolaté, who had such a profound influence on Leonard's view of the violence."

Raising her voice an octave, the ambassador continued, "Leonard and Consolaté Tangishaka would want their deaths to serve as a forceful reminder to everyone in Burundi that the violence is a disease that will not heal until all of us come together as one to stop it. We want all of you—every one of you—to express those feelings at the press conference."

With tears streaming down his cheeks, Michel Obadele, the Hutu point guard, said, "We will, Madam Ambassador. We will." The others nodded intently. And while their support caused Ambassador Foster to smile in gratitude, she knew that a murderous reaction was still a very real possibility.

I must hold steady . . . and lead, said the unremitting, internal voice that guided her every stride.

44

With Ambassador Foster standing by his side, Burundian President Peter Buyoya said solemnly, "Ladies and gentleman of the media, I have tragic news. Leonard Tangishaka, our brilliant young basketball player, and his beloved mother, Consolaté, have been killed in their home in Kayanza."

Standing in the front row, Finbar Finnegan felt like he'd been punched in the chest, and his throat tightened. When Finnegan had retrieved the message from Jesse Abbot about the press conference, he tried to contact Abbot at the Embassy. Unable to reach him, Finbar went straight to President Buyoya's office, arriving just after noon in the hope of getting an early tip. He found that the president's top advisors were all sequestered and lower-level aides weren't talking. The announcement was surely one of consequence.

Over the next hour and forty-five minutes, as more journalists arrived, rumors circulated through the hallway. The most prominent of the scuttlebutt was that Ambassador Foster was being reassigned. But when the president's office doors opened at 2:00, Finnegan took note of the morbid faces at the front of the room and also realized that Leonard Tangishaka was not among them. His eyes fell upon Jim Keating.

Finbar had last seen Jim at the post-game reception, when the coach had walked on air. Yet even before Buyoya began his announcement, Jim's forlorn expression forecast an unwelcome message.

When the president finished his statement, there was an instant of strained hush. A reporter from Reuters broke the silence. "What details are available?"

"We know very little," responded Buyoya. "What we do know is that the US Marines were told that Leonard and Consolaté were attacked by a band of guerrillas."

"Hutu guerrillas?" shouted a reporter from the rear of the room.

"We are not even certain of that. But as we get more details, we will, of course, make them available to you," a pledge Finnegan knew might likely be broken.

President Buyoya turned the microphone over to Ambassador Foster, who read a prepared statement:

"The tragic deaths of Leonard and Consolaté Tangishaka must be treated in the manner that Leonard and Consolaté would have wished. We must all react to these deaths by saying, loudly—with *one* voice—that the violence must cease. We must say this to our friends, and ask them—even tell them—to deliver this message to their friends.

"Consolaté and Leonard Tangishaka rejected the violence that has overwhelmed this country. All of us who stand before you today—Burundian and American, Hutu, Tutsi, and Twa—will honor their memories by rejecting the violence. We ask all citizens of this country to join us in this denouncement."

Jesse Abbot handed the statement, signed by the Burundian basketball team and other invited guests, to the media. President Buyoya then announced that a memorial Mass would be held

351

the following day at noon. He concluded the press conference by again imploring the media to "bring this message of nonviolence to the public."

As the group at the podium exited through the rear door, Finbar Finnegan slumped on a wooden chair, covered his face with his hands, and thought about Leonard Tangishaka. Proud of being the first journalist to discover Leonard, Finbar had developed great affection for the boy.

"He's so innocent . . . unsullied by that offensive sense of entitlement so many star athletes display," Finbar had said to bureau chief Sid Hawkins just after the Rwanda game.

Finnegan realized that he must compose himself and call Hawkins. He had introduced Leonard Tangishaka to the world but a few weeks earlier. Now he must convey the message of the young man's death.

Then he must seek out the facts.

———

With the Nimbona Court serving as backdrop, Finbar Finnegan delivered his report to *The World*. He spoke of the shock and sadness that had overtaken Bujumbura, and he addressed the wishful ideal of those who had been close to the deceased: "Their earnest hope is that the deaths of Leonard and Consolaté Tangishaka will somehow temper the violence."

While again airing footage of the boy's extraordinary play against Rwanda, Finnegan said, "Surely one game—one brief but brilliant debut and closing act—does not credential Leonard Tangishaka as a superstar. But there are those, like his coach, Jim Keating—undeniably a basketball scholar—who feel that Leonard would have reached the very heavens of his sport."

Finnegan concluded with quiet intensity: "To those who were privileged to have known this remarkable prodigy, as humble as he was gifted, he was the athlete dying young

of A. E. Housman's verse: 'Like the wind through woods . .
. Through him the gale of life blew high.' Finbar Finnegan
reporting from Bujumbura, Burundi."

The report was viewed by millions, most reacting with
the normal sadness that accompanies the death of an adoles-
cent with such promise. But in the west wing of a plush estate
many miles and borders from Bujumbura, a small group of
men smugly watched the account. When Finnegan was done,
the leader of the group switched off the large-screen TV and
proposed a toast.

———

A massive crowd gathered at St. Peter's Church in Bujumbura
to pay their final respects and celebrate the lives of Leonard
and Consolaté Tangishaka. Anticipating the large turnout,
Jesse Abbot had set up loudspeakers for those forced to stand
outside.

At a breakfast meeting, Ambassador Foster and President
Buyoya agreed that a formal investigation into the deaths of
Leonard and Consolaté must be carried out. Only two hours
after the Mass, a group of seventeen men boarded five Marine
jeeps and began their mission to Kayanza.

At Ambassador Foster's suggestion, President Buyoya
sent his personal physician, Dr. Natare Nicombero, to per-
form the autopsy. He also assigned five of his top Burundi
National Defense Force officers to the team of investigators.
Six US Marines, including Sergeant Rush and Privates John
White and Chris McKeon—the two men who had reported
the deaths to Ambassador Foster—also made the journey.
The doctor and eleven military men were joined by Mathias
Bizimana, Terrence Ndayisiba, Bill Foster, Jim Keating, and
Finbar Finnegan.

At the breakfast meeting, when Jesse Abbot proposed
that Finnegan accompany the group, Ambassador Foster

reacted with concern: "As much as I like Finbar, I'm not sure that a member of the media should be allowed such access."

But Abbot's persistence included the clincher: "This is a guy who'll know exactly what questions to ask—and exactly where to look for the answers. Plus, better that he goes with our protection than being in harm's way. Any security that CNN would hire would be questionable at best."

While the shock of the killings had brought about a momentary calm in Bujumbura, those making the trip were aware that, out in the country, few warriors even knew about the deaths, so remote were they from media reports or even word of mouth. And in many cases, those who had been informed were so steeped in their hatred of the other tribe that the tragedy would have no impact on their thinking . . . or actions.

In the lead jeep, Finnegan drew a comparison to the Troubles of Northern Ireland.

Refusing to use the name "Northern Ireland," coined by the Brits decades earlier, Finnegan said, "In the north of Ireland, the problem with maintaining non-violence is that even if the Irish Republican Army is a willing party in a cease-fire, there are many splinter groups within that organization. Any one of them—even a small band of two or three people—can decide to bomb a pub or shoot a soldier, knowing full well that such an act will derail the peace process."

He continued, "In Burundi, and you gentlemen in the Marine Corps would know this better than I, it appears that there is an almost infinite number of splinter groups within each tribe. In fact, with the Hutu insurgents, there is virtually no central authority. So, while I believe the murders of Leonard and Consolaté will actually calm things down in Bujumbura for a period of time, there is always the danger of a few causing great harm to many."

"Translated, that means we'd best be careful," said Rush.

"Exactly."

When the five jeeps approached Kayanza, the women and children who sighted the convoy through the deep brush scurried into their huts.

"We noticed the same thing last week," said Private White. "With the men all off at war, the mothers and kids are afraid."

Rush shook his head slowly. "It's so different than it was several months ago. I mean, when we first came here—and the men, even Charlé, were around—the children were so curious and friendly when they saw us, especially those of us with white faces."

Twenty minutes later, after navigating the treacherous stone road that led to the Tangishaka dwelling, the jeeps parked a quarter of a mile from Leonard and Consolaté's hut. Sergeant Rush motioned to White and McKeon to lead the way to the burial site.

As the group began their short hike, McKeon said, "The two warriors told us that the burials would take place over there—in that open area between the cocoa trees."

Everyone picked up the pace. Within seconds after they reached the site, Sergeant Rush stated the obvious, "There are no bodies buried here."

"Let's check the hut," said Captain Audace Niyangabo, officer-in-charge of the Burundi contingent.

The rest of the men followed Niyangabo to Leonard and Consolaté's home, only yards from where the grave was reported to be. The hut was in disorder: chairs broken, a ceramic bowl smashed, even the mud walls bore the imprints of bodies crashing against them.

Jim shook his head. "Looks like there was quite a fight here."

"Looks that way," said Finnegan. "But it's odd that there are no blood stains."

The Irishman's training included several criminology courses he took during The Troubles at the University of Ulster at Jordanstown, just outside of Belfast. He knew what to look for at a murder scene.

355

"In fact, a lot appears odd to me. It almost looks as if someone ransacked the hut to make it appear that a struggle took place. I mean, why would the chairs be broken but not the table, which is fragile at best? Why would the bowl be broken but none of the other crockery?"

"I agree," said Rush. "And it's clear we have some major work to do here. Best thing now is to break up into four groups. We need to search the entire region; try to find the graves, try to find the two warriors, talk to people about clues."

"Captain Niyangabo," continued Rush, "we'll need help with translation. So please make sure at least one of your men who can speak English is in each group."

After Niyangabo nodded his agreement, McKeon said, "Let's remember what I told Ambassador Foster—one of the two warriors was wounded."

"And it is likely," added Mathias, "that he would have sought medical help from a healer in the region."

Rush handed Mathias a large map. "Okay, Mathias, you and the captain break it down for us. Where does each team go?"

Mathias spread the map on the floor and, with Captain Niyangabo's help, outlined the area each team should search.

"The huts in Kayanza are one to two kilometers apart so it will take each party a good four to five hours—at least," Mathias said.

"Okay," said Rush. "Meet back here when you're done."

Five hours later, the four teams had all returned to the Tangishaka hut. Two startling facts were apparent: No one in the region claimed to know the whereabouts of the two warriors—or even their identities—and not one Kayanza healer had treated a wounded warrior in more than a month.

But one additional piece of evidence was even more remarkable: No one knew that Leonard and Consolaté Tangishaka had been murdered.

45

The group decided to spend the night in Kayanza and continue their investigation the next day. Four squad tents were pitched. In front of the fire, kept low as a security precaution, Finbar assumed the role of discussion leader and raised some important questions.

"Private McKeon and Private White—in light of what went on today, I must ask—are you both certain the dead bodies you saw were those of Leonard and Consolaté?"

"Absolutely," said McKeon. "We knew what Leonard looked like and we saw Consolaté in person the day before the murders. Plus, all of you saw the pictures. There's no doubt it was them."

"Did you see the wounds on their bodies?"

"No," replied White. "The bodies were draped in what looked to me like a white tablecloth—you know, a light cloth, like linen. We were told by one of the warriors, and correct me if I'm wrong on this, Mathias, that covering the bodies like that is customary before a Tutsi burial."

Mathias nodded, and the Marine continued, "Like I said back in Bujumbura, we asked the two warriors when and where the burials would take place. They told us the bodies would be buried the following morning just a few meters west of the hut—exactly where we searched."

After a pause, White said, "I guess we should have asked more questions."

"No," said Mathias. "You did the right thing. Neither of you could have known that they'd mislead you."

"Also," said Finnegan, "I have a strange feeling that had the two of you done more than just take pictures, you might've encountered some real trouble."

Clive Rush, still burdened with having recommended Leonard's visit home, felt that the Marines should have been more persistent. But he remained quiet, realizing this was not the place to question the judgment of McKeon and White.

"Well," said Finnegan, "let me ask you two one more question. Did the warriors seem surprised to see you?"

"Tough to say," said White. "They would have spotted us coming so they would have had time to compose themselves."

"Okay, then let me ask the whole group a question. Did anyone here feel that any person you spoke with today is hiding something?"

After a chorus of no's, Mathias said, "If they were murdered in the manner the two warriors described, it is surely possible that no one else would have seen it or known about it. There is a fair distance between huts, and, as we have seen, the women and children are so fearful that they are remaining close to their own huts. For my part, I am quite certain that if someone was hiding something from me today, I would have detected it.

"But I must also say that of the many odd things about this situation, the one most surprising to me is why a band of Hutu guerrillas would pick out a mother and a son—indeed a boy with enormous strength—and not attack anyone else in the area. What was their motivation?"

Jim Keating spoke up: "Wouldn't they have heard about Leonard—a Tutsi—and all that he would do for his country? Maybe they had the type of hatred that would not allow them to think a Tutsi would be such a healing force."

"Unlikely," said Terrence. A Hutu, he was feeling a bit uncomfortable with the direction of the conversation. "You must understand, Jim, that news travels very slowly in these parts. While people in Bujumbura might find out about a Leonard Tangishaka in a day or so—it is quite possible it would take several weeks—even months—for the word to travel out this far."

"Even though Finbar's report went out weeks before the game and there were newspaper accounts as well?" Jim's voice had a trace of frustration. He felt like he was listening to a scouting report fraught with key gaps.

"Yes," said Terrence. "It would certainly take more than just a week or two to plan something like this."

"Unless," said Finnegan, "the plan came out of Bujumbura . . . or somewhere else outside the country. And the question, of course, is why?"

"Why indeed," said Mathias. "And I also think it is strange that no one in the region knows of the two warriors. Most people I spoke with said that all the men were off fighting. They expressed surprise that any warriors would be here in this region."

"Another question," said Mathias, as he looked to White and McKeon. "What about the warrior who was wounded? How severe was it?"

"Well," said White, "his face was badly scratched, and he had a bloodstained bandage covering his left arm. Said it was grazed by a machete. But to be honest, I never actually saw the wound on his arm—just the bloody bandage."

Captain Niyangabo raised his own question, "And these two warriors claimed they lived in Kayanza?"

"Yes," said McKeon. "They said they were back in the region to check on their families—and to protect the other families, as well."

"Yet," said Niyangabo, "we cannot find any families who belong to them."

As several men shook their heads incredulously, Finbar had the last word before the group turned in, "Until we find the bodies—or those two warriors—we won't know much else about what happened. And, if there is more to this than we originally thought, which now appears likely, my guess is that we'll have great difficulty finding the bodies—or the two warriors."

Jim remained unsettled. But he was glad Finnegan had come along.

——

The men arose at daybreak, and Rush laid out the plan.

"Each team head back to the areas you searched yesterday and scour those areas for recent burials. And question everyone you see—again—particularly about whether anyone spotted those two warriors or anyone else new to the region. Meet back here at the campsite by no later than fourteen hundred hours—that's 2:00 for you civilians—so we can get back to Bujumbura well before dark."

Before the four teams headed out, Jim quietly shared an observation with Mathias: "It's interesting that the Burundian military men seem to defer to Sergeant Rush and the other Marines."

"Aaah, Jim," said Mathias, "for the most part, we in Burundi look at any American with authority as our leader. Have you noticed the respect that our president accords Ambassador Foster?"

"I hadn't thought of it in that way. But now that you mention it, I certainly have noticed how President Buyoya often defers to the ambassador. You could see it at the press conference."

"Exactly, Jim. Most Burundians know little about America, and what they do know all relates to a core perception of power and wealth. Because we are by and large an illiterate country, our judgments are often based on views that can be inaccurate and fleeting. Plus, because of the poverty and despair in Burundi, those views often tilt toward the negative—which is why Ambassador Foster has been so effective in terms of how we Burundians think of America."

"As a result of her humanity," Mathias continued, "many in the educated class, in particular, who might have thought of America as a country not only of power and wealth but, unfortunately, of arrogance, now look at your country quite differently. So, you can see what great and compassionate leadership can do. In the ambassador's case, it is on a diplomatic scale; in your case, it is on a sport and youth scale—every bit as important."

Though uncomfortable with such praise, Jim wished the conversation could continue, for he knew such analysis could help him better understand the various cultures and classes within Burundi.

"Mathias, could we pick up on this at a later stage?"

"Of course, Jim. It would be my pleasure."

At 1:00, Rush's team was the third of four to return.

"Anything turn up?" asked Jim.

"Nothing," sighed Rush. "Absolutely nothing."

"Same with our two groups," said Jim, shaking his head.

But fifteen minutes later, the last group appeared, and Finnegan reported an interesting development.

"We've discovered that two fifteen-year-old boys—both friends of Leonard and both part of the basketball group—have gone missing since the day of the murders."

"We actually ran into their mothers during our revisit to the various huts," added Mathias. "The mothers told us that for the last several days, they've been off looking for the boys with no success. That's why no one spoke with them yesterday."

Mathias went on to explain that the mothers were fearful that any number of "bad things" might have happened to the two boys—including being carted off to war by Tutsi warriors passing through the region.

"In fact," said Mathias, "now that I've learned about these two boys, my theory is that the two warriors Privates McKeon and White spoke with came into Kayanza to force young men into the Tutsi guerrilla unit. My guess is that when Leonard resisted, they killed him, then found the other two boys and made them join."

Most of the group thought Mathias's theory was reasonable. Finbar did not.

"I can't say exactly why, but some things still strike me as odd. Think about what these two warriors told John and Chris. First, they said they were from Kayanza, and that they were back to check on their families—but not one family in this region knows who they are. Second, they lied about where the bodies would be buried. And let's also remember that, based on what the two privates described, the bandaged wound of one of the warriors could well be fake."

"I see what you mean," said Mathias. "There are certainly many unanswered questions."

"And they're not gonna be answered here," said Rush. "Anything else we should do before we pack up?"

The men shook their heads, some training their eyes on the ground.

"No? Okay, let's load up and head back to Bujumbura."

———

Several hours earlier, while on search with his group, Jim had remembered something . . . something special. When he returned to the Tangishaka hut, he looked through the rubble for the item and found it. He carefully wrapped cloth around it and placed it in a safe place in the rear of the jeep.

———

Finbar Finnegan appreciated the special access that Ambassador Foster had granted him. But as a journalist, he was duty-bound to report his findings. When he returned to Bujumbura, he sought out the ambassador to relate his intentions.

"You're right, Finbar," she said. "You must report the facts. If anything, it will show that these murders might have been committed by someone other than Hutu guerrillas."

Finnegan's CNN report explained that the bodies of Leonard and Consolaté were missing and that a smog of mystery hung over the deaths. "While the photo IDs leave little doubt that Leonard and Consolaté Tangishaka were murdered, many questions will remain until the bodies are found." He placed particular emphasis on *murdered*.

Finnegan's piece concluded with a brief interview with Burundian President Peter Buyoya, who exhorted "anyone with information to contact my office. We have set up a special phone line for this purpose." The number was listed at the bottom of the TV screen.

Similar requests for evidence ran in the *Bujumbura Gazette* and in newspapers in Rwanda.

For several days, hundreds of calls flowed into the special number. The Burundi National Defense Force, with the help of the US Marines, followed up on every lead. But when nothing new turned up, at Ambassador Foster's urging, President Buyoya sent a thirty-two-man military unit back to Kayanza to search for more clues.

Three days later, the unit returned empty-handed.

46

Two weeks passed and not one clue surfaced. Jim struggled to fill his days and nights with productive activities. He persuaded Bill Foster to join him on a morning combination jog and run that covered two miles and many topics. After breakfast, he would work on his Kirundi vocabulary and view basketball films of various sorts, including a particularly good one from years earlier by Red Auerbach on fundamentals. The rest of the day was occupied by reading, check-in calls to Jesse for search updates, periodic viewing of CNN, an afternoon nap, and a walk at dusk.

Each evening, Jim would have supper with someone—Mathias, Jesse, Terrence, Clive Rush, or the Fosters. Increasingly, he valued the companionship and camaraderie that arose from thoughtful dinner discussion.

His day would end with more reading and, at times, watching a movie with Jesse Abbot on Jesse's VCR.

During the walk portion of one morning jog, Jim shuffled to a stop and turned to Foster. "Bill, I feel like they've got to put some zip into this search effort. It's getting . . ."

Before he could finish the sentence, Foster said, "You're right, Coach. And Cynthia is frustrated, too. She asked me to tell you about a session she'd like to hold this evening with the two of us, Jesse, Mathias, Terrence, and Finbar."

When Jim arrived at the ambassador's home that night, he found a pitcher of lemonade, some cheese and crackers, and a host eager to start the meeting.

"Gentlemen, we must assume that we will never find the bodies of Leonard and Consolaté. We must also realize that President Buyoya has limited resources, not to mention many other problems to deal with. He phoned me today to say that he must call off the investigation. While I was disappointed, I did tell him that I understood. I'm very sorry about this for, as much as all of you, I wanted to find the answers."

Several days before the meeting, Finbar had sensed that Buyoya would not take the investigation much further. He had called his bureau chief, Sid Hawkins, to relate his concern.

"Sid, aside from just hanging onto his job, Buyoya's confronted with issues that go far beyond finding those bodies. Yet I just know there's a major story behind the murders. Would you consider sending a team of our investigators here to uncover more facts?"

"We're a news organization, not a guerrilla force, Finbar. I have no reason to think that our people—who've never trained in the jungle—would have any success. Plus, at least from what I know, their lives would be in great danger."

Finnegan had been disappointed with Hawkins's reply. But as the meeting at the ambassador's home began to break up, he finally came to terms with his boss's position. He also laughed at the final comment made at the meeting.

"We need help," said Terrence. "You know, the forest god!"

Jim, too, enjoyed Terrence's suggestion. But, like Finnegan, he was disheartened that answers would not be found. On the front steps of the ambassador's home, Cynthia Foster pulled him aside and asked the same question she had posed several other times in the preceding weeks.

"How are you holding up, Jim?"

Employing the same rote response he had used to answer her previous queries on this issue, Jim gave her a reply that was not entirely true: "I'm fine."

———

Bill and Cynthia Foster were mindful that a consequence of Leonard Tangishaka's death could be Jim Keating's plummet back into depression.

"Barry Sklar sent me a fax expressing his concern about Jim," Cynthia said to Bill. "Barry feels that we must keep him busy. I can think of two ways to do this. The first, of course, is to encourage Jim to get the team back together."

"I agree," said Bill. "In fact, Mathias called me to say that the players are anxious to resume practicing. I'll talk to Jim. My guess is that he'd like to get going as well. . . . What's your second thought?"

With a look of mischief, Cynthia leaned over and whispered into her husband's ear.

"Hmm," said Bill, grinning at his wife's ingenuity. "An interesting idea. Well, you get it printed. In the meantime, I'll find Jim."

When Bill Foster reached Jim, the coach eagerly agreed to resume regular practice.

"Let's have a team meeting," he suggested.

In truth, Jim Keating *had* felt the specter of depression invading his senses. Leonard Tangishaka had been a near life force for him. And although Jim had concealed his emotions well, he had become inwardly unraveled over the murders, feeling there was but one slender psychological membrane separating him from hope and despair.

In the days that immediately followed Leonard's death, Jim's waking hours had taken on a disquieting pattern that no doubt related to his competitive nature. Early morning was the most difficult. He would lie in bed, knowing he hadn't gotten enough sleep, and would be unable to settle back to get more. During this "first period" phase of his day, he would remain in bed for about half an hour, then rise, mind racing, feeling that he was starting his day fifteen points behind, and that to advance to a state of equanimity, he would have to get certain things done—many of which were quite challenging. Were it not for Bill joining him, he would have skipped his morning runs. He also found that he had to push himself toward his other daily activities.

If, over the course of his day, he felt the reward of accomplishment, by evening, his emotional discomfort would abate to a few hours of moderate contentment, especially during the dinner conversation. And then, the cycle would repeat itself the following morning.

Yet when it became obvious that Leonard's body would probably not be found, Jim reflected on the significance of his work and began to find himself in a better psychological state. *I must move on.*

Without Leonard, Jim knew that his team would have no chance at winning an Olympic berth—a prospect that had so excited him. And even a trip to the States might be off, though the murders had generated significant US media coverage and, thus, great interest in Project Oscar. But in bitter irony, Jim also concluded that Leonard's death made his own presence even more important. He vowed not to succumb to despondency and, knowing that his contract would run out in three months, began to think about his possible future in Burundi. But from where would the funds come?

At the team meeting, his players confirmed his critical value to their lives. They made clear their appreciation to

Jim Keating . . . and expressed their hope that he would stay on.

Myo Niyongabo, a 5'8" Hutu, captured the squad's common sentiment when he said earnestly, almost devoutly, "You are our leader, Coach Keating—our savior." Jim noticed players nodding and smiling.

Moved by his players' allegiance, Jim said, "Gentlemen, I appreciate your support. Now, how about if we get together tomorrow night at six for a practice session?"

As they had done in the past when given news that pleased them, the players clapped loudly, and Jim headed back to his apartment feeling like he'd just dropped a fifty-pound backpack.

We may not make the Olympics, he thought as he walked toward his front door, *but this is as good a group of guys as I've ever worked with . . . and this work is by far the most meaningful I have ever done.*

As he fumbled for his keys, Jim was surprised at the sight of a blue envelope and gift-wrapped package affixed to the door by a large red bow. His curiosity was so piqued that he immediately opened the envelope.

To James Patrick Keating: You are cordially invited to join the Emily Dickinson Society of Burundi. Our next gathering will be on Wednesday night at 8 in Ambassador Foster's home.

Keating opened the package. It was a book titled *Selected Poems* by Galway Kinnell. Inscribed on the inside flap was a note from Cynthia Foster: *Jim, Galway Kinnell is one of our leading American poets—a Pulitzer Prize winner! I think you will like his work. Warm regards, CF.*

———

As the coach gazed at the invitation, Ambassador Foster sat alone in her study contemplating yet another enterprise for Burundian basketball—and Jim Keating. She then looked through her mail and found one letter postmarked Rome and bearing the perfect penmanship of a dear friend.

———

FRANCESCA CIMBRONE
21 VIA VENTO
ROME, ITALY

Dear Cynthia:

Your kindness since Nino's passing has been a much-needed fountain of *forza*. And my wonderful children have been there for me in every way a mother could hope. This includes frequent visits by my grandchildren; what better gift could one have?

But I do feel much pain and loneliness. To be honest, dear friend, there are times when I have felt without purpose.

And then I read the most extraordinary article in the *International Herald Tribune* about Project Oscar and the tragic death of young Leonard. I was so moved by the article, so saddened by the tragedy, and so proud to know the woman who created this magnificent program.

The American, Mr. Keating—he seems like such a good man, the perfect leader for Project Oscar. The article seemed unclear as to his future and the future of the program. Such a noble concept must continue.

Which leads me to a proposal: I know well from Nino's various ambassadorial posts that funds for such a worthy program are always a challenge. Nino has provided me well. As part of my proposal, I would like to make a donation to help fund the continuation of Project Oscar and Mr. Keating's work.

The other part of the proposal is more personal in nature, and I appreciate your indulging me, for I have given this much thought.

You know of my love of dance. Well, from the moment I finished the article, I began to read about the Burundian culture, only to confirm that dance has a special place in the minds and hearts of the Hutu and Tutsi. So I wondered, might there be a place for a Burundian program similar to Project Oscar, but with dance as the medium of goodwill?

And, if I may be so bold, might I be able to come to Burundi at my expense to explore this possibility with you and others? I have time and energy, and I would love to be part of such a movement.

One of your most wonderful qualities is your honesty. Please tell me what you think and I will respond accordingly.

Con Affetto,

Francesca

47

Sitting on his veranda with a glass of Perrier, calmed by the last glimmer of daylight, Jim Keating smiled at the engraved invitation.

Ever since the night in Kayanza when the ambassador had read under the dazzling stars, Jim had found himself attracted to poetry; intrigued by, if not somehow drawn to, the notion of trying it himself. He now realized that in the weeks since Leonard's death, his veiled interest must surely have been laid bare by a series of not-so-subtle hints to the Fosters. In one such instance, he told Bill how much he had enjoyed Cynthia's reading and asked, innocently he thought, about her poetry group.

"Meets every Wednesday night," Bill had replied. "And you know, Jim, Cynthia has looked at some of the documents you've written about Project Oscar. She's impressed with how clearly you write—feels you have a natural flair. I know she'd love to have you join the group."

Jim smiled. "Oh no, not a chance. I mean, Bill—hell—I was thirty years old before I knew that Joyce Kilmer was a man. I'd surely embarrass myself—and the ambassador, too."

Bill Foster had simply grinned at Jim's reply and, of course, had promptly reported the coach's coy interest to his wife. Shortly after Leonard's death, she had pulled Jim aside and said, "Jim, often in a time like this—during a period of mourning—it's good to have an outlet. For me, my outlet is my poetry. It's cathartic."

At the time, Jim had limited his response to a polite nod. But now, as he gazed out over Lake Tanganyika, he realized that somehow he had betrayed his quiescent interest in poetry. He finished his Perrier, picked up the Galway Kinnell book and headed to his bedroom.

Keating had never read a book of verse, and he had difficulty grasping the meaning of some poems in *Selected Poems*. But the more he read, the more he began to appreciate the pleasing rhythm of Kinnell's style—and to comprehend the many poignant messages that lay beneath the poet's words. And then, with a turn of a page, he came upon a poem called "Parkinson's Disease."

Jim's mother had suffered from this cruel affliction, and he vividly recalled the dignity and courage she displayed in her daily battle with the ailment. As he read "Parkinson's Disease" slowly, he thought the stanzas were written as if the poet had known Mary Keating; from her bright squint in reaction to food she enjoyed to her permanently clenched right hand. When he read the last line, "For him to pass from this paradise to the next," he felt a sudden rush of emotion and tears streamed down his cheeks.

Jim put the book down, wiped his cheeks, and turned off the light. Usually, he was so tired he would fall asleep as soon as he closed his eyes. But some nights, like tonight, when he turned off the light, the darkness would press in on him and fill him with loneliness.

I'm going to join the group, he decided.

———

Ambassador Foster's private line at the Embassy rang at 8:30 AM. Before Jim Keating could relate his budding interest in Galway Kinnell, the ambassador said, "So, Coach—you liked Mr. Kinnell's work, didn't you?"

"I did," said Jim, not surprised at her intuition. "In fact, he kept me up 'til after midnight!"

"You're not the first person to lose sleep over that man," she kidded. "So—is this call to say that you want to join the Emily Dickinson Society?"

"Well, um, Ambassador," he said awkwardly, "according to the invitation, you meet on Wednesday nights."

"Correct."

"Well, I mean . . . Wednesday is only two days off."

"Correct."

"Should I actually come this Wednesday?"

"Correct!"

Jim thought he heard her chuckling, but she continued in an earnest tone. "Seriously, Jim. We'd love to have you come to this week's session. Now, you must understand that one of our primary objectives is to listen to each other's poems—and critique them."

"Does that mean I should try to write something?"

"Exactly! But don't be too concerned. The whole point of poetry is to write what you feel. You know, Coach, poetry has many fine earmarks. It slows us down, helps us to question, to contemplate—and to discover. And, remember, a poem doesn't have to rhyme!"

"Kinnell certainly doesn't always rhyme," said Jim. "That took some getting used to—I grew up with Kipling. My favorite was 'If.'"

Cynthia laughed. "My favorite, too . . . and not a bad beginning. But rhyme or no rhyme, a poem should penetrate the senses, express a certain spiritual dimension—the best of them possess the 'music of the soul,' as Voltaire once called great poetry."

"A bit daunting, Madam Ambassador!"

Cynthia picked up on Jim's somewhat teasing tone, but also noted his underlying concern.

"Please don't worry about bringing a 'Galway Kinnell' on the first night. Just try to let your feelings be revealed on paper. And while you're struggling to get your thoughts out, take comfort in the fact that revealing oneself is a major challenge—even for old veterans like me. The more you work on it, the more comfortable you'll feel."

"Okay," said Jim. "I'd like to join."

"Glad to hear it, Jim. And you'll find that the group will help you with metrical form, imagery, alliteration, and other guiding principles of poetry. But between now and Wednesday night, just try to get something on paper that Wilma Sheehan, my old English professor at ISU, used to say, 'incriminates you.'"

Easier said than done, thought Jim.

———

National Team practice didn't start until six, so Jim spent the morning and early afternoon on his veranda struggling to compose his first poem.

Cynthia Foster had advised him well: "Don't worry about issues such as rhythm . . . we can get to these issues later. For now, get your feelings on paper—and write about something that moves you."

There is so much that moves me in one way or another, Jim thought. *Edna's death, getting fired, being labeled a racist, financial woes, coming to Burundi, feeling worthwhile again, losing Leonard.*

Could a poem—his first poem—incorporate all of those acute and indelible experiences? Despite knowing very little about the craft, Jim was sure that most poets would tell him to focus on just one thought—one experience. Yet he had noticed that in some of Kinnell's poems that the poet would focus on one thought and in others he would blend various experiences into one poem.

Jim would try both ways.

———

Over the last two decades, basketball—despite his love for the game—had given Jim Keating enough heartache to justify a divorce. But at the National Team's first workout since the Rwanda game—a game that seemed like an eon ago—Jim's romance with his sport was requited.

For ninety minutes, Jim's players responded to his every word, immersing themselves in an intense, especially enthusiastic practice. Their zeal caused Jim to reflect on a simple, self-evident truth he had first comprehended in the Catskills many years earlier—when he had worked with a callow Wilt Chamberlain on post-up moves.

Nothing is quite so rewarding as teaching this game to an eager young player.

When the session concluded, Jim headed back to his apartment, arriving at 8:30 PM. It would not be dark until 10, so he went out on the veranda. For the next hour or so, he struggled with a poem whose hatching, for him at least, was as tough—and often as aggravating—as coaching players with little skill or recruiting a kid who has little interest in your school. He finally went to bed, read several of Kinnell's poems, then fell into a deep sleep.

Jim spent the following morning in further pursuit of the elusive verses. While he was not making much progress and continued to find the experience somewhat frustrating, he also found it to be as Cynthia had suggested: cathartic, a challenge, but, at the same time, a release.

In the early afternoon, Jim met with Mathias and Bill to discuss getting Project Oscar back out into the rural areas.

He returned to his apartment at 4:00 PM, spent another hour working on the poem, produced something that he "wasn't totally ashamed of" and had a light dinner with Jesse Abbot.

"So, how'd it go with the poem, Coach?" asked Abbot.

Jim chuckled. "Jesse, I used to ask a friend how his golf game went. He'd say 'Well, I didn't embarrass myself.' I hope that'll be my answer to your question about the poem."

At 7:30, Jesse drove Jim to Ambassador Foster's home and his first session with the Emily Dickinson Society of Burundi.

48

"You seem a bit on edge, Coach," said Jesse as he pulled up in front of the ambassador's home.

"I am. I wasn't this nervous coaching my first game at St. Pius. You know, on the way over, I considered asking you to turn back."

"And risk my job! Seriously Jim, you should relax and enjoy yourself. As a matter of fact, I know that the ambassador and her friends are really pleased you're joining the group."

"They may not feel that way after I read my work. Anyway, thanks for the ride, Jesse. I'll see you at 9:30."

Since his early youth, when his beloved mother, Mary, had tried, often in vain, to convince Jim to sign up for such uninviting activities as ballroom dancing or piano lessons, he had steered clear of most non-sport-related undertakings that made him uncomfortable. But tonight, escape was not an option; Cynthia Foster was waiting at the front door!

Her attire was casual—jeans and an Indiana State University t-shirt that read: *At ISU, The Defense Never Rests!*

As always, she was attractive and, on this night, particularly cheerful. And just as she had done in their first meeting months earlier, the ambassador disarmed the coach with a warm greeting and a radiant smile.

"I am *so* glad that you are here, James Patrick Keating. Now you come with me; there are people eager to meet you."

Taking him by the arm, Cynthia walked Jim into the library, which was bedecked with posters of Emily Dickinson's most famous lines. Keating noticed one in particular: "If I feel physically as if the top of my head were taken off, I know that is poetry."

"I would like to welcome you, Mr. Jim Keating!" roared a tiny woman in the rear of the library. Other enthusiastic greetings followed—the perfect antidote to the awkwardness Jim felt.

As he shook hands with each member of the society, he noticed that the makeup of this small poetry group reflected the basic concept of Project Oscar. Of the nine poets, five were women and four were men. Along with Ambassador Foster, one other member seemed to be an American (a Peace Corps volunteer, Jim would later find out). Four seemed to be Hutu and three appeared to be Tutsi.

Before he could comment on the group's harmony, the ambassador apparently read his mind, "It's the Project Oscar of poetry, Jim."

Cynthia poured sherry into Waterford goblets, toasted the arrival of the new member, then invited everyone to sit in their customary circle.

"Who would like to go first?" she asked, and Erisa Mulifi, the elf-like Hutu woman who had welcomed Jim, responded, "I will go."

The next ninety minutes was an intellectual journey unlike any Jim Keating had ever taken. While he found

378

some of the poems difficult to grasp, the common element in all of the readings was the spirit the authors brought to their poetry.

"They really love this, don't they," Jim whispered to Ambassador Foster at a break.

"That they do! How about you? Are you glad you came?"

"Yes. I am glad I came—and I'm learning, too!"

When Mutara Karamera, a Tutsi physician who had joined the group only a few weeks earlier, read a work in Kurundi and then translated it into English, Jim was made aware of a complication he had never considered.

While Dr. Karamera was responding to some comments, Cynthia said, "Now that was interesting. You see, Jim, while certain poems in Kurundi translate well into English, others do not. Translation in poetry is a universal challenge. Ever hear the names Robert Hass or Czeslaw Milosz?"

"No, I haven't."

"Well, Hass is an American Poet Laureate, and Milosz is a Polish Nobel Prize winner. Hass, a brilliant poet in his own right, spends considerable time translating Czeslaw Milosz's poems from Polish to English, striving to capture the essence of Milosz's words."

The ambassador then took the podium for her reading. Before the gathering, she had explained to Jim the importance of proficiency in the two tasks facing the reader.

"Some truly great poets are simply uncomfortable with a microphone and audience. But if you can put content and eloquence together in the way that some of the great ones do—Rita Dove and Bob Hass as cases in point—a poetry reading is cerebral theatre at its best."

In Jim's unfledged view, the first readers had shown a wide range of ability, with no one really excelling in either category. The ambassador was at a whole other level. Just as she had done in the bivouac setting of Kayanza weeks earlier with her reading of the Oscar Robertson poem, she dazzled the small Emily Dickinson Society with her facile reading of a short but powerful poem on the loss of loved ones, in this case Leonard and Consolaté.

When she finished, heartfelt applause was quickly followed by a wide smile and foreboding words: "Okay, Coach. It's your microphone."

As Jim Keating headed to the podium, he thought back to an experience of many years ago—one that had caused him similar anxiety.

———

When he was a sixth grader at St. Peter's Grammar School in Worcester, Jim's teacher, Sister John Adelaide, had split the class into two teams—Holy Cross and Notre Dame. Drawing on the rivalrous instincts of her pupils, particularly the young boys, the nun had set out a week-long contest where every activity the class undertook was for points—from answering geography, math, and history questions to Friday's "cultural day." On cultural day, class members would volunteer to dance, play the piano, or whatever else might help their team achieve victory and earn a coveted reward.

At 2:30 on Friday, with class being dismissed at 3:00 and Jim's Holy Cross team 30 points behind, Sister John Adelaide declared, "Okay, a voice contest. Depending upon your performance, you can earn up to 50 points for your team."

She then threw in the clincher, "And the singers for both teams must be boys." When not one young man from Notre Dame volunteered, she turned to the Holy Cross team, only to be met with similar silence. Finally, Jim, his competitive spirit far more advanced than his crooning skills, walked to the front of the room, belted out an off-key version of "When Irish Eyes are Smiling," and took on the giggles of his classmates, even his fellow Crusaders.

But moments later, to the surprise of both teams—and Jim—Sister John Adelaide declared, "James, you displayed courage and a commitment to your team. Both of these attributes are important—and admirable. I am awarding you 50 points. Holy Cross wins and there will be no homework for the team this weekend!"

———

It had been a valuable lesson for Jim. While he never sang in public again, he had learned that taking a chance—even at the risk of embarrassment—could have its rewards. But tonight, as he placed his one-page, handwritten verse on the podium, he was as nervous as he had ever remembered.

After clearing his throat, he said softly, "You are all so knowledgeable. I hope I don't embarrass myself too much."

His nervous state was obvious, and Erisa Mulifi, the minikin Hutu, wanted to assist. "We are all with you, Coach," she said.

Her welcome remark helped Jim begin. He read his work slowly, his voice gaining resonance with each line. When he finished, a brief silence was followed by a most gratifying comment by Dr. Karamera. "Jim Keating, that was good . . . very good."

Dr. Karamera's praise was followed by applause and Jim felt the quiet pleasure of accomplishment.

Later that evening, on his way out of her home, Jim pulled Cynthia Foster aside. "Ambassador—the truth. How was it?"

"It was a fine start, Jim."

"But not a 'Galway Kinnell'?" he said with a grin.

"No, not a Galway Kinnell," she chuckled. "But a very good start. Now, here's a book with a simple title: *How to Write Poetry*."

Jim glanced down at the book and saw on the cover the name Cynthia Foster.

"Ambassador! You wrote this!"

"I did, Jim, although it will not be published until next year. What you have is called the galley or an advanced copy—which is really the final, uncorrected version before it goes into print."

"Wow, congratulations! Tell me, who will your readership be?"

"Well, I'm pleased—make that really pleased—that the Indianapolis school system is buying a thousand copies for use by teachers and high school English students at several schools."

"That is so great!"

"Thank you, Jim. And I hope it will be of some use to you."

"I'm sure it will, Ambassador. And I'll return it soon."

"No need, Coach. It's a gift."

On the way home, Jesse Abbot was glad that his friend was in such high spirits.

"I knew that she was writing a book, Jim. But she kept it kind of quiet. I bet it will be a big help to you," said Abbot.

"Like so many other things she's done for me."

"Oh, and by the way, Jim," he said, "The ambassador mentioned that I could come to one of the readings."

"Let's wait awhile on that," said the coach with yet another smile.

49

Satisfied with his first poetry reading, Jim Keating slept soundly and long. He was awakened the next morning by a three-car caravan moving slowly up the driveway toward his apartment. Parting the curtains, Jim spotted Ambassador Foster in the lead vehicle. Seconds later, when his eyes fell upon two teenaged boys in the back seat, he made the connection.

The two familiar young faces were from Kayanza—friends of Leonard's who'd been in the group that learned the new game from the American coach. They were surely the two boys who had gone missing. Jim was certain their visit related to Leonard's death. As he dressed quickly, he found himself trembling.

The car door swung open, and Ambassador Foster was the first to step out on the gravel driveway. Moments later, Jim met the group. "Coach, do you remember Mutara Kabaija and Habimana Yuhi?"

"I sure do," said Jim. As he shook hands with both boys, he noticed that their eyes reflected both fear and sadness.

"Last night, Mutara and Habimana were picked up by the Red Cross about thirty miles outside of Bujumbura," said the ambassador. "They were brought to my home about an hour after you left. By the way, Jim, this is Art Schokett. Art is one of the Red Cross workers who found them."

Jim shook hands with Schokett, and the ambassador continued, "The boys have been hiding since the murders of Leonard and Consolaté—and with good reason."

At this point, even though his curiosity provoked countless questions, Jim instinctively knew to restrain himself and calm the boys. "Please, let's go out on the veranda where everyone can sit."

Once the ambassador settled into a wicker chair, she went straight back to her story.

"They know a great deal about the deaths, Jim. For example, they know that Leonard and Consolaté were not killed by a machete or a gun, but by something far more cruel."

"What?" Jim was incredulous. How could anything be worse?

"We're not sure. They are still so fearful that they're having some trouble relating all the facts. But from what we can gather, let me tell you what we think happened."

The ambassador went on to explain that the two boys were walking to Leonard's hut at dusk on the evening of the murders. When they were some distance from the hut, and hidden by the forest, they heard loud cries—they have explained the noises as wails. They knew instantly that these wails came from Leonard and Consolaté, so they grew fearful and very cautious.

"About a hundred yards from the hut, behind a cluster of trees, they saw three Tutsi men—none of whom they recognized—and a fourth man whom they described as one of olive complexion and jet black hair," Ambassador Foster told Jim.

"The guy Mathias saw at the game," Jim thought aloud.

"That's what we're guessing. Both boys said this man was definitely in charge of the group."

She continued relating the rest of the story, telling Jim that Mutara and Habimana said that the three Tutsis appeared to be standing guard outside the hut. Their first instinct was to go for help, but they knew that there were probably no adult men in the region since nearly all were off at war. They also knew that they themselves could surely not overtake the large Tutsi men, and so they stayed in their hiding place all night and listened to Leonard and Consolaté's horrid cries.

The ambassador's voice was laden with grief, and, for a moment, she had to stop. But she quickly regained her composure. "By early morning, the wails had subsided and they knew that Leonard and Consolaté were dead."

When Cynthia Foster paused again, Jim asked gently, "Ambassador, do you have any idea what they died of? I mean—were they being tortured all night in the hut?"

At this point, Schokett interjected. "Jim, the fact is we don't know, and at this point, it's fruitless to speculate."

"But if you had to guess?" asked Jim.

"I'm afraid to guess," said Schokett grimly. "But we'll be able to find out. . . . Jim, the boys know where the bodies are buried."

Schokett stopped for a moment to allow Jim to digest that fact and then continued. "The boys told us that an hour or so after they knew that Leonard and Consolaté must be dead, a jeep with Americans pulled up one hundred meters or so from the hut."

"The Marines who reported the deaths?" asked Jim.

"Exactly," said Schokett. "And when the men in the hut—the three Tutsis and the olive-skinned man—heard the jeep, the boys said that two Tutsis approached it."

"What about the other two?" Jim asked. Schokett could see the veteran coach putting the pieces of the story together in his head. Jim's face conveyed an eagerness to learn all the facts.

Schokett and the ambassador took turns supplying Jim with the rest of what the boys had told them. They had said that the other men—one Tutsi and the olive-skinned man—hid out in the woods just behind the hut with rifles cocked. The Marines walked to the hut and saw both bodies draped in cloth. Had the Marines pressed the issue beyond taking pictures, the boys expected that they would have been shot dead.

Approximately thirty minutes after the Marines left, the four men dragged the bodies outside the hut. Then, another vehicle pulled up and maneuvered its way to the hut's front door. The boys' description of the vehicle indicated that the men were driving a Troubadour, which was often used on safaris in South Africa.

"It's a remarkable vehicle and *very* expensive," Schokett said. "It can literally wend its way through a forest. Narrow paths, dense tree cover, rock-filled roads—you name it. It's equipped with a laser scanner that alerts the driver to impending problems. On occasion, you'll see a Troubadour in Uganda or even Rwanda. But I've never heard of one in Burundi. It seems so strange that one would show up in the Kayanza region and be used to move two dead bodies. . . ."

Schokett shook his head and continued. "Once the vehicle approached the hut, the two men in the Troubadour got out to help the other four load the two bodies onto the rear of the vehicle. The boys said it took all six men to load Leonard's body."

Jim raised his hand as if to make a point.

"The two men in the Troubadour. What did they look like?" he asked.

"Good question," said Schokett. "Unfortunately, the boys were so afraid that they didn't get a good look at the faces of the two men. However, they were not so afraid as to lose their wits—or their courage."

Here, the ambassador picked up the story. Gesturing toward the two teens on Jim's veranda, she continued. "Jim, once the bodies were loaded in the Troubadour, the boys overheard one of the Tutsi men say where the vehicle was headed—to *les chutes d'eau grandes*—the great waterfalls. Because they knew a shortcut to the waterfalls, the boys were able to stay close—albeit at a safe distance."

She then added a disclaimer so that Jim would further understand the weight of the situation. "Now remember, when I speak about courage, please understand that if these boys had been seen, they would have been killed, or subjected to perhaps a worse fate—one that is now practiced in Uganda and, recently, even in Rwanda against children."

"What's that?" asked Jim.

Schokett answered for the ambassador. "My guess is that they would probably have been *rived*, which means they would have had their lips cut off so as never to speak."

"My God!" Jim exclaimed, instantly reacting to the mental image by placing his fingers against his own lips.

"But fortunately," Schokett continued, "they were able to follow the jeep and have a distant view of the burial site. They watched the six men dump the two bodies into a pre-dug grave. The grave itself—and the dirt that had been dug—were covered with bushes. After the bodies were dumped, the men heaped dirt and bushes on Leonard and Consolaté, and then got back into the Troubadour and drove away. The boys hid out for at least another hour and then they marked several trees near the grave so that they could identify the site."

After a moment's pause, the ambassador spoke up.

"Jim, there is more. After the boys marked the trees their curiosity led them back to Consolaté and Leonard's hut where they made an extraordinary discovery. Under Consolaté's pillow, they found a letter written to me."

The ambassador handed the note to Jim, who silently read Consolaté's last wishes despite his shaking hand.

To the American Queen,

I do not know if you will ever read this letter. Several weeks before I met you, I began to feel my body changing. I went to see a local woman just after Leonard left. She has been inflicted with the virus. She told me what it was like in the beginning, cold chills and burning fever. She also told me that Charlé was a carrier. I knew right then that I had contracted the virus, and this was confirmed by the Red Cross.

I did not know how to tell Leonard. But I once read that there are things that one can take to ease the pain and suffering, and I had to planned to seek your help.

I do not believe that this help is now important. You see, American Queen, when Leonard arrived home, we were taken by force by three warriors. They were with another strange looking man, not white, but olive. At gunpoint, the four men forced us to drink what appeared to be water. Our deaths are near, but so is God, of this I am sure.

Somehow, I feel the need to write this letter. Somehow, I am sure that you will read it and take action. I must stop now, as I hear the evil men returning.

With utmost respect,
Consolaté.

When Jim put the letter down, he shook his head but did not speak. Cynthia Foster was struggling to stifle her emotions. After a moment of group silence, she said, "Tomorrow morning, Sergeant Rush will lead a military unit to Kayanza. If the unit feels things are safe, a travel party, including the two boys and me, will head there. You're welcome to come, Jim."

Jim didn't hesitate. "I'll be ready."

50

Next morning before dawn, Sergeant Rush led a team of eight Marines to Kayanza. Five hours later, Rush radioed Ambassador Foster, who was waiting with her travel party at the Embassy.

"Things appear to be safe," Rush said.

"In that case," replied the ambassador, "we'll leave immediately and meet you at the Tangishaka hut."

The ambassador's travel party included four heavily armed Marines and four officers of the Burundi National Defense Force. The ambassador asked Art Schokett of the Red Cross to join old hands Jim Keating, Mathias Bizimana, Terrence Ndayisiba, Finbar Finnegan, and her husband, Bill. She insisted that both doctors, the Red Cross's Joel Fish and the Burundian physician, Natare Nicombero, accompany the group, along with the two boys, Mutara and Habimana.

Jim rode with the ambassador and Finnegan. In a light, bantering manner, the ambassador had insisted Jim take the front seat "because even though you're outranked, you're taller."

During the first couple hours, Finbar regaled them with stories of his youth in Ireland, but the mood became subdued as they drove closer to Kayanza. At 2:45 PM, five jeeps pulled within one hundred meters of the hut and were greeted by Rush and his fellow soldiers.

"We've had a good look around the region," said Rush. "There doesn't appear to be any danger."

Turning to the two boys, Schokett said in Kurundi, "Okay, lead us to the graves."

Taking the same shortcut they had used weeks earlier, the boys shepherded the group on a twenty-minute walk through the forest. When they arrived at the site, Mutara, the bigger of the two boys, went straight to the marked trees, turned around, looked slightly to the west, and then pointed his finger.

"Right there!" he said.

Rush and his men shoveled the dirt, heeding a request by Dr. Fish: "Please take care not to put a shovel into either of the bodies. Depending on how much they have decomposed, any new harm could impact the autopsy."

It took only another twenty minutes for the soldiers to unearth the bodies, which were still draped in cloth and exuded the wretched odor of death.

"Now," said Dr. Fish, "what we are about to see might make many of you ill. It's up to each one of you, but I'd suggest that you let Dr. Nicombero and I perform our duties. I'll call you over if we need you."

Most everyone followed Dr. Fish's advice, but Jim Keating did not move. As the Marines pulled both bodies from the small ditch to the level ground, they each held their breath to avoid inhaling the stench that saturated the air.

Sergeant Rush carefully slit the cloth that covered Leonard. Dr. Fish, having served in Burundi for two years, thought he was immune to the horrors of post-mortem examination. But when he saw Leonard's body, he gasped, causing Jim to lean forward for his own look.

Jim felt a surge of nausea, stepped back, dropped to one knee, and murmured, "I can't believe this." He turned and waved Rush toward him.

"Clive," he said softly, "Give a hand to the doc."

Fighting to maintain a stoic demeanor, Rush fell to his knees across from Fish and helped him gently remove the cloth from Leonard Tangishaka's mutilated body.

The others could no longer contain their curiosity. The group approached hesitantly and stared at a mass of skin that appeared as if it had been punctured by dozens of bullets.

Jim had seen bullet holes in bodies many years ago, but was perplexed by the holes in Leonard's body. Some were the size of a pencil eraser, some were larger and ragged, as big as a quarter. The reactions of the rest ranged from stunned silence to a hulking Marine vomiting within seconds of his glimpse.

"The lesions in the skin, Dr. Fish," said Ambassador Foster. "It looks as if they were somehow gored in by some small spike or spear."

"Ambassador, if you look closely, you'll see that those holes are not the result of something entering the body—but instead from something exiting it," the doctor said. "The only thing I have ever heard of like this is called Guinea worm disease. While I have never personally observed a case of this disease, I have read studies and have seen photos. The Guinea worm, spread through contaminated water, forms near the joints of the victims. After a time, it emerges from the body as a long ribbon-shaped worm in a brutal escape through the skin that is beyond painful. In fact, it's downright excruciating. It occurs in Africa and Asia, particularly in West Africa. Several years ago, former President Carter was quite active in a campaign to eradicate it. I remember him calling it one of the cruelest maladies on the face of the earth."

Dr. Fish continued. "But this . . . this is something far worse. These lesions are much larger than those of the Guinea worm. To my knowledge, no one else in this country or, for that matter, anywhere in Africa, has ever been afflicted by anything like this."

Visibly shaken, Fish said, "My initial thinking . . . given the actions of the men the two boys saw, is that this is not some runaway, never-before-documented natural occurance. On the contrary, it's as if some madman concocted this in a lab and tried it out on Consolaté and Leonard. But rather than doing any type of preliminary autopsy here, I'd prefer that we bring the bodies back to Bujumbura."

Dr. Nicombero spoke up. "I agree with Dr. Fish; there appears to be evil behind this. Also, you all recall how gaunt Leonard looked in the picture taken by the Marines? This explains that look, for this process would certainly suck the blood and tissue out of anyone's body, causing the face to appear that way."

"Plus," said Sergeant Rush, "it explains why those Tutsi men insisted to our Marines that the picture be taken with the cloth draped over Leonard's neck."

"Dr. Fish," said Ambassador Foster. "Let's get back to your point about a madman concocting this."

"Ambassador," he said, "if that is the case, and, as I said, my guess is that it may be, then we could be looking at something as serious as any form of germ warfare known to man."

The group fell silent, unsure of how to absorb and react to this sort of information.

The two doctors found the same gaping holes throughout Consolaté's skin. "Let's load both bodies in the largest trailer and head back to Bujumbura," said Fish. "We'll need proper equipment to perform the full autopsies."

On the trip home, Cynthia Foster sat next to Finnegan. "Finbar, depending upon what the autopsies reveal, I'm worried about a panic. How do you propose to handle your report?"

"I have to report the facts, Ambassador. If the autopsy bears out what Dr. Fish and Dr. Nicombero suspect—that this was concocted in a laboratory—then a well-presented report will not only help in the investigation, but also will help diffuse any panic. This is bound to leak, quite possibly by the bad guys. The worst thing that can happen is for misinformation to get spread around."

"On the other hand," said the ambassador firmly, "we aren't sure of much just yet. It would seem that your piece should wait or, if done, be done with great caution."

"Ambassador, whenever it is done, it will be done with great caution. Be assured of that—and for a lot of reasons."

When the jeeps reached Bujumbura, they went straight to the Prince Regent Charles Hospital. The hospital coroner, a Tutsi named Osano Bagatui, Dr. Fish, and Dr. Nicombero worked for five hours without a break conducting the autopsy.

When they finished, Dr. Fish called the ambassador. "It's pretty much as I thought. Whoever did this took the principles of Guinea worm disease and made it much worse. We isolated the bacteria and did some laboratory tests. What is particularly disturbing—as is pretty much confirmed by Consolate's letter—is that these bacteria can be ingested, sight unseen, from drinking water. And once they get into the bloodstream, there is no stopping their rapid growth."

He took a deep breath before continuing. "Ambassador, this is potentially disastrous—catastrophic would not be overstating the case—if we don't stop it."

———

Ambassador Foster asked Drs. Fish and Nicombero to join her at an emergency meeting she arranged with President Buyoya. Buyoya immediately raised the possibility of withholding information from the public "until we try to find who is behind this."

But following Finbar Finnegan's reasoning, the ambassador persuaded the president that a factual, well-documented report was far more advantageous.

"First of all, Finbar made the valid point that leaks are inevitable—including the real possibility of leaks being spread by those behind this. He also pointed out that the worst thing we can have out there is misinformation, for such misinformation will invite panic. While there is no guarantee that Finbar's report will produce meaningful leads, an airing on CNN might have that effect. Finbar is an excellent reporter who wants to see justice done. I am confident that he'll handle this story judiciously."

Turning to Fish and Nicombero, Buyoya said, "In the meantime, what can we do to prevent disaster?"

Fish's reply was as solemn as it was ominous.

"Mr. President, we can certainly develop some preventive measures to employ in your office, in the Charles Hospital, and other places in the Bujumbura area. But frankly, out in the rural areas, there's absolutely nothing we can do. And even in Bujumbura, our impact will be limited."

51

"I know we want to be first on this, Finbar," said Bureau Chief Sid Hawkins. "But this is one of those once-in-a-career tidal wave kind of reports. We've got to make damn sure that we're accurate."

Hawkins had come to enjoy his role as Finbar's mentor. But he also knew that the quality of this piece could impact both their careers—not to mention bring focus on a potential calamity as alarming as any Hawkins had ever covered.

"I'm goin' to be very, very demanding of you because this one's got to be perfect."

Finnegan's first step was to spend several hours with Dr. Fish and Dr. Nicombero. Finbar asked them to review the lab tests with him. There was a tacit understanding among the three that although Finnegan understood the fundamentals of these kinds of reports, he was, nevertheless, encountering an especially complicated case. The doctors also understood that Finnegan was a reporter. They were patient, almost plodding, in their review.

When they finished, Fish said grimly, "Problem number one is that we're talking about a microbe that multiplies in water faster than anything I've ever seen or heard. Problem number two is that while it can be detected with sophisticated equipment, it cannot be seen by the human eye."

"So," said Finnegan, "are you saying there's not only a possibility that a bunch of lunatics developed this microbe, but that these same people could drop these microbes into a reservoir and within days the reservoir would be contaminated?"

"I'm saying that depending upon the size of the reservoir, it could be hours, not days."

Fish let his statement take hold, then continued.

"But let's take it a step further. Let's say the bacteria is placed in wells and reservoirs in Burundi. A person drinks a glass of water and the bacteria is ingested into the bloodstream. It appears to us that the next thing that happens is that contact with the blood not only continues the multiplication process, but also enlarges the bacteria into the size of little gumballs you'd purchase at a candy store. And, of course, the next step is the most horrid of the process. These little balls want to escape."

"And the only escape route is through the pores?" asked Finnegan.

"Exactly."

"Can testing systems be put into place to monitor the water?"

"Burundi doesn't have the kind of equipment to do this. However, I've already contacted Red Cross headquarters in the States. There will be a worldwide effort to help set up the systems. Hopefully, in the next week or so, something will be in place, though I'm not sure how effective it will be. Plus, we can't monitor every reservoir in Africa."

"Or for that matter," said Finnegan, "countries outside of Africa. I mean, who is to say that these people, if in fact they're as evil as we're guessing, are just targeting Burundi—or other African countries?"

Fish nodded slowly. "You're right, Finbar. Who is to say?"

"Let me ask you one more question, Dr. Fish. On a global scale, are we virtually defenseless?"

"Well, I'll put it this way. To put reasonable detection equipment into place around the world, it will take billions of dollars, unprecedented cooperation among governments, and months—maybe years—of time. And the end result will be imperfect at best."

"So, what's our best hope?"

"Our best hope is to catch these people before they put their master plan into action," replied Fish.

———

After three days of exhaustive preparation, Sid Hawkins, who had flown to Bujumbura to oversee the preparations, said to Finbar Finnegan, "Okay, we're ready to go."

Next day, Finbar's exclusive was the lead story on the CNN *World News*. In his account, viewed by 60 million people in 130 countries, Finnegan took a guarded approach. He noted that there was no hard evidence, only suspicion, of a widespread plot—and that the potential impact of the bacteria was far from conclusive

In a prepared statement, which he read on air, Dr. Joel Fish said, "We are talking about the only two cases known to the medical community and the utilization of testing devices that are not of the standard of most countries. We cannot draw any conclusions beyond the fact that only two people have died as a result of this bacteria."

Nonetheless, the following morning, the "microbiciee bacteria," as Fish had called it, was on the front page of every major newspaper in the world.

President Buyoya and Ambassador Foster both took public positions of caution on the burgeoning crisis. At a hastily called press conference, Buyoya stated, "We are implementing a number of safety measures. However, at this time, we have no reason to think that this bacteria has implications beyond the deaths of Leonard and Consolaté Tangishaka."

But in the privacy of their offices, Buyoya and Foster feverishly worked the phones, calling on various international agencies to help in a situation that both leaders knew could have devastating consequences.

Over a forty-eight-hour period, battalions of Red Cross workers, UN peacekeeping forces, and other medical experts entered Burundi. The Red Cross workers took charge of dispensing more than five million bottles of pure spring water donated by Poland Spring, Perrier, and Evian. The UN reps were responsible for warning people throughout the country to refrain from using well or reservoir water until all preventive measures were put into place.

In the late evening of day two of the crisis, six UN cargo planes stocked with sophisticated equipment to monitor every major drinking supply in Burundi landed at Bujumbura International Airport. The equipment was on loan from several European Union countries, along with the United States and Canada. The monitoring procedure involved more than eighty lab technicians testing water supplies every ninety minutes. It was a massive and costly operation that would be hard to sustain for an extended period.

The relief and medical workers were joined in Burundi by a throng of media. Due to the short supply of hotel accommodations, many news teams bunked four or five people in one room. But the crowded accommodations did not prevent the press corps from trumpeting the microbiciee bacteria as a major world threat. "Operation Deliverance," the name coined by the media, was now the lead daily story around the world, and Dr. Fish, Dr. Nicombero, Ambassador Foster, and others directly involved were the reluctant recipients of their fifteen minutes of international fame—plus overtime.

Under top secret request from the United Nations, and a series of personal calls from the President of the United States and the Prime Ministers of Great Britain and Canada, three major medical research centers—one in New York, one in Toronto, and one in London—worked together to develop an antidote to the bacteria. But because the malady involved was known in only two cases, and due to the inferior testing techniques in Burundi, it was difficult to efficiently conduct the detailed analysis that would lead to a miracle drug that would kill off the bacteria.

A confidential conference call involving physicians and top government officials from the three countries was conducted under CIA surveillance to ensure that no tape recording or phone tapping took place. On the call, Dr. Paul Arnold of the Harvard Medical School stated, "We're looking into the possibility of creating a vaccine or other curative procedures. However, it could take months, even years, to accomplish this."

Even with the ironbound security measures employed by various governments, Wall Street still felt the winds of chaos that blew hard from Burundi. Volatile trading took place, particularly in stocks that involved bottled water or bacteria-related medical research.

At week's end, and despite the intense efforts of more than one thousand people, no microbiciee bacteria was detected in Burundi. The same was true after two weeks, three weeks, a month; at which time many volunteers and members of the media began to take leave of Bujumbura. At this point, a few journalists and several ranking officials of governments directly involved began to question the wisdom of such a comprehensive, if not impulsive, reaction to the murders of Leonard and Consolaté Tangishaka.

Senator Fred Hutchings of Wisconsin stated, "It is quite possible that these were merely two isolated deaths in a remote country that came as a result of something that we will never likely see again. It is also possible that the panic was for nothing. In my judgment, CNN, which broke this story, has a lot of explaining to do."

———

Six months passed with no new leads and a growing belief that Operation Deliverance was nothing more than a fluke of science in a small, out-of-the-way African country.

A poll commissioned by the *International Herald Tribune* revealed that 92 percent of those surveyed thought that the matter never should have been reported and had caused undo stress to millions of people. Many politicians second-guessed the amount of money spent on the project, and in an op-ed in *The New York Times*, Daan Basson, Secretary-General of the United Nations, confessed, "We might have acted hastily."

Even CNN tried to diffuse the criticism leveled at them by means of an oblique mea culpa. Barry Glenn, anchor of *The World*, concluded a primetime broadcast by stating, "Based on the information available to us at the time, CNN felt it appropriate to report on Operation Deliverance. While we still maintain the story has merit, we regret any panic that our reporting may have caused."

The public outcry also produced various degrees of fall-out for those at the genesis of the story. Ambassador Foster was called to Washington to testify before a special Senate panel convened to investigate Operation Deliverance. Only her sterling reputation—and documented evidence that she and her staff had scrupulously followed diplomatic protocol regarding release of information to the media—saved her from reassignment or, worse, forced retirement.

Ironically, because Burundi was so preoccupied in stemming the genocide still raging between Hutu and Tutsi, most Burundians quickly forgot about Operation Deliverance, and President Peter Buyoya retained his precarious hold on power.

Dr. Joel Fish and Dr. Natare Nicombero were the subject of criticism in some quarters of the medical community. But both physicians stood by their findings and their professional conduct during the investigation.

"We never made any public statements about a conspiracy," stated Fish in an interview in *Time* magazine. "We merely reported what we had discovered."

Nonetheless, the Red Cross, reacting to the harsh criticism of anything linked to Operation Deliverance, reassigned Fish to Kenya, where he silently vowed to continue research into an antidote. As for Nicombero, he remained in Burundi, his practice uninfluenced by outside reaction.

Finbar Finnegan, who had used proper caution in breaking Operation Deliverance, became the casualty of guilt by association. Sid Hawkins, fond of Finnegan and aware of the young man's considerable talent, was still forced to reassign his protégé to South Africa.

"Finbar, bottom line, we need to keep you out of the public eye for several months. I'd like you to come to Johannesburg, work out of my office, and conduct an investigation into post-apartheid South African sport. Hopefully, your investigation will lead to a major special on the role of sport in contemporary South Africa."

Hawkins himself was the subject of a critical memo written by the CNN ombudsman and circulated among the company's higher-ups. The memo proposed that Hawkins should have waited until there was more evidence that the bacteria had implications beyond Leonard and Consolaté. In a counter-memo, Hawkins vigorously defended himself, pointing out that he had followed CNN's rigid set of procedures regarding the release of a major story. He also noted that this was the first time that following the procedures, which he had helped draft, had failed.

Hawkins offered to resign, but a senior vice president refused to accept it, pointing out in his own memo that "Sid Hawkins is quite likely our most effective producer."

Finnegan was angry about the reassignment. He still believed in his story and vowed not to let Operation Deliverance pass without somehow finding more answers. Like Fish, he felt that the antidote research should continue. But for the time being, he had no choice but to accept the reassignment—there were simply no other job prospects.

As for Jim Keating, he was not affected, professionally at least, by the residue of the panic.

52

Despite the murders of Leonard and Consolaté, no signs of melancholy invaded Jim's senses—and he knew why. Following the accepted anti-depression practice of keeping busy, the coach filled his days and nights with basketball, poetry, and reading. Infusing these activities was a new sense of spiritualism.

Jim's love of reading now found him drawn to the writings of philosophers ranging from Saint Thomas More to Aristotle. The Fosters had an extensive library in their den, and Cynthia had encouragingly said, "Help yourself!"

He took particular interest in Aristotle's discussion of the Golden Mean. Trying to recover from the haymakers of Barcelona, Jersey State, and Leonard's death, Aristotle's treatment of the constant pursuit of the mean that lies between deficiency and excess resonated with Jim. And Jim's new affinity for poetry helped him come closer to that desirable balance.

Ambassador Foster continued her key role in Jim's active life. Suppressing the strain of the Senate inquiry, the ambassador not only maintained her enthusiasm for Project Oscar, but also kicked it up a notch. Her letters and personal calls to various grantors, including a special appeal to the UN Charities Division, resulted in more equipment and a cash gift by a US foundation to construct badly needed outdoor basketball courts in various sections of Burundi.

One location selected by the ambassador and Jim was the very dirt surface in Kayanza on which Jim had first taught the game to Leonard Tangishaka. The court would be named in honor of Leonard and Consolaté, and Mathias would make a trip to Kayanza to implore the warlords to refrain from blocking the court's use. Another site related to an important component of Ambassador Foster's grand plan, which was still known only to Bill and a few select others.

The grant covered the costs of the new courts, plus adjacent shacks to house the balls, nets, and other maintenance equipment. In a bold policy decision, the ambassador decreed that the honor system would be followed. THESE BALLS AND NETS ARE COMMUNITY-OWNED EQUIPMENT. PLEASE DO NOT TAKE THEM, read the sign on each shack.

The courts spurred even greater interest in basketball and, as the ambassador and Jim hoped, caused Hutus and Tutsis to continue to play together—a small but meaningful alliance germinated amidst the chaos of on-going conflict.

"The chipping effect in action," the ambassador said to Jim, who added, "Yeah, the kids are playing and the honor system is working. Barely a basketball has disappeared. Plus, our Marines on patrol in Kayanza report that those kids are using their court with no problem."

Jim ran youth clinics five days a week at various sites and trained the National Team at four weekly evening sessions. Though he'd just turned sixty-eight, and no player on the National Team was close to Leonard's caliber, the coach continued to teach the game with a relish he had not known since the early stages of his career. He also hoped to develop a girls program that would lead to meaningful basketball opportunities for young women in the country. Entrenched traditions would make this difficult, yet he saw much value in the idea itself, not to mention in the athletic potential of both Tutsi and Hutu women.

As for his rebirth of spiritualism, it was, he knew, the direct result of the brutal deaths of Leonard and Consolaté.

"My Catholic faith has not gone unchallenged," he wrote in the diary he began to keep after joining the Emily Dickinson Society. "Yet, despite my continuing disagreement with some aspects of church teachings, the recent pain that I have faced causes me to embrace the comfort and consolation granted by the Holy Ghost. And for the first time in my life, I am not in fear of my own mortality."

In gravitating toward another source of inner peace—his poetry—he would rise each morning at six. With the spectacular view of Lake Tanganyika as his companion, he would spend his first hour on the veranda writing, all the while taking tips from Ambassador Foster's most helpful book. Before retiring in the evening, he would re-check his early-morning work then read more of Galway Kinnell. Ambassador Foster had also introduced him to contemporary poets, such as Robert Pinsky and Eamonn Grennan, and highly regarded poets from the past, notably W. H. Auden. He made sure to record in his diary one of Auden's most thought-provoking lines: "If equal affection cannot be/Let the more loving one be me."

This line reminds me so much of Edna. Perhaps the best advice I have ever read for all relationships, including marriage. I must tell the ambassador about it . . . and Sarah.

To Jim's pleasure—and surprise—his poetry was improving, causing members of the Emily Dickinson Society to praise his work. The ambassador was still encouraging, but also more circumspect in her comments. This was fine with Jim—her candor was an important element in his development as a poet.

One night in April, at the end of a session at her home, the ambassador reminded the group, "Our annual Emily Dickinson Summer Solstice reading will take place on June 22 here at the Embassy. We will invite approximately 150 people. Each member of the Society will read two poems."

Jim had made a note about the session, but he'd put it out of his mind. Now, the thought of reading his work to such a large crowd caused him discomfort. On the other hand, he knew that such an event would motivate him to work more diligently toward his two "Galway Kinnells."

What he did not know was that Ambassador Foster was already planning to make this evening one that would reach a new level of meaning for Jim Keating.

V
Seeking the Truth

53

Johannesburg, South Africa

Raised a Catholic, Finbar Finnegan understood the literal meaning of Purgatory. But in recent weeks, the word took on a slightly different connotation when Sid Hawkins said, "Finbar, it'd likely take you a good while to get out of your Catholic Purgatory, but in this situation you can get out fairly soon—you just need to be patient."

In Finnegan, Hawkins and other CNN executives recognized they were the custodians of a major talent. Yet the news giant was still smarting from the fallout from Operation Deliverance. Because of heightened sensitivity at the home office, Hawkins's idea of personally overseeing Finnegan made sense to the higher ups in Atlanta. And so, Finbar was temporarily assigned to "Joburg," where Show Me Sid would keep the young Irishman busy with a new project regarding the state of sport in post-apartheid South Africa—and also off the air until the aftershock of Operation Deliverance had subsided.

"Sid, he's a gifted young man who, now more than ever, needs your supervision," said Robert Geissler, Hawkins's boss in Atlanta. "Keep him on track—and let's make damn sure that these sports reports are top shelf."

One of Finbar's specific assignments was to examine the discriminatory reign of Rugby Union leader Louis Luyt. Since Nelson Mandela, an avid sportsman, had gained power, he and Luyt had been locked in a fierce struggle over Luyt's refusal to open the sport to blacks. Despite legal pressure from the Mandela government, rugby had remained a predominantly white sport, and Luyt continued to loudly maintain his apartheid beliefs. Frustrated by Luyt's defiance, Mandela finally appointed a National Sports Council Judicial Commission to study allegations of racism and corruption in the Luyt administration. Luyt's response was to force Mandela into court, compelling the president to publicly justify the Commission.

"Even some of the most ardent of Luyt's followers found his action to be uncalled for," Hawkins told Finnegan. "However, it is fact that rugby—and Luyt—are important examples of die-hard pro-apartheid supporters refusing to accede to the wishes of the new administration. It's these kinds of conflicts that make South Africa one of the most fascinating human laboratories this side of Belfast—and a place where a good reporter like you can come up with some important stories."

While the assignment did have journalistic value, Finbar continued to seethe at being made the scapegoat of Operation Deliverance. He knew, as did Hawkins, that he had followed proper journalistic protocol in reporting a potentially major story.

In a memo sent to his superiors in Atlanta, Finnegan vented his displeasure: "My professional conduct throughout Operation Deliverance was properly cautious and above reproach. In my reports, I avoided generalizations and predictions, and I consistently let my audience know what was fact, what had been disproved, what was in dispute, and what was unknown. I am being singled out unfairly for what was, by all accounts, an exclusive that had possible international ramifications."

Hawkins, copied on the memo, called Finnegan to his office.

"Finbar, there's not one thing in this damn memo that's not true. Nonetheless, you—and CNN—are associated with Operation Deliverance. Now you've vented, and, fortunately for you, they appear to have accepted your right to vent. My advice is to put it out of your mind and focus on developing a first-rate story on the South African rugby situation. And remember this, if the people in Atlanta didn't realize your talent, they wouldn't have put you behind a desk for a couple of months—they'd have fired you."

Finnegan followed Hawkins's advice, confining his anger to staring several times each day at a portrait that he had received in the post a few days earlier. A note by its sender, Ambassador Cynthia Foster, accompanied the portrait.

"Enclosed is the rendering of the Mediterranean-looking man whom Mathias spotted at the Rwanda game and whom Mutara and Hibimana, the two Burundian boys, saw outside of the Tangishaka hut. Mathias and the two boys spent two full days with Daniela Retkova, an illustrator with UN Security Forces. The three all agree that the rendering is a lifelike portrait of this individual."

The ambassador concluded her note with a statement that Finbar knew to be accurate. "If we can find him, he might be able to unlock the whole mystery."

———

Finbar Finnegan found the new South Africa to be a country not without its growing pains and serious problems—basic safety being one.

Since the post-Mandela election turmoil, violent crimes, including rapes, had erupted, particularly in urban areas such as Johannesburg. The predominantly white media vigorously reported on the alarming trend, and the black government, while dealing harshly with offenders, often attributed the dilemma to decades of oppression.

Of particular interest to Finbar was the varied reaction of whites. Some viewed the situation as hopeless and took their leave—Australia and New Zealand were favorite stations of relocation. Others aggressively protested the upsurge to their politicians—both white and black. In most cases, the elected officials were helpless to offer aid, so strangled were they by the bureaucracy of an infant government. Still other whites, much smaller in number, looked at the predicament as penance for the sins of apartheid.

Yet all who stayed and who had grown accustomed to safe passage in their neighborhoods prior to the Mandela election had one thing in common, as explained by Sid Hawkins to Finbar: "Everyone, and I mean bloody everyone, no matter their neighborhood, has a modern security system."

Hawkins continued in an avuncular tone. "I know you like the diversity and excitement of Johannesburg. But my advice—strong advice—is that you take a place in Sandton. The downtown area is just too dangerous. And wherever you decide to situate, make sure that you join the masses and buy a damned good security system."

Finnegan knew Hawkins well enough to realize that his statements were not racist—just objective as well as practical, and he took the advice of his boss on both counts. He leased a luxury flat in Sandton, just twenty minutes outside of downtown Johannesburg, and purchased the most expensive alarm system he could find.

Yet despite these issues of personal safety, Finnegan *loved* living in South Africa. The climate was mild and dry—"salubrious," as Hawkins described it. Many of the women—black and white—were beautiful and, as Finbar was discovering, attracted to fair-skinned Irishmen. And a number of the sports he was researching, including his favorite, would offer important angles for his story.

"Sid," said Finnegan, "soccer and rugby might dominate the South African sports pages and even produce world-class teams, and I'm looking into the Luyt situation. But let me tell you something—basketball, while still not played at a very high level, is gaining remarkable popularity. Plus, I'm told the people connected to the game are a lively bunch."

Visibly, through sponsorship of youth programs and investment in the newly founded South African pro league (the first professional basketball league in the country), government officials and a new wave of young entrepreneurs were pushing the sport forward. Television coverage, both of the South African league and an occasional NBA game, contributed to the interest, as did the involvement in the league of several fine American players and coaches, like Sam Vincent, the former Michigan State All-American and ex-Boston Celtic.

The acknowledged leader of this "basketball revolution," as the media termed it, was an accomplished and fascinating twenty-nine-year-old named Albert Tshewete, whose acquaintance Finnegan would soon make.

———

The Roseleigh Basketball Complex, on the outskirts of Johannesburg, was the hub of Joburg hoop activity. The complex featured four lighted courts, as well as a renovated home that served as administrative headquarters for the entire South African school basketball league, a program that encompassed more than three thousand young players.

Roseleigh had another earned distinction: It was the best place in town to "get a game."

Within weeks of his arrival back in the city, Finbar Finnegan, always keen for a good hoop workout, had gravitated to Roseleigh. There, on a hot Sunday afternoon, he was introduced to Albert Tshewete, a compact and very quick 6'4" guard.

As opponents in a three-on-three game, Finnegan and Tshewete had employed the Doberman defensive practices standard on all asphalt courts throughout the world: hand checks, muggings on open lay-ups, and "nose jobs."

The latter improvisation had first been explained to Finbar by an American coach at a Dublin clinic years earlier. "A good nose job involves your hand grazing the schnozz of the shooter just before his release." Finnegan had tried the tactic on Tshewete, whose only reaction was a heightened resolve to win the game. When the South African banked home a ten-footer to seal the victory, he was mildly surprised that the competitive Irishman immediately approached him with an extended hand.

"Let me guess," said Finnegan. "You played ball in the States—and for a good coach."

"How did you know?" responded a surprised Tshewete.

"Since I arrived in Joburg a few weeks ago, I've been playin' the odd three-on-three game here at Roseleigh. You're the first guy I've guarded who knows how to move without the ball."

"Thank you. You play well yourself, especially for a guy who wears sun block," winked Albert.

It was now Finnegan's turn to be surprised—such a daring remark was surely not common between the races in South Africa. Yet Finbar recognized that the quip was made as a sign of friendship. He also knew that a basketball court was one of the few places in the country where such politically incorrect banter would be accepted.

Finnegan had picked up on something else unusual about Albert Tshewete. Despite appearing to be only in his late twenties, he was addressed by most of the other basketball participants as "sir" or "Mr. Tshewete."

"Why do they call you that?" asked Finbar.

"Aw," Albert replied sheepishly, "it's this job that President Mandela gave me."

"And what job would that be?"

"Well, I'm Director General of Home Affairs."

In South African government, the Director General of Home Affairs was in charge of immigration. For someone so young to hold such a lofty position must surely involve special circumstances. Journalist that he was, Finbar was curious to learn the full particulars, and Tshewete was just as interested in Finbar's background.

"Buy you a Coke?" Finbar asked.

"You're on," replied Tshewete, and the two headed to the nearby lunch wagon.

54

Finbar had made enough friends through basketball to know that accelerated bonding was a common offshoot of the sport. Under the shade of a white Karee tree at the Roseleigh Complex, that was exactly what occurred between Finbar and Albert.

As the two perspiring players drained their Cokes, Finnegan gently probed the background of his new friend. What he found was a remarkable story—and a surprising willingness on Tshewete's part to tell it.

Born in a shanty in the Triomf section of Johannesburg and raised by a single mother who worked as a domestic, Albert Tshewete had experienced a far different dimension of apartheid than most other black South Africans. His mother, Sophie, had been employed by the Nishes, a family of five who lived in Orange Grove, an affluent suburb of Johannesburg. William Nish had made considerable money as one of South Africa's most successful diamond traders. His work involved extensive travel, including frequent visits to the States before the Congressional ban on trading with South Africa.

During his many journeys, Nish had received a full dose of the anti-apartheid sentiment that prevailed in most other countries. At first, he was defensive about apartheid, in particular rejecting the comparisons made by many Americans between the apartheid system and slavery.

"We did not import slaves," Nish would counter. "The blacks came to our country when they needed refuge from countries such as Zimbabwe and Botswana. Apartheid was established by Prime Minister D. F. Malan in 1948—not to enslave the blacks but to create a system that would work for both sides—recognizing that we had a significant problem."

Nish held to this point of view for many years, until he came into contact with John Jenkins. Jenkins, an African American, had, in his own words, "studied his way out of the South Bronx." His intellect and diligence had earned him full academic scholarships to Choate, Harvard, and the Wharton School of Business at UPenn.

In his early thirties, and having achieved significant wealth as an investment banker, Jenkins decided to relocate to London because, as he explained to the *Wall Street Journal*, "I want to be part of the European Union economic explosion."

In London, he became involved in the import/export business and took a particular interest in diamonds. He met Nish through one extremely profitable deal, which soon led to other ventures involving the two.

As Nish and Jenkins became better acquainted, the South African found that he liked the American expatriate, a somewhat surprising development inasmuch as Nish had virtually no black friends in South Africa. As the friendship grew, Jenkins would cautiously raise the issue of apartheid. This caused Nish consternation, for defending his country's policies with other whites was one thing— but trying to justify apartheid to a black American was quite another.

Rather than being contentious on the matter, Jenkins followed his blueprint for all thorny issues. He did his homework so that when the subject was raised, his points would be logical and valid.

"I have read extensively of the history of South Africa, including Michener's *The Covenant*. My first point is that I do not subscribe to the notion that all South African whites are evil. In fact, in many ways, I now consider myself a Brit, or, at least, an Anglophile. God knows that the Brits have a long history of unconscionable oppression in many lands.

"Having said that, I'm also of the view that a system such as apartheid will prevent black South Africans from growing—intellectually or professionally. For example, I'll bet that if you took some time to find a young South African of color—and of great promise—you know, a motivated kid with high intellect and leadership qualities—then I'm quite certain you'll find that this youngster cannot advance in your system."

"I don't agree with that," replied Nish.

"Well," said Jenkins evenly, "may I respectfully suggest that you seek out such a young person and test my theory. Find someone who is bright and ambitious—and who wants to successfully move through the South African system of education and, ultimately, perhaps into the business or legal community."

"I will," said Nish in a decidedly firm and resolute tone.

Ironically, when he returned to South Africa, he found this person right in his own home on Christmas Day.

Albert Tshewete, then fourteen years old, came with his mother to the Nish house that Christmas for a special servants' dinner and gift ceremony. While the other staff children were eagerly opening their presents, Nish noticed young Albert sitting off in a corner reading, of all things, *The Adventures of Huckleberry Finn*. He approached the youngster and said, "Do you like Mark Twain?"

"Very much," replied Albert.

"What do you like about him?" asked Nish, quite innocently, he thought.

For a moment, Albert appeared reluctant to answer, and with good reason. But something inside him suggested that he should tell this man, his mother's employer, the truth.

"I like Mark Twain because his books offer interesting insights into black America in the nineteenth century."

At first, Nish was taken aback—not only with the cogency of the comment, but with the derring-do of the subject matter. For a fleeting moment, he even considered a mild rebuke to the boy for bringing up a topic that was generally off limits in conversations between blacks and whites in South Africa.

But Nish thought about his friend's challenge and decided instead to invite the boy into his private study for a discussion. Only minutes into their talk, Nish was amazed at Albert's depth of knowledge on a variety of subjects. Clearly, the youngster had read extensively. As the result of tutoring from a Mormon preacher, he had a firm grasp of math and science. In addition, Albert spoke four languages: Zulu and Sotho, both black languages; Afrikaans, spoken by both whites and blacks; and English.

Nish was also struck by the boy's physique. He was already 6'1", his legs were sturdy and muscular in the calves, and his upper body, while still wiry, looked as if it would soon ripple with muscles. His face was unusually handsome, with light, caramel-colored skin, unlike the much darker complexion of the Sotho tribe of his mother.

William Nish was a man accustomed to spending considerable time ruminating over important decisions. But in this case, as soon as the two finished their discussion, Nish decided to take on the challenge presented to him by John Jenkins. He would facilitate young Albert's application to some of the finest private schools in Johannesburg.

In making this decision, Nish knew that his actions would go against the wishes of his wife and, quite possibly, that he would face ostracism from others in his community. Yet, somehow, the successful white businessman had a strong sense that his black servant's son was worth the risk.

Within just weeks, William Nish found regrettable truth in the pessimistic forecast of John Jenkins. Despite testing higher than most white candidates, Albert Tshewete had been rejected at all four private schools in Johannesburg. While a variety of explanations had been given by the headmasters, Nish was well aware of the only pertinent factor.

"When you brought the subject up," he said to Jenkins, "I was confident that any qualified candidate would be accepted to at least one of these schools. My confidence related to the public statements of various educators about the importance of providing talented blacks with educational opportunities. But the fact is that Albert was rejected solely because of his color. I am as embarrassed as I am disappointed."

Nish then raised a calculated solution to the problem.

"Might there be an opportunity for Albert to study in the States?" he asked, knowing that Jenkins was a trustee at his prep school alma mater, the Choate-Rosemary Hall School in Connecticut.

"Send me as much information on the young man as possible. I'll see what I can do."

Four weeks later, Jenkins called Nish with good news. "Choate will give Albert a full scholarship."

Before Jenkins could add his personal offer of helping with the cost of airfare, Nish bellowed, "I'll take care of the flight."

What Nish did not say was that his philanthropy would remain a secret in South Africa. Weeks earlier, when it had become known that he was promoting a black candidate for acceptance into traditionally white private schools, he had received several threatening phone calls, one of which had been taken by his daughter. Alarmed by the calls, his wife Beverly had initially chastised her husband for "placing your family at risk." Yet, upon righteous reflection, she had softened her position. When Nish told her about the offer at Choate, she had agreed that paying the airfare was a proper gesture.

"But let's remember, William, that there are still many people in South Africa who would be angry about your support. If we're going to do this, it must be kept quiet."

A few weeks later, the fourteen-year-old packed his things and nervously awaited the day of his departure. The night before, Mr. Nish came to speak to him in an effort to calm his nerves.

"Young man," Mr. Nish said. "I'd like to tell you what my daughter's high school commencement speaker told her about going away to school, particularly because this speaker drew upon the written words of your favorite author, Mark Twain. Over the next week or two—or even month or two—it is likely that you will be lonely. As my daughter was reminded, loneliness can be your ally—it can help you grow up. Remember when one of your favorite characters, Huck Finn, lit out for the 'territory,' by which, of course, he meant the wilderness?"

"Yes," Albert replied.

"Well, Huck would soon find out what you will find out as well—you cannot be immobilized by loneliness—or fear. There will be many wildernesses in life, Albert—within and without; don't be put off by any of them."

———

At Choate, Albert shined in the classroom and also became an outstanding basketball player. His hoops career took root only days after his arrival, when the coach, taking note of the new student's height, convinced him to give the sport a try. A natural athlete, Albert easily adapted to the game. By his senior year, he had become a coveted recruit of many of the Small Ivies like Trinity, Wesleyan, and Williams in New England.

Albert chose Bates College, received a full academic scholarship, and blossomed into a top New England Division III performer. More importantly, his grades were exceptional, and, upon graduation, he was accepted into a joint program at the Harvard Law School and the Fletcher School of Law and Diplomacy at Tufts. Four years later, he graduated with honors, armed with a degree in international law and diplomacy that would allow him to return to his native land and take on apartheid. He never considered another career path; he wanted only to help the cause.

When Albert returned to Johannesburg, his achievements in America were the subject of a feature story in *The Voice*, a new black-owned newspaper. Nelson Mandela, months out of prison and soon to be elected South Africa's first black president, read the piece and summoned Albert to his office. Mandela was so impressed with Tshwete that, pending his imminent election, he offered him a position as a legal assistant in the Justice Department. Over a twelve-month period, Tshwete earned several promotions and finally the appointment as Director General of Home Affairs.

During this period, Mandela took a personal liking to the young scholar. The president was struck by Tshwete's brilliance, and he also observed another important quality: Albert Tshwete had acquired the licit, logical skills that could help to forever immunize the virus of apartheid.

"Rather than raising our voices or our machetes," Mandela had said to his protégé, "we must use a far more potent weapon—our divine faculty for sweet reason."

And, of course, the two also shared another common interest—a love of sport. When the newly elected president decided to form the South African National Sports Council, he appointed Tshwete to the board of directors.

"We want this council to make sure that the old apartheid practices do not persist on the playing fields or in the gymnasiums," Mandela had said. "Now, please understand that I'm not worried about basketball, for I see a more advanced level of fairness in your game. Also, over a period of time, I sense that we will be able to field competitive teams. In fact, you may be interested to know that an old friend of mine in the states, Richard Lapchick, will soon bring a group of NBA stars to South Africa—including Patrick Ewing."

"This will surely help," Albert had said, too modest to add that it was he who had first contacted Lapchick about the trip.

"On the other hand," the president continued, "there are sports such as rugby that seem very reluctant to open their doors to blacks."

"So what do we do, Mr. President?"

"What we do is force them to open their doors," Mandela replied. "Through our court system, let's try to pass new laws that will, for example, mandate that a national rugby team select a fair percentage of blacks."

"You know, of course, Mr. President, that this policy will mean that some of the best players will not be chosen."

"That is true, but what we must also remember, Albert, is that for decades, some of the best scholars, the best doctors, the best attorneys were not chosen—or even given a chance. Leveling the playing field in rugby is, unfortunately, just one measure of the retributive justice that is part of ending apartheid. So tell me, Mr. Attorney, can this be done through the courts?"

"Yes, Mr. President."

———

Finbar, spellbound by Albert's story, was disappointed when Tshwete said, "Okay, enough about me, tell me about yourself."

As soon as Finnegan told Tshwete that he worked for CNN, Albert responded, "Ahh, you looked familiar, but I could not place your face. I've watched many of the reports on Operation Deliverance, and you know something? My instincts still tell me that there is much more to the story."

"Mine, too," laughed Finnegan. "And that's putting it mildly."

"Well, in any case, regarding your assignment to put together a series on sport in post-apartheid South Africa—it's a great topic—and obviously one of interest to me. As I think you can sense Finbar, I can help you with your stories. In fact, within the next day or two some important things may be happening in the rugby union."

"I'd appreciate any help you can give me," said Finnegan. "And by the way, this William Nish—he sounds like a courageous man. Can I get to meet him?"

Albert Tshwete's expression immediately turned grim. "I'm afraid not, Finbar. Only months after I left for the States, William Nish was murdered. The case has never been solved. It's another reason why I came back to South Africa."

55

Two days later, Finnegan's phone rang at 7:00 AM.

"Sorry for the wakeup call, Finbar, but remember when I told you about the possibility of some major happenings with rugby?"

Finnegan grunted what sounded like a yes.

"Well, I just got word that the Rugby Union will hold a 10 AM press conference, supposedly to address their racial problems. Louis Luyt may resign. I have to be there to represent the NSC."

Tshwete's urgency ushered Finbar to coherence. "I'd like to go with you."

"Thought you might. We'll have to leave early because we may run into some veld fires. I'll pick you up at nine."

Veld fires were an odd practice that Finnegan had never heard of before his Johannesburg assignment. In late autumn, government workers would, in the words of Tshwete, "ignite any state-owned property adjacent to a road with grass on top of it." The process would char the grass so that, by early spring, the knolls and meadows that abutted South African highways would be lush and green.

"But what about the environmental implications of these fires?" asked Finnegan as he settled into the front seat of Tshwete's Mercedes 230. "I mean, in Europe and in the States, burning grass and leaves was banned years ago."

"We know that," Albert replied, "but the veld fires are a tradition in our country. Even though some of our environmentalists raise a stir each year, it's not likely to change. We like the green springs the veld fires produce."

Finnegan wanted to point out that there were modern, environmentally safe techniques to ensure green grass. But sensing Tshwete's firm viewpoint, the Irishman held back, fearful he might harm a relationship that was still budding. But there was another topic that Finbar Finnegan could not hold back on.

"Albert, you mentioned that William Nish had been killed. Can you tell me more about that?"

For a moment, there was silence.

"One evening, in my first year at Choate, just before the American Thanksgiving, John Jenkins, the friend of Mr. Nish who I told you about, came to my room. I was to stay at his family's home over the holiday, and at first I thought Mr. Jenkins might have mixed up the pick-up date. But as soon as I saw tears in his eyes, I knew that his visit must be related to Mr. Nish."

Tshwete paused for another moment and took in a deep breath.

"The autopsy stated that Mr. Nish died of internal injuries—the result of a car accident in which, allegedly, his brakes had failed. But I have never believed that. Mr. Nish's home was on top of a hill in Orange Grove. Each morning when he would leave for work, he would drive down that rather steep hill. Now remember, my mother had told me many times that Mr. Nish always took good care of his automobile, which, by the way, was a brand-new Mercedes—hardly a vehicle that would have brake problems."

He continued. "Anyway, on this particular morning, his car crashed through a guard rail at the bottom of this hill, and he died instantly. There is another thing about it—something typical of Mr. Nish. At a certain point less than halfway down the hill, he could have turned into a cul-de-sac and likely found his safety. But he had to know there were school children at that corner waiting for their morning bus. I think he didn't take the turn in order to save their lives. Instead, he went on and was killed."

Finbar could see a wave of emotion beginning to overtake his new friend, but Albert remained composed enough to finish his story.

"You know, Finbar, when I was a child, before I met Mr. Nish, I hated all white people, the only exception being the Mormon missionary who taught me to read and write. But after I got to know Mr. Nish, I realized I was wrong about whites. My hatred toward them turned to a hatred of the system of bigotry that so overwhelms this country. As you may be able to sense, my life's mission is to crush this system. Yet I also came to realize that to be a leader, you must think with compassion about the other side—you must get into their heads, try to think as they do."

He added, "Believe it or not, I understand how many whites fell for the specious philosophy of apartheid; how many were just blinded to its injustice. And I also understand how this makes what Mr. Nish did for me all the more remarkable."

"It surely was remarkable," said Finnegan. "But tell me this—do you have any idea who did it?"

"Well, there were several extremist groups in those days—one that did its dirty work in Johannesburg. This group was, and still is, called Wit Wolve, which means white wolves. The Truth and Reconciliation Commission, which has been reporting on this group's alleged use of chemical and biological weapons on blacks, has also uncovered a number of murders allegedly committed by Wit Wolve." Tshwete took a deep breath. When he continued speaking, his tone was stern. "Understand, people in Wit Wolve are intelligent, cunning, and *very* well funded. The way Mr. Nish died would have been typical of their work."

"A moment ago, you used the term 'still is.' Are the Wit Wolve still around?" asked Finnegan.

"I believe so. After the Mandela election, they supposedly went underground. But, as I said, they are extremely well funded and the consensus is that they're still very much alive."

"Are they still being investigated?" asked Finnegan.

"Oh yes, but because of their money—and their power—it's been more difficult to break their ranks than the ranks of other extremist groups. But that doesn't mean that we've given up," Tshwete said emphatically. "Or that I've given up hope of finding the murderers of Mr. Nish."

There was another period of quiet until, several minutes later, the Mercedes pulled alongside a veld fire that seemed out of control. The fire's smoke seeped through the car's closed windows and created a fog-like condition that Tshwete had difficulty navigating. Concerned, Finnegan blurted out, "These veld fires, Albert. They're bloody dangerous!"

Tshwete smiled and calmly steered his way through the fire. Several minutes later, he pulled his Mercedes to the front of the Intercontinental Hotel in Sandton.

———

The press conference began with a thunderclap announcement by Michael Lyons, press secretary for the South African Rugby Football Union. "Our organization has accepted the resignation of Louis Luyt."

There was a quaver in Lyons's voice—and for good reason. Luyt had become a millstone around the neck of Mandela's watchdog National Sports Council. But he also had his share of backers in the Rugby Union, many of whom were at the press conference.

When Lyons opened the floor for questions from the media, James Merrill, a hulking fullback, stood and snarled, "I'm not from the press but I've got something to ask. Is it the opinion of the National Sports Council that we should field a team of inferior players just to make certain that an equal number of blacks are on the bloody field?" Merrill's harsh tone was as contentious as his question; an undercurrent of tension charged through the room.

To Finbar Finnegan's surprise, Albert Tshwete, seated next to him in the front row facing Lyons, and known by all in attendance, raised his hand and calmly asked, "Mr. Lyons, may I respond on behalf of the National Sports Council?"

Lyons nodded, and Tshwete rose from his seat and turned to the audience.

"Ladies and gentleman, we have a mandate at the National Sports Council to ensure that rugby, and all other sports, incorporate the principals of equality. Unfortunately, it is true that this mandate will cause some competitive disadvantage at first, particularly to some athletes at the national level. But over the long haul, it will bring about the level playing field that every fair-minded South African—black and white— seeks for our country."

The statement, delivered in a composed yet commanding manner, seemed to guide the overall mood in the room back toward civility, a condition reflected by Merrill's silence and the polite tone of the next questioner.

"But Mr. Tshwete," asked John Farr, assistant coach for the National Team, "how long will the long haul be? You see, sir, many of our players are concerned that their careers will be over by the time this objective is achieved."

"It is a fair question, Mr. Farr, and I wish I could say how long this process will take," Tshwete responded. "What I can say is that the council does not subscribe to the position of some others—that because our population is 75 percent black then all national teams must be 75 percent black. However, we are saying that all national teams must have black—and white—representation."

"But Mr. Tshwete, you are, by all accounts, a fine basketball player. How would you feel if this policy resulted in an inferior white player making the National Team before you?" asked Robert Bloss, a white reporter for the *Johannesburg Mail and Guardian*.

The personal nature of the question, and the ensuing silence, signaled another rise in tension. But Tshwete remained composed. Before answering the question, he momentarily flashed back to an ethics course at the Fletcher School at Tufts and the right-versus-right conundrums inherent in many complex issues.

"Let me try to respond to Mr. Bloss's question. Those of you who take the position that it is unfair if even a few qualified players are not selected in favor of less qualified players— you are not wrong. But those of us who take the position that for decades the oppression of apartheid prevented all blacks from having *any* opportunity are not wrong either."

Tshwete moved to the center aisle and addressed the crowd with a stronger voice. "Let me pose a question in sports vernacular: If two people were in a boat race from one side of a lake to another, and one started at the dock and yet the other was given the opportunity to start in the middle of the lake, would that be fair?"

The room remained silent.

"You see," Tshwete continued, "to me at least, that is what the cancer of apartheid did to blacks in this country. The charge of the NSC is to give that person who started back at the dock a fair chance. This will require, among all of us, patience—and compromise. But, at least in my judgment, it is the right thing to do."

Finnegan did not completely agree with his new friend's reasoning. However, he was not about to challenge Tshwete's points, particularly in such a precarious and distrustful environment. Instead, his attention was drawn to another questioner seated in the rear of the room, a reporter from *The Sowetan.*

As Finbar turned his head to get a better listen, his heart nearly drummed through his chest.

Standing behind the reporter was a man who bore a remarkable resemblance to the illustration Ambassador Foster had sent. Finbar immediately wondered if the man recognized him or, if not, had noticed Finbar's surprised facial expression. Uncertain of either possibility, but knowing that the real culprit would surely know of Finbar Finnegan, the Irishman decided to act as quickly and unobtrusively as possible.

Turning slowly back to the front of the room, Finbar handed a note to Albert, who had returned to his seat.

Don't turn around. I think the man I've been looking for is in the back of the room. I'm going after him. Stay here—no commotion, okay?

Tshwete's first instinct was to insist on aiding his friend. But he knew that Finbar was right—that his own departure would surely cause a stir throughout the room. And so, he reacted as Finbar hoped he would, showing no emotion other than a soft whisper. "Be careful."

With his head down, Finbar quietly rose from his chair and began to walk to the back of the room. Seconds later, when he looked up to find his quarry, the man was gone.

56

Nazr Fadeli had been in his current position for four years since his employer had recruited him straight out of the Afrikaner Weerstandbeweging, better known as the Afrikaner Resistance Movement, a militia active in South Africa since the 1980s. His original job description was simple: enforce the noble principles of apartheid, principles abandoned by the South African government. Of late, his role had expanded to that of troubleshooter, a promotion that had landed Fadeli in Burundi as overseer of a laudable experiment with exiting implications far beyond this small, landlocked African country.

Born in Palestine, the son of a Sunni Muslim father and Bedouin mother, Fadeli and his family had moved to South Africa when he was in his early teens to escape the rapidly expanding land seizure of the despised Jews. He saw the Israeli encroachment as not simply illegal, but immoral. For Fadeli's mother, whose ancestors had especially deep roots in the Arab culture, the Jewish settlements created a rancorous, malignant hatred.

As a student at the all-white University of the Free State in Bloemfontein, capital of the Free State of South Africa, his mother's malevolence inspired his emerging affinity for apartheid's virtues, so much so that Nazr had made a frequent vow to his classmates: "I will do all in my power to prevent the blacks from taking over South Africa the way the Jews have stolen the Holy Land."

His fervent support of apartheid was accompanied by another passion—a love of sport. At 5'10", and of sturdy build, Fadeli reveled in contact sports and ended up a center fullback on the university rugby team. And while he found the rugby pitch an ideal venue to release his pent-up anger over the perilous apostasy taking over his country, his favorite spectator sport was American football, the result of South African TV picking up NFL games on a delayed basis.

By the late '80s, Fadeli saw the foundation of apartheid weaken at the hands of the imprisoned Mandela, his demon cohorts in the African National Congress, and those meddling foreigners whose hypocrisy had brought about the crippling sanctions. Fadeli decided to volunteer with Wit Wolve—a privately funded and entrenched top secret organization dedicated to quashing anti-apartheid activity.

Fadeli invested a considerable amount of his spare time as a volunteer. On rare occasions, at a meeting, planning session for noble retribution, or secret attack on a militant black group—"preventive strike" as it was called within the organization—he would overhear the phrase *Die Voorsitter* (The Chairman). Curiously, when the term came up, it was whispered, suggesting that queries about the eminent figure were unwelcome.

As Fadeli became more involved in the work of Wit Wolve, and more zealous in his commitment to suppressing the anti-apartheid movement, he would occasionally summon the courage to ask off-handed questions about Die Voorsitter. From what he could piece together, The Chairman was a wealthy, powerful individual, passionate about his privacy and equally passionate about the utilitarian value of apartheid.

Fadeli wanted to move up in the organization's ranks, and one morning his steadfast allegiance to the mission was finally requited. An unexpected call from a general in Wit Wolve requested Fadeli's presence at a meeting of the organization's senior command. At the meeting, Fadeli met The Chairman, who was surrounded by a group of unsmiling aides.

Appearing to be in his late sixties, but fit, tanned, and alert, The Chairman politely asked Fadeli a series of questions aimed at gauging the degree of Nazr's support of apartheid. At the end of the session, The Chairman stared intently into Fadeli's eyes. "I would like to offer you a job in what I call my security force. Your rank would be that of captain, and the job will pay double what you now earn in the militia."

The Chairman went on to explain that the position would entail myriad responsibilities including, when necessary, justified assaults on those who wished to ruin the rightful, godly way of life in South Africa.

Fadeli accepted instantly—and gratefully.

Within months of becoming a true insider, he discovered that the scope of The Chairman's work was as wide as it was commendable. The projects of Wit Wolve included a top-secret biological and chemical weapons program, as well as covert distribution of an anti-fertility pill that the organization spread liberally through the black neighborhoods, camouflaging it as a treatment for dysentery.

There were other important experiments: As an example, Wit Wolve's active laboratory developed a shirt infused with poison. In a trial test, the shirt was given to a black activist who, after wearing it for several hours, suffered a spasm of the coronary artery and died of a heart attack.

And then there was The Chairman's avid interest in sport. This fervent attraction, a long-standing tradition in his family, led to a fascinating scientific discovery, which then led to the successful experiment in Burundi. After the initial CNN report on Project Oscar, Captain Fadeli had been given the honor of overseeing this important experiment. He had arrived in Burundi for the Rwanda game and the highly anticipated debut of Leonard Tangishaka. He had left at halftime to call headquarters with the message: *We must go forward.* The result, of course, was a successful first step in a form of retribution and repression that could be used in a variety of circumstances by Wit Wolve.

The Chairman took a particular interest in rugby; he knew rugby was one of the last and best hopes for white domination in any South African sport. He also knew that this sport had been unfairly penalized by the immoral international ban jointly imposed by the Rugby League International Federation and the International Olympic Committee. The ban prevented South African athletes from playing outside of the country, a serious competitive disadvantage.

The Chairman was unequivocal in his admiration of Louis Luyt. When he had learned of Luyt's forced ouster, he was furious and had dispatched Captain Fadeli—his sports expert—to attend the press conference and learn more of the facts. Fadeli arrived slightly late so as to discreetly position himself in the rear of the room and not attract attention. Get the facts, and then report back to me, was his only order from The Chairman.

When he spotted Finbar Finnegan and the correspondent's chilled reaction, Nazr recognized him instantly as the "Talking Head of CNN"—the one who had tried to do so much damage to the honorable experiment in Burundi.

Fadeli was not aware that Finnegan was in South Africa, let alone Johannesburg. He inwardly seethed that others within the Wit Wolve empire, whose job it was to track such movements, had not discovered the presence of this menace. Surely, The Chairman would be equally upset.

When Fadeli spotted Finbar, the witless reporter had completely given himself away with his startled expression and awkward attempt to hide his surprise. Fadeli knew that if Finbar approached him, a troubled situation would ensue. And so he left immediately, dashing out of the back door and into the window-darkened limousine that awaited him at the rear of the hotel.

He was convinced that his getaway had been clean, yet when he returned to headquarters he also knew that it was his duty to report his discovery to The Chairman, including the fact that he saw Finnegan passing a note to their bête noir, Albert Tshwete.

"You are right, Captain Fadeli. It is very upsetting that our people did not realize what should have been an easy detection. Nonetheless, we must react accordingly."

"Should we kill this Irishman?" asked Piet Van Vuuren, another aide.

"God, no," replied The Chairman. "This would only attract more attention and lead people closer to our covert operation, especially if he has befriended Tshwete. . . . No, because Finnegan recognized Captain Fadeli, we must transfer the Captain to our operation in the Seychelles. Captain Fadeli, are you okay with that?"

"I am," replied Fadeli.

"In that case, Piet, take Captain Fadeli to his home, where he can gather his belongings and then head to the airport. Our private jet will take both of you to the Seychelles. Since we have some staff there already, we can easily continue our planning from our Seychelles base."

When Nazr Fadeli left the room, The Chairman picked up the phone and gave his death order. He hung up, leaned back in his chair, and said to the group, "It's a shame. Fadeli was a good employee—loyal and diligent. But we cannot take any chances of being discovered, particularly with the next phase of our essential experiment so close at hand."

Six hours later, Nazr Fadeli boarded the private jet. He was dead upon arrival at the D'Arros Island Airport in the Seychelles.

The following morning, after a restful sleep, The Chairman made five untraceable calls, each bearing the same coded message.

VI
Finding Light

57

Bujumbura, Burundi

In the month or so that Jim Keating had to prepare for his public reading, he approached the task with a rigid, athletic discipline that had characterized his life. Each morning, he faithfully wrote for an hour; each evening, he reviewed his work of that morning and contemplated another writing project—a letter of encouragement to Robert Frazier.

Frazier was struggling as head coach at New Jersey State. In keeping with the ambassador's philosophy of love and forgiveness, Jim felt that reaching out to him was the right thing to do. Before drafting the letter, he would discuss his intentions with Cynthia at some point after the Summer Solstice Reading, for she would surely provide good guidance.

Jim also planned to seek out Bill for advice on another matter. The item Jim had retrieved from the Tangishaka hut was Consolaté's beautiful and lifelike watercolor of Leonard. Jim would ask Bill if Cynthia's birthday, which he knew was only days after the Summer Solstice reading, would be the best time to surprise her with the painting.

Along with his writing and coaching, Jim found he was enjoying—more and more—the simple pleasures of life: a walk, a glass of cold water, birdsong—everyday delights that, in the past, he had seldom appreciated. The birds were fascinating, an especially enjoyable distraction. Josiane had set up a birdfeeder on the veranda. Jim took particular pleasure in two infrequent visitors: His favorite was the Blue-breasted Cordon-bleu, a gorgeous bird with azure blue from its breast to its tail and a beige back and wings. A close second was the Tanganyika Weaver, all yellow with a black mask.

Jim had written a number of poems and had to choose two for the reading. As June approached, he sought out the ambassador to ask her counsel.

"If I were you," she replied confidently, "I would go with 'First Love' and 'Finish Strong.' In my view, Jim, these are your two finest."

Pleased—and relieved—to have his choices confirmed, Jim smiled. "Mine, too!"

The day of the event, Jim rose at 6:00 AM, practiced his reading from 6:30 to 7:30, and went for his twenty-minute jog around the grounds.

After a cool shower and breakfast of Mealie, an oatmeal-like porridge similar to the hominy grits he'd learned to like in the Army, he headed to the veranda, poems in hand. Easing his rejuvenated body into the rattan armchair Josiane had found to fit his rangy frame, Jim rested the poems on his lap and gazed out over Lake Tanganyika, a view that always filled him with tranquility.

He would miss it, but not in the way that he would miss the sense of fulfillment he'd derived from teaching the game he loved to young men he had grown to love. Nor would he miss it in the way that he would miss the camaraderie of his inner hoops circle of Bill Foster, Mathias Bizimana, Terrance Ndayisaba, Jesse Abbot, and the others who had embraced his presence. And he surely would not miss it in the way that he would miss one of the most admirable people he had ever known, whose compassion and goodwill had shored up his self-command.

There were attractive elements to his returning to Worcester. Thanks to the pay he had received in Burundi, he would have enough money to live more comfortably. And, no doubt, he could find part-time work at the Ionic Ave. Boys' Club or at a local school, coaching and mentoring young people. But the appeal of his hometown would not, he knew, diminish his sense of melancholy over leaving the most rewarding job he'd ever had.

After an hour or so of quiet review of his poems and more reflection, Jim headed off to the Nimbona Court. He took care not to stretch his vocal cords before the reading. When the practice session ended, Jim headed back to his apartment, only to see Corporal Jim Roberts in an embassy car exiting through the gates. Jim was surprised when Roberts did not stop to chat, but instead smiled and drove on.

Jim was still wondering where Roberts was headed when he opened his apartment door and was startled by a familiar voice. "Hello, Daddy."

———

As early as two months after his arrival in Burundi, Jim had offered to pay Sarah's way to Africa for a visit. But she had stubbornly refused his help, making clear that her teaching job would afford her the opportunity to save enough for the flight.

Though he did miss her greatly, Jim was proud of his daughter's resolve. He was also pleased that the distance separating them had, indeed, brought them closer together, a condition reflected in the tender sentiments that each expressed in letters and on calls.

When Jim had first told Sarah about his new avocation, she was overjoyed. "Galway Kinnell is a Princeton grad and one of my favorites, too!"

Sarah had followed up by sending her father other books of poetry she thought he would like, including the works of Jack Ridl, a sports poet. Jim had known Jack's father, the late Buzz Ridl, a renowned basketball coach at the University of Pittsburgh. He took delight in reading Jack's poignant verses about growing up the son of a great coach.

Through many conversations with Jim, Ambassador Foster was also aware that Sarah would not accept any financial assistance from her father. The ambassador finally decided to take matters into her own hands.

In a confidential letter to Sarah, she wrote, "Your dad has told me that you will not accept his financial help. However, through the State Department, I have been able to make arrangements for a diplomatic discount on a round-trip air ticket. This is a perfectly legitimate perquisite that we offer to immediate family members of individuals who have performed with distinction here in Africa. If you are able to come, I know your dad would love to see you. Hopefully, you can arrive just in time for his reading on Summer Solstice Night. Let's keep it a secret, though!"

The day she received the letter, Sarah wrote back to Ambassador Foster, expressing her gratitude and agreeing to the offer.

———

After a long embrace, and a failed attempt at holding back tears of jubilation, Jim reveled in his daughter's narrative about her life since his move to Africa. She filled him in on matters ranging from her teaching position to Ambassador Foster's unexpected letter, to the challenges and opportunities that lay in her future as an aspiring writer. Sarah made no mention of her boyfriend, and Jim did not ask, sensing that she would bring up the relationship when she was ready.

It was the longest uninterrupted conversation that Jim could ever recall having with his daughter. He became so engrossed in their discussion that he forgot his anxiety about the impending reading.

After a couple hours of catching up, Jim could see that Sarah was weary. He escorted her to the small guest room for a much needed nap and then went out to the veranda to finalize his preparation.

The first poem that Jim had decided to read, titled "First Love," was about his lifelong romance with basketball. The second poem, "Finish Strong," addressed the harsh challenges of aging and his personal strategy to confronting those challenges.

In the past, reading these poems in the solitude of the veranda, Jim had sometimes found himself fighting back mild fits of grief, for both evoked a plethora of emotions. But though he felt a sense of anxiety returning, he vowed that he would hold his voice steady at the reading, a task that would now be more difficult due to the presence of his daughter.

As he continued his preparation, he was pleased to feel his qualms give way to a rush of adrenaline—the same sensation he'd felt the morning of the Rwanda game.

When Sarah awoke, Josiane made a traditional Burundian delicacy of red kidney beans mixed with green bananas, followed by Bananas Burundi, a favorite native dessert made with cinnamon and orange juice. When father and daughter were finished, Jim said, "Okay. It's game time. Jesse will be knocking on our door any moment."

Sarah was amused by Jim's unchanged habit of relating most of life's experiences to sports, silently taking pleasure in her dad's endearingly unadorned style.

Jesse Abbot drove Jim and Sarah to the ambassador's home. When Abbot pulled his car past the security gate, the site of the overflow crowd that had congregated on the rear lawn caused Jim's heartbeat to quicken.

"Looks like at least three hundred people," said Abbot, "including President Buyoya."

"I didn't know he was coming," said Jim, slightly uncomfortable at the thought of reading before a head of state.

"Oh, and by the way," Abbot said to Jim as the coach was exiting the car, "there's another special guest I know you'll enjoy seeing."

Just then, Jim heard a familiar voice. "You didn't think that I was going to miss the debut of a master poet did you?"

Jim immediately recognized the voice of Barry Sklar, who, now standing in his view, held a glass of wine in one hand. A luminous smile lit his face.

The two dear friends hugged, and Barry then said, "Seriously, Jim, when the ambassador told me about this reading, it helped me decide to come and check things out personally."

As was her custom, Ambassador Foster had planned well. A massive blue tent, on loan from the president's office, provided shade from the early evening sun. At the west end of the tent, rows of chairs were set up for the guests, and a special section was cordoned off for President Buyoya, his wife, and the readers. An elevated podium with a microphone was situated directly in front of the chairs. Draped high above the podium was a sign—painted red, white, and blue—that read: WELCOME TO THE FOURTH ANNUAL EMILY DICKINSON SUMMER SOLSTICE READING.

As more guests arrived, members of the ambassador's staff employed their contingency plan by bringing out additional folding chairs. Servants walked through the crowd with heaping trays of hot and cold hors d'oeuvres. And for the first time in months, Operation Deliverance was not at the center of conversation. Instead, the talk was about poetry and the mood was one of light anticipation.

Too nervous to eat the hors d'oeuvres, Jim sipped slowly on a glass of Perrier only to be caught off guard by an unexpected and well-known greeter.

"While I confess to knowing little about poetry," said President Buyoya, "your ambassador has piqued my curiosity. I am particularly looking forward to your reading."

As Jim pondered whether he should be flattered or uneasy over the president's interest, Bill Foster, dressed nattily in white slacks and a bright shirt with a floral design, rang a decorative ship's bell and said, "Ladies and gentlemen, please take your seats. The readings will begin in five minutes."

Jim moved toward his seat in the front row. With a turn of his head, his eye fell upon the ambassador in amiable conversation with a woman he had never seen.

A stunning woman.

58

Cynthia Foster had agreed to assume the dual role of reader and master of ceremonies. She would read first and the others would follow, based on a draw of straws.

With well-modulated eloquence, the ambassador read two of her newest poems—the first about her love for her husband, the second about the strain of Operation Deliverance. The words of the second poem, emollient and heartfelt, had special meaning to everyone in the audience. When she was finished, her poignant treatment of this sensitive topic produced a thundering ovation.

As bearer of the smallest straw, Jim Keating would be the final society member to read. While waiting, he tried hard to focus on the poetry of his fellow members, cheering joyfully for the ambassador and the others who preceded him. But as he mobilized his mind for what would be, for him, an uncharted experience, the positive adrenaline he had welcomed while on his veranda transformed to a serious case of jitters.

The reader just before Jim was Dr. Mutara Karamera, who finished with a stirring poem about growing up a Hutu in a country governed by Tutsis. "Through the Eyes of Another" was critical of the Tutsi regime of his youth. The diverse audience, including President Buyoya, accorded him a courteous applause, causing Jim to reflect on something the ambassador once said to him, "Listeners of poetry are generally a polite and tolerant lot—at least until they are on their way home."

Seconds later, that thought was purged by one more daunting: *It's my turn.*

"Ladies and gentlemen," said Ambassador Foster, "I am pleased to call to the podium our final reader. Jim Keating joined the Emily Dickinson Society several months ago. Since becoming a member of our ranks, he has worked diligently on his verse and he has become a fine poet. I know that you will enjoy his readings of two very special poems."

Scattered applause followed the introduction, and Jim walked uneasily to the podium. He glanced at his daughter, who shot back a smile, and then at Barry Sklar, who gave him a thumbs up. The coach cleared his throat and then looked down at the typed, double-spaced page on the podium.

"My first poem is about my introduction to a game that is special for many of us here this evening. The poem is called 'First Love.'"

In a strong, clear voice he had used so often in gymnasiums on three continents, Jim recited:

He once read
that love
required
an object.

Aside from family
the first object
of his devotion
was not a schoolgirl

but a rubber sphere
taut with air

Dan Doyle

and tiny, protruding dimples
to aid his grip.

He dribbled it
when dry,
palmed it
when wet.

It accompanied him
on the journey
from push shot
to jumper

served as a catalyst
for choosing sides
and seizing lessons
from laurel and loss.

At evening's close
torpid from
the day's pounding
on hot or frigid asphalt

the rotund bunkmate
rested
still and sure
atop his bed.

When a shard
of glass
punctured its
rubber skin

Al Banks
the gas station owner

helped him apply
a four-tailed bandage

to halt
its oxygen
from seeping out
and deflating his joy.

He watched it age
the protruding dimples
transforming first
to a smooth, seamless surface

soon deformed
by boil-like air bubbles
that subverted
its stable bounce.

As the fullness of life
unstrapped its
full-court press
of joy and woe

he would remain
forever faithful
to that first object
of his love

a starbright, Spalding basketball
which he first saw
resting under
the Douglas Fir

on Christmas morning
1933.

The poem produced a roar of applause. Several people, including Barry Sklar, stood to express their delight.

Feeling more confident, Jim said, "Thank you ... thank you so much. Now, as for my final poem, called 'Finish Strong,' well ... let me just read it." His remark produced gentle laughter.

On the matter
Of aging
The metaphors
Abound:

Last lap
Fourth Quarter
Home Stretch
Final Round.

Less in view
An unclouded tract
To guide me to the finish line
With dignity intact.

And so I set
An unwavering goal
A state of mind
I may control.

Rather than wallow
In restive lament
My call to arms:
Stay relevant.

When Jim finished, he tried to pick up the pages and get off the stage as quickly as possible. As he fumbled for a moment, the applause began to ascend. To his astonishment, it quickly rose to a crescendo. He looked into the audience, only to see his daughter standing in jubilation and mouthing the words "I love you, Daddy." Barry Sklar clapped with even greater vigor, then Jim's eyes locked on the woman who had been talking with Ambassador Foster. She was smiling broadly, nodding and clapping animatedly.

Moments later, when the ambassador reached the podium, Jim was surprised to see tears welling in her eyes. Unable to speak, she simply hugged him.

————

When the readings ended, Summer Solstice socializing renewed full-scale, and Jim was the focus of special interest. Among the first to offer congratulations was President Buyoya. "May I pull you away from your bearers of well-earned praise?"

"Certainly, Mr. President," Jim said, wondering what the president wished to convey.

"You know, Coach Keating, I am now sixty-eight years old. I just wanted to tell you that I loved both poems and that 'Finish Strong' had special meaning to me."

The compact message, delivered with earnestness, touched Jim deeply. He felt both a male and an age bond with Buyoya, seeing the human side of a leader known to most as an autocrat.

Jim thought back to another comment Ambassador Foster had made about poetry: "It can pierce the most hardened of hearts."

The congratulations picked up again, but several minutes later the backslapping was replaced by a gentle touch on the shoulder. Jim turned and was greeting by a smiling Ambassador Foster.

"Jim, may I introduce you to a very dear friend. This is Francesca Cimbrone."

59

"Mr. Keating," said Francesca. "I am so pleased to meet you. Your poems . . . they were wonderful."

What a lovely voice, thought Jim. Seldom would a voice cause him to take notice. But Francesca's was special, the timbre melodious, laced with vitality and goodwill.

And then there was her appearance.

Jim guessed Francesca to be in her mid-fifties, and he felt certain that a life of fitness and moderation had helped preserve her striking features. She was tall and tan with glossy dark brown hair that was slightly curled, cascading softly to her shoulders and framing a face of harmony and intelligence. Her eyebrows arched subtly over soft brown eyes that resonated with kindness. Her nose was delicate and slightly angled; her lips sugarplum and full; her teeth perfect and snow white.

She was one of the most attractive women Jim had ever seen and her presence was spellbinding.

Come back to Earth, Jim said to himself. But such reentry was not easy, and a line from his favorite poet came to mind: "By the force of beauty we are root and branch reduced."

That favorite poet then spoke up again. "Jim, Francesca and I have been friends for more than thirty years. Her dear husband, Nino, who passed last year, was also my good friend. Nino was the Italian Ambassador to France and a wonderful man."

"I am so sorry for your loss," said Jim, and Francesca nodded her gratitude.

"Francesca has traveled here for a reason," said the ambassador. "She would like to share with you the details of a wonderful plan she has developed. It would be a dance version of Project Oscar."

The idea struck an immediate chord with Jim. "Well . . . yes, of course. That sounds like a great idea . . . a really great idea. I . . . I'd like to hear all about it."

"I am so happy you are interested, Mr. Keating," said Francesca, and the ambassador followed up.

"When things settle down here in an hour or so, perhaps the three of us could meet in my study and Francesca can tell you more about the plan."

"That would be great," said Jim.

"Thank you . . . thank you so much," said Francesca. "And may I call you Jim?"

"Yes . . . by all means."

"And please, Jim. Please call me Francesca."

She smiled, but along with the movement of her lips, her eyes seemed to tighten slightly as though she were—if only for the briefest moment—sharpening her focus on Jim Keating.

As the two women moved away, a thought burst forth in Jim's mind.

She looks so familiar.

———

When Cynthia took Francesca off to meet other guests, Jim continued to enjoy the attention accorded him. Yet he found himself wishing the crowd would thin so that the ambassador would feel comfortable starting the meeting.

As well-wishers surrounded him, he noticed Barry Sklar and Sarah at the far end of the tent, in a conversation that seemed to please his daughter.

Moments later, Barry made his way to Jim. "Coach, can I borrow you for a few minutes? I have something I'd like to run by you. Okay if we walk around the grounds?"

"Sounds important, old friend."

"It is important," said Barry, as he rested his hand on Jim's shoulder.

The two made their way to the rear of the home, passing by the hoop Bill Foster had installed.

"He entices anyone who visits into a game of HORSE," said Jim. "I love Bill. He's a great friend."

As they continued toward the garden, Barry said, "Well ... the real reason I flew over relates to Bill ... and the ambassador ... and Mathias and Terrence, and most of all, the many young lives you've touched, including Leonard's. But no more suspense. Let me get to it."

The two sat down on stone benches, surrounded by mixed clusters of orange and red hibiscus. Barry leaned back slightly and turned toward Jim.

"What you've done here is amazing. It's exceeded even my wildest expectations, and my expectations were pretty damned high to start. Anyway, about a month ago, we received an anonymous matching donation to continue Project Oscar and honor Leonard's legacy. It came from a person who had learned about the program, and who, as the letter said, 'was impressed and promptly impelled to support this initiative.'"

Jim raised his eyebrows at the news.

Barry continued. "Knowing that getting the funds matched through State would take some time, I contacted a friend in DC who oversees a family trust. I shared the details of Project Oscar, and two weeks ago, my friend got back to me to say that the trust would match the grant. So, Coach, we now have enough money to keep the program going for at least a couple more years. And, I'm guessing I can get State to kick in some extra money to even expand it a bit."

A mix of thoughts tumbled through Jim's mind. He had been ready to return to Worcester; that was the game plan. But now . . .

"I know this is quite a surprise, Jim. But let me tell you more," Barry insisted. Jim recalled the initial conversation he'd had with Barry when he had first presented Jim with the job offer in Burundi. Barry had quickly related all the facts to Jim, enticing him with the details before Jim could say yes or no.

Barry went on to tell him that the funding they received would mean that they could extend his contract for three years with a 6 percent per annum raise. Even though everything would come from outside funding, both grants would still go into the federal coffers, which meant that Jim would still be on their payroll. His medical and retirement benefits would stay in place and he'd receive two all-expense paid trips home each year.

"I know you're set to go back to Worcester, but please give this some good thought. You're making such a difference here. And by the way, I told Sarah about this and she plans to talk with you. Well, make that more than just talk with you!" Barry chuckled. "And I also met Francesca. What a great idea. And what an impressive woman."

Jim looked straight into his friend's eyes. Though he needed more time to process the facts, he wanted to tell Barry that his gratitude was exceeded only by his love of his old friend. And while his male censor blocked any emotional expression, his face conveyed the message.

"You know, I've agreed to a meeting in a short while with the ambassador and Francesca to discuss the dance program."

"I know," said Barry, with a playful grin.

———

When Jim entered the study, the ambassador and Francesca rose to greet him. While these two accomplished women obviously came from vastly different backgrounds, their worldly wisdom and sorority-sister bond resonated throughout a workroom that had become a hub for a wellspring of creative ideas, including the one to be discussed.

"Tea, Jim?" asked the ambassador as Jim took his seat.

"No, I'm fine." He was anxious to learn more about Francesca's plan.

"Jim," Francesca began, "I was so impressed when I read about what you are doing—so affected. If I may, I have a concern that I would like to raise at the outset."

As she spoke, Francesca looked straight into Jim's eyes. Once again, her harmonic voice and hypnotic air made him feel nearly powerless. Yet at the base of her demeanor lay an authentic aura of humility and kindness that allowed Jim to quickly snap out of his trance and focus on her message.

Combining perfect English with just a hint of an Italian accent, Francesca continued. "Project Oscar is a concept owned by the two of you and all the others who have made it so successful, so meaningful. I would not want my idea to compete in any way."

Feeling more at ease, Jim said kindly and confidently, "You know, from what you've said, I sense it could enhance Project Oscar."

From there, the conversation soared. Carefully, but enthusiastically, Francesca laid out her plan. Young Peace Corps–like Italian dancers would come to Burundi for six-month stints. They would cultivate ancient Hutu and Tutsi dance rituals. At the same time, they would introduce original and creative routines, from Europe to North America. The capstone would be the integration of a burgeoning dance movement.

Francesca's excitement was palpable. As she spoke, she shared descriptive photos she had brought along. Jim was fixated by her movements, at once swift and smooth.

"My goal is to have many dancers from both tribes working together toward a major production to be held in Bujumbura and beamed throughout Africa, if not the world. And at the end of the show, I see us using this new concept called mob dance, which involves a great many people dancing to a semi-choreographed routine, but all the while allowing a degree of personal creativity. One of the great advantages of the mob dance is that it can involve the participation of literally thousands of people all at once!"

Francesca's élan and sincerity caused Jim's shyness to evaporate. "This is a brilliant plan, Francesca. I can see it making a world of a difference."

Jim realized that Francesca's beauty and grace of expression complemented the winsome goodwill she projected. In her company for mere minutes, he felt a connection developing that went beyond the practicality of shared interests.

As Ambassador Foster watched two of her favorite people interact, she suppressed a smile and thought to herself: *Well, well, well!*

———

Before falling to sleep, Jim lay peacefully in his bed, his stillness the pleasant aftermath of one of the most perfect evenings of his life. There had been certain times in his past—hours or, at best, perhaps a day—when he felt similar tranquility, when everything seemed to come together in seamless accord.

One Christmas came to memory. It had snowed heavily, the drifts forming a buffer around the Keating home on that Holy Day. His Saint Thomas team was off to an unblemished start, Edna was fulfilled, and, on her first Christmas Day, Sarah personified his mother's favorite Gaelic phrase: Grá Gan Choiníoll—unconditional love.

Tonight's magic was an experience he would never have anticipated when fighting through the depths of his recurrent despair. Sarah, Barry, the reading, the ambassador's heartfelt embrace, President Buyoya's touching message, and then . . . Francesca.

Incorporated into Jim's late night musings about Francesca was his view of the romantic path that some, if not most, men follow. For younger men, Jim thought, the first allure is beauty, be it face, body, or a combination of the two.

Second, discerning men, even young men, understand the importance of intellectual compatibility.

But as a man matures, a third component emerges and becomes increasingly treasured: goodness—sheer, utter goodness.

At this stage of his life, Jim could not imagine being attracted to a woman who was not an inherently good person. Francesca Cimbrone did not merely possess goodness; it radiated from her like a flower's fragrance.

Then, just as he nodded off, Jim remembered . . . and smiled. A flower! Of course. With drowsy bliss, he fell into an untroubled sleep.

60

Jim woke early, excited about the possibilities of the day. On the way out of yesterday's meeting, the ambassador had suggested that he stop by in late morning for more discussion.

"I don't want to rush you, Jim," she'd said. "I know this is an important decision, but I do have some other thoughts I'd like to share that might be helpful."

At breakfast, Jim had a wonderful conversation with Sarah, who left no doubt about her position.

"Daddy, Worcester will always be there waiting. But this . . . this is now a mission . . . and a wonderful mission at that. And by the way, the ambassador introduced me to Francesca. What a gracious lady. And what an exciting idea. I could see the two of you working so well together."

"Yes . . . yes, she seems like a wonderful person," said Jim in a neutral tone.

Sarah wanted to share other thoughts about Francesca. But in this case, she could see by Jim's guarded response that less was clearly more.

At 11:00 AM, Cynthia Foster greeted Jim Keating at her front door. She was wearing pleated khaki pants and a Project Oscar t-shirt, and she radiated joy.

"Thanks for coming, Coach. As you can see, I decided to go casual today!"

The ambassador led Jim into her study and immediately got down to business.

"First point, Jim—and an important one. Finbar sent me a fax this morning. He indicated that he is almost certain that he saw the Mediterranean man in Johannesburg."

"My God," said Jim, his adrenaline racing.

"My exact reaction, too. The fax did not have many details, only that Finbar is going to his superiors in Johannesburg in the hope that he will be allowed to get back on the case. He said he would keep me posted."

The news stunned Jim, and he needed a moment to gather himself.

"We'll hope for the best, Coach. But if it's okay with you, I'd like to move to the main point of the meeting."

"Of course."

"Okay, I'll begin with full disclosure! I'm hoping to convince you to stay and let me tell you why."

Leaning forward in her chair, and making direct eye contact, she began her entreaty.

"Jim, Project Oscar has become the singularly most important unifying force in this country. Let me paraphrase one of my favorite thoughts from the French filmmaker Claude Chabrol: The murders of Leonard and Consolaté have defined in the minds of many Burundians the absurdity of that gap between the awesome finality of death and the trivial reasons men adduce for killing—or putting themselves in the way of being killed. And may I add to Mr. Chabrol's point by saying that for many in this country, this absurdity now equates to outrage—which is good.

"So," continued the ambassador, "we need Project Oscar to go on, Jim. We need it to grow. We need it to celebrate Leonard's memory . . . and we need your leadership."

Delivered with earnest and gentle force, the ambassador's statement enlivened Jim's senses. But then his mind took another turn. At sixty-seven, the coach was bound to convention. His bags were ready to be packed, his flight was booked, and there were people in Worcester expecting his return.

The ambassador anticipated the uncertainty, and she was ready with a game changer. "Jim, could you join me in the library for a moment?"

In the library, Cynthia Foster led Jim to a large picture window that overlooked the side driveway and Bill's hoop. When the ambassador and Jim looked down at the court, they saw but one player engaged—a tall, slender athlete wearing a basketball cap and bearing the smooth stroke of a classic shooter.

The ambassador remained silent for a moment, allowing the coach to size up the prospect.

"Nice touch and follow through," said Jim. "But I don't recognize him, especially with the hat on."

"The two of you actually met, albeit briefly," said the ambassador in a tone laden with mischief.

"Geez, with a shot like that, I thought for sure I'd remember the kid."

"Well Jim, you're looking at a player who took every sentence of your lesson to heart and then, with no small amount of difficulty, spent hours practicing pretty much alone."

"Alone?" asked Jim.

"Pretty much," repeated the ambassador.

Just as Jim's mind was finally approaching the obvious, the ambassador rapped loudly on the window. In one swift motion, the player dropped the ball to the ground, removed the baseball cap, and then, with a radiant smile, looked straight at Jim Keating and waved.

For a moment, the Coach was speechless and then, "Ambassador, that's, that's . . . the girl . . . the one we met out in the country . . . in Gitega."

"Correct, Coach! Remember . . . her name is Omella Kurabitu," Ambassador Foster said. "In my view, she may be the best prospect we have in Burundi. Over the last several months, I've conducted a bit of a clandestine mission—and for a lot of reasons. When she did not show up that day in Gitega, I could sense from her brother, Alain, that she desperately wanted to try the game. A month or so later, Alain got word to one of the Marines that her parents might be rethinking their position on no play. And so, I traveled there, met with her parents, and received their permission to train her. I've been heading to Gitega every other week since, and it has been a joy. By the way, we will be constructing a court there next week. And while we've made good progress, I know that I can only take her so far."

Jim smiled and simply shook his head in admiration.

"Coach, just like Project Oscar has made small but important strides in scaling that high wall of hatred between Tutsi and Hutu, I'd like us—you and me—to scale yet another wall: the vile wall of prejudice that prevents women from pursuing their dreams. In this case, the dream of a young lady to become a world-class basketball player. And, if it's okay with you, I'd like to include Francesca's program in our overall plan."

"A great idea," Jim said with a nod.

"You know, Jim, as we've already seen, basketball can become a small but important contributor to reaching this objective. And so can dance. And by the way, if Omella is as good as I think she will be, she can become one of the movement's leaders."

The ambassador took a step toward Jim. Clasping his hands in hers, and staring straight into his eyes, Cynthia Foster launched her final shot. "James Patrick Keating, Project Oscar needs your coaching, which is why I hope you'll follow me back into my study, sign the contract, and get down to the driveway and back to work."

With deeply felt gratitude and a renewed sense of purpose, the coach pivoted, followed his dear friend, and did exactly what she asked.

———

Later that evening, Ambassador Foster made a short entry into her journal:

June 23, 11:40 PM

So pleased that Jim will stay. He is such a good man and Project Oscar has so much promise. My God, I cannot imagine the project moving forward without him.

Still need to tell him about Ted Williams and my long-ago crush on him. But I need to have time to discuss it with Jim, and to tell him about an old boyfriend, who was white, and how this was so forbidden in that era. I must also tell him that the only person I told about my crush on Ted was my sister, Carolyn, who told me not to tell anyone else. She reminded me of how saddened I was when my white boyfriend ended our relationship due, I knew, to pressure from his white friends.

I need to tell Jim of my surprise and, to be honest, my disappointment with myself in holding back about Ted . . . finding that this mindset still existed within me. I need to tell him that I know full well that such a mindset makes no sense . . . but it's still there . . . forever lurking. By sharing this information, I hope it might help Jim better understand some of the deep-rooted pains that African Americans face.

But this whole issue . . . well, it still makes me so sad.

61

The meeting took place in The Chairman's retreat home, situated thirty miles outside of Johannesburg, surrounded by forty acres of dense forest. Security was ironclad, nothing could penetrate the high walls topped with glass shards and a roll of concertina wire.

The Chairman entered and the five men already in the room, all billionaires, stood and saluted.

"Please sit, gentlemen. First, I want to confirm that all of those who were part of the Burundi experiment are dead. . . . We have eliminated any threat of a link to the experiment."

The Chairman then pulled from his satchel five envelopes and passed them out.

"What you have before you is a one-page executive summary of the plan. Please open your envelopes and read the plan."

As they read the summary, smiles creased their faces. When finished, The Chairman collected the envelopes and summary and immediately shredded them.

"Now, gentlemen, may I propose a toast?"

He ceremoniously uncorked a bottle of champagne and poured six glasses. After a moment, he slowly raised his glass, and the others followed suit.

"To the mission," he said gravely, "which we are now ready to begin."

All in the room felt a rush of exhilaration.

All except one.

62

His veranda had become Jim's favorite place to meditate, to lean back and let his mind slip into a pleasant plac-idness. The view to Lake Tanganyika was spectacular, but in between his rattan chair and the lake was another scenic view: Josiane's garden.

It was an exquisite garden, a spectacular mixture of small patches of purple lobelia and mint-green clover amid bands of bougainvillea, Leonidas roses, and hibiscus. Jim's favorite was the spiked orange aloe because it attracted several species of hummingbirds. When Josiane had first come to work for Jesse Abbot, she had suggested a garden, and Jesse readily agreed. The result was a magnificent mix of colors, planted and cultivated in perfect harmony.

Jim had long admired gardeners. They met a key require-ment of a worthy undertaking—they were incrementalists of the best sort: careful, precise builders. In Jim's view, they possessed so many admirable qualities: patience, diligence, selflessness, and, most certainly, a love of nature. And, as he noted in Josiane's work, gardeners seemed to derive great pleasure and fulfillment from the task.

Jim had enjoyed the addition of poetry to his life so much that he had contemplated adding another hobby, one that was relaxing and not overly time-consuming. And one with a purpose, for Jim was forever about purpose. The more he thought about it, the more it seemed that gardening was the perfect choice, and he had discussed the prospect with Josiane, who was encouraging.

As he was thinking more about his entry to this new avocation, Jesse came around the corner, smiling broadly. "We found the book, Jim! It was in the University of Burundi library. They sent it over this morning. Got to get back to the Embassy, but I wanted you to have it right away."

"Thanks, Jesse."

The book was a collection of the works of El Greco. During Jim's coaching stint in Spain, he'd come to realize that El Greco was accorded rock star status in the Spanish art community. The first owners he worked for, the Lopéz family, were major players in the art community who donated generously to various museums. From time to time, Jim would hear whispers about their private collection, including several El Greco paintings they apparently did not show except on rare occasions.

He recalled one such occasion . . . a magical occasion.

In his first year as coach in Spain, Jim was invited to a dinner party in celebration of the twenty-first birthday of the family's oldest son, Jose, whom Jim had grown to like. After dessert, Jose's mother, Andrea, said to the guests, "May we all adjourn to the library? Our family has something very special we would like to show you."

Jim recalled the anticipation he felt heading toward the Lopéz library that evening. He remembered sensing that he was about to see something important—something unique—and his instinct had been spot on. When he entered the library, perched below perfect lighting was a painting that was, even to Jim's untrained eye, awe-inspiring. He knew instantly that he was in the presence of preeminence and recalled being overpowered by the moment.

The painting was one of El Greco's most famous originals, brought out by the Lopéz family from a bank vault in Barcelona in celebration of this ceremonial evening.

Navigating his mind back to the present, Jim picked up the pace of his page-turning of the coffee-table book of paintings. Moments later, there it was! And to his delight, his memory had proven accurate. He gazed at the image of a remarkably beautiful woman: El Greco's legendary portrait, "Lady with a Flower in Her Hair."

True to his recollection—and his quiet pleasure—the beautiful woman El Greco had painted four centuries ago was a near perfect likeness of Francesca.

Jim leaned back, looked up at the blue Burundian sky, and exhaled. He could not quite fathom his current emotional state, only that it was deep and absorbing.

Moments later, he regained a semblance of equanimity and saw Josiane heading to the garden with a pitcher of lemonade. Jim had already told her that he wanted to plant a small grouping of flowers to honor people special to him. He explained that there would be two plantings, one now and one in a month's time. The second planting would honor his "African Dream Team—people like Bill, Mathias, Jesse, and Terrence."

Josiane had smiled. "I will carve out a patch for you, Mr. Coach. A fertile patch."

"*Urakoze*, Josiane. Many thanks. I'll pick some and you can tell me if they'll grow here."

Laughing, Josiane said, "We have sun and water and good soil. You can pick almost anything."

Jim decided his first planting would recognize six people who were a part of his African journey and who touched him profoundly: Edna, Sarah, Cynthia Foster, Barry Sklar, and Leonard and Consolaté Tangashika. With Josiane's help, he would select plantings that would remind him of each of them.

Several days earlier, he had retrieved a book he'd seen in the Foster's library, *The Language of Flowers*, and, after a couple of hours on the veranda one morning, he felt good about his choices.

While pouring Jim a glass of lemonade, Josiane asked, "Have you made your selections, Mr. Coach? For I can go now to make the purchase."

Jim handed her his list. "I have, Josiane, and I think I've gotten the perfect matches."

In Edna's memory, he selected a blue salvia, but only after considering a dwarf sunflower. The book had the salvia aligned with "I think of you," while the sunflower was "adoration." "Adoration" was appropriate. Throughout their marriage, Jim loved Edna to distraction. At games, he would sometimes even glance at her in the bleachers and have to fight to regain his concentration on coaching. But "I think of you" encompassed all the times the thought of her would lead to extended reveries, happy distractions from the more challenging aspects of his life.

He mentioned his reason for this choice to Josiane.

"Mr. Coach, plant both. Together they will make a nice combination."

Jim's throat tightened and he clenched his teeth to fight back tears. He then said simply, "Thanks, Josiane, a good idea."

For Sarah, for whom his love was mixed with admiration and pride, he chose a red carnation; the carnation was his favorite flower.

His choice for Cynthia Foster was serendipitous. She often came to mind when he saw the Bird of Paradise simply because of its striking, almost regal shape. Jim was pleased that *The Language of Flowers* associated it with "joyfulness." From the beginning, the ambassador had impressed Jim with her irrepressibly upbeat, positive attitude, signaled so often by a captivating smile and hearty laugh.

Barry was easy. He ran his eyes through the pages of flowers until he found one associated with "gratitude." And so, for his friend who had helped turn his life around, it was the Bell Flower.

The thought of Leonard unleashed a flood of emotions. He would need an entire garden to match these emotions. Could he possibly find just one flower to represent the feelings of a coach, friend, and, yes, a father? Slowly, Jim sifted his sentiments and finally decided on "pride" and the Amaryllis.

And for Consolaté, he chose a Dahlia, signifying elegance and dignity.

He passed the sheet of paper to Josiane, who looked at it and said, "It is a good list, Mr. Coach. I shall go now."

As Josiane turned to leave, Jim looked up quickly from the book of paintings in his lap. "Josiane," he said, "could you look at a picture?"

As she moved toward him, Jim handed her the cumbersome book. "That one, Josiane."

"She is such a beautiful woman, Mr. Coach."

"The flower in her hair, Josiane. What kind is it?"

"It is a jasmine," she said admiringly.

"Would a jasmine grow in my patch?"

"Yes, most definitely. It would grow . . . and it would flourish."

Without hesitation the coach said, "Then please, get one."

As Josiane turned away from Jim, she felt a rush of joy at his decision.